C000179826

EVERY BREATH YOU TAKE

ALSO BY SHEILA QUIGLEY

Run for Home
Bad Moon Rising
Living on a Prayer

To find out more visit
www.theseahills.co.uk

EVERY BREATH YOU TAKE

Sheila Quigley

C

Century · London

Published by Century in 2007

1 3 5 7 9 10 8 6 4 2

First published in Great Britain in 2007 by
Century
The Random House Group Limited
20 Vauxhall Bridge Road, London SW1V 2SA

www.randomhouse.co.uk

Addresses for companies within The Random House Group Limited can be
found at: www.randomhouse.co.uk/offices.htm

The Random House Group Limited Reg. No. 954009

A CIP catalogue record for this book
is available from the British Library

ISBN 9781844138487 (Hardback)
ISBN 9781844138494 (Trade paperback)

The Random House Group Limited makes every effort to ensure that the
papers used in its books are made from trees that have been legally sourced
from well-managed and credibly certified forests. Our paper procurement
policy can be found at: www.randomhouse.co.uk/paper.htm

Typeset in Sabon by SX Composing DTP, Rayleigh, Essex
Printed and bound in the United Kingdom by
Mackays of Chatham plc, Chatham, Kent

For Darley

Acknowledgements

Thank you to all the wonderful people at Random House.

Special thanks to Paul Lanagan, historian extraordinaire, for organising a wonderful tour of all the murder spots in the books as part of the Houghton feast celebrations.

Prologue

Early February, bitterly cold, with a frost that gave everything it touched a shimmering cover of tiny pinhead diamonds. Weaving tendrils from the thick fog which was rolling through the streets and alleyways, turned the hard edges soft, giving them an almost ethereal look. In this bleak and soulful landscape the sound of his breathing was harsh, ragged, asthmatic even, as his warm breath hurtled out into the frosty air of the alley like stream upon stream of ghostly ectoplasm.

There were a few people about in the main street, some in better states than other's. A drunk tried to hail and cab and swore loudly as it sailed past him. 'Hey, fucking wanker, it's me, Jimmy. Mr Fucking James O'Brian to you, you useless fucking prick.'

The cab though was long gone, on his way to the other side of Dublin. Still snarling and shouting, Jimmy, Mr fucking James O'Brian to you, lurched from side to side as he made his way to Temple Bar, unaware that he was being watched.

In the alley the watcher followed O'Brian's progress, green eyes tight slits against the cold, a sneer on his face. He reached inside his jacket and pulled his black polo neck jumper down

1

over his waist and shivers, it had slid up over explosing his bare flesh to the elements. He shivered again as he stepped back and crouched behind the low wall.

To wait. For her . . . Ha.

It had not been the first time he'd hid nor the first time he'd suffered rejection.

The bitch.

He spat on the ground. The very thought of her agitated him and caused his breathing to become erratic.

As it always did.

He needed to regain control, it happened every time, he knew that it was linked to his anticipation of what was to come. Closing his eyes he took a deep breath as he counted to ten, preparing himself he clenched his fists then realised them, just another aspect of his preparation.

Mediative, calming, soothing.

The fog was thickening fast, but he'd done his homework, he knew every inch of this glorious alley, which could not have suited his purpose any better if he'd designed it himself. Apart from, he wrinkled his nose, the overriding stink of piss.

He took his tool wallet out of a long pocket he'd sown into his jacket, opening it up he spread it almost reverently on the ground. Four very sharp knives of different weights and sizes lay comfortable in their sheaths. A pair of long handled autopsy scissors snuggled next to them.

He nooded calmly almost serenely at his implements.

He was ready.

This was her route home every night from the bar she worked in. He watched her walk towards him, tall and slim, with long blonde hair captured in a pony tail that frizzed at the ends in the cold damp air.

She drew abreast of him and he leapt.

Jumped clear over the wait high wall and in the space of a

single heart beat instilled a fear in her that she had never known before.

'What the?' she gasped, her face registering total incomprehension, as he lifted his arm and struck her bringing her to the ground.

She landed on her back, too shocked to react for the moment she stared at him her terrified eyes locked on his. In a desperate bid for freedom she tried to scramble to her feet, with a snarl he pulled back his fist and punched her mouth hard, splitting her lips wide open and smashing both her front teeth. Reaching she spat bits of teeth and blood into the gutter. He grinned, she didn't look so pretty now . . . Ha.

He picked her up, her slim frame limp and almost malleable in his arms. Carrying her the few steps to the wall he threw her over as if she was nothing more than a heavy laundry bag. Quickly he followed and a moment later he was astride her. he opened his tool kit and spread it on the ground.

With practised ease he unzipped her leather jacket, then ripped open her pink blouse, exposing her chest. She wore a flimsy bra of almost the same shade of pink as her blouse, which he easily tore away. Her breasts spilled out into the freezing air. He caught his breath and stared at her for what seemed the longest time.

Then he sneered, she was beneath him in more ways than one. Reaching over he picked the third tool from the right, the sharpest, the longest his favourite. Smiling he ran his gloved finger along the edge.

Then he looked at her face, her eyes were open. Her body shook with terror and her eyes pleaded with his, as her ruined bleeding mouth hung open in a silent scream. She watched as her death, only seconds away, began to descend.

He plunged the knife into her heart, felt resistance for a moment but the blade had been honed to a brilliant sharpness. Viciously he twisted the knife first to the left then back round.

3

From the ever-widening slit blood spurted out of her body, spraying his face and chest as the life ebbed out of her. He watched her face as she died, saw the exact moment her eyes glazed over and he was content.

Calmly, his face devoid of any emotion, he pulled the knife out, wiped the warm bloody blade on a piece of litter that had blown his way, placed it in the sheath, then drew out the smaller cutting knife. Quickly, with the expertise of a pro, he opened her body from her throat to her navel. One by one he snapped the two two ribs on each side of her chest, the sound muffled by the fog.

A few minutes later he was staring at her ruined heart. He lingered only a moment though, then with his autopsy scissors he cut the blood vessels. The aorta – the largest artery in the human body – had a slight slippery resistance to the scissors, but it was only slight, and the rest proved easy. In just a few more moments he held her ruined, treacherous heart in his hands.

With a feeling that was almost ecstasy he placed the heart on her stomach between her navel and her pubic hair. He studied the placement for a moment, re-examined his decision not to take pictures as he always did, then, with a slight nod, rationalised that pictures could be found and they would most certainly incriminate him.

He wiped his rubber gloves on her blouse before taking them off and stuffing them into a pocket in his tool kit. From a lower pocket he took out a clean pair, snapped them on then took an envelope out of his jacket. From the envelope he gently shook a white rose in full bloom on to his palm. Almost reverently he placed the rose in the cavity from which he had ripped her heart.

Part One

1

'Sure yer don't want to sit beside the window Luke? Cos I don't mind an aisle seat.'

Detective Inspector Lorraine Hunt of Houghton-le-Spring police grinned cheekily at Detective Sergeant Luke Daniels. They had just boarded a plane at Newcastle airport. They were bound for Ireland, and were waiting for the plane to take off. It was a wintry February day, grey and cold, rain lashed the windows of the plane, and Lorraine could see baggage handlers outside, clad in thick woolly jumpers that they wore under their fluorescent orange waistcoats. Other passengers were boarding the plane, putting their hand luggage in the overhead lockers and taking their seats. Lorraine glanced at the other passengers, there were a few who looked nervous, but no one else seemed quite as apprehensive as the man seated beside her.

Not for the first time, Lorraine reflected on how Luke was always surprising her. He looked hard; he was tall, muscular, built like a brick shithouse, as her godmother Peggy often said, but his dark-brown eyes betrayed his sensitive nature. He was a handsome man, a handsome black man whose gold tooth glittered when his smiled, but his eyes were his best feature. Lorraine knew the effect that they had on the female population of Houghton – policewomen, suspects, even prisoners weren't immune to his charms. And Lorraine couldn't blame them, she wasn't exactly immune herself.

Lorraine had seen Luke hold his own under pressure. She had seen him perform acts of bravery in the call of duty, but put him in a plane and he was terrified. It wasn't quite an irrational phobia – Lorraine thought it wasn't flying but crashing you should be afraid of – but it was surprising, nevertheless, that the man that she had worked with for years and had just embarked on a tentative relationship with, had this fear of flying. Certainly, Lorraine would never have guessed. In fact, if it weren't for his teenage daughter, Selina, they wouldn't even be here.

Luke managed to open his eyes long enough to watch the flight attendants point out the exits and go through the emergency procedures as the plane taxied to the runway. Lorraine couldn't help noticing that he gripped the armrests so tightly the tendons stood up on the back of his hands. A moment later they were airborne.

Lorraine knew the pressures that Luke was under. She knew that not only was he terrified of flying, he was also stressed by Selina bolting from the house after they had had a massive row. She had only returned to steal cash from his wallet. There had been an anxious twenty hours before hearing where she had ended up. Lorraine and Luke had called in every favour they could from the policemen and women they knew in the north-east, even calling detectives they knew as far away as Scotland and London. And then, finally, the Garda in Dublin had called. They had picked up Selina for causing a public nuisance. She was drunk out of her mind and they had left her to dry out in one of the cells. Lorraine booked her and Luke a flight on the next plane. Sure, Lorraine reasoned, Luke is stressed, but at least now he knows where Selina is, and it's not as if she can do any more trouble stuck in a cell. Perhaps she could lighten things up a bit – make Luke smile, it's not as if they could do anything more from here until they reached Dublin, but Luke was winding himself up so tightly with fear and stress, Lorraine thought he might explode.

Lorraine made her voice sugary sweet, a hint of a hidden velvety smile in it, and said, 'Yer can open yer eyes now Luke love, the wings haven't fallen off . . . Well . . . Not yet anyway . . .'

'Lorraine . . .' Luke's voice was a warning.

Lorraine's smile turned into a wicked grin. 'What?'

Luke opened his eyes and frowned at her, he focused on her face. The plane had broken through the clouds, and the sun was shining through the window, creating a light that turned her naturally blonde hair into a halo, though saint she was not. Would a saint who said she loved him torment him like this? Her deep-blue eyes glinted with mischief.

God she's never looked so bloody gorgeous, he thought to himself, his fear of flying leaving him for a moment.

Luke had loved Lorraine for a very long time. Ever since he first saw her, in fact. But at that time she was with her husband – now ex, thankfully – who had hurt her badly, and made her distrust her own feelings. And he knew that the fact that they worked as closely as they did was an issue. Even now, there were those amongst his colleagues who thought that two people who worked together should never try to take their relationship further. He suspected that Superintendent Clark had his reservations. But it was getting to the point where they had had to do something about their feelings or he would have had to seriously think about another career, just so he could ask Lorraine out. But that had been unthinkable; being a policeman was what he was, he couldn't imagine any other life. And then, just when he and Lorraine seemed to be going somewhere, his daughter Selina arrived on his doorstep.

He hadn't even known she existed. In fact, he didn't even know that her mother was pregnant when they had split up. They had been so young, they had been so careless, so in love, and then Selina's mother left Houghton and was out of his life for good. The first time he knew he had a daughter was when social services knocked on his door. Selina had no one – her mother was dead, and she had been living on the streets for months, drugged out of her mind and doing God knows what to get the cash. It had been a hard and harrowing road getting her off the junk, and when she finally got it out of her system, he had been terrified that she would go back to her old ways. She had been violent, manipulative and angry – so angry. But, against all the odds, before their fight, Selina had seemed to be getting herself together. Selina had been going to a group therapy session, and she had even made a couple of friends. Luke hoped to God that this latest episode was just a one off, that it had only been alcohol she had taken the night before; that she wasn't back on the smack.

He knew that he had a responsibility to her, a responsibility that soon turned into love, even if he couldn't trust her. He had agonised over whether it was fair on Selina to start a new relationship with Lorraine while he needed to take care of her, but Lorraine was so much part of his life anyway, it wouldn't make much of a difference to Selina whether or not they were together. In fact, Lorraine had been a godsend; she and Selina got on great together. Sometimes a bit too well, if he was going to say the honest truth.

He sighed. *It's me Selina doesn't like*, he thought. *Even though I'm trying to do the best by her. I just don't even know where to start.*

Lorraine's smile softened when she saw Luke's frown and heard him sigh heavily, she placed her hand on top of his, which was still clenching the armrest. But what was worse? Him obsessing over Selina as he had done over the last twenty-four hours? Or his fear of flying? Lorraine knew just how much Selina had worried him since she came into his life a couple of months ago. Anything was better than the mental torture Lorraine knew Luke would be putting himself through at the moment.

'Chill Luke, it'll be all over in a blink. A hop, skip and a jump as they say. Thirty minutes tops. Unless we run into some turbulence, that is . . . or maybes,' she shrugged and shot him a beatific smile, 'another plane.'

Luke groaned loudly enough to make the passenger across the aisle, a small bespectacled man with a brown beard, throw him a worried glance.

'Thanks a lot, Lorry,' he muttered through gritted teeth as he turned his face towards her and buried it in the crook of her neck.

He sighed again. *This is murder*, he thought, *in fact, if I had my hands on Selina right now I'd strangle her for putting me through this bloody nightmare.* Luke had never liked flying, had been terrified of it ever since he could remember. Only a dire emergency would get him up in the air. If it hadn't been for Lorraine insisting on taking the flight, he would have let Selina rot in the jail she was being held in for the extra seven or eight hours it would have taken to go by ferry.

Praying hard for the plane to go faster, anything to get it over with, then panicking a little in case it went too fast.

'I'm gonna kill her,' Luke said under his breath.

Lorraine realised that her tactic of taking Luke's mind off his daughter wasn't working. She sighed. She had held her tongue for the past few weeks, but if she was Luke, she would handle Selina very differently. Selina was a troubled young woman, of course she was, and she had had a hard life, but Lorraine had talked with her enough to know that there was

11

a good kid underneath all that anger and bravado. Luke was laying down the law just a little bit too hard, in Lorraine's opinion, which must be difficult for a seventeen-year-old girl to take, especially one who was used to a large amount of freedom, even if that freedom was on the streets. All Selina seemed to want from Luke was for him to try to understand what she was going through. And, essentially, that had been what the fight had been about.

'Listen Luke,' Lorraine said cautiously, 'when you see Selina, try not to be too hard on her. I know how difficult it's been for you, but it's hard on her too. She's been stupid, but loads of teenagers do stupid things. Just listen to her side of the story before yer go off on one. She's a great girl, I think, yer've just gotta give her a chance.'

Luke clasped her hand. His hand was so large it swallowed hers. 'Lorraine, darling woman. There is something you and Selina should know. You aren't supposed to like each other. It says so in all good magazines and countless books on the subject, but she backs you up and you back her up. Far from natural if yer ask me.' He smiled wanly.

Lorraine chewed her lip for a moment, and then said, 'Yeah well, that's what yer do when yer like somebody,' then added hastily, 'of course I'm not backing her up on this. She is way out of order and you've got to do something to make sure that she knows she can't pull a prank like this again. All I'm saying is to not go overboard. She's young and thoughtless and selfish but that's what teenagers are. And even though she was a drug addict, she's still a teenager. She's not suddenly going to start acting mature just because she's got off the junk.'

'Please don't defend her,' Luke snapped, then wanted to bite his tongue off when he felt Lorraine tense up against him. 'Sorry,' he muttered.

'I'm not defending her, have yer not listened to a word I've said?' Lorraine took her hand out of Luke's grasp, sat back in her seat and gazed out of the window.

'Oh God,' Luke thought.

Lorraine was right. She wasn't a bad kid, not underneath it all. In fact, until a couple of days ago, things were calming down, she'd even smiled once or twice, a miracle in itself. And she had shown an interest in learning to play the guitar, and Luke had taught her a couple of easy chords, placing her fingers on the strings. That had been a good day, one of the few, where he had felt a real bond between them. She had picked up the chords really fast, so she was musical. Even if she couldn't sing. And she also seemed to be interested in design. He'd bought a few magazines that he thought she might like and left them lying about and had been quite happy when he'd noticed they had at least been picked up and flicked through, and just the other day, he had come across some rough sketches that looked as if Selina was trying her hand at designing clothes. She seemed to have some natural talent.

So things were looking up, he'd listened to Lorraine and tried not to come across as a heavy-handed father. He'd bought some home drug-test kits off the internet, and Selina had tested clean day after day, even though there was always hell to pay to get a urine sample, but he insisted. It had been part of the deal when he allowed her to go out of the house. He had even been thinking about reducing the amount of times he tested Selina for drugs to twice a week.

But then there was the fight. It was the most almighty row. Luke had come home to find Selina and Mickey holding hands on the living room couch. He had gone ballistic and had taken Mickey by the scruff of his neck and had physically thrown him out of the house. Selina had turned on him then, 'What are you doing you bastard?' she had screamed. 'We weren't doing anything, just watching TV.'

13

He had yelled back, saying things that he didn't really mean, the frustrations of the last months coming to the fore as he called her ungrateful and selfish. What was she planning to do? Get pregnant like her mother had? What the hell was she expecting him to do then?

Selina had stormed out of the house then, giving Luke some time to calm down. Mickey bloody Carson, of all the people to take up with. Not that Mickey was a really bad sort. He just wasn't going anywhere, the only saving grace Carson had at the moment was that Luke was certain the kid didn't do drugs. And it wasn't as if he had caught them in the act or anything, they were only holding hands. As he waited for Selina to come home, he started to feel embarrassed about the way he had overreacted. As he had drifted off to sleep on the couch, he promised himself that he would apologise to Selina, hell, he'd apologise to Mickey if that's what it took.

But when he woke up, he discovered his wallet out of his jacket pocket and lying on the kitchen bench. The hundred pounds he had taken out of the cash machine the night before was gone, and so was Selina, and a quick glance through her bedroom told Luke that she had taken her rucksack and a few clothes with her.

Luke drove round to Mickey's place, fuming. But Mickey denied everything – he told Luke when he opened the door to him that he hadn't seen Selina since Luke had kicked him out, and, from the scared look on Mickey's face, Luke believed him.

He sighed inwardly. What the hell was he gonna do with her? No way was he ever that difficult at sixteen. It was frightening what kids got up to nowadays. OK, so he had done stupid things – even got a girl pregnant although he hadn't discovered that fact about his life for seventeen years – but he had never had that bottled-up furious energy that Selina seemed to be able to draw on.

The phone call from the Irish Garda had been downright embarrassing. A policeman introducing himself as Inspector Ian Wade had told Luke that he had Selina in the cells. She had been caught throwing up by Temple Bar, and had lashed out at the policewoman who had asked her if she was OK.

He'd wanted to curl up in a corner and die. Now he knew what it was like to be on the receiving end of such a phone call, he'd lost count of the times he'd made them himself, but thank God Selina was safe. He couldn't understand why she had chosen Dublin to run to though – unless it was the furthest she felt she could get from him with the money in her pocket.

With a heartfelt sigh he opened his eyes and found Lorraine staring at him with that slightly quizzical look on her face that he loved so well. He felt his heart stop for a moment, then asked in a very suspicious tone, 'What?'

Lorraine shrugged. 'Looks like we're almost at Dublin airport. Just thought I'd warn you.'

Sure enough, the captain's voice came across the speakers telling them to ensure their seatbelts were fastened. They were due to land in ten minutes.

Lorraine watched him squeeze his eyes shut. Like most bad flyers it was the taking off and the landing that were the worst part about flying. She felt her annoyance towards him fade, and held his hand.

Selina was a little minx. Luke just had to handle this carefully though, try to stay on the middle line. He took his responsibility seriously and was determined to make a success of Selina's life even if he had to live it himself. And Selina was just as determined as Luke was that she would do her own thing.

Lorraine smiled as she remembered the evening when she and Luke had finally become an item. They had been circling round each other for months. Lorraine had been put off men by the discovery that her ex-husband John was gay, and that

15

their marriage was a travesty. The split had been awful and had left her with a deep distrust of men, and a deep distrust of herself. If she was so wrong about John, couldn't she be wrong about other men too? But through it all Luke had remained solid, a rock in her time of need. The attraction between them had grown stronger over time, although both had lied to themselves that it even existed. On Christmas Day, Luke had come for dinner with Selina, who was recovering from going through cold turkey and was looking very sick and pale. Lorraine's heart went out to her. She had seen enough teenagers who had abused drink or drugs to know that there was always more to their story than what was at face value. Between Christmas and New Year's Eve, Luke and Lorraine had each taken a well-earned holiday and the three of them had taken walks together, their faces bitten and red by the cold winter wind; they had sat in Luke's house drinking endless cups of tea, or had just sat in companionable silence at Lorraine's house, watching old black and white movies on the telly.

Lorraine had lived with her mother, Mavis, since she had left John, and Peggy, Mavis's best friend, and now possibly permanent lodger, lived there too. Lorraine had said that she didn't want to do anything much that New Year's Eve, but 'the Hippy and the Rock Chick', as Lorraine had dubbed Mavis and Peggy, weren't having it. They decided to lay on a spread, invite a few friends round, and celebrate the end of a difficult year in style.

Lorraine had felt inexplicably nervous on the night. Mavis and Peggy told Lorraine that they had invited Luke and Selina, but they were late in arriving. Two of Lorraine's colleagues were already there, her young constable Carter turned up earlier with a bottle of cava, and Sanderson had just appeared with his wife. Lorraine knew that it wasn't going to be a big party, but she had taken more than the usual care with her appearance that night anyway. Dressed in jeans and a sparkly top, she looked casual but beautiful, the gold of her top catching the highlights in her hair, which she had left down for the evening.

The doorbell rang, and Lorraine went to open it. It was Luke and Selina, who already looked healthier and better fed than she did when she had turned up on Christmas Day. Luke smiled at Lorraine as he bent down to kiss her on the cheek. 'Wow,' he whispered into her ear. 'You look beautiful.'

Selina went to speak to Carter, who had placed himself next to the food. Meanwhile, Mavis and Peggy were in their element, laughing and joking with their friends and neighbours. At one point someone put Abba on the stereo, and a couple of brave, or possibly, drunk people had started to dance. Selina tried to pull Carter on to the dance floor, but he had bashfully declined.

Lorraine and Luke watched them, smiling. They spent the party together, talking and laughing, Luke topping up Lorraine's drink every so often. But she didn't feel drunk, just a pleasant sense of well being that came with being looked after so well. And when the countdown to New Year's arrived, it seemed the most natural thing in the world for Luke to bend down and kiss Lorraine on the lips. They had broken apart only to find that now they were the centre of attention, with Carter, Mavis and Peggy, Sanderson and his wife, even Selina and the other guests all looking at them with stupid grins on their faces.

And that was that. At first she'd worried that a personal relationship would affect their working one, but there was no discernible change, although she knew that there were a few people at work who didn't approve. Nothing had been said, but there were a few stray looks now and then that she caught. She reasoned to herself that the gossip and the atmosphere would die down in time. They could manage somehow to keep their work and their professional life separate, and if she ever did favour him, it wouldn't be because he was her man, but because he was a damn good cop. At work she was the boss, after work she finally had her rock to cling to.

Even if he was an Eagles fan.

The plane started its descent and Luke froze. For one shocking moment he could have sworn the engines failed and the breath caught in his throat. Lorraine squeezed his hand. Then they were down, rolling along the runway. Luke let out a huge gasp and fought an overwhelming need to jump off the plane and kiss the ground.

2

The frozen remains of a small snow shower clung to the edges of the grass along the Broadway, but, cold as it was, Mickey Carson, shoulders hunched deep inside his black Rockport jacket, sat outside on a wooden bench, feet on the seat, elbows on his knee, head in his hands. His unruly black curls were caught at the nape of his neck in a pony tail. Mickey reckoned he'd saved over ten pounds on haircuts over the last three months. 'Trouble is,' as he often moaned to his mate Robbie Lumsdon, 'where the hell's the ten pounds?'

Mickey was oblivious to the sight of two pretty young girls, both looking his way, nudging and giggling at each other across the road. A couple of weeks ago, he would have been well pleased to have got some attention from a couple of lookers like that, but things had changed. Mickey didn't even notice them. To him, they did not even exist. Mickey was in love. The problem was, the love of his life was in another country.

Both Robbie and Cal Black had teased him relentlessly when they found out that Selina, his girlfriend of two weeks, had taken off.

'Whoa mate, I've heard about a different county, but a different country!' Cal had laughed, not ten minutes ago.

'It's just friggin' Ireland yer know. Just across the water, not the other side of the world,' Mickey had retorted.

Robbie had grinned, not nastily, but still a grin.

When they had asked if he fancied a game of pool, he'd refused. So now he was sitting here all by himself freezing his friggin' arse off and thinking about Selina.

They had met two weeks ago. It was a Saturday. He had been walking down the street, minding his own business when he turned the corner and ran straight into Selina. He'd bowled her completely over, and then he was bowled over, by how beautiful she was. Small and petite, with beautiful, clear skin stretched across her delicate features, and big dark eyes that he could sink into. He put out his hand to help her up, apologising profusely all the time. But she was fantastic, she actually laughed about it. He offered to buy her a drink to make up for it and they had gone into a nearby café and he bought them a can of coke each. Thank God he had some dosh on him. They talked and laughed and seemed to get on really well and yet he'd never been more flabbergasted when he'd got the nerve up to ask her to see him again and she'd actually agreed.

And now she had bolted to Ireland, after that massive row she had had with her father. Mickey had been shit scared when he opened the door to Luke Daniels that morning, looking even angrier than he had the night before. When Luke had told him that Selina was missing, his heart had plummeted. Selina was gone, he should have known it was too good to be true.

But then, just an hour after Luke had left, his mobile had beeped. It was a text message from Selina. He kept it and looked at it every few minutes or so:

Had 2 go. Dad 2 mad. In Dublin til he calms down or £ runs out. C U, miss U, Sel xxx

He had texted her straight back saying that he missed her too, but had had no reply. At least, he thought glumly, it says that she misses me. Kisses too.

'Hiya Mickey,' came a voice from behind him. Mickey groaned aloud. He didn't need to turn around to see that it was Dave bloody Ridley, Houghton's resident conspiracy theorist. Mad as a nest of snakes. The last thing he needed was to listen to him and thoughts on alien abductions.

'Got a belly ache?' Dave asked, sidling round from behind Mickey and sitting on the bench.

'No,' Mickey said. He hoped that his body language would give Dave the hint that he was not in the mood for talking today.

'I see, touchy today.' Dave rubbed at his rheumy eyes with his hand.

Mickey sighed. Wished he'd gone with Cal and Robbie. Wished for about the tenth time that day that Luke hadn't caught him with Selina. Wished he had loads of money – he must wish that one about a hundred times every day.

None of which was poor Dave's fault.

'Sorry Dave.'

'S'all right,' Dave slurred, and patted Mickey's knee.

Mickey looked at Dave cautiously. *I swear to God, if he mentions alien abductions just once I'm outta here.*

But for the moment Dave seemed content to sit and watch as the people of Hougton-le-Spring hurried about their business.

Mickey started to shiver, 'Think I'd better go Dave, else I'll be frozen in this spot forever . . . What do yer think mate?'

'Don't worry, yer thaw out in the spring lad.' Dave gave a slow wave as Mickey uncurled himself.

'Yeah, up yours Dave. Are you gonna sit there all day or what?'

When Dave didn't answer Mickey shrugged and turned away.

The stupid old sod will move when his snot turns to ice, he thought as he followed his friends' footsteps to the snooker club.

He was just passing Woolworth's when he spotted Amy Knowles coming out of the door. Selina had made friends with Amy at the addiction clinic in Sunderland a month ago. Mickey supposed she was all right, quite pretty really, with her natural fair hair and big blue eyes, a few weeks ago he might have even fancied her. But he was in love with Selina now, and it was real love, nothing like the crushes he used to get on other girls. Besides, although she looked like a teenager, Amy was in her early twenties and had twin boys who were about five years old. She had them with her today. Two bonny little lads, with Amy's blonde curls.

Mickey stopped dead in his tracks, she might have heard from Selina. 'Amy,' Mickey waved.

Amy turned and saw Mickey, smiling she came down the steps towards him. 'Have yer, er, heard from Selina?' Mickey asked, one eyebrow raised in a question.

'I got a text message from her this morning,' Amy said, 'just telling me where she was and that she's fine. But,' she went on when she saw Mickey's disappointed face, 'I'm sure she'll be back soon.'

Mickey sighed, and Amy touched his arm, 'Don't worry Mickey, she might even be on her way home now, for all we know.'

'Do yer reckon?'

She shrugged. 'Maybes. I bet yer her dad will be on her tail. He'll bring her back, don't you worry.'

Mickey nodded, his spirits lifted. He said goodbye and carried on along the street.

Gotta get a job so her dad will like me, he was thinking as he turned the corner by Greenhow's hardware shop. And his oldies were starting to bug him now, every time he saw his dad the same question, time and time again. Got a job yet?

But where? It wasn't as if Houghton was dripping with jobs and he really didn't want to leave the area, especially now that he had met Selina. He knew one thing, a factory was the last port of call. He couldn't stand being cooped up.

Hands deep inside his pockets, his head tilted down to try and escape the biting wind, Mickey walked along the street, scouring his mind for ideas of how to make Selina's dad like him.

3

Lorraine and Luke caught a cab from the airport, which took them straight to their hotel. After checking in they dumped their bags in their room and took another cab to Pearse Street Garda Station. Lorraine watched Luke's profile as he gazed out the window. His muscles were working in his jaw. He seemed even more tense, if that was possible, than he had on the plane that afternoon. And was getting tenser still the nearer they got to the station. 'It'll be OK Luke,' Lorraine murmured. Luke answered with a tight smile, his eyes fixed on the road ahead.

When the cab stopped at the station, Luke was out of it like a shot, striding purposefully towards the entrance. Lorraine paid the driver, stepped out of the taxi and hurried to catch him up. Luke went up to the front desk, where a white-haired officer in uniform was completing some paperwork. Lorraine reached his side as Luke said, 'Inspector Wade please. Tell him it's Detective Sergeant Luke Daniels from Houghton-le-Spring. He's expecting me.'

The man behind the desk glanced up and said something so quickly and in a brogue so thick that Lorraine could see that

24

Luke was struggling to understand him. But she could work out what he was saying, possibly because she wasn't nearly as wound up as Luke.

'Yes, that's right,' she said quickly. 'You've got a girl here, in your cells. Luke is her father, we're here to pick her up. But first we've got to see Inspector Wade.' Luke flashed her a look, but she couldn't read it.

'OK,' the policeman growled and picked the internal phone up.

Very shortly afterwards, a tall, dark-haired man with startling green eyes entered the office through a door behind the desk.

'Inspector Wade?' Luke asked.

'That would be me.' Lorraine couldn't quite place the accent. There was Irish in it, of course, but it was nowhere near as strong as the policeman on the front desk.

Wade and Luke shook hands, then Luke introduced Lorraine. Wade raised an eyebrow slightly when Luke introduced her as his senior officer and Lorraine, reading his mind, bit back a retort. This was Luke's show, his daughter, she was merely along for moral support.

Giving Lorraine a half-guilty, lopsided smile as if he understood what had flashed through her mind, Wade turned back to Luke. 'Yes, your daughter.'

Luke cringed inside, praying she hadn't been mouthing off. He tried to smile but knew that it came out as a sort of frozen grimace, then winced when Wade picked up the phone and barked orders into it.

'She won't be long,' he said a moment later as he put down the receiver. 'Would you like to come through into an interview room? We don't have much space here and it'll be private.'

The white-haired officer lifted the hatch in the desk and ushered them through. Lorraine and Luke found themselves in a corridor painted pale green. Wade was waiting for them by a door. He waved them into the room and indicated two seats that were tucked into a nondescript pale brown desk. Lorraine pulled the nearest chair out and sat down, the thought passing uncomfortably through her head that this would be where the suspects usually sat. She didn't like the feeling of being on the other side of the desk. Luke pulled out the other chair, and sat down on it heavily, his arms folded across his chest. Lorraine wondered whether he felt as claustrophobic as she did.

Wade took his seat opposite them. With a sly grin he said, 'Feels a bit different to be on the other side of things, doesn't it?'

Lorraine had the uneasy feeling that, yet again, Wade had somehow sensed her thoughts. Was she really that easy to read? She didn't like it.

Wade placed a thin manila folder in front of him, put his elbows on the desk and said, 'She'll be here in a moment, but I thought it might be worthwhile having a bit of a talk to you first.'

'She, er, she hasn't been giving yer any grief, has she?' Luke asked.

Wade smiled. 'No more than most.' He opened the file in front of him and said. 'It's just as I told you earlier. She was picked up in Grafton Street in the early hours of this morning. She was being, um,' his eyes flashed up from the paperwork in the folder to meet Lorraine's for a moment and then flicked back down again, '. . . sick on the side of the road. Anyway, Constable Gorman offered assistance, Selina lashed out at her and then keeled over. No one was hurt, but it was quickly established that she didn't have anywhere to stay and didn't know anyone. We kept her in the cells to dry out and, if truth were told, give her a bit of a fright at the same time. Has she been in touble before?'

Luke snorted and Lorraine put a hand on his arm to restrain him.

'What, er, exactly was found on her?' Lorraine asked.

Luke shrugged off Lorraine's hand and said, 'What Lorraine means to say Inspector Wade, is were there any drugs found on her?'

Wade looked surprised. 'No,' he said, taking another look at the file. 'Nothing like that, in fact.'

'And you don't think that she was on anything aside from alcohol?' Luke persisted.

Wade sighed. 'Well, you can't know for sure, not unless you test them but there were no indications of anything else in her system. You could ask her, of course . . .'

Luke gave a sigh that was more like a growl and folded his arms even more tightly across his chest than before.

'And there's something else,' Wade said, a small smile playing around his lips.

Lorraine glanced at Luke who was glaring at Wade as if he was responsible for everything that Selina had been up to since she had come to Dublin. 'Well, come on out with it then.'

Wade coughed into his hand. Looked Lorraine in the eye and said with a very solemn face, 'Selina was also found with a pair of leprechauns in her possession.'

'What?' Lorraine said. She stifled a giggle while Luke looked at her with horror.

'Yeah,' Wade went on. 'Real good quality ones as well . . . Seems your daughter likes nothing but the best.'

Before Luke, who was starting to seethe, could say anything, Lorraine said, 'What are you implying, Inspector?'

Wade shrugged. 'I'm not implying anything. But Selina had two leprechauns on her when she was picked up, thirty euros in her pocket, and no receipt. I happen to know that these leprechauns sell for about sixty euros each, so unless your daughter had more money than I suspect she had—' a quick look at Luke's face told Wade that he had suspected right, 'then I'm not sure that she came by them in the, ahhh, accepted way. However, as Selina wasn't caught in the act, my suspicions are just that, suspicions.'

Before either Lorraine or Luke coud reply, there was a knock on the interview room door. Wade left his seat and answered it. It was Selina and a social worker, who was dressed in a baggy pink woolly jumper. The social worker clutched a large brown paper bag to her chest. She introduced herself as Sally Kennedy, and sat on a chair that had been placed against the wall.

Luke glared at Selina, but even under these circumstances, he was struck by her resemblance to her mother. Selina was extremely beautiful, her caramel-coloured skin belying her mixed heritage. And she had proved how intelligent and resourceful she was by managing to get as far as Dublin. God, he was angry at her, but that anger was tempered by compassion. She had been let down badly in the past, whatever tack he took with her now had to be the right one. For her sake, he had to do the right thing by her, whatever that was, and even if she didn't like what he had planned for her. He had seen too many casualties of an unfeeling system to let a girl, whom he hardly knew, but who he had grown to love, become yet another victim. Although he hadn't even known she was alive until a short time ago he still felt partly responsible for the life she had lived until now. And wholly responsible for the life she would lead from now on.

For a moment she met his eyes. Thank God, he thought, at least she has the grace to look ashamed.

Luke tried to keep his voice even. 'So, I hope you've got one hell of a headache.'

Abashed, Selina stared at her hands.

'And these leprechauns, how did you come by them?' Luke was aware of Wade, Lorraine and the social worker's gaze upon him. He was also aware that, despite himself, he was sounded as if he was interviewing one of his suspects. 'It's

OK,' Luke continued, trying in vain to soften his voice. 'Just tell me the truth.'

Selina shrugged. And then, raising her head defiantly said, 'Found them. In a rubbish bin outside Brown Thomas. And anyway, I thought they would make a nice gift, for you and Lorraine,' she said, her face reddening.

Lorraine put her hand over her mouth, while Wade raised an eyebrow at Luke. Lorraine was certain he was trying to suppress a grin.

Luke swallowed hard and glared at Selina. How did parents deal with something like this, parents who knew their children, parents who had been part of their lives since the day they were born, not shoved on them when they were very nearly full grown? He simply had no idea of what was the best thing to do. He couldn't even trust his instincts – he didn't even *have* instincts as far as Selina was concerned, he was that out of his depth. Luke's voice was gruff when he said, 'That kind of present miss we can well do without. Thank you.'

Selina shrugged. 'That's cool.'

'What?'

'I sai—'

'I heard what yer said,' Luke was practically shouting as he glared at Selina.

She shrugged again, her face sullen and closed.

Lorraine placed a calming hand on Luke's arm, she could feel the tension building up in him and could barely remember ever seeing him so angry.

Wade broke the silence. 'These are her belongings.' He held his hand out for the brown paper bag, Sally Kennedy handed them over quickly as if she was pleased to be rid of the responsibility.

Wade looked at Selina, offered her a ghost of a smile and said, 'Could you please check that these are the items you had in your possession when you were picked up?'

29

He shook the contents of the bag on to the desk. A half used packet of mint flavoured chewing gum, one small folding hairbrush, Lorraine raised her eyebrows at the brush, recognising it as one of hers. A tube of lipstick, a few coins, thirty euros in notes and a photograph.

Lorraine felt a quick rush of warmth when she saw the photograph was a recent one of her and Luke, taken, in fact, at the New Year's party. But Luke was looking at the objects on the table, with an angry look on his face. 'Where the hell's that purse I bought yer for Christmas? The cream one with a cat on it?'

Selina shrugged. 'Dunno. Lost it.'

'Lost it,' Luke repeated, with a chill in his voice. Lorraine winced. She knew how Luke had agonised over what to give Selina for Christmas, so Selina's nonchalant disregard for one of his gifts must have hurt.

Selina glanced over the items on the table. 'What about the leprechauns?' she asked.

'Well,' Wade said slowly, looking at Luke as if for approval, 'we're not sure whether we believe your story. I mean, who would throw away such fine leprechauns, to be sure?' His voice changed into a stereotypical Irish brogue, and he gave Selina a quick wink. 'So, in the spirit of that, I think you could, err, donate them. I'll tell yer what, I'll auction these off for charity, at the next Garda benefit ball. What do you think of that?'

Selina's expression said 'not very much', but she didn't raise any objections. Finally she said, 'So what's gonna happen now?'

'Can yer read her caution Wade please, and then we'll get out of here,' Lorraine said hurriedly. Again Luke threw her a glance that she couldn't quite read.

After the caution was read and Selina had packed up her things, Lorraine said goodbye to Wade and Sally Kennedy while Luke took Selina out of the police station, his hand gripping her upper arm.

An hour later, they were in their hotel room. Selina was asleep next door. Luke sat in a chair, his tie loose, the sleeves of his white shirt rolled up above his elbows. He looked as drained as Lorraine felt, and there was something hopeless in his eyes as he stared unseeingly at the blank television screen.

Lorraine sat at the table, sick to death of reading the room service menu for want of something to do. She had tried from day one not to interfere between father and daughter, but it had not been easy, and sometimes it was impossible. She could see that Luke had the makings of a very good father, and that he loved his daughter, but he was severely lacking in practice and confidence.

'So,' Lorraine said. 'Fancy some overpriced food? Or we could go downstairs, see if there's anything in the bar . . .' She suggested food more as a way to break the silence rather than out of any real hunger.

'Well, that's a good idea,' Luke said sarcastically. 'Selina can then just waltz right out of here, go back on the streets, and we're back where we started.'

'Hang on,' said Lorraine, 'there's no need to take out your anger on me.'

'No, you're right, it's all my fault,' Luke muttered sullenly.

'God, Luke, I wasn't saying that either.' Luke's anger and tension had been gnawing at her all day. She tried really hard to ignore it, she knew how difficult the last few months had been for him, but still, she did not appreciate being talked to like that, nor did she like the looks he had been throwing her since they arrived in Dublin. 'You need to know I'm on your side, Luke. I wouldn't be here if I wasn't, but you're angry at me as well as being angry with Selina, and I don't understand why.'

Luke didn't look at her, just stared resolutely at the television, the muscle in his jaw clenching and unclenching. He looked just as surly and defiant as Selina had in the police station that afternoon. For the first time, Lorraine could see the family resemblance. Evidently, stubbornness was also hereditary.

Finally, Luke looked at Lorraine. 'I know you just want to help,' he said. 'But I've got to work things out in my own way. Selina and I have got to find a way of living together, and we can only do it by ourselves. I want your support, but when I want your advice, I'll ask for it.'

'If you're saying I'm interfering, Luke, you're totally out of order. Interfering has been the las—'

Luke held up a silencing hand. 'I know that's what you think, Lorraine, and I know that you don't mean to, but you just do interfere, without thinking about it. You and Selina get on so well, and it's great that you're friends, but I can't be her friend, I have to be the one who provides security and discipline, otherwise, she's never gonna get herself back on track. And even if I'm wrong, even if I make mistakes, you have to back me up in front of her, otherwise, it's just not going to work.'

'Come on, Luke, when did I not back you up?'

'You and that inspector, what's his name; Wade. You both almost burst out laughing when Selina told you that she had got those leprechauns as a present for both of us. Couldn't you see that that just reinforces her behaviour?'

'Luke, I think you're overreacting . . .'

Luke shook his head, almost in disbelief. 'I know you think that, I know you thought that when I kicked Mickey out of the house, and I know that you think that Selina's just a teenager and bound to make mistakes, but she's made some pretty big ones in her time. You weren't there when she was going through cold turkey . . .'

32

'No, Luke, I wasn't,' Lorraine folded her arms across her chest. 'And why was that? Because *you* didn't tell me, that's why, *you* were the one who wouldn't let me in . . .'

Luke made a pass at the air as if waving away her statement. 'Right,' he said. 'Yes, that's true. But yer had other things to deal with. I couldn't deal with anything else. I had to sit outside her door and listen to her scream bloody murder.'

'But Luke, she's over that now, and you've got to let her have some room, you've got to show that you trust her, otherwise she's going to do this all over again.'

Luke sighed heavily and ran his hand over his eyes. 'You see, this is exactly what I'm talking about. You can't help but interfere. You've got to put yer oar in. I have to learn how to be a father to Selina for myself, can't you see that? And I can't do that if you're constantly undermining my judgement or making me look like a fool in front of my daughter.'

Lorraine felt as if she had been slapped. 'What are you saying, Luke?' She had left Houghton this morning feeling so happy and secure in her relationship, knowing that her and Luke could face anything together, even a daughter who had run off from home. But now Luke seemed to be suggesting otherwise.

Luke sighed. 'I don't know what I'm saying.' He looked straight into her face and she could see the pain in his eyes. 'I love yer, Lorraine, yer know that. But Selina comes first, I have to do what's right for her.'

'Are yer breaking up with me?' Lorraine asked, her voice a whisper. She couldn't quite believe what she was hearing.

'No – I don't know. I don't want to but I can't see how this can work at the moment.'

'Well, what about if we cool it for a while, yer know. Give you and Selina a proper chance to really get to know each other without me being in the way. It's got to be hard for her, and for you. There's adjustment to be made on both sides.

33

Maybes you both need a little space. I . . . I might be in the way.' Lorraine said all this with horror in her heart.

Luke sat perfectly still, his eyes on the fireplace. *Say something damn it.* Lorraine glared at his profile.

Another long moment ticked by, and Lorraine was just about ready to take it all back and say that, to hell with it, it might be difficult but surely, if anyone could make it work they could . . . but then Luke lifted his eyes to hers.

His face was solemn when he said, 'I think you're right.'

After the argument that they had just had, Lorraine was expecting – dreading – that he would agree, but it was still something of a shock. God, she thought. Is this really it? Does cooling it down mean that it'll cool off altogether? The past few weeks hadn't been easy – they hadn't really had that honeymoon period when couples first get together where all they can think about was each other. Lorraine always knew that Selina came first, and she had never resented that fact. And now, the fact that she cared enough about both Luke and Selina to offer help and advice had been thrown back in her face. 'Wow,' she said slowly. 'So this is really it.'

'I don't mean for us to finish, good God no! You know I love yer Lorraine, but maybes we should only see each other on weekends, or something. Just until she settles down and properly finds her feet, if yer know what I mean.'

'Yeah, Luke,' said Lorraine. 'I think I do.' Even though it all sounded so logical, that it made sense that Luke and Selina needed a chance to get to know each other, it still made her feel very sad.

'Well, that's it,' she said brightly. Luke held his arms out as if he wanted a hug. She walked past him, with a smile on her face that felt horribly false, but she felt that if she didn't smile, then she would start to cry, and she couldn't do that in front of Luke, not when he was going through hell. If his daughter was going to be nightmarish, if work was going to take up most of his time, then she wanted to be the one thing in his life that he didn't have to worry about. 'Listen, I'm just going out to clear my head. Don't wait up.'

The last thing she saw when she closed the door was Luke's face looking back at her, looking sad, and somehow defeated.

Downstairs Lorraine was sitting at the bar, already regretting her rashness, her jean-clad legs gripping the stool, her knuckles white from clenching her wine glass.

Should have known, she thought staring at the different coloured bottles behind the bar. *It was too good to be true.* She sighed. *Pull yourself together*, she told herself. *We're not teenagers anymore. Both of us have come through a lot. We've both got history and baggage. I just thought that because we knew each other so well, that we'd bypass all that shit. Just goes to show that when it comes to love, I don't know a single thing. Shit, let's be honest, it's me running away like a bloody teenager when really he's just looking for a way around the problem, she's his kid for God's sake.*

She drained her glass and placed it on the bar.

'Can I get you another?'

Startled, Lorraine quickly looked round. It was Inspector Wade, dressed immaculately in an expensive-looking suit.

'This is my local watering hole,' he offered, by way of explanation for him being there. 'The place I unwind to of a night and try to forget what a shitty day it's been. In fact, Detective Inspector Hunt, you'll find that about forty per cent of the people in here are Garda. All of them doing their best to blot out another working day.'

'That bad?'

Wade nodded. 'I suspect it's pretty much the same wherever you go.'

Lorraine returned his nod. She'd seen her fair share of

human depravity, people were people, good and bad, wherever you went.

Wade caught the barman's eye. 'Pint of the usual Ian?' he said. Without waiting for Wade to answer he began filling a pint glass with a rich, dark liquid.

'Guinness?' Lorraine asked, more for something to say than out of any burning need to know. Anything to take her mind off Luke. She couldn't get out of her head that look that he had given her when she left the hotel room. She knew he must be hurting; she was hurting too. But there didn't seem to be any other way out of it.

'That's right,' Wade smiled at her. The smile, Lorraine noticed, didn't quite meet his amazing green eyes. Those same eyes raked the room until he spotted an empty table in the bay window. 'Fancy sharing a table?'

Lorraine thought about it for a moment, then decided, why not, what the hell.

She unwound her long legs from the stool and followed Wade as he weaved his way through the tables, saying hello to this one and nodding at that one. Lorraine could feel eyes bore into her back and just knew in moments they would be gossiping about her, wondering who she was. Police stations were the worst places in the world for gossip, she knew her own was rife with it.

Yeah well, if they think I'm green eyes' latest conquest, they can think again.

They sat down. Wade took a deep drink of his Guinness, looking in her eyes the whole time. *Is he flirting with me?* Lorraine wondered. *Doesn't he know that Luke and I are together, or does he just think that we're good friends?* Then she caught herself. *Were* together, she amended. *And so what if he's flirting*, she thought rebelliously, the one wine that she drank on an empty stomach making her feel slightly more gung ho than usual. *I can flirt if I want to, no one's stopping me.* But the thought sounded hollow, even to herself. Wade was good looking all right, and charming, but there was something about him that was a bit off. Maybe it was his odd accent that she couldn't quite place, maybe it was that he simply wasn't – and could never be – anything like Luke.

Wade put his glass down on the place mat and smiled again at Lorraine. It was as if he was about to say something, but didn't quite know how to start. Lorraine smiled encouragingly. Finally Wade blurted out, 'You really don't recognise me, do you?'

Whatever Lorraine had been expecting him to say, it wasn't this. She frowned. 'No, I don't think so. Should I?'

Ian Wade looked at her for a long moment. 'Think about it for a bit, I'm sure it'll come to you soon.'

Lorraine slowly shook her head. 'No, nothing. I'm sorry . . .'

Wade laughed, 'No worries,' he said, putting his hands up as if he was defending himself, 'I get it all the time. Actually it's good that I'm so forgettable. Great for undercover work.'

Lorraine smiled at his weak joke. 'Well, go on,' she said after a couple of silent seconds had passed. 'How do I know yer then?'

Wade leaned in, as if confiding a dark secret to Lorraine. 'I used to go to school with you.'

'What!' Lorraine said. 'In Houghton-le-Spring?' Wade nodded as he took another sip of his beer. And then she thought to herself: that explains the accent at least, and the odd word slips. But it was still amazing – to meet up with someone in the same line of work as her, from her part of the world, in a completely different city.

'Small world, isn't it?' Wade said, and once again, Lorraine had that uneasy feeling that Wade had intuited what she had been thinking. Lorraine looked at him with puzzlement. 'I'm wracking my brains but I just can't recall you at all.'

Wade shrugged, 'Well, I remember you though. You were so pretty, all the boys fancied you.' He smiled as Lorraine laughed. 'No, it's true! But you either didn't care or didn't know that they did. I think that made you even more attractive to all those hormonal adolescents.'

'Well, you've definitely kissed the blarney stone!' Lorraine took a sip of her wine. 'But what about you? Were you in the same year?'

'Same year, same class. But to be fair, I was really shy, I wasn't one for sports and I didn't go to parties. I left Houghton when I was younger, when I was about sixteen or so. Actually,' Wade took another sip of Guinness, 'I'm not surprised you don't remember me. I was actually quite boring.'

Lorraine smiled.

'Hey, this is when you say, "oh no you're not" . . .'

Lorraine laughed, and when Wade asked her if she would like another glass of wine, she said yes.

Two hours later, they had talked about what some of their old schoolmates were up to, although Wade had lost touch with almost everyone in Houghton. They had giggled together about some of the more annoying teachers and had talked about school life in general. It felt fantastic to talk to someone who didn't have any claims on her at all, though as much as Lorraine wanted to unburden herself, something about Wade held her in check. So when he said, 'So, what's the story between you and Detective Sergeant Luke Daniels, then?' Lorraine hesitated. She wasn't really sure whether she wanted to talk about Luke to this man, but being slightly tipsy, she thought, what the hell.

'He's, well, he's kind of my boyfriend, but after today, well, I don't know what's happening.'

'Selina a bit of a handful? You guys don't really get along?'

Lorraine sighed. 'Well yes, she is a handful,' she said slowly, 'but we get along great. She's a laugh, really energetic and talented, fiery and stubborn, actually *just* like her father. But underneath it all, she's not the problem. She's a good kid, just needs to find her own way in the world. I think it's more because of Luke and me, really. We've fancied each other for so long now, that there's all these expectations – other people's as well as our own.'

'Reality doesn't measure up to the fantasy,' Wade nodded his head in sympathy. 'I get that.'

'That's not quite it,' Lorraine frowned. 'I think we both went into this knowing each other well enough. It's not that I don't think that we won't be together, I just think that it's the wrong time for us, perhaps.'

Lorraine became aware of Wade's knee touching hers. She drew it away and looked into Wade's face. He was looking at her in a way that she didn't really like. 'Oops sorry,' she said, faking a yawn. 'I, er . . . I think I'll go up now. I'm shattered . . .' she yawned again. 'I've got an early flight in the morning.' She stood up from her chair and held her hand out. 'Thanks for the drink. It's been really nice talking to you.'

'Do you really have to go? It's still early, by Dublin's standards at least.'

Lorraine nodded. 'I'm afraid so.'

But Wade was persistent. 'You know, Dublin for all its sins is a beautiful city. Especially at night time. I could show you the sights.'

Yeah, I'll just bet yer'll show me the sights an' all.

'Thanks, but I really am beat. Bye.'

'Well, let me walk you to the lift, at least.'

Lorraine nodded, her smile tight. He just wasn't getting the hint. And that wasn't all. As they waited for the lift, he took hold of her hand and brushed it with his lips. Lorraine stared at the top of his head. *Whoa boy*, she thought, *slow down*.

Although, if she admitted the truth to herself, she did feel rather flattered, who wouldn't? Ian Wade was a good-looking man.

Not as good looking as Luke though.

Luke. Before today she had found herself smiling whenever she thought of his name, but now there was a big jolt in her stomach as she realised that he probably wouldn't be waiting in the bed for her, or holding out his arms to embrace her, making her feel so warm and safe and loved. She hadn't cried yet, and perhaps it was the booze, but she felt herself tearing up at the thought that she and Luke weren't properly together anymore.

But I think Wade may have got the wrong idea though. What with me telling him me troubles an' all.

The lift finally arrived, and deciding that she needed to make a quick getaway, she tripped as she quickly stepped into the lift and came very close to hitting her head on one of the mirrored walls.

'Are you all right Lorraine?' Wade asked, following her into the lift. 'Might be best if I help you to your room, get you settled in?'

'No, no . . .' Lorraine said, feeling foolish. What would Luke think? She pushed him back out of the lift, muttering, 'It's OK, I'll be fine. I only had a few yer know, it's not as if I'm tipsy or anything. Well maybes just a little bit, but I'm fine, really. So . . . er . . . Bye then.'

She smiled at him as the lift doors closed between them.

'Jesus,' she said out loud. That was a close call.

Very quietly she slipped into the room. From Selina's room there was silence, from the room she was supposed to be sharing with Luke, there came a gentle snoring.

She went to knock on Luke's bedroom door, but then thought better of it. Irrationally, she felt angry with Luke. It really was over. She could face that, but what really hurt was that he didn't even try to fight for her. And now here he was, sleeping like a baby. Her face set in a stubborn mask, she quietly went into Selina's room, grabbed a spare quilt and made herself as comfortable as she could on the settee. Which, seeing as her long legs hung over the edge, was not very comfortable at all.

'Damn you to hell Luke Daniels,' she muttered, just before she closed her eyes.

He opened the door slowly, eased the key silently out of the lock and, remembering the exact place the door creaked – and the extraordinary hearing of old Mrs Holland who lived next door, he stepped quietly into the house.

He threw his bags into the bedroom, then headed for the kitchen and opened the fridge.

'Hmm.' Mouth watering, he looked at the plate full of fresh meat, liver, kidneys, you name it. He loved cooking and he was ravenous.

He looked at the knife rack and was mesmerised for a moment, then he went over and one by one pulled the six knives out of the rack. Carefully choosing the one he wanted he put the others back and collected everything he needed from the fridge.

Tonight he would prepare a surprise. 'Ha.'

Part Two

4

Selina viciously poked her toast soldier into her soft-boiled egg, looked at it, grimaced, and then bit into it. *God, he even makes soldiers, would you believe*, she thought. *Obsessing that I have to eat breakfast every day.*

She sighed. She was certainly in the dog house though. Had been ever since they had got back to Houghton three days ago. So, to appease her father, she dunked a piece of toast into the egg and ate it. *Better eat the stupid egg or old moany face will have something else to complain about.*

She sighed, which caused Luke to look from behind his newspaper. 'What?' he asked, looking suspiciously at her.

Shrugging, Selina sucked butter off her fingers before replying, 'Never said anything.'

'Huh.' Luke grunted.

God, Selina bristled inside, how bloody long is he gonna sulk for?

I only got drunk, Selina thought. *And it was just a couple of friggin' ornaments for Christ's sake. OK, and the hundred quid. But I've apologised and I wasn't on the junk. Anyway, I*

45

don't need to answer to him. I managed quite well without moany face for nearly seventeen years.

She sighed, blurted out, 'Look . . .' then hesitated. It had been awkward at first, wondering what to call him. Dad didn't seem right, especially after sixteen years without one, so mostly she skirted around it, like people do when they know they should remember your name but can't for the life of them think of it. When it became absolutely necessary, she called him Luke, even though it always felt awkward.

When he heard her speak, he glanced up, and father and daughter eyed each other like restless sparring partners.

'What's wrong with Mickey?' she demanded, 'Why don't you want me to see him? That's what I want to know.'

Luke folded his newspaper, rose from his chair then picked his jacket up and shrugged it on, all the time looking at Selina.

'Jesus,' she flung her hands up in the air, 'doesn't anyone ever get a second chance around here?'

'What do yer think yer getting now?' Luke, face stern, glared at her.

'So, can't you answer my fu— question?' She'd stopped herself just in time, but he knew what she was going to say.

'A question yes, a demand no. And certainly not a question asked with a gutter mouth.' He moved to the door.

Selina sighed, OK, so she had been stupid, but he had hardly talked to her since they had come back from Dublin. She understood that he wanted to punish her, but at the same time, she needed more than the monosyllabic answers she was getting from him lately, 'OK, OK, I'll try and tone it down. So, where's Lorraine? I haven't seen her since Ireland, has she upset you an' all?'

Luke froze, then spun round from the door. If she thought he'd looked angry before, now he looked downright frightening. She held herself perfectly still as Luke took a step towards her. *At least that got a reaction*, she thought.

46

Luke's voice was quiet when he spoke, as if he was trying his hardest to keep control. 'Anything between Lorraine and me is just that, between Lorraine and me. So keep yer nose out of it.' Seeing Selina's bewildered face, he softened. 'And as for Mickey Carson, I've changed me mind. Yes, yer can see him, but on one condition.'

Conditions, Selina thought. *Of course, there's bound to be conditions.* She stared at her father, wondering what was coming next.

'I will pick you up at two o'clock tomorrow afternoon and take you to Shiny Row College for an interview.'

'College!' Selina's mouth hung open; that was the last thing she had expected.

'Yeah, it's a place of learning.'

'Yeah, I know what college is,' Selina said sarcastically. 'But dream on. I'm not gonna go to any poncy college.'

Luke shrugged, and smiled to himself. He knew he had the upper hand at last. It had taken some thinking through, but he'd made enquiries yesterday, and since then it had just been waiting for the right moment to spring it on Selina. He fully believed that the devil made work for idle hands; his grandmother used to say it constantly. Not just that, he also thought that Selina had talent, but without someone to take that talent and show her how to utilise it properly, it wasn't going to go anywhere. To be honest, he knew that stopping her from seeing Mickey was an empty threat. But if it helped to get Selina into education, then it was a threat well worth making.

'The choice is yours, either yer go to college and yer can meet Mickey Carson afterwards, or don't go to college and I'll have you and Mickey tailed where ever yer go . . . He'll sharp get sick of yer then.'

'But . . . But that . . . That's blackmail.'

'Yer better believe it.'

47

He turned back to leave just as someone knocked on the front door. A moment later he returned holding a long-stemmed white rose in bud, in a plastic tube.

'Obviously not for me,' he said, putting the rose on the table. 'Mickey fiddling the dole again?'

Selina stared at the rose, she hung back from the table where Luke had placed it, a suspicious frown on her face. Realising she was not going to answer him, Luke left for work. He did wonder why Selina didn't look happy to receive the rose – but that was teenagers for yer. The colour wasn't right or something, or getting a rose was deeply uncool. He snorted. Selina could be so irritating sometimes, she couldn't even be grateful when she received a gift.

Hearing the front door slam, Selina moved to the table, goose bumps prickling the skin on her arms, the hairs on the back of her neck bristling. She nibbled at her knuckles for a moment as she stared at the delicate flower.

'Please, let it be from Mickey,' she murmured.

Pure fright burned in her eyes. Then she shivered. There was no card. Slowly she picked the rose up, and as she did a thorn pierced the tube and entered her thumb.

The man stood across the street, his eyes hard stone chips that glowed with burning hate. He watched as a tall black man came to the door and took the rose from the smiling florist's hands. The man nodded his satisfaction, his lips curled in a sneer.

Thought you had escaped girl, he thought to himself. So easy to follow you, you and your pathetic little ex-druggie friend; you and your even more pathetic new boyfriend, what a fucking wimp. Nobody escapes from me. Not her, not him, and especially not you.

He pulled his dark hood up over his head, the drizzle of the last hour was steadily turning into a deluge. Not that he minded the rain, oh no, the rain was good cover, the rain hid a lot, and washed even more away.

He was bored now. He'd seen enough. He knew now where she lived. The sneer turned into a spiteful grin as he turned and walked away.

5

'So, yer see boss . . . Boss, boss are yer listening?' Carter leaned over Lorraine's desk and peered closely at her.

Carter, the young uniformed police officer who had been taken under Lorraine and Luke's wing over a year ago, was trying really hard to break Lorraine out of whatever mood that she had been in since she and Luke had returned from Ireland. Carter had a face full of freckles, bright red hair and adored Lorraine and Luke, in that order. 'Boss.'

'What?' she snapped, when she realised how far in her face he was.

'Yer weren't here, boss.'

'Course I bloody well was,' Lorraine retorted.

'What was I saying then?'

'We don't have time for these sort of games, Carter. This is a police station. We have work to do.'

'Knew yer weren't listening.'

Shit, Lorraine thought, what the hell had he been rambling on about? Knowing it would have something to do with his obsession about local history, she took a guess.

'St Michael's Church.'

Carter looked impressed, then threw his spanner into the works. 'Yeah, but what exactly about the church?'

Lorraine was saved from answering as Scottie, Sunderland's top pathologist rapped with his knuckles on Lorraine's office door, which was already open and came in. Scottie was a huge bear of a man and had more hair on his body than his head, strands of black hair peeped out of his cuffs and over his collar. But, although he looked large and gruff, he had a big heart and a kindly face. He'd been brought up in the children's home in Houghton-le-Spring, of which he was now on the board of governors, so he knew well what it was like to be a product of the system, lost and forgotten, and he really wanted to help.

His long-time assistant Edna, who was well past retiring, had become his surrogate mother; not only did he work with her, they shared a house on the outskirts of Durham. It may seem to be an unusual relationship, but it worked very well for both of them; they could keep an eye on each other. Scottie was also a very good friend of Lorraine's, and was always in her corner. Lorraine appreciated his loyalty.

'Scottie!' she said with genuine delight. 'Good to see you.' But as pleased as she was to see him, it was unusual to see him inside the police station, usually Lorraine went to him, to view a body and to discuss what had happened to it. Or, they would meet up at a crime scene. The fact of the matter was that she mostly saw him in connection with one death or another; it was very strange to see him out of his normal context.

'Hello, my love. How are we today? As always you look good enough to eat.'

Lorraine smiled. Scottie was a very likeable person, and it was hard not to smile around him. Lorraine also knew that sometimes Scottie was the only attendee at the funerals of the lost and lonely who passed through his very capable hands. He had a genuine concern for the dead, and it was this respect that Lorraine admired, that and his attention to detail.

'So, business or pleasure Scottie? Not that it's not good to see you, but you don't normally come down to the station.'

'Well, it's sort of both, Lorraine, I er . . . I wondered if, that is, if you're free, you would come with me to a charity dinner tomorrow night. Edna, God bless her, has that damn flu bug that's doing the rounds. I'm sick of telling her to get the injections, but she keeps refusing to. She's going to be all right, but she really just needs to rest up at the moment. So I, er, wondered, if you've got nothing on maybe you could come with me? I know it's short notice and that you're probably doing something with Luke, but if you're not,' he raised his eyebrows in a hopeful gesture, 'you could come along with me as a friend? I don't really fancy going to these things myself.'

Shit, what the hell, why not, Lorraine thought. It's better than sitting in with the Hippy and the Rock Chick, watching re-runs on the telly. 'Well, actually, I'm not doing anything tomorrow night, so OK.'

Carter and Scottie looked as if neither could quite believe what she was saying. 'OK? Did she say OK?' Scottie raised his eyebrows questioningly at Carter.

Carter nodded solemnly.

'Wow, yes, OK, that's great Lorraine, really appreciate it . . . Pick you up at half past six tomorrow then . . .' he backed quickly out of the door, as if staying one more minute would give her the chance to change her mind.

Carter looked at Lorraine, worry in his eyes, his frown drawing his many freckles even closer together. 'What about Luke?'

'What about Luke? Jesus we are not tied at the friggin' waist, yer know. And I'll also have yer know it has nothing at all to do with Luke who I choose to go out with, OK . . . Nor has it bloody well got anything to do with you. Christ between them two at home and you two here, anybody would think I was a flaming teenager.'

52

'Sorry, boss,' Carter mumbled. He blushed, his face almost matching his bright-red hair.

'Yeah,' Lorraine frowned at him. 'Well, I'll talk to you later Carter, cos right now I'm supposed to be having a meeting with Clark.'

Carter gave a half smile and nodded as Lorraine stepped past him, knowing that his big mouth had dropped him up to his knees in shit again. He prayed that Clark would have some news that would take the heat off him a little bit – obviously nothing serious or threatening to the community – but anything other than that would be good. Lorraine had been in a foul mood these past few days and Luke hadn't been much better. Carter just wished that they wouldn't take it out on him so much.

Lorraine hurried along the corridor and stopped outside Clark's office. She pulled down the sleeves of her navy pin-stripe suit, straightened the collar of her white cotton blouse, then ran her hands over her hair, smoothing it back where it had escaped from the band at the back of her head.

She knocked on Clark's door, and he gave her permission to enter.

Lorraine went in and sat in the chair facing Clark. He was studiously avoiding her gaze, keeping her waiting while he finished off some paperwork. It was an annoying tactic of his, designed to put her in her place, to make her feel as if he had much more important things on his mind than his senior officer. Lorraine knew exactly what he was doing, and usually, his pettiness only irritated her. Today, it was all she could do not to reach over his desk and snatch the pen from his hands. She settled for saying, 'You wanted to see me, sir?'

Clark, with great deliberation, put the cap back on his pen and leaned back in his chair. He regarded her for a long moment – another tactic – and she bore it impatiently, waiting for Clark to say whatever it was that he had to say, so she could get back to her work. That was the difference between her and Clark, he was a consummate politician, manipulative and slick, whereas Lorraine became a cop because helping people was all that she had ever wanted to do. She knew that dealing with bureaucracy was an inevitable part of her job, but some people positively enjoyed it. She tried to remain calm. She had an idea of what this meeting would be about. Chances were it would be about Clark's lackey, Sara Jacobs, who at this moment was on suspension because of her big mouth. If Lorraine had her way, she wouldn't be on suspension, she'd be stripped of her badge altogether.

At the end of last year, the teenagers of Houghton were terrorised by a man who promised them love and freedom, but had given them fear and slavery instead. If things had gone to plan, he should have been given a fair trial. He was a very evil man, and some young people who had followed him had disappeared. Perhaps if he was still alive, he could have told their families what had happened to them, given them some sort of closure. But it wasn't to be. Instead, he had been killed by the grieving mother of a boy he had had murdered.

Jacobs had let slip to Debbie Stansfield that her son Richard's death was not, as had been first believed, a suicide, and so Debbie had taken the law into her own hand and was now sitting in a jail cell in Durham awaiting trial.

Finally, Clark cleared his throat, another one of his habits that Lorraine found very annoying, then said, 'How are things, Lorraine?'

Lorraine groaned inwardly. *Has he heard something then? Has he heard about me and Luke splitting up? Good God, I hope not. The last thing I need is Clark's false sympathy when I know that he'd be crowing with happiness inside.* She pasted a false smile on her face. 'Very well, sir,' she said in tones of honeyed politeness. 'And how are you?' *God, we sound as if we haven't seen each other for months!*

'Well, Lorraine.' Oh dear, here it comes, she thought. He smiled as he went on. 'It looks like Houghton police are going to get our moment of glory at last.'

Lorraine frowned. So this wasn't about Sara Jacobs after all. She dreaded to think what the hell he was so bloody happy about. Clark was obsessed by image and loved the media spotlight. She hoped it wasn't going to be anything like a fly-on-the-wall documentary or something of that nature. It would be exactly like Clark to agree to something like that, not thinking about how the film crew would impede the day-to-day running of the station.

So she was less than surprised when Clark said, 'A reporter from the *Sunderland Echo*, with her editor's good wishes, has approached me. She wants to run a series of pieces on real police work, you know the hard bones of the job.' He rustled some papers on his desk until he found the one he wanted. Lorraine was guessing what was coming, and her heart sank.

'Ah yes, here she is, Kate Mulberry, quite a nice name don't you think?'

When Lorraine didn't answer he pushed his glasses back up his nose and went on with a smarmy smile, 'I've decided to put her with you and Luke Daniels. That way, she can see the real guts of the job.'

Lorraine took a deep breath. 'I'm sorry, sir, I don't think that's a good idea.'

Clark looked perplexed. 'Well, who else would I assign her to? Dinwall? Sanderson? Myself?' At this last comment, he laughed nervously. 'No, you're the only ones who would do. You and Luke are the new, modern face of policing, and that's the one that we want to show to the public.'

'Well, that's sort of my point, sir,' Lorraine went on. 'What we show the public, I mean. I don't care if she follows Luke and me about,' *yes, I bloody do*, 'but we won't have any control over what she writes about, or how she portrays us.'

'For God's sake, Lorraine, don't be so bloody paranoid. Don't you think I've thought this through? It's not an investigative piece, it's just going to be a couple of articles about your work and how that fits into the community. I see it as only a positive thing. God knows we need all the good publicity we can get after that, ah, incident, last year.'

Lorraine sighed. If it had to happen, then it was better that this Kate Mulberry should stick around with her, where she could keep an eye on her. She'd better warn the troops to be on their best behaviour. 'When does she begin?'

Clark nodded, pleased that he had won Lorraine over. She could certainly be, at times, the most difficult and stubborn woman on the planet, but she was taking this so well. 'Tomorrow morning, first thing.'

She stood up, 'OK, is that it sir?'

'Well, apart from one other matter.'

Oh God, Lorraine thought, alarm bells ringing in her head. She could tell what it was about, just by the tone in his voice. 'And that is?'

'Yourself and Detective Sergeant Daniels.'

Fuck. Lorraine thought. *He has heard something. Police stations are the worst places in the world for gossip. I've always thought it.* 'So, what about me and Detective Daniels?'

Clark laughed, 'Come on Lorraine, the whole station knows that something is up between the pair of youse. Yer hardly speaking to each other . . . what's going on? A lovers' tiff?'

'*Tiff?*' Lorraine said incredulously.

'Well, I don't know what you want to call it. The fact is, that I knew from the beginning that this was a bad idea. Two people, working so closely with each other, you were mad to think that it wouldn't blow up in your face at some point.'

Lorraine seethed. She was almost at breaking point. 'Well,

sir,' she said sarcastically, 'it's not really any of your business what Luke and I are up to.'

Clark, who had been leaning on his chair, brought it down to earth with a thump. 'Actually, no,' he said with a sternness in his voice, 'you are completely wrong about that. When it's the talk of the station, that's exactly when it becomes my business. People are noticing that there's something wrong, and people are commenting on it. You've been biting people's heads off, and Luke has been glowering round the place like a wounded bear, which just isn't like him. It doesn't take a genius to put two and two together. Frankly, I don't think you should have had that "fling", or whatever it was, in the first place, but now it's done, now it's over – put it right. You're the superior officer, it's up to you. I don't care how yer do it, just do it. I don't want my two best officers at loggerheads, especially when this young Kate Mulberry is going to be around.'

Lorraine was quiet for a moment. Clark was well aware of how passionately his best officer could take things. He sat back again in his chair waiting for her outburst, and was mildly surprised that when it came it was more like a damp squib.

'OK, sir,' she said, then she rose and headed for the door. She closed it quietly behind her, and leaned with her back to it for a moment.

God! The cheeky bastard. I won't give any of them the satisfaction of thinking that anything that they've been saying is affecting me in any way. But bloody hell. I've got to talk to Luke, try to make it so that it doesn't affect our work. Her heart sunk at the thought. They had managed to avoid talking about Ireland – they had managed to avoid talking at all, in fact – but Lorraine knew that that couldn't go on for much longer.

She silently frowned her way along the corridor to her office. Spotting her Carter caught up, and walked behind her into her office. 'Everything OK with Clark?' he asked.

Lorraine stood behind her desk, shuffling paper so as not to look the young policeman in the face. She was sure that he hadn't been the one to gossip, and really, she didn't care about that, but she was still smarting a little from the dressing down in Clark's office.

Finally she said, 'It's not great news. We're going to have a reporter hanging around our heels for the next couple of days. Get the gang together, will you? I need to tell them about it, make sure that everyone is on the same page with this.'

'A reporter?' said Carter.

'Yes, Carter, didn't you hear me the first time?' Lorraine said irritably, and then remembering what Clark had said, sighed and looked up at her young constable. 'Sorry, Carter. Just got other things on my mind. Yep, someone by the name of Kate Mulberry wants to do a profile on the station. Clark thinks it's a good idea, I don't. But I don't have a choice on the matter. She's going to be tailing me and Luke, and maybe a few other officers, if I can offload her on to them.'

'It might be all right boss, she might be a canny lass,' Carter said.

'That's two might's in one sentence Carter,' Lorraine said, but she tempered it with a smile.

Carter sighed, he adored Lorraine and respected her judgement in all things. 'But what can it harm boss? We've got nowt to hide, everybody knows yer run a tight ship. Anyhow, time these people from the newspapers saw how hard we really work, rather than running us down every chance they get. And it could have been worse, what if they had sent that other one, yer know him with the deerstalker hat.'

'I know, I know. It's just the sheer irritation factor. Do they think I have time to chaperone bloody reporters about? God, I could strangle the sodding editor who came up with this one. Bloody reporters.'

*

Not so long ago, Luke would sit in Lorraine's office, where they would talk through their cases. But now, of course, that camaraderie had evaporated. Luke had come into the station like a bear with a sore head, and Sanderson, seeing his mood, had quickly taken him into the locker room, where he told Luke to get whatever he had to say off his chest.

At first, Luke had been reticient, but then he found that he was pouring his heart out to Sanderson, who had sat quietly listening. Sanderson, a small neat man with sandy-coloured hair, had known Lorraine from her very first day in uniform and had taken her under his wing. He became more like an uncle than a colleague to her, and would back her up, whatever the situation. Personally, he thought that Luke was being a bit stubborn. Sure, if he was in Luke's position, he'd take all the help he could get, not throw it away, like Luke seemed to be doing.

'Christ man, yer've been trying for a year to get together, the times I could have banged both yer heads against the wall. And now yer go and blow it.'

'Thanks, Sanderson, last time I come to you for any sympathy.'

Sanderson sighed. 'Look, Luke. I just don't get it. Yer've got a great girl in Lorraine, yer know that, and she's taking an interest in Selina and wants to help. I just don't see what yer problem is. Get it together, man, you'll lose her otherwise, and it'll be the worst thing that could happen to yer.'

This didn't boost Luke's confidence at all, and he went into the incident room with his heart heavier than ever.

Lorraine looked up when she saw them come into the room. 'Daniels, Sanderson,' she said, with a slight edge to her voice. 'Nice of you to join us. Find a seat.' She was sitting on the corner of a table at the top of the room, and her eyes followed them as they found a seat and sat down.

'It seems,' she began finally, 'that from tomorrow morning we will have a reporter with us.'

There was silence for a moment, then a collective groan went up around the policemen. Lorraine raised her hand. 'I know, I know. But Clark thinks it will be good for the image of the station.' Here James Dinwall let out a large snort. 'Yes, Dinwall, my thoughts exactly. But we don't have a choice. The young woman's name is Kate Mulberry, and I want you all to treat her with respect. And yes, that does include you too, Dinwall.' Everyone in the incident room laughed. Dinwall thought of himself as a bit of a ladies' man. 'She has access to the station, but not unrestricted access, I want a police officer to keep an eye on her at all times. And if there's anything that she wants to see that you're not certain about, run it past me first. Are we all clear?'

Muttered affirmatives and nods came from the assembled policemen, and Lorraine stood up to leave. 'Oh, and Luke?' Lorraine said pleasantly. Luke looked up, surprised. 'When yer have a minute, can I see yer in my office?'

Lorraine caught some of the looks that passed between the men, but she didn't care. Consciously avoiding Luke's gaze, she walked out of the incident room and into her office.

Luke followed her just a few seconds later, and shut the door quietly behind him. 'Yes, boss?' he said.

'How's Selina getting on?' Lorraine asked.

Luke nodded, and said, 'Fine, thanks for asking. Is that what you called me in to talk about?'

Lorraine took a deep breath. 'First of all, Luke, I'm going to apologise. I was out of line with you and Selina.' Luke went to say something but Lorraine put up a hand to silence him. 'Please, Luke,' she said softly, 'this is difficult for me. Let me say my piece. I know that we're taking a break, and I agree that it's the best thing that we can do, in this situation. But we have to work together, and we can't let whatever's happening between us affect the station, like it's been doing.'

'Lorraine, I . . .' Luke's voice trailed off. He so wanted to take her into his arms, but then he remembered Selina, and how she had to be the most important person in his life, even if that meant letting the love of his life go. '. . . I think you're right. I'm sorry too,' he said.

'I don't think it's ever going to get back to the way it was,' Lorraine carried on, 'but I'd like to try. You're a great policeman, Luke, and we work well together. Let's not give the station any more gossip than it already has, OK?'

Luke nodded. 'Thanks, boss,' he said. He smiled wanly at her and left her office. Lorraine put her head in her hands and willed the tears not to fall.

He stared at the white rose. Never had he seen anything so pure as a white rose in full bloom.

'The rose,' he said, perhaps to the rose or perhaps to himself, 'is a symbol of purity and love, and has been spouted as such by poets since fore ever . . . Liars . . . There is no such thing as love.'

He picked the rose up and began pulling the petals off one by one.

'There is only lust.' More petals fell to the floor.

'And there is only revenge . . . Ha.'

6

Selina took a deep breath and walked into the room. The room was in a drop-in centre, which was situated in a prefab just out the front of the Hall Lane Children's Home. It was, like the rest of the home, deeply institutional. The walls were painted a creamy grey, and were smudged and scuffed. The floor was covered with carpet tiles, some were coming up at the edges, and were the kind of orangey-brown colour that had been popular in the late part of the seventies. The room was brightly lit from fluorescent lights that were set into the ceiling.

On the walls were posters with lurid pictures and vivid writing, warning of the evils of drugs. Selina knew all about these evils, knew too well how easy it was to slip into taking them. Drugs offered, at the beginning anyway, a solace and comfort that you couldn't find anywhere else. But she knew that it was a lie. That drugs were never the solution.

But was this the answer? She was attending a group that was held for young people with substance abuse problems. When old moany face had told her that she had to go, she resisted. She didn't actually scream at him or anything at that

63

– she had learned pretty quick that that wasn't the right tack to take with him, but at the same time, she had told him that these sort of groups were a joke, that they didn't work and she couldn't see the use of attending. Anway, she was off the junk now, so why did it matter?

Luke had sat down with her and explained that it was important that she got support. That he knew how easy it was to go back to your old ways, and he wanted Selina to find strategies for coping. That was why he thought this group was so good. She could meet other teenagers in her position, and work out ways of avoiding situations where she might be tempted. Noticing that Selina still wasn't convinced, he had told her to give it a go. If she thought it really wasn't worth her time, then they'd try something else. Reluctantly, Selina agreed.

And, she had been pleasantly surprised. Carl Hanson had been more than welcoming the first night that Selina had attended the group. She had sat beside a pretty girl with blonde hair, who looked as if she was Selina's age, but then Selina had found out later that she was a few years older than her. The girl had nudged her in the ribs. 'Carl, he's a nice guy. But really skinny, don't yer think?'

Selina had agreed. Perhaps that's what made taking advice from Mr Hanson so much easier than listening to her father. He looked fragile, battered, as if he had been subjected to the worst that life could throw at him. And he accepted what you had to say, without judgement or morality. You could say to him that you were craving crack, and he'd just nod and tell you how to get past that craving.

And the group had been useful, too. Although Selina hadn't felt like contributing much, she thought that what Carl Hanson had suggested was practical and sensible. And she found herself nodding in agreement at some of the stories; some of the things the other kids had done weren't all that different from the stupid things that she had done. It felt good to know that she wasn't the only one out there. She hated to admit it, but maybe old moany face was right.

After the class, she had walked home with the blonde girl. Her name was Amy Knowles, and she had been clean for a bit longer than Selina, although she admitted that she still had days when it was all she could do to stop herself getting another fix. 'But I've got twins, boys,' said Amy, her face lighting up. 'So I just picture their faces and think: if you can't do it for yerself, do it for them, and that seems to help.'

After that evening, Selina and Amy became good friends, and Selina started looking forward to the nights when the group was held. But today she felt a gnawing sensation in her gut – and the thought that she had been followed here hadn't left her alone. Perhaps it was just paranoia left over from the drugs, but she thought it had more to do with the fact that she had been sent a white rose from someone. Hopefully Mickey, but that would be too much of a coincidence. There was only one person she knew who ever sent white roses to her, and she thought she was rid of him.

She took her seat beside Amy. 'Haven't seen yer since yer got back from Ireland,' Amy whispered. 'You OK?'

'Yeah, fine,' Selina whispered back, not sure whether or not to tell her about the gift that she had received that morning. If it was Mickey who sent her the rose, then she had nothing to worry about, but if it was who she thought it was, then she had every reason to be fucking terrified.

7

'So,' Kerry Lumsdon said to Mickey as she flopped down on the settee next to him. 'What's this Selina girl like?'

Kerry was a slim seventeen-year-old, with shoulder-length, gypsy black hair that she mostly wore in a pony tail. She dreamed of one day running for England in the Olympic games, and had recently been doing very well in quite a few regional events.

'It's none of yer business,' her younger brother Darren said, swinging his head round from their new television. 'Is it, Mickey?' Darren was a few shades darker than his brother and sisters, all of the Lumsdons had different fathers.

Kerry jumped up and clipped Darren's ear. Darren howled and looked at their older brother Robbie for help.

Robbie, who looked enough like Kerry to be her twin, shrugged, and said, 'It's yer own fault. Yer should have known she'd give yer a clout . . . idiot.'

'Shut up.' Emma, the fifth-in-line and the redhead of the family screamed, tearing her green eyes from the snarling alien on the screen to glare at them all with an expression astonishingly like that of the growling alien.

'You'll be next, yer little bitch.' Kerry threw a cushion at Emma.

Mickey grinned. He loved being here, he was an only child and he missed this kind of horse play; plus he used to fancy Kerry like mad. Kerry was at the head of a long list of babes that Mickey had fancied but had never dared ask out. But not now, now his thoughts were full of Selina.

'I'm bringing her round in half an hour or so. She's at the drop-in centre now,' he said, answering Kerry's question.

'Who?' Emma demanded.

'Nowt to do with you,' Kerry snapped.

Emma stuck her tongue out at her sister.

'I've warned yer before, I'll bite it off.'

'Wouldn't dare,' Emma replied.

Kerry made a move towards her, snapping her teeth, and Emma squealed.

'Yer must be mad bringing her here, she'll think she's walked into the nut house,' Robbie said, looking his family over and shaking his head.

'Yeah, probably.' Mickey stood up, 'But it's bloody freezing out there and we have nowhere else to go mate. Anyhow, yer did say yer wanted to meet her properly.'

'Yeah,' Robbie agreed. 'See yer later then.'

Ten minutes after Mickey had closed the Lumsdons' front door, he was stood outside the new library in Newbottle Street waiting for Selina. His heart thrilled when a few minutes later, he watched her walking towards him.

Selina was pleased to see Mickey already there. She glanced back the way she had come. The street, apart from a couple of stray cats fighting outside the betting shop doorway, was empty. She couldn't, however, shake off the strong feeling she'd had since leaving Amy, that she was being followed.

Living on the streets as she had, you learned to trust such feelings. Your survival instincts sometimes were able to warn you that the friends you had had yesterday were not today's, especially if they were in need. And although there had always been a room at her grandmother's, for the last two years she had usually been too high to go home.

She smiled at Mickey, her eyes settling on his face. She really liked him. OK, so he wasn't exactly the drop dead gorgeous type but he was quite good looking in his own way, he had character, and that was what was important. The best thing was that he was funny, even if most of the time he didn't even know it, which was a definite plus as far as she was concerned. Most of the guys she'd known had been far too spaced out to even appreciate a joke, never mind crack one. He was kind, and she thought with a smile, not a bad kisser.

That's all they had done though, kiss, which was why she had been so angry with old moany face for coming in, jumping to conclusions, and going off on one just because he had seen her holding hands with Mickey.

Then her mind did a backward flip, and she was seeing the white rose that had arrived this morning. With the image of the white rose came that of her old boyfriend and the thought of him brought prickles of apprehension up and down her spine. Eccles had been the sort of person you would run a mile from, that's if your head wasn't fucked up with drugs. Anything or anybody was fair game to Eccles, he especially loved mugging old ladies, and kids on their way to the shops or school were considered fair game. There were a lot of other things that it was said he was into, many more scary and dangerous things. But Selina hadn't cared at the time. As long as he could provide her with her next fix, then she couldn't care less what he was into.

There were a lot of losers on the streets, but Eccles had been something else. He was into weird things, stuff that she didn't really want to go into with him, even when they were together. He'd had a thing about roses, God knows where that particular obsession had come from. The last she'd seen of him had been in an old allotment shed, he'd been out of it with a needle stuck in his arm.

She sighed, thank God she had come out of it all in one piece. Thank God for her da— for Luke. Not that she was ever about to tell old moany face that she was grateful in any way . . . That would be totally uncool.

Deep in her heart on the darkest of nights, she'd wanted a way out. When she'd been alone, she had cried for a way out. Every time she'd seen a mate dragged off the street and into a cell, a hospital or a nut house, she'd gone to sleep that night, after countless hours tossing and turning in some rat hole, vowing that the next day she would get help. But the next morning had seen her off again, begging, stealing to feed her habit . . . She had never got to the point where she had sold her body, but then, she had been with Eccles, which was almost the same thing. She knew, though, if she was still on the streets, that Eccles would have probably made her go on the game to get some cash for the junk – she knew other girls whose boyfriends had forced them on to the street. Selina knew that there was one point where she wouldn't have cared what she did, so long as she had the junk to make it all better afterwards.

Please God if you are up there, don't let me go on it again, she prayed silently. *I'm sorry for everything I ever did. And please let the rose be from Mickey . . . Please.*

She shook her head, trying to shake the thoughts away, she was only five yards from Mickey now and she did not want any poison from her past life to ever spoil what was building between them.

'All right?' Mickey asked with a grin, when she reached him.

'Yeah, cool.'

Mickey always felt awkward when they first met up, he

never knew quite what to do with his hands, he felt totally clumsy . . . *All right. I am totally clumsy.*

God I so want to kiss her.

Maybes her cheek?

No better not, don't push it. She lets me kiss her good night, don't want to frighten her off.

He was standing with his hands in his pockets, trying his best to look cool, and nearly gasped out loud when she linked her arm through his.

'So,' Selina smiled up at him, 'I thought we were gonna chill with some mates of yours?'

'Oh aye . . . It's . . . er . . . it's this way . . . Down the Seahills,' Mickey nodded, then in his eagerness he spun round so fast that Selina nearly lost her footing.

'Sorry, sorry,' heart sinking Mickey froze. *Shit, I'm gonna spoil it already, she's not gonna want me if I break her frigging ankles.*

'It's all right,' she laughed, but inside she was dying to know if Mickey had sent the rose.

But if I ask if it's from him he's gonna wonder if I'm thinking it might be from somebody else. Shit!

She decided to leave it and see if he brought it up. She knew though that she wouldn't be able to leave it for long.

They set off and Mickey had never felt so proud as he strutted down the Burnside with Selina on his arm.

'Did you er . . . Did yer get it then?' Mickey asked suddenly as if he'd been building his courage up to ask.

Thank you, God. Selina thought, as the whole world fell off her shoulders. 'You bettcha Mickey.'

Grinning, Mickey nodded, and they hurred on.

Soon they were approaching the Homelands estate and barely three minutes away from the Seahills where Robbie Lumsdon and his family lived, when Mickey his heart sinking fast, spotted Masterton an his gang, who were obviously on their way up to Houghton and seeking trouble every step of the way.

'Oh no,' Mickey groaned under his breath.

'What?' Selina asked, staring at the approaching group of half a dozen youths.

'Whatever yer do, don't make eye contact,' Mickey hissed frantically. But it was too late, Stevie had already seen Mickey, and he had certainly seen Selina.

'Whoa there, what's a good-looking chick like you doing with that fucking ugly numb nut?' Masterton shouted. His silver face rings glinted in the fast-approaching twilight. Masterton had a veritable pin cushion of a face, he had two rings in one eyebrow and one in the other, as well as various studs through his nose and lip. Once there had been two in both eyebrows, until the day he crossed swords with Kerry Lumsdon. She'd whipped one out, then had taken off, leaving Masterton bleeding, dazed and wondering exactly what the hell had just happened.

Masterton moved closer, leering at Selina and this got Mickey's back right up. 'Piss off Stevie, yer git ugly shite. Nobody wants yer here,' he yelled without thinking, then watched Masterton's face turn from a sickly pasty white to a deep shade of scarlet. He thought, What the hell have I just said . . .

Mickey's eyes skipped quickly to Stevie's gang, most of them were wearing hoodies that covered most of their faces, they were all obviously high. One, wearing what was once a pale-blue hoodie but was now a dirty grey, jumped up and down yelling, 'Fight, fight, fight'. In moments, just like a bunch of wild animals smelling fresh blood, the other members of the gang jumped in.

'Oh God,' Mickey groaned, of all the times to bump into this set of creeps. His imagination ran riot, he could see himself thumped and kicked, stabbed and mauled to death.

71

Squashed flat like a beetle on its back. His heart started to race.

Selina though, was staring at Masterton as hard as he was glowering at her. She'd come up against the likes of him before. Usually they were all wind and water . . . Usually.

Mickey tugged her arm. 'Come on Selina, we're gonna have to leg it . . . I hope yer can run in those heels.'

'Why should we run?'

Mickey stared at her. Was she for real? 'Cos, er, yer know there just might be too many of them.'

Masterton was walking towards them now, his body swinging and swaying with a confidence gained solely from the contents of a needle, his gang bounding around him as if they had springs in their trainers.

'Come on bastard, think yer hard do yer? I'll show yer who's hard.' He flung his arms out and waved his hands in towards his body in a gesture Mickey had seen in hundreds of gang movies. '*Come on!*'

While Masterton was challenging Mickey to a fight, one of his gang, known only as Toad, was moving towards Selina.

'Fuck off,' she snapped, when she saw how close he was.

He giggled insanely, his green eyes wide and staring. Up close he was a lot older than she had first thought, not a kid at all, probably late twenties or early thirties. What the hell he was doing in a gang of kids, she just didn't want to know.

Mickey gulped hard, they were converging on all sides now. Tiny bubbles of fear-drenched sweat popped out all over his body. He feared that at any moment one of them could pull a knife.

God only knows what shit they're on. He pulled hard on Selina's arm, praying that if she could run only half as good as Kerry could, it would do.

What Selina felt at that moment was guilt. She'd been here before, only she'd been on the other side, giving out the same sort of shit as Masterton and his cronies were dealing out to them. And she'd fairly dished it out. Hell she'd thrown it with force. Talk about karma.

She'd never felt any guilt when she and the gang she'd ran with tormented others, young or old. That's what drugs did, destroyed your soul, made you feel invincible, you thought you could conquer the world and everyone in it. So invincible, you thought you were a god.

The next morning if there was guilt, another fix got rid of it. But seeing this today brought it all back. Made her so ashamed of the things she'd done, that she wanted to get lost again in the solace that drugs offered. It was so tempting. To forget. To lapse into the warm trance that was almost like death.

She sighed so heavily that Mickey looked at her oddly.

But then she shuddered. No way was she ever going back to that life. She'd been to hell and back these last six or seven weeks. And yes at the beginning she hadn't wanted it. But as the cravings had eased, she'd begun to see sense. She'd been given a chance, one she never thought she would get. And if it meant going to college, damn it, then she would go. She would grab this one chance with both hands and prove that she was worth it.

'Go on,' she snarled at Toad, then swung her head round to the others. 'Fuck off the lot of you. You're all pathetic fucking losers. All of you. Go away. Go on. Fuck off.'

For a moment they all stopped and looked at Masterton for guidance, and for a brief, luxurious moment Mickey thought Selina had won the day.

Then Toad started giggling that unhinged giggle of his, and Mickey wanted to throttle him. As if this had been a signal, they all moved in. Trapping Mickey and Selina.

'What the fuck is going on here?' Robbie Lumsdon peered out the window of Cal Black's car as they came round the

73

corner of the old farmhouse and headed towards the Homelands.

'It's Mickey, and that must be his new lass . . . not bad,' Cal whistled.

'Uh huh . . . So what the hell are they doing with Stevie Masterton and his friggin' gang of creeps?'

'Actually, I don't think they are with them . . . More like they're getting ready to brawl, I think we might have just saved our mate's bacon.'

The ear-cringing screech of tyres on tarmac gave Robbie and Cal the attention they wanted. All of Masterton's gang, and Mickey and Selina, flinched.

All except for Toad, who slowly turned his head until he was staring at them through the windscreen with eyes that were far too bright. He laughed that mirthless laugh of his.

Cal, well over six feet, and strong with it, got quickly out of the car.

'All right Mickey?' he said loudly, only he was looking at Masterton when he spoke. Robbie got out of the car, and kept a wary eye on Toad. He knew if anything was coming, it would be sparked off by him.

'Yeah, oh yeah.' Mickey feeling as if his blood was circulating for the first time ever, began to edge towards the car, he had a hard grip on Selina's arm taking her with him.

'Course he's fucking all right,' Masterton yelled, suddenly finding his tongue. He looked round weighing up the odds and finding them still in his favour. 'What the fuck's it got to do with youse two friggin' pests anyhow?'

'Just leave it out Stevie, we're not after any bother like,' Robbie said. 'All we're doing is just picking up a couple of mates, that's all.'

'So yer want some bother, eh, is that it?' Stevie stuck his chest out then spat on the ground. 'Any time yer like, cos believe me I still owe youse Lumsdons some.'

Most of the others had shrunk back when the car had arrived, and the only one standing between Mickey, Selina and the car, was Toad. If it had been one of the others and he'd been on his own Mickey would have took a chance. He knew he could move faster than this drugged up mug in front of him. But Toad . . . Toad was known to carry a knife and he was crazy enough to use it. Rumours were that he also carried a bottle of acid. Mickey noticed Toad's right hand was already in his pocket. Heart in his mouth, because he knew that Toad was wired and that he would do something.

Mickey, shaking uncontrollably, decided to make a run for the car. He squeezed Selina's arm hoping she would understand.

Understand she did, but instead of running towards the car, she jumped forward taking Toad by surprise. She swung her right leg forward and with every ounce of strength she possessed kicked Toad between his legs. He went down instantly screaming like a stuck pig.

Turning she pushed Mickey and they ran for the car, Cal already had the engine running and before they had even shut the doors he was screeching back up the street, praying that nothing was coming in their direction.

8

'Come on dog,' Lorraine said, slipping Duke's lead on. Duke, a large black and tan mongrel that Lorraine had ran over in her car one night just before Christmas, happily wagged his tail. Unable to trace his owner, Mavis and Peggy had insisted that Duke move in.

'How the hell I got lumbered with this job while the gruesome twosome in there sit with their bloody feet up, I'll never know,' she grumbled.

'We heard that,' Peggy called from the sitting room where she and Mavis were watching the end of *Emmerdale*.

'Sweet Jesus! The woman's got hearing like a bat.' Shaking her head, Lorraine closed the door behind her.

Heading along the road she kept out of the fields because of the darkness and the damp. What a bloody long, miserable winter.

Smelling a rabbit, Duke pulled on his lead. 'Stop that right now,' Lorrraine admonished him. Duke hung his head but did what he was told and they walked on, Lorraine's thoughts turning to Luke as they always did.

God, it was so bloody hard. She had only been with the man

for a few weeks, nowhere near as long as she had been with John, and yet the hurt that she was feeling was so much more painful than how she felt when her marriage ended.

Sighing she bit her lip, alone like this she could let her defences down. The tear that rolled out of her right eye was allowed to fall on her denim jacket unchecked, as did its partner from her left eye a second later.

She stopped for a moment while Duke sniffed around a tree. She bit her lip. *Really, I'm just as much to blame as Luke. He's only trying to do the best thing for Selina.*

She wiped her eyes with the back of her hand and when she dropped it to her side, Duke licked it. Lorraine tutted, then with a small quick smile she patted the top of his head, and they turned for home.

Bloody men.

Lorraine shook the drizzle out of her hair as she hung Duke's lead on the peg she had put on the back door a few weeks ago to give Mavis and Peggy a hint. Not that they had paid much heed.

She checked her face in the hall mirror, Good, no sign of tears. She smoothed her hair back from her face and after putting a bowl of water down for Duke, she went into the sitting room.

'Something to eat, love?' Mavis asked.

'No thanks Mam, I'll probably have an early night, read a book, get some sleep. Have yer finished the new Ian Rankin, Mam?'

Mavis nodded and handed the book over.

'So, not seeing the delectable Luke tonight then?' Peggy asked, her left eyebrow arched, as she sensed there was something that Lorraine wasn't letting on. 'I would have thought a real flesh and blood man like Luke would be better to go to bed with than a pretend one. Besides, Rebus is to old for you.'

'Jesus Peggy, get real will yer. Where's the law stating I have to see Luke Daniels every night, Mrs Nosey?'

Peggy pulled a face, 'I know I would.'

'Yeah, we all know you would, and a few others an' all.'

'Are you suggesting that I am unfaithful?'

'Who you Peggy? Of course not, pure as the driven snow, you are,' Lorraine said, sarcastically.

Peggy tutted, and drew her cardigan around her shoulders.

Pleased to have the last word, Lorraine said, 'OK girls, I'm off to bed,' left the room and quickly took the stairs two at a time.

She undressed slowly, her mind elsewhere and slipped into her pink satin pyjamas, a belated Christmas present from Luke, and lay down on top of her bed.

Staring at the ceiling she inhaled deeply then released it in a rush of air.

She really missed Luke. Since New Year's Eve it had felt so right. She had felt loved, and protected. She had thought that he had felt the same way too. Had she misread all his signals? She thought not, but, obviously, it wasn't working out for him. *I am a bloody idiot, opening me big mouth without thinking. Now it looks like I've gone and lost the only thing I want in my life.* She turned over and punched her pillow into shape, then spun round and flopped back on to it.

If it's ever gonna work in the future, we've got to be more open with each other, that is, if he wants me back. Lorraine chewed her bottom lip and then an unwelcome thought slipped into her head. *What if he doesn't? What if he was looking for a way out?* God! She'd never thought of that.

She sighed. *Nah. He just panicked over Selina. Really I should go visit her, see how the kid is. Can't be much fun for her if Luke's as grumpy at home as he has been at work.*

Work. The word triggered the memory of being in Clark's

78

office that morning. 'Shit,' she said out loud. 'That bloody reporter.'

What the hell to do with her? *Sanderson has great people skills, I'll try and get him to show her the ropes as much as possible. Too much time with me I'll probably tell her to fuck off, that'll look good in the paper.*

She sighed and turned over. It was rare that Lorraine got an early night, and although it had just gone eight o'clock, she began to drift off. Soon, book forgotten, she was fast asleep.

Selina got home that evening about nine o'clock. She greeted Luke with a huge smile on her face as she came in the door, and laughed at his surprised expression.

Aside from that encounter with Masterton and his gang, she had had a great time. She had finally met the Lumsdons, and had been touched by the shy way that Mickey had introduced her to them as his girlfriend. The house was chaos, with everyone talking and yelling at once, but, like Mickey, she loved it. It had such a different feel to the house that she lived in with moany face – though, she admitted to herself, she might have had something to do with that. She especially liked Kerry and Robbie, who were a laugh, the pair of them. It felt good to be around ordinary people, who argued and joked and talked together, just as normal people should. And Mickey, well, he was way cool.

Selina went upstairs to her bedroom, and had opened her sketchbook, when she heard a light tapping at her door. It was Luke. 'Yer all right?' he said awkwardly, standing in the doorway, not really wanting to cross into her territory. 'It's just that I didn't expect yer home so early.'

Selina smiled and shrugged. 'I just thought I'd have an early one.'

Luke nodded and turned to leave. 'Oh, I forgot. This came

for yer in the post.' He handed Selina a letter and shut the door quietly behind him.

Selina held the letter in her hands, staring at it for a moment, before turning it over. There was no postmark or return address, it must have been hand delivered. With a slightly uneasy feeling building in her stomach, she opened the envelope.

It was a card, a Valentine's Day card. On the front was a cartoon of a cute cat, holding balloons that read: 'A Valentine's Wish for You.' She opened the card and read the message:

I wish that I could make you understand just how much it's meant to me even just meeting you. You're not supposed to sign these things, but you know who it's from, so I will anyway. Mickey.

He had even drawn a little cartoon of himself. It was really sweet.

But even though Selina loved the card, her heart plummeted. This must have been what Mickey had meant when he asked her if she had received her gift this afternoon. And if Mickey didn't send the rose, there was only one other person who could have. Eccles. Despite the warmth of the house, goose-bumps stood out on her flesh.

9

The smell of frying bacon filled the air, as James Dinwall sat with his feet up on a chair in the police canteen. It was early morning and he wasn't feeling great. His stomach was playing up and the food smells made him feel slightly nauseous. Added to that, the sound of plates being collected and cutlery clanging together was enough to make him wince.

A bored, petulant look on his face, he held a huge mug of tea in his hands – no milk, one sugar – and was sounding off to the desk sergeant Allan Peters, who was sitting next to him. They both had ten minutes to go before their shift started.

Peters, a tall, thin man with a pasty complexion and a misshapen nose that seemed too big for his face, winced as he drained the dregs of his coffee and put the plastic cup on the table. 'By God that's foul stuff and no mistake,' he shivered.

'So, what the fucking hell do yer drink it for?' Dinwall practically snarled at him.

'Jesus, what's the matter with you?'

Dinwall shrugged, 'Sick as a chip that's what I am.'

'What's bothering yer? Yer usually not as miserable as yer are today.'

Dinwall tutted, stared into his tea for a moment, then looked at Peters. 'Do you think that Daniels gets preferential treatment since him and the boss have got it together, if yer know what I mean?'

Peters shrugged, 'Well, word is that they're not together no more. And anyway, I don't think it was like that anyway. Not really, Luke's a good copper, and the two of them have always worked well together. Anyhow, what makes yer ask that? I thought yer got on well with him?'

'I do, but twice this bloody week already, I've been sent out on shit jobs while he gets the cushy numbers.'

'Oh, pick yer dummy up. The boss isn't like that, and yer know it. What's the real problem?'

Dinwall sighed, 'It's the wife.'

'You been playing away, *again*?'

'What do yer mean?' Dinwall asked as if he was pure beyond words. Then he sighed. 'She's jealous that's all. Can hardly look at another woman without her jumping down my neck.'

Peters just shook his head, then raised his eyes to the roof a moment later when a young blonde girl came round collecting cutlery. Dinwall couldn't keep his eyes off her and she bent down to pick a knife that had fallen on the floor. When she stood up, and caught him staring at her, she snapped, 'Piss off, creep', and quickly went back into the kitchen with her tray of dirty dishes.

Peters sighed, 'Yer just never give up do yer.'

'What's yer problem? I've got eyes, don't I? Not harm in viewing the merchandise.'

'Yeah, do that around the boss and see if she thinks it's fun. Bet yer anything yer like she'll punch yer friggin' lights out.'

'Thank God not all woman are Karate black belts then. Anyhow what's it to you, you sanctimonious old git?'

'I have a daughter her age,' Peters jerked his head in the

direction of the young girl who was behind the counter, 'and believe you me I wouldn't let yer near her.'

Dinwall snapped his fingers as if a great insight had suddenly dawned on him. 'That's why we never play cards at your house is it? Well, well. All I can say is I hope the poor kid doesn't look like you.'

Peters picked up his paper cup, stood and walked over to the rubbish bin. After he'd thrown it in, he came back, leaned over the table and said, 'Know something Jimmy boy, sometimes yer nowt but a pain in the fucking arse.'

He walked out of the canteen, and left Dinwall staring at his back. 'Must have been something I said,' Dinwall muttered.

Luke put a can of coke on Lorraine's desk and smiled at her. 'Here you go, boss. Thought you'd like it to, yer know . . .'

'Thanks,' Lorraine murmured, her heart skipping a beat. She could feel her face flushing. *God, it's not fair. I wish my body didn't react to him the way it does. I hate the hold that he has over me.*

She took a sip of her coke, then put it to one side. Luke sat down in his customary chair beside the desk, and looked as if he was about to say something to her, but he accidentally knocked the table, which made the coke spill over on to her paperwork.

'Sorry, boss,' Luke said, taking his handkerchief and trying, in vain, to wipe up the mess.

Lorraine sighed, 'Don't worry about it,' but Luke heard her tone. He knew it wasn't going to be easy getting back on Lorraine's right side. *God but I love her*, his mind thought treacherously, *even though if looks could kill I'd be dead on the spot now. Them baby blues can certainly flash fire when they want.*

He sighed. How were they going to get through this mess? If it wasn't for Selina, then he knew that the two of them

83

would be happy, but the fact of the matter was that he had a daughter and he had to do the best by her. Which meant putting his life on hold for a while, however difficult that was going to be.

They were just cleaning up the last of the spilled coffee when Carter came into Lorraine's office followed by a young woman. She was small and slim with short, curly, auburn-coloured hair and enormous hazel eyes. She had freckles dotted on her nose and wore a huge smile on her face, which looked freshly scrubbed. She was dressed in a green top with black trousers, and carried a large and battered brown leather satchel over one shoulder. The effect was that of a particularly precocious thirteen-year-old girl, playing at being a journalist. Lorraine sighed. *Here we go.*

'Boss, this is Kate Mulberry.' Carter was beaming at Lorraine and Luke almost with the same high-wattage smile as Kate's. *Well, like that's hard to guess*, Lorraine was thinking as she forced a tight-lipped smile on her face and and held out her hand. Kate's grip was surprisingly firm. 'Detective Inspector, I'm very pleased to meet you,' she gushed. 'I've read up on a lot of your cases, and I must say that I'm impressed.'

'Well, um, thanks,' said Lorraine, at a loss for words. How old was this kid? Twenty-two? Twenty-three? She was too full of bounce and energy for Lorraine's mood to take at the moment. She noticed that Luke was stifling a smile as his hand was shaken by the young reporter. *Cheeky sod*, she thought.

'Right,' Mulberry said a moment later when Carter had left the office. Luke stood by the door, and Kate sat in the chair he usually took. 'I'd love to start with an interview, if I can, and then I thought that you could take me round the station, show me a few sights. And perhaps then we could go out on a call?' Kate had taken out a small, spiral-bound notebook and was checking things off a list. 'I'd really like to be where the action is, see first hand how the police operate.'

I'll give yer action, Lorraine thought. She glared at Luke, who seemed to think that the whole thing was particularly funny, but changed her expression to one that she hoped Kate would read as pleasant yet stern. 'I think that, before we go on, we should set a few ground rules.' Kate nodded enthusiastically, her pen poised over her notebook. 'First of all, under no circumstances whatsoever, are cameras allowed in the station. I'll have to confiscate the one you've got there,' Lorraine could see the lens pointing out of Kate's satchel and held out her hand. Kate's face fell, but she took the camera out of the bag and handed it wordlessly to Lorraine, who passed it to Luke. 'Detective Sergeant Daniels here will return it to you at the end of the day. I don't want to see it in the station again.'

'Secondly, it's not open season for you here. There will be areas to you that are out of bounds. We have a number of ongoing investigations, which, you'll appreciate, need their details to stay out of the papers. Any leaks could mean anything, the suspect might scarper, for instance. So don't stick your nose in where it doesn't belong – got that?'

Kate was making a note on her pad, her eyebrows raised. Lorraine didn't wait for an answer, but continued. 'Thirdly – and most importantly, I can't have you interfering in the day-to-day running of the station. You're here to observe, not to interfere, always remember that. I've told my officers to come straight to me should yer be getting in the way, and if that happens, yer out. Consider this yer one and only warning.'

Kate had stopped writing and was looking at Lorraine levelly. Lorraine suddenly saw more than just a freckled girl, she saw grit and determination in her eyes that made Lorraine reassess her initial assumption. It looked like the girl had backbone, and when she opened her mouth to speak, she confirmed it. 'Inspector Hunt,' Kate said calmly, 'I appreciate you allowing me to come into the station. I also appreciate that you might think that I'm going to be a disruptive influence. I can assure you that's not my intention. I simply want to write the best article I can. I am going to write the article how I see it, and, of course, your help in making sure that I see all I need to see would go a long way towards making sure that the police are portrayed in the best possible light.'

Lorraine almost laughed out loud. Was she being threatened? *Cheeky cow.* She'd better be on the watch out for this one. Obviously, strong-arm tactics were not going to work. She took a deep breath, smiled, and looked into Kate's eyes. 'I'll see what I can do. About the interview, well, now's not a good time. We do have the morning briefing though, and you're welcome to sit in on that.'

Kate smiled, and was transformed back into the young, bubbly girl who had entered the office. Lorraine was surprised to find herself liking the young woman, even if she was a reporter, and quite clearly ambitious. She seemed to be able to get what she wanted, and Lorraine admired that. On the other hand, if she stepped out of line, she'd soon know about it.

Lorraine got up out of her seat, gathered up some papers, and walked to the door. Luke held it open for Lorraine and Kate, and the three of them walked towards the incident room to begin the morning briefing.

Naked in front of the mirror, he studied his body. Taking pride in his smooth torso, his eyes lingering on the four white roses neatly tattooed on his chest. Below these four were another two, faded now. He ran his fingers over each of the six tattoos. They were home-made, and he had tattooed each one himself, the first an early attempt made with a sharp needle and a bottle of ink, the drawing crude, yet, he thought, still effective, even if the edges had gone slightly blurry with age.

The newest tattoo still had a small scab clinging to one of the petals.

That was fine.

It would drop of its own accord.

He smiled as he dressed. Picking up his car keys from the dresser, he slipped them into his jacket pocket.

Tonight he would cruise.

And none of them would even know he was there . . . Ha.

10

Darren Lumsdon slipped quietly into the sitting room and sat on the chair by the window. Kerry and fifteen-year-old Claire were sitting together on the settee. He did his best to not let on that he was in the same room, most of the time they would be content if he was on a different planet anyhow.

Silently he picked at the scab on his right knee. The left was covered with yet another fresh plaster. Because of the rain, today they had used the all-weather pitch for football training, hell on the skin.

When he realised that they were talking about the run-in last night between Mickey and the Masterton gang, his ears pricked up.

'She didn't?' Claire said in amazement.

'She did, right between the legs an' all.'

Claire clapped her hands in delight. 'That creep Toad's had that coming for a long time. Last time I was in the corner shop he was in the queue behind me and the creep was pressing up against me, don't yer just hate that? So, what happened next, did he get out of the gutter and go for them? Or did he just lie there?'

'Don't know, they all escaped in Cal's car.'

'Cool . . . So what's she look like then, this Selina person?'

Kerry shrugged, 'Well, she's quite pretty I suppose.'

Fucking drop-dead gorgeous, more like, Darren thought, as he watched his sisters through lowered lids.

'Is she just? I bet Mickey's falling all over her, making a fool of himself as usual.'

They both giggled. Darren marvelled at how well the pair of them seemed to get on these days, well, most of the time anyhow. Last year they were for ever at each other's throats. He lifted his other knee to check that the plaster was still in place and his stomach rumbled loudly.

Uh oh, sussed.

Both heads spun round. 'What yer doing yer little creep, spying?' Kerry shouted at him.

'Doing nowt, just checking me legs out. It's allowed isn't it? Anyhow, I can sit here if I want. I live here an' all yer know, it's not just your house.'

'Yer've been cocking yer lugs again, haven't yer?' Claire snapped at him.

'Wasn't . . . Anyhow I heard yer's last night so I already knew so there. And, they all better be careful an' all cos I know for a fact that Toad carries a bottle of acid as well as a knife, and he won't forget what Mickey's girlfriend did in a hurry.'

With that he walked out, football tucked under his arm, knowing he'd given them something to think about.

It had been a busy morning. Lorraine and Luke had taken Kate Mulberry to the local fire station. They had some mug shots to show the local fire brigade. Two nights ago, out on a call, they had been bombarded with stones on the Washington highway, nobody had been hurt, thank goodness, but it had meant that the fire engine hadn't arrived on the scene in good enough time, and the house, although not burned completely to the ground, had suffered such bad structural damage that it looked like it needed to be torn down. The second in command, David Mack, swore he had eyes like an owl and would recognise at least two of the horrible little bastards. And he had. He didn't need to go too far into the shots to pick out Terry Rivers and Damon Welsh, two fourteen-year-olds who had been in trouble before, and looked like they were both heading down the road to ruin. Lorraine made a note to get Carter and Dinwall to pick them up.

The next port of call was the court. Lorraine and Luke were police witnesses in a case where a twenty-one-year-old man had broken into a house and threatened its occupant, an elderly man with a heart condition, with a razor. Thankfully, the old man wasn't injured, but the thief had scared the living daylights out of him, stolen every penny he owned and smashed up some photos on his mantelpiece.

'The thing is,' Lorraine said to Kate as they walked towards her car, 'that little bastard only received a community sentence for a hundred hours. That's all very well and good, but what about the victim? I know for a fact that elderly victims of crime often suffer enormous emotional and psychological trauma, but nothing is really done for them, is it? It's all about rehabilitating the offender, and trying to get him on the right track. But I've seen people never recover from crime.'

Lorraine noted as she walked that Kate had to run in a sort of half-trot to keep up with her. She pointed her keyring at the car and unlocked the doors with an electronic bleep. Kate said breathlessly, 'So, what's the answer, do you think? Are you advocating a lock the door and throw away the key policy?'

'No,' Lorraine said carefully. This sort of sentence made her sick to her stomach, but she was aware that anything she said could be taken out of context and misinterpreted. 'I just think that victims also need support. More support than what they get at the moment. But the police don't have the resources and, quite honestly, it's a job for social services, not us. And for someone to know that the person who has stolen their money and ransacked their belongings is back on the streets with no more than a slap on the hand,' she shrugged. 'Well, it's difficult for them, that's all.'

'So, where to now?' Kate said as she clambered into the back seat.

'Back to the station, time for lunch,' said Luke. Lorraine sat in the driver's seat and took a look in the passenger seat at Kate. She was frantically scrawling in her notebook, no doubt trying to get every word of the conversation down.

When they got back into the station, Lorraine had asked Dinwall to take Kate through the steps of processing a suspect once he was arrested. She needed some time away from Kate and her endless barrage of questions. The girl was exhausting. As she was about to start eating her sandwich at her desk, there came a knock on her door, followed a moment later by three quick ones, Carter's trademark. 'Come in,' Lorraine shouted.

Carter was half way in the room when he waved his thumb over his shoulder, 'Found this one out the front boss, says he knows yer.'

It was Inspector Wade, who was leaning on her door frame, and smiling at her in a particularly charming way. Just at that moment, Luke happened to be passing the door. When he saw who it was, he stopped, his jaw practically unhinged. Standing up, she came out from behind her desk and held out her hand. 'Ian,' she said. 'I think you are just about the last person I thought I would see today. What on earth are yer doing here?'

She saw that Luke was standing in the corridor watching the proceedings with his arms folded across his chest, his face glowering. Wade shook her hand and held it for just that second longer than was absolutely necessary, and Lorraine could see that every muscle in Luke's body was tensing. She couldn't help but be pleased by Luke's reaction. Wade might have been the one with the green eyes, but Luke's metaphorical green eyes were flashing fire.

'Actually, boss,' Luke said before Wade could say anything, 'I'm off for a couple of hours. Gotta pick Selina up.' He looked at Wade and what he said next was definitely for the Irishman's benefit. 'College interview.'

'Oh good.' Wade's smile seemed genuine. 'That's the secret, keep them busy, then one day they wake up and realise that they have finally grown up.'

'Oh, do they,' Luke said in a flat tone. He threw Lorraine a look, and she nearly burst out laughing. Luke's jealousy burst off him like bright green sparks.

He left without another word and, smiling to herself, Lorraine motioned for Wade to sit down.

'So, yer haven't answered me. What yer doing here?' she asked him after he had made himself comfortable.

'Visiting family in the area. It was arranged a few months ago,' he added hastily.

'Right,' she nodded.

'I thought that while I was here I'd perhaps pay you a visit, you know, take you out for a meal, or something,' he shrugged, all the while gazing intently at her.

Oh, she was tempted, definitely. And it was extremely flattering to be tracked down by someone, all the way from Ireland. Who wouldn't be flattered? Wade was one handsome hunk of a man, as Peggy would say. And Luke, well, should she really put her life on hold for him? There was no guarantee that they would get back together, was there? And a casual dinner with a colleague couldn't hurt, could it? But truth be told, she wouldn't say that she was attracted to Wade. She could see how other women would be, but he was too smooth for her, too slick. And he lived in Ireland, so she couldn't really see anything happening there. Besides, she would be thinking of Luke the whole time, she knew she would. No, it was better to say no to the dinner and hope that Wade wasn't too disappointed.

And she even had an excuse. 'I'm sorry, tonight's impossible. I'm going to a charity dinner with an old friend, I really can't let him down.'

'Sorry to hear that . . . Another time maybe?' Wade sounded disappointed.

'Well, maybe,' she said. 'But yer've gotta know – this would just be as friends. I'm not really looking for anything – I'm still working out what I'm feeling about Luke.' She hoped that was enough to put him off. 'But would you like a look round while you're here, see how we do things in Houghton-le-Spring? We still have some stocks in the back yard where we put prisoners and throw tomatoes at them on alternate Thursdays. It's quite an enthralling show.'

Wade was quick enough, 'Tomatoes? We've found that eggs work the best, the smell, you know, really sticks.'

Not long afterwards she was waving him off in the car park. She stared after the car as it left towards Sunderland, then she headed back to the office. Kate Mulberry popped her head in at one point to say that she was going to head out with Dinwall to talk to Terry Rivers' family, which was fine with Lorraine. She was planning on spending most of the afternoon catching up on paperwork.

At five, she made her way towards her car. She'd already decided what to wear tonight and Scottie was picking her up at six thirty.

She stuck to her little black dress. It came down to her knees and was cut very low in the back. But it was a smart and sexy look, definitely not trashy. She caught her hair in a jewelled clip at the side of her head, but left the rest down. Around her neck she fastened a delicate twist of silver, and kept her make up fresh and natural. She looked at herself in the mirror. She didn't look too bad, even if she did say so herself.

'Oh my God, yer look good enough to eat. I should take a picture for yer mother,' Peggy exclaimed as Lorraine came downstairs just as Scottie pressed the bell.

'Should I let Luke in?' Peggy asked.

'It's not Luke.'

'What?' Peggy grabbed the door before Lorraine could get to it and pulled it quickly open.

'Oh it's you.' Peggy looked him up and down, but there was no disguising the confusion in her face. 'Yer scrub up well.'

Scottie, in black tie and tails looked very smart indeed. He'd even had a haircut, so his black mane of hair looked reasonably tidy, for a change. 'Hello Peggy, Mavis not in?'

'No, she's taking a pottery class.' She turned to Lorraine with raised eyebrows and a look that said, *what the hell is going on?*

'Mind yer own business,' Lorraine answered as she swept past Peggy.

Pulling a face at Lorraine, Peggy closed the door. 'Something fishy going down here, you mark my words,' she said to Duke who wagged his tail as he followed her into the sitting room.

She switched the news on and pressed the record button on the video for *Emmerdale*. She and Mavis would watch it together later, after they had discussed what was going on with Lorraine and Luke. Peggy couldn't wait for Mavis to get home.

It was exactly the kind of function that Lorraine hated. The charity evening was held in a large ballroom in one of Sunderland's finest hotels. As Scottie and Lorraine entered the room, they were handed a glass of champagne. Sipping it,

Lorraine looked around the room. It was a little too stuffy for her taste. The style was Victorian and the room was painted green with the mouldings picked out in white. Large chandeliers, dripping with glass and light, hung from the ceiling. Waiters were employed to ensure that everyone's glass was topped up, and some others handed round canapés on silver trays. Lorraine tasted one, a tiny pancake covered with smoked salmon and cream cheese. And although it was delicious, it didn't put a dint in her stomach. She was famished, and wished that she had thought to have a piece of toast before she left the house that evening.

Gazing around the ballroom, she noticed that everyone was dressed up to the nines. Gold jewellery sparkled from the necks of elderly ladies; men wore beautifully cut suits and impressive-looking watches on their wrists. It was a far cry from the men and women who Lorraine dealt with on a day-to-day basis, although the policewoman in her had an inkling that there was a fair share of thieves and conmen in this lot – they just used off-shore bank accounts and double-book accounting as their weapons, but the effect could be just as devastating.

Lorraine was standing on her own, nervously twiddling the glass of wine in her fingers. Scottie had left her for a moment to talk to one of the trustees. Sipping her glass of champagne, she tried to look as if she belonged there, but the truth was, she felt completely out of place. She would much rather be sitting on the sofa in the living room with Mavis and Peggy, gossiping and watching telly, or even down at the station, catching up on some paperwork. *Or*, a stray thought popped into her mind, *with Luke*. But she shook the thought out of her head.

'I hate these things, don't you?' said a voice behind her.

Lorraine turned round to see a man in his mid- to late-thirties at her shoulder. He wasn't as glossy or as sleek as the other people at the function. His brown hair needed a cut, his suit had seen better days, and hazel eyes stared out of a pair of glasses that had been fashionable perhaps ten years ago. But he had a kind smile, and he was someone to talk to, so Lorraine smiled back, gratefully, at him.

'To tell you the truth,' she said, 'I'm just not used to this sort of thing.'

He shrugged. 'No, I'm not either.' He held out his hand. 'Carl Hanson.'

'Lorraine Hunt,' she said, shaking his hand.

Hanson looked at her quizzically. 'You're a policewoman, aren't you?'

Lorraine laughed, 'And you're a mind reader!'

'No, no,' Hanson smiled, 'it's just that, well, Selina is in one of the groups that I take . . .'

'Oh,' said Lorraine, realisation dawning on her face, 'yer hold that support group that she's been going to. How's she doing?'

Hanson shrugged. 'To be fair, I don't really like to discuss my sessions with outsiders. It's a trust thing, you see. But Selina has mentioned you – glowingly, I might add – and I've been meaning to get in touch anyway. Obviously, I deal with a lot of troubled teenagers, and it would be good if—'

But Hanson was interrupted by Scottie. 'I'm sorry, Lorraine, love. Couldn't stop him talking. Anyway, you'll be pleased that dinner is just about to be served. Carl,' he said, shaking his hand. 'I think you're seated at our table.'

They walked together into a separate room and took their seats. Introductions were made. Lady Sybill, one of the directors of the children's home, was a tiny bird-like woman, whose sparse hair had been blow-dried so that it surrounded her head like a halo. She wore a green velvet dress, which looked like it had been made for her when she was younger and perhaps a little heavier; it hung limply on her shrunken frame. However, she had a winning smile, which must have broken a few hearts in her time, and an open manner that made Lorraine instantly like her. However, her son, Simon, was a balding, chinless wonder with a flaccid handshake. He spent the evening clearly bored but unwilling to join in on the conversation. Also at the table was Andrew Gardner, a recently retired fireman, and his wife, Candace. Lorraine had dealt with Gardner on a couple of occasions, and didn't like him. He was a cynical bastard, who hated the world and everyone in it. His wife looked worn out.

'So, what do you do, dear?' said Lady Sybill to Lorraine.

'I'm a detective inspector,' Lorraine said. 'With the Houghton police force.'

'Ohh, how daring, a real live police woman.' She clapped her hands in delight. 'Never met one of them before. A real detective, how fascinating.'

'Dare say yer've never had the opportunity have you Lady Sybill.' Andrew Gardner said, finishing his drink and catching the waiter's eye.

Lorraine glanced over at Hanson, who pulled a tight grimace. She smiled warmly at him. She wondered vaguely, for a moment, why he was the only one at the table who didn't bring a partner, but then put it to one side.

'And what do you do?' Lady Sybill directed the question at Hanson.

'I work at the children's home, Lady Sybill,' he answered. 'I'm a behavioural psychologist, specialising in child development.'

'Hanson's relatively new, but an already valued member of staff,' said Scottie. 'The kids love him, don't they?'

'I don't know about that,' he said self-effacingly, 'but I really enjoy working with them. Sometimes I think they teach me just as much as I teach them.'

Andrew Gardner snorted. 'Some of these kids though, yer've got to wonder. Just look at them these days, no respect.

And yet, they've got it easy. Rationing was still about when I was a kid, we just had to make do. But these teenagers these days,' he shook his head, 'don't care about property, don't care about other people. The only thing they care about is themselves. Born rotten, that's what I say . . . Born rotten and spoilt brats. Think they can do what they bloody well want and the rest of us have to put up with it.'

'I don't think you can say that,' said Hanson gently. 'There's other pressures on kids these days. Drugs, families breaking up, lots of the kids you're talking about are just angry and don't know how to express it.'

'I don't think anybody's really born bad. Do you Lorraine?' Scottie asked.

'Well, I wouldn't be at all surprised if Mother Nature throws up the odd emotionless human now and then.'

'How would that make them bad?'

'Because if yer totally cold to other people's feelings, which the truly selfish are, yer couldn't care less what yer do to them.'

Hanson shook his head. 'I just can't believe that,' he said. 'If that was so, those people that you're talking about would have no capacity for change, which would mean that what I'm doing would make no difference. No. I've seen a lot of troubled kids, and it's all got to do with how they were raised.'

Scottie nodded in agreement. 'And lots of them just don't have the start in life that we did, either.'

'Don't give me that, Scottie,' Andrew Gardner replied. 'Look at yer – yer didn't have the best start in life either. And yet, now yer a pathologist. How did that happen unless there was something in yer that made yer want to do better for yerself.'

Lorraine looked at Scottie. Gardner was right. For a kid from nowhere, Scottie had done extremely well for himself. *Not bad, Sunshine.*

Scottie shrugged. 'I was lucky. I had people who took me under their wing. But others aren't so lucky. However, I firmly believe that yer can change yer life around, any time yer like.'

Lady Sybill nodded her head, 'I know just what you mean,' she said. 'I bumped into a man the other day, he was in the children's home about twenty years ago. He was extremely disturbed. I remember there was an incident when he was caught torturing a stray cat, which really worried his carers at the time, but now he seems to have put all that behind him. We held an extraordinary meeting of the governors to sort out what to do about him. But looking at him now, he truly seems to have turned his life round.'

Andrew Gardner shook his head yet again. 'Mark my words,' he said, 'yer might think he's all goodness and light now, but yer can't say from a meeting on the street whether or not he's changed his spots.'

'Well, he was giving a tramp some money when I passed by the florist shop late that afternoon,' said Lady Sybill. She turned to Scottie, 'I called in to order some flowers for Edna, just to say get better soon.'

'I meant to say,' Scottie answered. 'She loves them. Really brightened up her day,' and with that, the dinner arrived.

Two hours later, the dinner finished, Scottie and Lorraine left the party. They walked out into the dark night. It wasn't raining – for once – and Lorraine liked the coolness of the air against her skin. Scottie gallantly opened the front door of his car and Lorraine got in. She wouldn't have said that she had enjoyed the party, but it was nice meeting Carl Hanson, and Lady Sybill was an old dear, even if she was a bit batty. They drove in companionable silence for a while, until Scottie said, uncharacteristically, 'Yer know, I really could have punched Andrew Gardner one tonight. He's an unthinking old bastard, and I have no idea why he even wants to go to this sort of charity dinner.'

'Oh, he's old school,' Lorraine said. 'He was probably pulled up by his bootstraps himself, made something of himself from nothing, that type of bloke. They're usually the hardest on the people that have it hardest in life. They expect that if they can do it, then everyone else should be able to, as well.'

Scottie shook his head. 'No, that's not it, Lorraine.' He took a deep breath. 'I really shouldn't say this, but because I know yer won't say anything, I'll tell yer. I'm upset at Gardner because, well, Hanson is, shall we say, an old boy of Hall Lane Children's Home.'

'Really?' said Lorraine. 'Well, shouldn't Gardner see what he's done for himself? He seems like the kind of person who really cares about the kids.'

'He is,' Scottie agreed. 'But all this talk about whether you're born bad or made that way was really insensitive seeing that Gardner was right there. Some people had it pretty bad, but from all accounts, Hanson's family was exceptionally troubled. It's no wonder that Hanson is so strait-laced. He's probably terrified that if he lets himself go one little bit, he'll end up like his family.'

'What was it?' said Lorraine. 'Abuse?'

Scottie sighed. 'Listen, I'm on the board of governors, and when Hanson's job came up, we sorted through the applicants, and saw that Hanson was one of the best. Extremely well qualified. When we saw that he had been to Hall Lane, we pulled his records and, well,' he paused. 'Let's just say that he and his brother had a pretty traumatic time. His brother moved out of the area entirely as soon as he could.'

'Poor Hanson.'

Scottie shrugged. 'He probably gets it all the time. I'm sure

100

that comments from people like Gardner just roll off his back. But that doesn't stop me from being angry on his behalf.'

Scottie pulled up outside Lorraine's house. 'Well, love,' he said, back to his usual jovial charm. 'Thanks very much for stepping into Edna's shoes at the last minute. You're a godsend.'

'It was a pleasure,' Lorraine answered. 'I had a fantastic time.'

'Liar,' said Scottie, and Lorraine laughed.

They said good night and Lorraine waved at the twitching curtain from Peggy's room as she walked down the path. Fifteen minutes later, she let her head sink into her pillow and was immediately asleep.

He breathed in the heady scent of the white rose in the vase on the windowsill. The rose was short of perfect and he demanded perfection. He would have to buy more tomorrow, a minor set back but a set back none the less. Imperfection made him angry.

Suddenly, the cat belonging to supersonic ears next door, landed on the windowsill startling him. He hated cats.

'Hissss.'

The cat froze, watching him, then with a screech, as if she sensed some primordial evil in the human, she leapt for the wall and disappeared into her own yard.

'Ha.'

11

Luke picked up the letters from the front door mat, quickly glancing through them, two were obviously bills, gas and electric. *Shit a brick, doesn't seem five bloody minutes since I paid the last lot.* He tore the electric bill open, stared at it for a moment, gasped then said out loud. 'My God, I must be wired up to death row.'

'What?' Selina asked from the hall doorway.

'Bloody bills, that's what . . . Damn and blast, I refuse to open the gas bill.'

'Should I?' Selina held out her hand.

'No I'll keep the bad news for tonight. Anyhow, there's a letter here adressed to you.'

He handed her the letter, saw her frown, and wondered himself who it was from. *Who knows that she's living here? Unless Carson is sending her snail mail. There was that card from him the other day. But mostly the kids use e-mails or text messages these days. Carson probably hasn't got a computer. Neither has Selina. Could be a hell of a carrot on a stick, maybe I should suggest it to her, that she could have one, if she's good.*

Selina opened the letter, stared at its contents in surprise for a moment, then lifted her eyes to Luke with a puzzled frown on her face.

'What?'

She handed him the envelope. Luke took it and looked inside. 'What the?' Slowly he shook the contents on to his hand, a dozen or so white rose petals, already their edges curling and turning pale brown, fell on to his palm.

'Who . . .? Why on earth would anybody want to send dying petals through the post, eh? For Christ's sake who ever it is has gotta be a bloody sicko.'

Selina stared at the envelope, her hands clenching and unclenching, 'It might be someone I used to go with from . . . before . . .'

'What do yer mean before? Is it somebody yer used to go out with when yer were on the streets? Is that who yer mean?'

'Just this, this person I knew before, an idiot if yer must know . . . And yes a druggie,' Selina snapped, misinterpreting the look on Luke's face.

'I didn't mean that . . . Never mind, why would he want to send yer something like this, without even a letter of explanation inside eh? It's pretty creepy if yer ask me.'

Selina shrugged. She was getting fed up with all the questions, plus she was pretty spooked out herself, and she wanted Luke gone so she could have time to think this through. 'Cos that's the sort of things he does.'

'Might be Carson?'

'No, Mickey wouldn't do that . . . He'd know the petals would be dead before they got here.'

'Yer sure he's that bright?'

'It's *not* Mickey.'

Luke could see by the look in her eyes that she was adamant the petals weren't from Carson. 'OK, not Carson, but how the hell did this guy find you?'

Selina shrugged again. Luke looked at the envelope and saw, with a shudder, that it had a Sunderland postmark. Whoever it was from Selina's past, had posted it here.

Lorraine was just parking into her space at the police station when she saw Kate Mulberry in the rear view mirror, walking towards her, her big brown satchel slung over her shoulder. Lorraine sighed deeply to herself, shut her eyes for a long second, and got out of the car.

'Hi, Inspector,' said Mulberry brightly. 'I was thinking that today we could do that interview, but it'll have to be either before or after lunch. Superintendent Clark is taking me out.'

Lorraine smiled thinly. 'I'll have to see how busy I am this morning.' She walked towards the police station, noticing that Kate's heels were tapping double quick time on the pavement. Even though Kate was wearing heels, and Lorraine was in flat shoes today, she was still shorter than Lorraine by a good few inches. A wicked idea popped into Lorraine's head. 'Actually, I was thinking that you could go and shadow PC Jessop for this morning. He's a dog handler.'

Kate nodded. 'Good angle for a story, great human interest. People love animals.'

Yeah, thought Lorraine, *more than they like people sometimes.*

Just as they were heading into the station, a voice behind Lorraine said, 'Hello there.'

'Hello Ian,' Lorraine said with a smile.

'Hi, I'm Kate Mulberry.' Kate pushed herself in front of Lorraine and held out her hand. 'I'm a reporter for the *Sunderland Echo*. Are you with the police as well?'

'On holiday, at the moment,' Wade replied smoothly. 'I'm with the Garda in Dublin.'

'That must be really fascinating,' Kate gushed. 'Actually, perhaps while you're here, I could interview you and Lorraine about the differences and similarities between Irish and English policing. Could be a really interesting article from both sides of the fence. Would you be interested? I suspect I could use it in the *Echo* and also sell it to one of the Irish papers . . .'

Lorraine, almost laughing out loud at the young woman's energy, cut her off before she could bowl Wade over with her enthusiasm. 'Kate, if you go round to the side of the police station, you'll find Jessop waiting for you I'm sure.'

Kate nodded her head and went in the direction that Lorraine pointed to her.

'Best of luck,' Wade called after her, then turned to Lorraine and laughed. 'She's a bit full on, isn't she?'

'A bit of a pain in the arse, more like,' said Lorraine. 'But I'll say this for her, she's ambitious. Can't see her staying too long in Houghton. So,' she continued, 'what brings yer here today?'

'Well, you, actually. I wondered whether you might be, um, you know, free tonight.' Wade saw the look on her face and put his hands up. 'I know yer not ready for anything more than friends, but really, yer the only person I know in this town, and Kate's got a good idea – we should talk about policing, see if there's anything that we can learn from each other.'

'Well I . . .' *Oh shit, what the hell. It's only a meal.* 'Yeah, actually I am.'

'Good, seven o'clock all right? I'll need your address.'

As Lorraine gave it to him, she wondered what Peggy would make of this handsome green-eyed Irish man knocking on the door tonight.

Claire Lumsdon and her best friend Katy Jacks were in the local shop. Katy was trying her best to get the owner Mr Stanhills to allow her to paint a mural on his wall.

'She's really, really good,' Claire said, tossing her mane of blonde hair.

'It's rubbish. I've seen it on shop walls before,' Stanhills said, his fat cheeks wobbling every time he spoke.

'No, it's not,' Katy answered, with a pout.

Stanhills shrugged, he'd always been a pushover for a pretty face. 'OK, I've seen one or two that look all right, but how do I know yer won't make a mess of it?'

'Have yer seen that new flower shop, down Fence Houses?' Claire said.

Jim looked at Claire. 'She done that?'

Claire nodded her head and Katy stuck what little chest she had as far out as she could.

'Well,' he wavered, then tutted. 'No, I better not. What will the council say?'

'It's your wall. Yer can paint it if yer want,' Katy said.

'How much?'

Katy had never thought of payment, she'd done the flower shop for free because she wanted to paint. 'Fifty quid.'

'Fifty quid,' Jim echoed. 'Who do yer think I am, Rockerfeller?'

'Who's he?' Claire asked.

'Never mind. Twenty-five.'

'Twenty-five, and yer pay for the paint,' Claire said quickly.

The shopkeeper sighed, but nodded his head. A bright lick of paint was just what he needed to get the place looking up to scratch. 'Done,' he finally agreed.

'Yeah,' both girls yelled as they slapped hands mid-air.

Stanhills shook his head as he went back behind his counter, already wondering whether he'd done the right thing.

Claire and Katy left the shop, but their smiles soon faded as they saw Toad and two of his gang leaning against the wall that Katy wanted to paint.

When he saw them he frowned, his eyes turning to slits. 'Oh, if it isn't Carson's gang.'

'We ain't in nobody's gang, but if Mickey had a gang we'd sooner be in his than yours, yer ugly creep,' Claire sneered at him, while Katy turned pale and looked as if she were about to faint.

'Cocky twat, aren't yer. Do yer know what I've got in me pocket?'

'Do yer know what I've got in me hand?' Stanhills said.

They all spun round to see Jim Stanhills slapping a baseball bat in the palm of his hand. 'Now, move along, and if I see yers pestering little girls again, I'll swing for yer. Go on, move.'

Toad was the last one to lift his back from the wall. Glaring at Claire he said, 'Tell Carson's chick I'm gonna have her . . . And you,' he turned to Jim, 'I'll have you an' all.'

'Get away, go on, with yer slimy threats, yer horrible little creep. Time yer grew up and stopped acting like a bloody kid. I'm not frightened of you and yer gang. Go on, fuck off before I call the coppers on the lot of yers.' Stanhills waved his baseball bat in the air.

Toad curled his lip then spat on the ground, before he turned and swaggered slowly after his two pals, who were prudently at least fifteen yards away. When he reached them he turned back and shouted to Claire, 'I mean it, you tell that fucking bitch she's gonna get it.'

'Move,' Stanhills shouted, his face turning bright red with the effort. 'And if I see any more of yer drug deals going down near my premises, I will tell the coppers, sick to death of yers, pathetic bastards.'

Toad and his cronies sneered back at him, making obscene gestures back at the shopkeeper before they turned around and walked down the road. When they were out of sight, Stanhills let his bat fall to his side. Out of breath, he shook his head at the girls. 'Pile of shite that bloody lot. Make sure youse two girls keep well away from him, poison that's what he is.'

108

Still shaking his head he went back into his shop and slid the baseball bat under the counter where he kept it.

Katy leaned against the wall. Her face was deathly pale and she was still trembling. 'He's not gonna forget us. I know he won't,' she wailed. 'He'll not forget Stanhills either now. He'll stab us, or blind us, or both.'

'Get a grip Katy,' said Claire with more courage than she felt. 'He's all mouth.'

'No, he's not. And you know it.'

12

Lorraine fought with the cling film that was wrapped around her ham and tomato sandwich like a second skin. She finally managed to get it off and was just about to take a bite when there was a tap on her open door. She looked up. It was Luke. The days when he had just walked in, pulled his chair up to the desk, sat down and talked to her, were gone.

'Come in,' she said, aware that she sounded incredibly formal. 'I'm just having lunch,' she added, somewhat redundantly.

'Yer sure? It's a bit, well,' Luke looked uncomfortable. 'Well, I'm not exactly sure whether or not it's police business.'

Lorraine nodded, her heart suddenly feeling as if it was about to take flight. Was Luke thinking what she had been thinking? Could he possibly be asking her to take him back? She knew that, if only he would give the word, she would be back in his arms like a shot. 'That's fine,' her voice quavered only slightly. She was finding it hard to keep her emotions in check. 'Shut the door, if yer like.'

Luke hesitated, and then shut the door, and sat in his old seat, almost like before, but his face was grave.

'So?' she said, eyebrows raised, her sandwich still poised in mid air.

'It's like this, Lorraine.'

She waited, hardly breathing, for him to say the words that she was longing to hear. But her heart sunk when he said, 'I'm worried about Selina.'

'Oh,' Lorraine said quietly, feeling devastated and stupid by her assumption that Luke was about to ask her back. But then, what else would he want to talk about, if not Selina? Luke was taking his responsibilities very seriously. And she couldn't fault him for that. 'Well, what's happened? She's OK?'

Luke nodded his head, but not very confidently. 'She seems to be, but I'm not sure she would tell me if anything was truly wrong. A very strange thing happened this morning.' He proceeded to tell her about the white rose petals that Selina had received through the post.

'So what do yer think, weird or what?' Luke was staring intently at her, as if willing her to agree with him.

Lorraine hesitated before she spoke. She'd seen a lot less amount to something devastating, more than once. People get strange ideas into their heads, even the sane ones. And Selina had baggage.

'Well . . .' She looked at Luke who was obviously worried and tried not to worry him more by saying quietly, 'It's probably nothing.'

Luke sighed heavily. 'I don't know, Lorraine. I didn't like Selina's reaction. She thinks they're from an old boyfriend, someone from,' he paused, 'someone from the days before she came to stay with me. And whoever sent it posted it here.'

Lorraine paused a moment before saying, 'It's probably no more than intimidation, Luke. And yer know as well as I do that there's not much yer can do about rose petals. Have yer got the envelope?'

111

Luke nodded, and took it out of the front pocket of his jacket. 'It's got my fingerprints on it, and Selina's.'

Lorraine nodded, opened a drawer in her desk and took out a plastic bag. She opened it and Luke slipped the envelope inside. She called Carter into her office. 'Yer see this,' she said, holding the bag out to Carter, 'I want yer to get forensics to pull what they can from this, fingerprints, anything. And they're to treat it as a priority, OK?'

Carter nodded, and took the envelope from Lorraine. His eyes widened when he saw the name and address. He glanced quickly up at Luke, who stared at him levelly. 'What's this about?'

Lorraine looked at Luke questioningly, who closed his eyes for a second and then nodded. Having got permission, Lorraine said to her young constable, 'Selina received some rose petals in the post this morning. She thinks it might be someone from her past, someone bad, but there's not much we can do. However, I think it would make us all feel better,' she glanced up at Luke, who was staring at the ground in front of him with a look of angry desperation on his face, 'if we just see what we could get out of this. And Carter,' Carter looked up. For once his young, freckled face looked deadly earnest. 'Not a word about this to anyone. Make sure forensics know that this is confidential too. We've got an eager young reporter out there, and I don't want her to pick up on this and make a story out of something that's potentially nothing. OK?'

'I'll get on it right away,' Carter said. He glanced quickly back at Luke again, and then left Lorraine's office without another word.

Lorraine and Luke sat in silence for a moment. Then Luke said quietly, 'Thanks, Lorraine.'

Lorraine smiled. She could see that this was really worrying Luke. It was awful, it was another reminder of the desperate life that his daughter had lived on the streets. She thought of the conversation that she had had at the charity ball the night before and thought that it didn't matter how much you were prepared to change, sometimes other people wouldn't let you forget what you once had been. *Poor Selina.*

'So how did it go at the college?' she asked, partly to change the subject, partly because she was genuinely interested.

Luke brightened up, 'She's taking a foundation course in design. It could lead to anywhere, really. She might be able to do hairdressing after that, or she could go on a fashion design course. They don't start until September, so it's good she's got something to concentrate on before then.'

'That sounds great.'

'I've also come up with a good idea. I'm buying her a computer to help her with her studies, and so she'll want to stay in more.'

Lorraine wanted to laugh, although really it wasn't all that funny. It was as clear as day to her that Luke was trying to compensate for all the years that he hadn't known that Selina was around.

'Good idea, but yer can't keep her inside forever . . .' Lorraine stopped as she realised that she was overstepping her bounds slightly. She didn't want Luke to think that she was telling him what to do, or interfering.

Luke didn't seem to react badly to this advice, though. 'That's true, Lorraine,' he began, 'but that's exactly what I want to do, keep her inside, keep her safe, make sure that she knows she's . . .' he stopped, as if he was unable to say the word, '. . . cared for,' he said finally.

'Well,' Lorraine hesitated but then thought, *what the hell. He's come to me for advice, I'm going to give it to him.* 'She's come through a lot these last couple of months and I think she's strong enough to keep on the right path. This college thing's really good news. But for God's sake Luke, yer have to give her space.'

Luke sighed and sat back in his chair. 'Do yer want to know what the latest argument I had with her was?'

Lorraine smiled, 'Go on, tell me.'

'Just after she got that letter, no more than five minutes later, mind you,' he said in disbelief, 'she was asking me if she could go clubbing tonight. No alcohol, no drugs, she said – as if after that weirdo letter that's what I'd be afraid of!'

'So yer said no.'

'At first, and we had a big argument about that,' he smiled. 'But the kid's smart, you've got to give her that. She said that I'd be playing into this guy's hands, if I never let her out of the house anymore. That he'd have won.'

Lorraine laughed. 'Selina seems to know you well.'

Luke ran his fingers over his head. 'Yeah, she got me with that one. And she said she wouldn't be alone, that Amy and Mickey Carson would be there too.'

'So, what did yer say?'

'Said I'd think about it,' Luke gave her a wan smile. 'I'll probably say yes though. A crowded club, she's promised she's not gonna drink, and I'll make sure Mickey keeps an eye on her, make sure no one sticks anything in her water or anything like that.'

'So, yer come to terms with the Mickey situation then?' Lorraine was surprised – a lot had happened in the past couple of days.

Luke snorted, 'Don't think I've got much of a choice.'

'Do yer know something Luke,' Lorraine said suddenly, 'I haven't got a clue what you have against the kid. I could name at least two dozen losers that she could have taken up with within a mile radius of here. Think about it, their names will come to yer I'm sure . . . Then start worrying.'

'Yeah, you're right, but I'm not convinced about him yet, and I'm not convinced about this Amy person either. The last thing I wanted was for her to make friends with somebody else with a drug problem.'

'Luke, yer have to give Amy a chance. And how else is Selina gonna ever meet anyone else, if yer never gonna let her out of the house.'

Luke sighed, thought for a moment, then grumbled. 'Yer probably right. But Selina has made so many mistakes.'

'That's right, and she'll no doubt make a few more, all you can do is show her the right way, and for God's sake lighten up and give her a break.'

There was a strained silence between them for a minute, then Luke completely changed the subject. 'So what's Wade sniffing around for? That's strange an' all.'

'Do yer know something Luke,' Lorraine said, trying to keep her tone light, 'if yer keep banging on about everything being strange, I'm gonna end up thinking we live in the friggin' Bermuda triangle.'

Lorraine tried not to think about what Luke would say if he heard that she was going out with Wade tonight. *Shit, should cancel it really, don't even know why I agreed to go.* Then she remembered. Fuck. I haven't got his mobile number and I don't know where he lives. *Oh, what the hell we'll only be talking about police business.*

Carter gave his usual knock then put his head around the door, 'Sorry to disturb yer, boss, but the RSPCA have phoned. A cat has been found, with its heart cut out. They want to know if we've had anything like it before.'

Both Lorraine and Luke looked at each other. Lorraine shook her head, 'I would remember that all right . . . That's horrible, the nasty depraved bastard.'

'I've never heard of that before either, well, not up here anyhow. Sharp find out though. There's a job for yer Carter, search the database see if yer can come up with something,' Luke said.

'OK.' Carter turned back to Lorraine. 'Boss.'

'Yeah.' Lorraine answered, still thinking about the poor cat.

'When we catch him can I have him for five?'

'Yer'll take yer turn, Carter.' Lorraine couldn't get the vision of the dead cat out of her head. 'Wonder where they've taken the poor thing?'

Luke shrugged, 'Probably to their head office. Why?'

'Just wondering if it was a neat job.'

'What!' Luke screwed up his face.

'I mean was it done in a hurry or was time taken and the job done to perfection. In other words, was it a practice session, yer know, keeping his hand in. Or a trial and error job in preparation for something else?'

Luke saw where her thinking was taking her, and he felt his body shiver with apprehension.

Selina dressed carefully in a brown skirt that hung low on her stomach exposing her navel and a cream top with long sleeves that fitted very tightly. Not too much make up, just enough to give a little extra colour, and not enough to set old moany face off. She was excited, Mickey was taking her to a club where her favourite DJ was working. The last time she'd seen him had been in that bar in Ireland.

Selina leaned into the mirror, putting lipstick on her lips and rubbing them together. She smiled at Amy's reflection in the mirror. 'Sure you won't come?'

'Nah, I can't. Dad's had the boys all day, he's bound to be at the end of his rope. Amy folded her legs underneath her so that she was sitting cross-legged on the bed. 'You're looking fantastic though, love that top.'

Selina wrinkled her nose, and Amy laughed. 'Stop that,' Amy said. 'Yer know yer gorgeous.'

'Yer should come!' Selina flopped down on the bed beside

her friend, grabbed a pillow and held it to her stomach. 'Just for a little while? I told Dad you'd go.'

'No. I'm not playing gooseberry,' Amy replied with a laugh.

Selina hit Amy with the pillow she had been holding, 'Yer know Mickey won't mind.'

'Yeah I know, but you two just want to be together at the moment, don't yer?' Amy replied. 'Yer really like him, don't yer?'

Selina smiled and, her cheeks turning pink, said, 'Yes, actually, I do.'

'Thought yer did, he's a canny lad, fab black curls.'

Selina giggled. 'Come on, come with us,' Selina pleaded. 'The DJ is really hot, and it'll be fun! I promise that Mickey and I won't make you feel uncomfortable.'

Amy hesitated, then shook her head. 'I can't. It's not fair on Dad to have the boys all day.' She unwound her legs from under her and got up from the bed. 'Next time, yeah?'

Amy saw herself to the door, leaving Selina to get ready.

Selina went into the living room as her father was putting on *Hotel California*, by the Eagles. She was starting to warm to his music taste, athough she'd never tell him that. Luke turned around when he heard her come in, and for a moment, it was eighteen years ago, and he was looking at his first love, Selina's mother, the resemblance was that strong. He fumbled with the CD case, and it fell to the ground.

'You look,' he said finally, 'very beautiful.'

Selina smiled nervously. She had never really had a father figure in her life – until now – and she never really knew how to react to Luke. When Luke had told her that it was fine to go out tonight, she had almost flung her arms around his neck, grateful that he should take a chance on her, even after she had bolted to Ireland just the week before. But then she had held back, not sure whether that was the right thing to do or not.

'Was that Amy I saw leave just before?' Luke asked.

'Um, yes,' said Selina hesitantly. 'She can't make it after all. But it's still OK if I go with Mickey?'

She heard Luke take a deep intake of breath, and then let it out slowly.

'You're going to Blacks, is that right?'

Selina nodded. It was a club for sixteen- to eighteen-year-olds, and although it didn't sell alcohol, it sold an enormous amount of water, which usually was an indication that the revellers were partaking of something much less legal and far more dangerous. It had been closed down twice. Selina knew that Luke had his reservations about her going there.

'OK, just make sure yer in by eleven.'

'Eleven!' She couldn't help feeling dismay. Eleven was usually when the club started to get going.

Luke frowned at her. 'OK, midnight. If I have to come looking for yer, believe me I will.'

It was better than nothing, but still, midnight. It wasn't so long ago that she had started partying at midnight. There had been nights that had stretched into afternoons, where she hadn't come down until four or five o'clock, when she had danced until she had blisters on her feet that broke and bled, blisters that she didn't even notice having until the drugs were out of her system. She held down a small rush of anger as she felt the chains rattling around her but tried hard not to let it show on her face. For years she had been used to coming and going as she pleased. Not that her grandmother didn't care, well she did a bit, the odd times she was sober.

OK. Just chill and go with the flow, the last thing I really want is to be back out there on my own. Fucking Cinderella it is.

'Thanks – it's a fab DJ who's playing tonight.'

Luke nodded. 'Nothing on the Eagles, mind yer.'

Selina groaned and rolled her eyes up to the ceiling. Just at

118

that moment, there was a knock on the door. 'That'll be Mickey,' Selina said. 'I'll see you later . . . Lu . . . Da . . . Dad.'

'Take care, love,' Luke said quietly. It was the first time she had ever called him that. He had noticed that she had avoided the word, or called him Luke only when necessary. He suddenly felt enormously elated. He felt, for the first time since he had met Selina, like a real, proper father.

13

The knock on the door came exactly as *Emmerdale* was starting. 'Who the hell's that?' Peggy moaned as she hurried to the door.

She opened it to find a handsome, green-eyed man smiling down at her.

For a moment she was thrown, but only for a moment, it never took Peggy long to get right back on form. 'And what can I do for you?' she said flirtatiously.

'This is the right address for Detective Inspector Lorraine Hunt?'

'It's all right Peggy,' Lorraine said practically in her ear, causing Peggy to jump. 'I'm here now.'

Peggy looked Lorraine up and down, her eyes showing a mixture of perplexity and amazement.

Lorraine was the kind of woman who could make even the simplest jeans and shirt combination look stunning. It was what she was wearing now – dark blue jeans, a loose white shirt with a belt tied loosely around it, small pearl earrings in her ears. She looked casual, yet chic. She reached over and put her hand underneath Peggy's chin and closed the other woman's jaw with a smile. 'See yer later Peggy. I won't be late, but don't bother to wait up, there's a good girl.'

'Cheeky madam,' Peggy muttered under her breath, but said, 'Bye,' as sweetly as she could to Ian Wade, as she closed the door. 'Mavis,' she shouted up the stairs a moment later. 'Yer not gonna believe this!'

'So, where are we going?' said Lorraine as she hopped into the passenger seat of Wade's rental car. It was a small, nippy red Nissan Micra, and Lorraine approved of his choice, seeing that the factory that made them gave jobs to a lot of folk in the Sunderland area.

'Ooo,' said Wade, 'I thought we should push the boat out a bit. I've booked us a table at the Newcastle Malmaison, what do you think?'

'Um, that's lovely, Ian, but – yer know, I thought we were going out as friends – this isn't really a *date* date, is it? Malmaison's very expensive, and I'm not really dressed for it.'

Wade smiled tightly. 'I just thought I'd, yer know, treat yer. You deserve it.'

Lorraine smiled, but really, she was apprehensive. She thought she had made it clear to Wade that she wasn't really ready for anything yet, and besides, she didn't think that, even with Luke completely out of the picture, she'd even fancy Wade. He was handsome, sure, but just not her type.

The food at the Malmaison was spectacular and Lorraine enjoyed every mouthful of her steak. But the evening was flat, she knew it and Wade knew it; even the champagne, which was even better than the champagne at the dinner the evening before, did nothing to energise either one of them. It was obvious Wade had something on his mind, he was nowhere near as talkative as he'd been that night in Ireland, and Lorraine had a hunch that he would rather be somewhere else. *Then why was he so insistent on taking me out for dinner?* she

121

wondered. *Why on earth did he take me here, instead of just a quick ploughman's at the pub?*

If it wasn't his constant fidgeting that gave the game away, the amount of times he looked at his watch, certainly did. And Lorraine's thoughts were mostly centred on a certain Luke Daniels, and the fact that she'd probably made a huge mistake agreeing to go out with Wade tonight.

'Would you like some more?' Wade asked, the champagne bottle already poised over her glass.

Lorraine was about to say no, she'd had enough, when Wade sighed and put the bottle down. He looked at Lorraine for a moment, gave a reluctant shake of his head, before saying, 'I'm sorry Lorraine, but I really have to go. Something's come up. Unavoidable, I'm really sorry. I should have told you when I came to your house. In fact that was my intention, but you looked so lovely that I couldn't bring myself . . .'

Lorraine was confused. This was certainly strange behaviour, and she couldn't believe that Wade was, essentially, going to ditch her at a very expensive restaurant in front of tables of very expensive people. 'I just don't understand, Wade, why take me here at all? I thought it was just going to be a dinner between a couple of mates, but then you took me here and now you're leaving? This is really weird.'

He stood up. 'I don't blame you for being angry, believe me. I just have to go, but perhaps it's for the best? Or, ah, maybe, we can do this another time? I do come over quite frequently.'

'I just don't know about that, Wade.' It all sounded like bollocks to her. He was all gung ho when he came to pick her up this evening, it wasn't until they had got into the car and Lorraine had said that she hoped he knew that it wasn't a proper date that he started acting withdrawn and surly. Maybe he was upset that she didn't want to be more involved with him? Maybe he really had got the wrong end of the stick and was devastated that she saw him as just a friend?

Whatever the reason, it was very strange, and Lorraine didn't like it.

'I'll order a taxi for you.'

'Yeah, you do that.'

'You're sure that's all right?'

'It'll have to be, won't it.'

'Look Lorraine, I really am sorry, I can't explain but it is important.' He was already on his way as the last word came out of his mouth.

Jesus! Hope he's paid the friggin' bill.

Mickey had managed, though it took a lot of perseverance, to get his aunt Brenda to drop him and Selina off at Blacks, which was on the outskirts of Sunderland near Doxford Park. That way he had enough to get them both in the door, and enough to get them a taxi home.

And now they were inside. Mickey had heard a lot about the place, it belonged to a cousin of Cal's, a cousin he and the rest of the family had very little to do with. Cal had told him plenty about what went on, and he'd warned him: 'Just keep yer head down, say no, and they probably won't bother yer again. Plenty other fish there what's eager enough.'

And Blacks was the right name for the dump, he thought looking around him. The walls were painted black, just like the name of the club, and battered seating was on either side of the room. A bright disco light was above the dance floor, and lights flashed red, green, orange and pink, and followed each other all around the walls. The DJ was up in a booth, spinning some discs, and the bass in the music seemed to echo the beat of Mickey's heart. He could feel it all the way from the floor, up his legs and into his chest. He didn't feel entirely comfortable here. But Selina seemed happy enough. A girl pushed past them wearing large silver hoops in her ears, big enough to swing on.

Mickey grinned at the picture in his head of Selina swinging off one ear and him swinging off the other.

He lifted his foot to follow Selina through the crowd of screaming, whistling, arm-waving teenagers, and it was sticking to the floor.

'Eww.'

'What's the matter?' Selina asked, the strobe lighting high-lighting her face, making her movements seem slow and deliberate.

'Me feet are sticking to the manky bloody carpet,' Mickey moaned.

'Yeah, bit of a doss house isn't it . . . So don't forget to wipe your feet on the way out.' Then she jumped when a very tall boy bent almost in half and whistled in her ear.

Mickey scowled at him, but the darkness hid his face, and the boy who was obviously out of it, danced away grinning his head off and talking to whoever it was he imagined was by his side. When Mickey, shaking his head, turned back to Selina she had disappeared.

The door slammed shut and Duke lifted his head from the rug in front of the fire; his time of sleeping alone in the kitchen was long gone.

Mavis looked at Peggy as they heard Lorraine pound her way upstairs.

'Mustn't have gone well, then?' Peggy looked at the clock and then at Mavis, her left eyebrow raised in a question.

'Wonder when she's gonna tell us what the hell's going on between her and Luke, and why we haven't seen hide nor hair of him since the pair of them went to Ireland.'

'I reckon they've had a falling out.' Peggy nodded wisely.

'Never! How did yer figure that one Peg?'

'No need for sarcasm . . . Pass the popcorn will yer Mave?'

Mavis leaned over and passed the bowl to Peggy, Duke sniffed the air.

'It's bad for yer Duke.' Peggy looked at him and his tail thumped the carpet. 'Oh go on then, just one piece.' She threw it at Duke who neatly caught the treat.

As Duke was tasting his first piece of popcorn, Mickey was frantically searching the overcrowded hall for Selina. There had to be at least four or five hundred people squeezed into Blacks, all of them jumping, whistling and screaming, only the odd ones were making an attempt at what might be called a proper dance.

DJ Adza, a local hero, put Eric Pryde's 'Call on Me' on the decks and if possible the place went even wilder, people dancing frantically to the classic track, mixed with a modern edge.

Mickey made his way to the edge of the crowd, and at that moment spotted Selina coming out of a side door. His heart sank. What was in there, an office of some kind?

Was a fat greasy creep of a man sitting behind a desk giving out drugs?

'Selina,' he shouted, but he couldn't breach the noise around him. Quickly he set off after her; he caught up as she stopped and peered through the crowd, looking for him. When she caught sight of him, she waved. He breathed a sigh of relief and pushed through the crowds towards her.

'Mickey.' She smiled, obviously pleased to see him, 'I thought I would never find you again.'

'Where did yer go?' He looked at the door and this time made out a black motif in the supposed shape of a lady on the door as one of the strobe lights momentarily flashed on it.

He felt stupid. He shouldn't have even thought she would go looking for something. She'd told him a bit about her life before, and he truly believed that she was sincere when she swore she would never touch drugs again.

125

'I did tell you I was going to the loo, but you mustn't have heard,' she yelled into his ear.

'What?' Mickey lifted his head up and smiled at her, feeling a warm glow spread all over him, from her soft breath.

Selina smiled and shook her head. It was too loud to talk, so she kissed him on the cheek instead. Mickey took a chance and quickly turned his head and kissed her on the lips. She smiled at him. He smiled back, and started waving his arms about in mockery of most of the kids there.

'So you want to dance?' she shouted as loud as she could.

'Oh yeah . . . Cool.' Mickey grinned at her, but inside he was feeling as nervous as hell.

Oh God, the only time I've danced is in front of me bedroom mirror. And that time me Robbie and Cal got shit-faced and we danced till we fell down.

He glanced quickly around. *Well, anybody with half a brain can do better than what most of these morons are doing!*

Full of confidence Mickey started to dance with Selina. In moments she was giggling at his movements.

'What?' Mickey asked. By now he was thoroughly enjoying himself.

'Nothing.' She spun round to hide her smile, even though her shoulders were shaking, giving away the fact that she was laughing at his dancing. She thought that, just a few months ago, she would have made fun of anyone who danced the way Mickey did, and with a jolt realised that it was because she liked him so much that she didn't care if he looked ridiculous. It was all part of his quirky charm. As long as they were together, that was all that mattered. The thought made her feel good inside, better than any drug.

Her life had finally taken a turn for the better, and she supposed this college thing might be all right. The foundation course didn't look that interesting, but it didn't look that bad either, and it had been the only option. She could decide to do design or hairdressing in September, either sounded like it would be fun.

An hour later they were still dancing, when crashing above the music, and the whistling crowd, the fire alarm went off. Some of the kids, those stoned out of their minds, just grinned and carried on jumping, thinking the noise was coming from the DJ for their enjoyment. The sober ones tried to get the message across to their friends just what was happening. A few made their way calmly to the doors, others simply panicked.

Panic spreads as fast as a bush fire and is just as lethal. Selina was swept along with the crowd, and Mickey nearly got his arm torn off trying to hold on to her.

He watched as they came tumbling out of the club, a thrill of satisfaction coursing through his veins as he heard a bone snap here and another one there, the accompanying screams of pain nearly sent him into overload. The chaos was even better than he expected, he had planned it perfectly, jamming the back exit shut so that there was only one way out.

Then the one he was waiting for came out at a run, that runt she'd gone in with was nowhere in sight.

He smiled as she headed in his direction.

Everything had gone according to plan. He'd set the fire alarm off then hastily got out of there, hoping she'd head this way but follow her and take her down another alleyway if she hadn't. And anyway, there was so much confusion, no one would be looking out for a lone girl. People were selfish, they only looked after themselves.

Soon, soon she would be his. 'Ha.'

14

Lorraine opened her arms as Luke reached for her. She smiled. Luke was burying his face in her hair, kissing her neck, his fingers running down her body in the way that she remembered from the all-too-short time together. 'I'm never gonna let you go,' he whispered into her ear. 'I love you, Lorraine.'

'I love you too, Luke,' she murmured.

'Lorraine, Lorraine.' Luke's voice was urgent and not at all suited to the mood.

She opened her eyes, jolted out of her dream. 'What the—?' Luke was standing over her, and Mavis and Peggy were in the doorway.

'She hasn't come home,' Luke's voice was frantic. 'What am I gonna do?' he rushed on. 'I phoned the club and nobody's answering the bloody phone. The dump is probably run by a bunch of flaming morons.'

Lorraine had only taken in half of what he'd said. She sat up and glared at Mavis and Peggy, 'Do yer mind? The pair of yers cluttering up the doorway, for God's sake.'

'Sorry,' they both muttered as they scuttled away. 'Cup

of tea, Luke?' Mavis shouted as she and Peggy headed downstairs.

Lorraine shook her head then rubbed sleep out of her eyes. 'What's going on, Luke?' She blearily looked at the time on her alarm clock. 'It's quarter to one in the bloody morning, for God's sake.'

Luke took a deep, calming breath. 'Yer don't understand, Selina was meant to be home at midnight. I waited for her, but now she's late and I'm worried that, with those petals and everything, that something mght have happened to her.'

'Luke, I'm gonna tell yer what I – and you for that matter – tell parents whose kids are late home. They're probably just having a good time and haven't thought to call home. She's late, but Luke, not that late.' *For God's sake let the kid breathe*, she thought to herself. *He's gonna bust a blood vessel if he stresses so much over every little thing that Selina does.*

'But yer don't understand,' Luke continued, 'anything could have happened. She could . . .' He left what could have happened to Selina hanging in the air. Lorraine knew what he meant.

'OK, OK,' Lorraine said. 'Just calm down a little. I take it you've tried her mobile?'

'She forgot to take the bloody thing with her,' Luke said. 'I called it just past midnight and heard it ring in her bedroom.'

'Do youse two want a cuppa or not?' Peggy yelled up the stairs.

'Oh, fuck it.' Lorraine swung her long pyjama clad legs out of the bed. 'Come on,' she grabbed hold of Luke's hand, 'Let's go downstairs, see if we can make some sense out of it.'

Luke shook himself and followed her down the stairs. When they were seated in the sitting room, facing each other, Mavis and Peggy brought them out a cup of tea each and then scuttled back into the kitchen. Lorraine said, 'OK, yer said she had to be in by midnight, she's three quarters of an hour late.

What would we do if we got a call at the station saying a sixteen-year-old was less than an hour late?'

Luke shrugged, starting to calm down and beginning to feel slightly ridiculous for creating such a fuss and dragging Lorraine out of bed, then wishing he was actually in the bed with her. This whole father business was nothing but a giant fucking headache.

'Laugh,' he replied finally, then sighed.

'Precisely. Is she with Mickey Carson?'

'Aye and I'll kill the little flaming toe-rag when I get me hands on him. I went to his house before I came round here, his parents haven't seen him. Usually he stops at the Lumsdons' a couple of nights a week.'

'Have yer been there? They might be snuggled up watching a video.'

'No, I came here first.'

'OK, I'll get dressed, but phone home first, just in case she's sitting there wondering where the hell you are. If yer don't get an answer just keep on trying.'

While Luke phoned home, Lorraine went upstairs and quickly dressed in her jeans and a pink jumper. Yawning she tied her hair up in a ponytail, then went back downstairs. When she saw Luke's face, she realised that there had been no answer. Despite herself, she began to get an uneasy feeling in the pit of her stomach. Luke's paranoia was catching.

After the all clear had been given, Mickey had gone back into the club and searched every nook and cranny. With the lights on he could see just how filthy the place really was, and without the aid of perfume and aftershave mingling in the room, he could smell the damp and foisty air. There was no sign of Selina.

When he'd come back outside it was like looking at a disaster area, eleven ambulances, all of them with their lights blazing, were parked at the curb. The sound of sirens as police cars came and went added a frightening dimension to the scene.

Jesus!

Too late to search the ambulances that were already moving off, his heart pounding like a hammer in his chest, he'd pushed past the milling kids, some who didn't have a clue what was going on, and ran to the first ambulance.

Two boys, one with his arm in a makeshift sling, the other with a large gash above his right eye and blood all over his face and green T-shirt, had gazed at him confusedly as the ambulance man closed the door. 'Looking for yer friends son?' he'd asked.

Mickey had nodded. 'Yeah a girl. Any girls in these ambulances?'

The ambulance man gave a small smile as he replied, 'Oh, I'd say there's at least a fifty per cent chance on that one, Sunshine.'

The friendly sarcasm went right over Mickey's head as he ran to the next ambulance. His heart did a back flip when a girl who had looked a bit like Selina had lain there unmoving with breathing equipment over her face. But she was wearing blue and, when Mickey looked closely, didn't look like Selina at all.

He'd examined every ambulance and found no sign of Selina, and now, just about ready to drop, he reached the hospital gates after a fifty-minute walk. If it meant searching every ward in the hospital for Selina, he'd do it. He had to know that she was all right.

Lorraine and Luke were approaching the Seahills when they were flashed down by a patrol car.

'What the?' Lorraine said, amazed when Sanderson and Carter jumped out of the patrol car and headed towards them. Lorraine pressed the button for the window to roll down.

'You've heard then?' Sanderson asked. 'I've been phoning your mobile but it keeps saying it's switched off, and the house phone was engaged.'

Lorraine took her mobile out of her pocket, looked at it with disgust, 'Damn. I dropped the bloody thing yesterday and it hasn't been the same since . . . Anyhow heard what?'

'We're actually looking for Selina,' Luke put in before Sanderson or Carter could answer. 'Have yer seen any sign of her, she's with that Mickey Carson.'

Sanderson was quiet for a moment and Carter was jumping from foot to foot with anxiety. Sanderson cleared his throat, then said, 'There's been an incident at Blacks club . . .'

'That's where they were,' Luke said anxiously. 'What happened?' He was practically out of the car now in his eagerness to find out what Sanderson and Carter knew, and if they didn't hurry up and spit it out, he just might strangle the pair of them.

'The fire alarms went off.' Sanderson held his hand up as Luke started to look like he was about to explode. 'It's OK, there was no fire, it was just some idiot messing around.' Above Luke's sigh of relief he went on, 'But there were at least twenty or more kids hurt in the panic to get out.'

'Oh God . . . Come on, we have to get to the hospital,' Luke said. His face wore an even more panicked expression on it than it had previously.

'It might be OK, Luke, she might be one of the ones who didn't get hurt. She might still be at the club, or she might be on her way home,' Lorraine said reassuringly, but then stopped. There was something in Sanderson's face that she didn't like. Then she realised that he was keeping something back, and although she had a hunch she would dread finding out what it was, she said, 'There's more isn't there Sanderson?'

He nodded, while Luke frowned his impatience. It was Carter, standing still for the moment who quickly said, 'A body has been found behind the club, she's been beaten up, very badly beaten up. We don't know whether or not she's alive or dead.'

'How, how old is she?' Luke asked quietly, as the blood drained from his face. 'A girl, a woman, an old lady, for God's sake, Carter!'

'They, er, they never said, least I never heard what they said.' Carter put his head down, and stared at his shoes as if willing his feet to keep still.

'A teenager,' Sanderson said quietly.

Lorraine closed her eyes and put her head back on the headrest. After a couple of deep breaths she opened them and looked at Luke. He had the look of someone in deep shock and her heart went out to him. She had the horrible feeling, a feeling bordering on certainty, that Selina had to be one of the kids hurt at the club or, God forbid, it was her body behind the club.

15

Carter had barely brought the squad car to a stop, when Luke jumped out the door and ran towards the hospital entrance. Lorraine and Luke had got into the panda knowing with the sirens going they would get to the hospital that much quicker, and Sanderson followed in the other car.

When Lorraine and Carter walked into the hospital, a few moments behind Luke, their eyes couldn't believe the mayhem they were seeing. 'Bloody hell,' Carter said, looking around him.

The waiting room was full to the brim with the walking wounded. Those who were the most badly hurt were already being seen to by the doctors and nurses, who looked frantic. Some of the kids had been patched up to various degrees, and were waiting for their friends. But there was still a lot of people to be seen, and there were kids who were in a bad way anyway, who were quite clearly drugged out of their mind. There were a lot of minor injuries; skin torn off arms and legs as they had been dragged or pushed screaming through the unyielding metal doors of the club.

One poor girl, sitting in the corner, and obviously still in shock, was holding the right side of her face on with her hand. Her two friends who stood beside her looked unscathed, which was amazing for the amount of flesh they were showing. A name was shouted by a young black nurse who looked exhausted, and the two girls helped their injured friend to her feet. She shuffled slowly, leaning heavily on her friends, towards the waiting nurse.

Lorraine sighed. The luck of the draw. *Poor bugger, she might never be the same after this night.*

Luke had buttonholed a policeman, and was giving him the third degree. As Lorraine watched, the policeman pointed down the corridor. Lorraine, with Carter trailing behind her, made her way through the battlefield and followed Luke.

Lorraine looked at the kids as she passed. The blood bank would be sorely depleted tonight.

'Poor bastards,' she muttered.

'What, Boss?'

'Bet yer fucking life I have that place closed down after this, most of these kids are gonna be scarred for life . . . I hate the damn dump, last time we raided it they had the friggin' taps turned off, how bloody sick is that?'

Carter nodded his agreement. His eyes wandered around the room hoping to see Selina, hoping that she was one of the many kids milling about. Praying she wasn't the one who had been found behind the club. But, heart sinking, he couldn't see her.

They caught up with Luke just as Carter was figuring out why they had the taps turned off. 'Oh, so the kids will buy water. That's nasty, eh. What about the ones who can't afford to buy it?'

Lorraine looked puzzled at Carter, then she remembered what she'd said minutes ago. 'They dehydrate, Carter, and if God's watching and they're really lucky, they end up here.'

Luke was reaching up to pull the curtain back from the

cubicle. But before he could, the curtain opened and Mickey Carson stepped out. Mickey did a double take, receiving the shock of his life to find Luke's face not three inches from his own. Even though he'd half expected to see him there.

'Jesus Christ,' he muttered.

'Is it her . . . Is she?' Luke demanded, unable to finish the rest of the sentence. He had gone through hell on the way here. Of course it was her, why else would Carson be here.

The last thing he'd wanted in this life was to be given, out of the blue, a sixteen-year-old daughter, especially one with the stubborn street-instilled grittiness that Selina had. But, what he didn't tell Lorraine, and the reason why he had known that something had happened to Selina, that he wasn't just being overprotective, was that, for the first time, Selina had called him Dad. That seemed like such a little thing, but in fact, it meant everything. They were beginning to bond, they were developing trust. And they had negotiated the time that Selina was going to arrive back home together. It just hadn't seemed like something someone who was planning on not living up to her promises would do. And she had sealed that by calling him Dad. His heart was in his throat. If anyone had hurt his little girl, then he was going to kill the bastard.

Sweat broke out on his brow and he felt himself unable to move. His heart felt as if it was being squeezed by two giant hands.

Please God, don't snatch her away.

Silently, terrified of Luke's reaction when he saw Selina, Mickey pointed to the cubicle. Luke shook himself and with mounting fear, stepped inside, his eyes raking in everything in front of him. A very tall policeman with a dirty-grey moustache that was yellowing on the ends, stood on one side of the bed. He flashed Luke a suspicious squint-eyed look accompanied by a weak smile, which showed a whole mouthful of nicotine stained teeth.

137

Slowly, dread flushing his veins in much the same way a panic attack brings the strongest to their knees, he looked at his daughter. A machine beeped steadily on showing a strong heartbeat. Her eyes were closed.

The dread receded with a swiftness that made him gasp. 'Selina,' he said out loud. He hurried to the side of her bed, opposite to where the policeman was standing.

Her eyes looked as if they were swollen shut; that she'd taken an horrendous beating was obvious. But she was breathing on her own, her chest moved up and down, up and down. He reached out to touch her hand.

'That's far enough.' The policeman leaned slightly over the bed, as if protecting Selina.

'It's all right she's my . . . my daughter.' Luke took his ID out of his jacket pocket and handed it over.

The policeman examined it and relaxing, handed it back. 'Sorry, Sir.'

'OK OK, we, er,' he swallowed hard. 'We were told it was a body.'

Before the policeman could reply, the curtain opened again and Lorraine stepped in, Carter close behind her. 'Oh, thank God she's all right,' Lorraine said.

'You betcha.' Carter grinned.

Luke was holding Selina's hand now and grinning his pleasure to everyone in the tiny cubicle.

Lorraine quickly established that the policeman's name was Sergeant Martin Pierce. 'Can you tell us exactly what happened officer?' Lorraine asked. 'When we got the call it was to say that a body had been found behind the club.'

'And that's what we thought it was at first, she wasn't moving. We – my partner and I, that is – went round the back of the club as a matter of course, checking that everything was all right. We nearly tripped over her. Big Jim swears there was no pulse, but mind yer, Big Jim's ready for retirement and he was probably looking in the wrong place.'

'Thank God yer found her when yer did though, if she'd been left all night . . .' Luke's voice trailed off. On their way to the hospital the heavens had opened, and it was still pouring.

'Big Jim Malloy?' Lorraine asked, looking quizzically at Pierce.

'Aye, know him do yer?'

'Very well, he's a good man. It'll have been his idea to search round the back even though all the action had took place out front, he never leaves anything out, so I'm surprised that he made the mistake about the pulse.'

'Aye, problem is,' Pierce patted his flat stomach, 'Big Jim's got trouble bending, too much weight, if yer know what I mean.'

Lorraine smiled. Big Jim had once dated her mother Mavis, she knew all about his fondness for all things sweet. He used to do a magic trick with sherbet dips. Mavis could have done much worse, but it was not to be.

'There's er, something else yer should know about, Marm.'

Luke was just about to leave the cubicle to find a doctor to ask about Selina's condition when he was stopped by the policeman's words. It wasn't so much what he said, but the way he said it. He noticed that Lorraine and Carter were also staring at Pierce. There was something in his voice that had raised the hairs on all of their necks.

'We found something that we thought was really odd, if yer know what I mean. We have it down at the station if yer want to see it, Big Jim bagged it. Thing is, it was in pristine condition. Perfect even, and with everything that was going on, how delicate it is, well, it's a bit odd that it managed to survive . . . unless it was left by the perpetrator . . .'

Luke felt a growing unease in his chest. He thought back to that morning and his daughter's reaction when she had seen the petals in the envelope. He thought about how coincidental it was for his daughter to get beaten almost to death the day that she had received them. And then he thought about her previous life and all the things she must have done, and all the unstable, ruthless people she must have known. His mental processes were whirring around like crazy, and a cold sweat broke out on his body. One part of his mind registered that Lorraine was looking at him worriedly, but the rest was fully focused on the ramifications of what Pierce had said, and what that meant for Selina. He raised his head and looked him in the eye. 'Don't tell me. Was it petals from a white rose?'

Lorraine and Carter looked at each other, and then they looked at Luke, who was clenching and unclenching his fists.

Martin Pierce looked perplexed. 'Well, not quite, but yer on the right track. It was a single white rose. How the hell did yer guess?'

At the beginning, it had all gone exactly the way he had meant it to. Taking the girl, throwing her down in that sordid alleyway and punching her in the face, trying to destroy those flawless features, all of that went just as he imagined it would. She had been too shocked to react, but that didn't matter, the screams coming from the club, the sirens as the fire engines and the ambulances arrived on the scene, all managed to heighten his excitement. He almost couldn't wait for it to be over, this feeling, which he'd replay and replay in his head until it wore out and needed refreshing, was deeper than love, and less fleeting than sex.

And then his blood had run cold. 'What you doing with me girl?' came a strong Mancunian accent, and he had looked up to find, not the skinny runt she had been with, but a small, wiry skinhead who looked mean and ugly.

He stood up and bolted. The skinhead, he reasoned, would stay with his girl, but he was wrong about that too. He climbed over the fence at the end of the alleyway, only to have his foot grabbed by the skinhead. He kicked him off, and dropped to the ground. And then he took off, running past call centres as fast as he could to reach his car, the skinhead close behind him, until finally, his lungs bursting in his chest, the skinhead caught up with him and knocked him to the ground. He scrabbled on the hard pavement to get up and get away, but the skinhead was on top of him, pinning him to the ground. The skinhead's forearm was in the back of his neck, and he turned his face, so that he could breathe. The skinhead was speaking into his ear, he could smell his assailant's breath, it smelled of decay.

'No one hurts me girl,' the skinhead had muttered. 'No one but me. Yer not gonna get away with this.'

The skinhead ran his hands down his body, then stopped when he found the package in his coat pocket. 'What do we have here,' the skinhead sneered.

The skinhead got off him and walked a little way off. He opened the leather pouch and gave a low whistle when he saw the knives and the autopsy scissors. 'What were yer planning to do with these then?'

'Give them back to me,' he said, holding out his hand. 'They're my tools.'

'Yer tools, eh?' replied the skinhead. 'And yer were going to use them on me girl?'

His hand dropped slightly, but his eyes remained locked on the skinhead's. He didn't answer him.

'Have yer used these before?' the skinhead asked, and again he didn't reply, letting the silence speak for him.

Finally, the skinhead closed the pouch up and gave it back to him. 'Show me,' he said. 'I'd like to know what yer do.'

So, he had lost the kill, but he had gained an apprentice, someone he could use. He didn't really think that the skinhead was all that bright, he could easily get rid of him when the time came. And he could be a convenient fall guy, should the situation arise.

Looking in the mirror he ran his fingers over his smooth chin as he stared into his eyes. Losing the kill had been unfortunate, but he hoped the message would get through to the one he wanted it to. She wasn't safe, no one she knew was safe. He could see her now in his mind's eye, brushing her mane of blonde hair. She was near perfect. A mirror image of the first one. She was the one. The one he had come to England for. And he had given her chances, three chances, in fact, not to reject him. But she had, and like the rest she would pay. But firstly he would scare her, let her know who was in control.

His fingers touched the place on his body where the two faded roses were.

'I will have you,' he murmured. 'But first,' he put his jacket on and moved to the door. 'First I have to meet the apprentice . . . Ha.'

16

Dinwall had been at the station all morning, getting in early rather than facing the wrath of his wife over breakfast. For once her suspicions were totally unfounded, and Dinwall felt hard done by. Last night he had to sleep on the fold-out sofa in the living room, and he had a sleepless night. It wasn't because the sofa bed was uncomfortable – it was – but his mind kept on going back and forth over the arguments he'd had with his wife. She had veered between yelling at him and calling him a filthy bastard, and crying uncontrollably. He couldn't think what it was that had sparked her off – unless she'd heard of something that he'd done in the past.

He sat in the chair he always sat in, reading this morning's edition of the *Sunderland Echo*, which had a brief summary of the incident at Blacks nightclub, and did not see Kate Mulberry until she flicked his newspaper with her fingernail.

'Hi,' she smiled. 'Want a fresh cuppa on me?'

Dinwall sat upright, feeling his feet tingle as they hit the floor. It was almost time for his shift to start. He looked at the young woman sitting next to him and thought, *she's not bad, yer know, bet she's got a great little body under those clothes,* then he stopped himself, *Gotta behave, gotta stop looking at other women. Lynn's the only woman for me. From now on this is the new and improved James Dinwall.*

'No thanks,' he smiled 'I'm about to start me shift.'

But she wasn't listening, she picked up his discarded copy of the *Newcastle Journal*, read the front page and just as Dinwall was getting up to go, she yelled, 'Bastard, bastard,' stamping her foot with each expletive.

'Em, something wrong?' Dinwall asked, trying hard not to cringe as he became aware of the sudden silence and the way everyone was looking at them.

'This,' she poked her finger at the paper, 'It's my bloody story, but the *Sunderland Echo* doesn't come out until well after dinner, one of them bastard's in the office has stolen my story. The bastard.' She threw the paper down, batting away tears of anger and frustration.

'Oh dear,' Dinwall shrugged and made to leave but Kate put a restraining hand on his arm.

'Listen, this story could really break the whole underage club thing open, Johnston, the bastard has hardly touched it – I mean, it's all about the injuries, but not about what caused them . . . What do you think?'

Taking her notebook out of her pocket and with pen poised, she waited for Dinwall's response.

Despite himself Dinwall was flattered that such a pretty young thing was showing an interest in his opinion. He sat back down.

'Well, er . . . These clubs yer know,' he tutted, and shook his head. 'Well dodgy if yer ask me. Drug dealing is rife, but closing them down,' he shook his head again then sighed, 'It's only gonna put them back on the street with nothing to do. At least at Blacks they're contained. Swings and roundabouts . . . Er, that by the way is my opinion, and not necessarily the police point of view.' Dinwall covered himself.

'Oh yes.' Kate nodded and moved closer. 'There's a much larger story to be told, and you are just the right person to help me with it. Why don't you take me down to the hospital, and we can see whether we can get any information out of the victims who are still there?'

Dinwall looked dubious. 'It's not really the done thing, there's coppers that'll have been there all night, why don't yer wait till they start coming in?'

'But why don't we go down there anyway?' Kate smiled in a way that made Dinwall anxious to leave. She really was a very pretty girl.

'I mean, someone of your obvious experience and capabilities might be able to uncover something new. And if I'm there to report it, then perhaps you'll finally get the recognition you deserve.'

A bullshit artist himself, Dinwall knew when he was being bullshitted. He laughed at her audacity. She was young, she was flirting with him and stroking his ego, and if it had been a couple of weeks earlier, she might just have had him round her little finger. And it wasn't as if he wouldn't like to go there – if his wife wasn't on the verge of throwing him out, he would have jumped her bones like a shot. He leaned close to Kate, so close he could smell the freshly laundered scent of her clothes and the toothpaste on her breath. She leaned in closer too, he could see the anticipation in her eyes. 'Nice try, but not good enough.' He got out of his seat and walked towards the doors.

'Fine,' she snapped back at him, but he kept on walking. She tapped her pen on the table, annoying a policewoman on the next, who glared at her over her cup of tea. 'Fine,' Kate muttered again, this time to herself. 'If Dinwall won't take me, then I'll go there alone.' She picked up her notebook and pushed back her chair so that it made a loud screeching sound on the linoleum floor. She strode purposefully to the doors, putting her notebook in her satchel and slinging it around her shoulders. All she wanted was that one amazing story, the story that would get her noticed by the editors in Fleet Street and Canary Wharf. What she wanted, more than anything, was to get a job on a paper like the *News of the World* or the *Daily Mirror*. Her idol, Piers Morgan, had worked on both, hell, he had been the editor of both, and at an obscenely young age too. Kate knew she was bright, she knew she had the drive and the talent, she just needed to create that one big break for herself. Although she knew that a follow-up story on the victims of a stampede in a nightclub wasn't going to do it.

Just as Kate was leaving the building, she met Lorraine and Carter. They both looked exhausted, and somehow drained. Carter's freckles stood out starkly on his face. 'You've been at the hospital,' Kate said excitedly, digging around in her bag for her notebook.

'Put that away,' Lorraine said crossly. 'I've already told Alf Johnson all I have to say on the matter.'

Kate frowned, put her notebook away, and followed Lorraine back inside. *Damn Johnson. If I go any further, I'll be stepping on his toes, and he'll accuse me of stealing his story.* And it wouldn't have been the first time. In fact, Kate had been dressed down by her editor for doing just that, accusing her of lacking focus and going where the most high-interest stories were, rather than putting in time, paying her dues.

'So, Inspector,' Kate began. 'What do you think caused the stampede?'

Lorraine groaned. OK, it was the duty of a reporter to be nosy, but Kate Mulberry pushed her to the limit. She stopped walking, and Carter followed suit, crossing his arms across his chest.

'Listen, Kate, I've said this to Johnson, and I'll say this to you. We don't have a clear idea of the exact circumstances of the incident, but from our early interviews with some of those involved, it looked as if one of the two exits was blocked, and then the fire alarm was set off. Whether the nightclub owners were negligent in blocking the door, whether the alarm was set off by someone who had malicious intent, or was just being stupid, we can't say until we look into it further. And right now, that's all I've got to say on the matter.'

Lorraine continued down the corridor to her office, Kate and Carter following behind. 'Inspector,' Kate said, 'I've still got to do that interview with you, is now a good time?'

'No,' Lorraine snapped. She was too on edge with the events of the night before to be nice. 'Some other time. Why don't yer shadow Dinwall today? Carter – come into my office.'

And with that, she shut the door in Kate Mulberry's very indignant face.

Once they were inside her office, Lorraine told Carter to sit down. He looked more than beat, he looked upset, and angry too. 'How are yer holding up?' she asked him softly.

Carter shrugged. 'OK, I guess. I mean, poor Selina, seeing her like that. And Luke . . .' He shook his head.

Lorraine knew exactly what her young constable was saying. They were both worried about Selina. Physically, they knew she was going to be OK, although it would probably take her a long time to recover fully from her injuries. Three of her ribs were bruised, her eyes were swollen tightly shut, and her face was a mass of bruises. In fact, she and Mickey made a right pair.

The doctor wanted to keep her in for a couple of days at least to ensure that no complications arose from her injuries. But how she was going to cope with her attack mentally, they had no idea. She had come round while they were there, but was still groggy from the medication, and it would be a while until Lorraine could ask her about her recollection of events. She knew that she was going to have to tread carefully. By the time they had left that morning, Selina had slipped again into a deep, healing sleep.

'It's gonna get out that Selina was attacked,' Lorraine said. 'I don't think that we can keep it under wraps now. But what I don't want leaked out is the fact that there was a white rose at the scene, and that petals were sent to Selina. This has to stay between you, me, Big Jim Malloy, Martin Pierce, and Luke, OK?'

Carter nodded. 'Goes without saying, boss.'

'Great,' Lorraine leaned back in her chair. 'I'm gonna get you to grab the CCTV footage from the area, also I'll get someone to talk to the club's owners, see if they have any CCTV cameras of their own hooked up.'

'What are yer thinking, that the person who set off the alarm was the one who attacked Selina?'

Lorraine nodded. 'Luke's right. The rose thing is too much of a coincidence. If we can confirm that the person who set off the alarm was the same person who attacked Selina, then we can see if we can pull off an ID from the CCTV footage. And then we've got him.'

'I'll get on to that right away,' said Carter, and before Lorraine could suggest it said, 'and I'll see whether there's anything I can find out about the white rose connection.'

'Good, yer read my mind.' Lorraine looked at her young constable with concern on her face. 'Carter, you look really beat. Do yer need to go home, rest up for a bit?'

Carter shook his head. 'No,' he said firmly with a resolve in his voice that Lorraine had rarely heard before. 'I'm staying. I want to find whoever did this, for Luke, and for Selina.'

17

'Here love,' Sandra Gilbride said, handing Mickey a tangerine she'd peeled for him.

'Nowt wrong with his fingers yer know,' Emma Lumsdon said spitefully, glowering at Mickey. She'd done her stint of kindness when she'd buttered him some toast earlier, and brought him a glass of milk. Just cos he was worried about his girlfriend. But that was ages ago.

'You leave him alone, yer nasty pasty,' Suzy the youngest Lumsdon snapped at her sister.

'Now girls, time for school.' Vanessa shooed them out the door.

'Think I'll just stop off and eat oranges,' Emma declared.

'School,' Robbie hissed loudly in her ear as he came downstairs and passed her in the doorway.

She stuck her tongue out behind his back before storming through the door.

Robbie shouted after her, 'Selfish little cow.'

'God help us all when she reaches puberty,' Sandra said, patting Vanessa's arm.

'Aye, I would rather have ten teenage boys than one teenage

girl in the house. Speaking of teenage girls, has there been any more news, then Mickey?'

Mickey shrugged. 'Don't know really. She was unconscious when her dad arrived, after that I walked back here.'

'So, how bad was it then?' Sandra asked, frowning. Two of her own boys went to the same place now and then.

'Oh bad, real bad. Thought I wasn't gonna get out alive. Everybody was pushing and shoving, everyone was screaming.' He turned to Robbie, 'Yer remember that lad we used to go to school with, wore them git jam-jar glasses, tiny kid.'

'Mattie somebody, he was always by himself.'

'Aye, we asked him a few times if he wanted to come places didn't we?'

Robbie nodded, as Mickey went on, 'Well he hasn't grown much, only looks about twelve, anyhow I saw him go under, he was just in front of me, so I grabbed his shirt and yanked him up, else he would have been a gonner probably stamped to death . . . That's when I lost Selina.'

'So, really you're a hero well done Mickey.' Vanessa patted his back.

But it didn't cheer Mickey up. 'Selina's dad won't think so, cos if I'd kept hold of her then she wouldn't have been attacked, would she?'

Carter stared at the screen, a cup of coffee beside him. It was his third since he'd come back to the station this morning, and he was starting to feel unpleasantly jittery. But he ignored it. He had run a search on the police database for England, Wales and Scotland, and had come up with nothing that was connected to a white rose. He sighed and rubbed his eyes. *Think, think*, he urged himself, but he was just too tired. He sighed. *Perhaps I'm being too specific*, he thought, *I need to think outside the box*. He typed in 'rose' and then, his fingers tapping the keys of his computer lightly, typed in '+ stalker'.

151

Over a hundred entries popped up. *Better than nothing, but it's going to take me a while to get through all these.* He sorted them by date order, and then started skimming through the entries.

The first several entries were from all over the country from women who had complained that they were being stalked. Typically it started off with them receiving innocuous gifts – like roses – but then their admirer had quickly escalated his campaign of terror. It made for distressing reading, but it wasn't what Carter was looking for.

And then he hit paydirt. A policeman in Wales had noted, in his report, that a woman who had been victimised by the unwanted attentions of a cab driver, had, at first, received roses in bunches of dozens, but had soon found roses cut up on her doorstep. The policeman had written:

Although there is no connection, this reminds me of the case in Dublin, where the killer stalks his victims by sending them first a rose, then its petals, and then kills them, cutting out their heart and leaving a rose in its place.

Carter gasped, eyes wide. He stared at the screen for a frozen moment, then quickly took down the name of the policeman who had written the report, Constable Gwyn Waldron. But something was bothering him – why hadn't they heard of this killer before? Surely it would have been in the papers. He went on to Google and typed in ''white rose', 'serial killer', 'Dublin'. There were hundreds of results, but none of them relevant.

'Whatcha looking at?' said a voice from over his shoulder.

Carter quickly closed the screen and turned round to face Kate Mulberry. She was looking remarkably inquisitive, even for her. 'Uh, nothing,' he said. 'Just surfing the web,' he added unconvincingly.

Kate Mulberry took a seat across from him. 'I heard about Luke's daughter,' she said. 'That's awful for him.'

Carter nodded nervously. 'It is,' he said. 'Awful.'

Kate smiled, 'Don't worry so much, Carter, this is off the record.'

Carter nodded, and tried to look casual.

'There's a rumour going round,' Kate said nonchalantly, 'that something strange was found by the body. Something that shouldn't have been there. I don't suppose you know what it was?'

Carter sighed. 'Kate, yer know that I can't tell you anything that relates to an open investigation.'

Kate laughed. 'Well, it was worth a shot,' she said, and got up out of her chair. 'See you later, Carter.'

Carter waited until Kate had left the room, then left his desk and walked to Lorraine's office. He had something to tell her, something that he knew that she would like even less than he did.

Kate watched as Carter left his desk and walked down the corridor to Lorraine's office. She glanced quickly round to check that there was no one watching, and dashed to Carter's computer. She opened up his web browser, and, on a hunch, clicked on the history icon at the top of the screen. She read the most recent entry – 'white rose', 'serial killer', 'Dublin' – Google Search – and smiled to herself. It looked like she just might get that big break after all.

Lorraine was just about to get her coat and leave for Blacks. She wanted to lean on the owner heavily, and make sure that he handed over any CCTV footage of the night before. But then came a knock on the door, and Carter popped his head around it. She saw the look on his face and motioned him to come in. He shut the door quickly behind him.

'What have yer found,' she said. The feeling of unease that had begun with Martin Pierce telling them of the white rose found at the scene of Selina's attack had been building up steadily all day.

'It's not good,' said Carter. 'I think it might be far more serious than we feared.' He told her about what he had found on the police database and handed over the number of the station where Gwyn Waldron was to be found.

Lorraine glanced at Carter. 'Shit, do yer know what we might be dealing with here?'

'It could be just a coincidence, boss,' said Carter.

'Yer know what I feel about coincidences, Carter. I'm going to ring this Welsh constable, see if he can shed any light on this whole situation.' She looked at the young man's face, which was rigid with worry. 'Don't panic just yet, Carter. Let's talk to this Gwyn Waldron, see what he has to say for himself.'

Lorraine dialled the number of the Holyhead Police Station and, after giving her name, asked to speak to Gwyn Waldron. 'You're in luck,' said the lilting voice at the other end of the line. 'He's having lunch at his desk today.'

Lorraine waited a minute before a deep voice came on the other end of the line. 'Gwyn Waldron here, how can I help you?'

Lorraine introduced herself again and said 'Constable Waldron, I understand that yer wrote a report on a stalker who had sent roses to a young woman. Yer said that they have similarities to another case, one that you had heard about from Dublin. Could yer please tell us more?'

'Well,' said the voice on the other end of the line. 'I was in Dublin helping with a raid that the Garda and the Holyhead police were co-operating in. There was a drug ring operating out of Dublin, importing cocaine into Wales. Anyway, we managed to break the ring, and we all had a drink to celebrate. I got talking to one of the Garda, and he told me about the serial killer.'

'And what else do yer know about it, what else that's not in the report?'

'That's all I know. But Sean O'Neill is the person I talked to in Dublin. Now he might be able to help you . . . So what's this about?' he asked.

'If I could tell yer, I would. But thanks very much for all yer help.'

Lorraine forced herself not to look at Carter, who was twitching nervously in his seat. She dialled the number of the Dublin Garda, and was put on hold to speak to Sean O'Neill. A woman's voice answered, 'Sean O'Neill's phone.'

'Hello, this is Detective Inspector Lorraine Hunt, calling from Houghton police station. I was given Sean O'Neill's name in relation to a killer in Dublin whose signature is a white rose. Can I speak to him?'

The voice was silent on the other end of the line, then finally said, 'Sean O'Neill is on duty at the moment, but I'll get you to speak to Inspector Harry Collins, he's in charge of the investigation.'

Lorraine had to wait a long while before she was connected to Collins. She pulled out the drawer of her desk and rooted around in it for a pencil stub, feeling as stressed as she did today, she craved nicotine with every fibre of her body.

Finally a curt voice was heard on the other end of the line. It belonged to an Irishman with a pronounced brogue, but through it Lorraine could hear barely restrained anger. She introduced herself, and then asked about the report that Gwyn Waldron had written. 'Is it true?' she finally said.

There was no response for some time. Lorraine thought she had been cut off, so she said, 'Inspector?'

'What's this about?' came the barked reply.

'I don't think I'm in a position to tell yer, I'm sorry.'

There was a short, mirthless laugh on the other end of the line. 'Inspector Hunt, you are sorely trying my patience. I have tried to keep the details of the killer under wraps for two reasons. To make sure we don't have any copycat killings and to not alarm the public. You call me, from Sunderland no less, demanding answers but aren't prepared to tell me why. I don't have time for this. Goodbye—'

'Wait,' said Lorraine before he could hang up. 'OK.' She sighed. She wanted to contain the news to that small group of people who already knew, but realised that she would have to tell Inspector Collins, otherwise he wouldn't reciprocate with any information that could help her case. From the sounds of it she could count on his discretion – he could certainly rely on hers. 'I'll tell yer. I'm worried that we have our own killer on our hands. And his modus operandi seems to be exactly the same as what Gwyn Waldron describes in his report. He must have been disturbed because he didn't kill her – we're waiting on the CCTV footage. But a white rose was found at the scene, and I'm worried that either he must have moved from Dublin to Houghton, or we've got a copycat on our hands.'

There came a heavy sigh from the other end of the line. 'The white rose, it was in full bloom, yes?'

'Yes,' confirmed Lorraine. 'And there's more. I—' she tried not to let the emotion sound in her voice. 'I know the girl and she received some petals in an envelope the day before her attack.'

'That sounds like the killer, all right,' said Collins. He still sounded gruff, but nowhere near as angry as he had before. 'But hang on, you call the victim a girl, how old is she?'

'She's sixteen.'

'Well, there's a difference for a start. All the victims are women in their mid-to-late-thirties, all with blonde hair, all quite slim and tall. They come from differing walks of life, but all fit that physical description to the letter.'

Lorraine shuddered. 'Selina's quite small and dark. And as

yer say, a lot younger than the victims in Dublin. So do yer think we're dealing with a copycat here?'

'It looks like it to me. It's unlikely that he'd suddenly change both his location and his choice of victim.' Collins's voice took on a thoughtful quality. 'But if it is a copycat, then the only way he could have found out about the killer is from Waldron's report on the database . . .'

'. . . which you can only access if yer belong to the police in some way.' Lorraine finished for him. She rubbed her forehead, trying to smooth away the stress headache that was building there. Every answer just turned up more questions, and she wasn't liking the direction the conversation seemed to be leading. Could it be possible? Could Selina's attacker be someone in the station? The ramifications of the news reverberated throughout her mind. It became even more imperative that she kept the information under wraps.

'You said you know the victim,' came the voice on the line.

'Yes,' answered Lorraine. 'She's the daughter of my best sergeant, Luke Daniels.'

'I'm very sorry to hear that,' the voice was less gruff now, and much kinder. 'Listen, give me your e-mail address and I'll send you a summary of our investigation. I hope it'll help. And, I hope, of course, you'll do the same for me, should you dig up any new information.'

Lorraine thanked him and placed the receiver down. God, she was tired. She sunk her head into her hands.

'Bad news, boss?' said Carter.

Lorraine looked up. She dropped her arms, letting them rest on the table. She felt tired and a little defeated. Sure, they now knew what they were dealing with, but it seemed like the tip of the iceberg. There seemed to be three options. Selina's attacker was either someone who had come from Ireland to track her down, but as she wasn't his preferred type, it seemed unlikely. Or he was a copycat killer, who had somehow got the details of the killings from the police database, which pointed to someone who had access to it – perhaps a hacker, but it was more likely to be a colleague. Or maybe it was someone within these offices who bore a grudge against Luke and wanted to hurt him in the worst way possible, by attacking his daughter. Lorraine's tired mind was awhirl. She sighed and filled Carter in on the other side of the conversation, and told him her fears.

Carter smiled weakly. 'What makes yer think it's not me?'

'Because yer face is as easy to read as a picture book,' Lorraine smiled at the young constable. 'And it would mean I would be the worst possible judge of character if yer were.'

'Still,' Carter said. 'It's horrible to think that it might be one of us. Do yer suspect anyone in particular?'

Lorraine slowly shook her head. 'No. There's not a single person I work with that I think it could be. Yer realise now that we have to be even more careful about this leaking out, Carter.'

Carter sucked in air through his teeth. 'I'm trying me best, boss, but there's already rumours flying round. Kate Mulberry asked me, off the record, if yer can believe that, whether it was true there was an unusual object left by Selina's attacker . . .'

'Oh God,' Lorraine groaned. 'That's the last thing we need.'

'I put her off,' said Carter, 'but yer know what she's like.'

Lorraine's computer beeped. It was the e-mail from Dublin Garda. She printed off a copy for her and Carter, and ran her eyes over it. Then she got up from behind her desk and took her coat from the hook on the door. 'See whether or not the CCTV footage has come in, and get Sanderson to go to Blacks. I'm heading to the hospital. I need to tell Luke about this.'

Sanderson knocked on the back door of Blacks nightclub. It was opened by a surly looking man, dressed in a grey jacket and dirty jeans. He had blond hair, sideburns and a moustache. A cigarette was stuck to his bottom lip. 'Who are you?' he sneered. It was obvious from his accent that he was from Ireland.

'Name's Sanderson, Houghton police.' He produced his ID and showed it to him. The man looked at it, took his cigarette out of his mouth and blew smoke into the air. Sanderson put his ID back in his pocket and said, 'And who are you?'

'Name's Donald Carr,' he said. 'The boss told me you lot would probably be in today. Come in.' He held the door open and Sanderson walked past him into the club.

'So, what do yer do here?' Sanderson tried to breathe in through his mouth. The smell was damp and mouldering, with a sweet undercurrent of something even more rank, and the floor was sticky underneath his feet.

Carr shrugged. 'Barman, odd job man . . .'

'Cleaner?' Sanderson suggested.

'Ha.' Carr led him into an office that was only slightly less dank than the rest of the club. An ashtray of used butts sat on the corner of a desk. Posters of past events were blu-tacked to the walls. It was grim and uninviting.

'I've come for a tape. We need any CCTV footage you've got of last night's club.'

Carr nodded. 'The boss thought yer might. He already told me to give yer what yer need.' He went to a cabinet in the wall, opened it, and pressed a button on a video recorder. 'Here yer go. There are four cameras in the club, and this shows all four pictures at once.'

'Thanks,' said Sanderson, pocketing the tape. 'I've got to tell yer, that was easier than we've come to expect.'

Carr laughed. 'The boss wants me to tell yer to make sure that yer take his co-operation into account when yer come to investigate the club.'

'Should have guessed,' Sanderson said wearily. 'So what can yer tell me about last night?'

Carr shrugged. 'Nothing more than yer already know. I was

behind the bar serving water when the alarm went off. Was a typical night up until then.'

'And what about the blocked exit? What can yer tell me about that?'

'Beats me. It wasn't blocked when I went out for me break earlier in the evening.'

Sanderson raised his eyebrows. 'Really? What time was that?'

'About nine, nine thirty.'

'And the alarm went off about eleven thirty?' Sanderson took out his notebook and waited for Carr's answer.

Carr scratched his head. 'About then, I think.'

Sanderson thanked him and said that they would be in touch. Walking outside, he took great gulps of fresh air. He took a look at the exit. The back door had a large scratch on it. He touched the scratch and paint came off in his hand. He rubbed his fingers together, thought for a moment, and then called into the club for Carr.

Carr came outside, looking mildly annoyed. 'Yep?'

'Yer went outside about nine thirty, yer said?'

Carr nodded, 'That's right.'

Sanderson cast around, looking for something that matched the scratch on the door. He found a large iron bar that had been thrown to one side. On it was red paint. Sanderson took a handkerchief from his pocket and lifted the iron bar. 'I'm gonna take this, OK?' Carr shrugged assent. 'And don't come out here, I'm gonna call my boss, get the forensics team out.'

He stared at his knife, the long one, his favourite. Frowning he held it up to the light.

Was that a spot of blood?

How the hell had he missed that?

He picked the cloth up and started to polish it when he heard old Mrs Holland next door shouting for her cat Blackie.

He smiled, looked into the blade as he muttered, 'Kitty isn't come home. Kitty isn't ever coming home . . . Ha.'

18

Lorraine stood outside the entrance to the hospital as she listened to Sanderson's news on the mobile. 'So it looks as if the door was jammed from the outside,' she said, 'which would mean that the perpetrator could then set off the alarm and shepherd the clubbers out the front door. Good work, Sanderson, and yes, get forensics out there immediately.'

Putting her mobile back in her pocket, Lorraine hurried as quickly and as quietly as she could down the hospital corridor. Selina had been moved to a side ward overnight, and even though Luke had insisted that Lorraine and Carter leave to get some sleep, they had kept him company until they left for work. Lorraine should have been feeling the effects of little sleep, but she was running on nervous energy and little else. More than anything she wanted to make sure that Selina and Luke were both OK.

Lorraine found them asleep. Selina looked pale and drained, her head covered in bandages, there was also a thick bandage on her left arm. Encouragingly, though, the machines had been taken away. Luke was dozing in the chair at her side. She smiled. He looked so peaceful and rested. She hated to wake him up. *God, I care about him*, she thought. Quietly she walked over to Luke and gently ran her finger over his cheek. His eyes flashed open immediately.

'Lorraine.' It came out as a gasp.

'We have to talk. Can Selina hear us?'

Luke looked at his daughter, and shook his head. 'Don't think so. They've given her something to keep her under, reckon she should come to, sometime tomorrow. Have yer seen Carson yet? If he's got anything at all to do with this I'll personally strangle the little toe rag.'

'Luke, if you really thought Mickey had hurt Selina you would have found him last night. Anyway, someone has to stay here, because Selina can't be left alone for a moment.'

Luke looked back at his daughter, studying her face intently, but Lorraine knew he was digesting what she had just said. After a short while he swung his gaze back to Lorraine, his face deadly serious. 'Why? What's the matter?'

She sighed and sat down in the chair next to him and dug around in her bag for the e-mail that Inspector Harry Collins had sent from Dublin. She handed it over to Luke.

'There have been three murders in Ireland, the last one only days before we were there,' she said quietly. 'All three victims had their hearts cut out and a white rose in full bloom placed exactly where the heart should be.'

Luke looked up from the e-mail in horror when he realised what Selina's fate could have been. Lorraine recounted the conversation that she had with Collins. 'I wouldn't panic about it yet. We either have a serial killer who's relocated himself from Dublin, or a copycat, or . . .'

Luke frowned. 'Or?'

Taking a deep breath she went on, 'The thing is, Luke, the Garda haven't released any information to the press for fear of causing a panic – or starting off a copycat. The only way whoever did this knew everything that the killer did is if they had access to the police database.'

'Jesus Christ!' Luke looked up sharply 'What are yer saying, Lorraine?'

'I'm saying that the third option is that there might – *might*, mind you – be someone in the police station who's out for you, getting to you through Selina. And I'd hate to say it, but out of the three, that's the option that I'm hoping will turn out to be right.'

Luke shook his head. 'I don't believe that it's one of us, not for a second.'

'I agree. But me mind's been whirring around, and I can't see what else, other than those three options, it could be.'

'And if it is a serial killer, or someone who's copying him,' Luke looked at Selina, hesitated a moment before saying quietly, as if talking to himself, 'he made sure they suffered before they died.' Luke thought for a moment. 'These victims in Dublin, did they have anything in common with Selina? Could she be his type?'

Lorraine took in a deep breath, and then let it out slowly. 'No, Luke, that's one of the reasons why I'm suspecting it's a copycat.'

Luke looked over the e-mail again and read it more carefully. He then lifted his gaze and stared with concern at Lorraine. 'These women who were murdered, it says here that they were women in their mid-thirties, with long, blonde hair, tall and slim.'

Lorraine nodded.

'Lorraine,' there was real worry in his voice. 'I'm not being funny, but these descriptions of these women, well, it could describe you too, almost exactly.'

At that moment Mickey Carson was sitting on the settee recently vacated by Vanessa when she and Sandra went shopping up Houghton. He had stayed the night unbeknownst to anyone, convinced that the police would be looking for him to blame him for what had happened to Selina. Vanessa and Sandra thought he'd arrived for breakfast.

'What am I gonna do?' he wailed to Darren. 'They'll blame me, yer've heard what the coppers are like when it's one of their own.'

Darren sighed, 'Just tell them the truth, Selina's dad must know that there's no way that yer would hurt her.'

Robbie came down from the bath with a towel wrapped round his waist.

'Can I have a bath?' Mickey asked.

'Aye, but yer better be quick, if yer don't want me mam coming back and finding yer here.'

'How long yer gonna hide out here for?' Darren asked.

'Don't know' Mickey replied ruefully. 'That's why we're not gonna tell yer mam and the others, they'll think I've gone home if they don't know I'm here, then they can't tell lies to Selina's dad when he comes looking, can they?'

With great exaggeration Darren looked slowly around the room, then at Mickey and even more slowly shook his head. 'Eight people in a tiny council house, that's not counting the ones who come and go, and you think yer gonna remain invisible?' It was Darren's turn to be amazed. 'And the very best of luck to you mate.'

'What else can I do?'

'Hand yerself in,' Robbie said from the kitchen where he was rummaging in the laundry basket for a clean pair of socks.

'How can I hand meself in?' Mickey wailed. 'I haven't done nothing.'

'That's why yer can hand yerself in,' Robbie came back into the sitting room with a clean pair of jeans, a blue Nike T-shirt over his shoulder and two odd socks in his right hand. 'Hurry up then, Mickey, we've gotta go up the Broadway and see what's up for grabs.'

'What if I'm seen up Houghton, what'll I do?' Mickey's voice held an edge of panic.

'Mickey, they're probably not even looking for yer, anyhow I thought yer were gonna phone the hospital and see how Selina's doing.'

'Got no credit on me phone. You used it up, remember, phoning Cal the other night.'

'Might be able to pick a cheap phone card up.'

'Huh,' Mickey snorted as he headed towards the stairs, 'and that's like looking for bloody gold dust.'

Lorraine left the hospital and drove to Houghton where she had arranged to meet Carter in the Co-op car park. He was standing in an empty bay with a red and white parking cone next to him. When he saw Lorraine's car he grinned, lifted the cone up and moved to one side, drawing frowns from people walking by.

'Carter,' Lorraine chided when she got out of her car.

Sometimes, even though he always meant well, she could bloody well kill him.

'What?' he asked, his face a picture of innocence.

Lorraine looked skywards, 'Never mind, just get rid of the bloody thing.'

Carter walked to the next row of cars where the patrol car was parked, and put the cone in the boot. 'Got yer a space though, didn't it boss? Yer know it's always murder trying to park up here.'

'Yeah, OK . . . So what more have yer found out?' They started walking towards the Co-op.

'Well, at this time of year, look,' he waved his arms around. 'Can yer see any flowers?'

'Get on with it.'

He made his big announcement with a flourish. He was obviously pleased with himself. 'It stands to reason, the only place yer can get roses this time of year is at florist's.'

'Yeah, unless forced in a greenhouse.' But Lorraine was starting to see where Carter was heading.

'Thought about that an' all. But if he's Irish, then the greenhouse will be in Ireland. So where did he get the roses in England?'

They bypassed the Co-op and Mautland Square and turned into a small street, the sole occupants of which were a travel agents, an optician, a video shop on the corner and two florist shops on opposite sides of the road.

'OK, Sherlock, you take the left and I'll take the right.' Lorraine turned into Apple Blossom while Carter crossed the road to Flowers By Brenda.

Ten minutes later, Lorraine noticed Carter peering through the shop window. When he saw he had her attention he shook his head. Lorraine guessed he'd got nowhere. After a few minutes' more conversation, she said goodbye to the florist.

'Anything boss?' Carter asked when Lorraine joined him. He could tell by her face though that she had found something out. They headed back towards the cars.

'It seems, Carter, that a tramp came in and bought half a dozen roses, all in bud. Before he took them away with him, he had one delivered in full bloom to Luke's house. Apparently he was very insistent that the one to be delivered was in bud and it had to be really fresh, like it had just been picked.'

'Did she give a description?'

'Aye. She didn't know him personally, though she has seen him around before. He's definitely a tramp, she says yer could practically smell the mildew on him when he came in, and it looked like he hadn't shaved or bathed in months. Long black

167

overcoat, grey woolie hat, with a hole in the side. It could though really be any colour, could look grey with muck,' she sighed. 'We should get someone on to that, see if they can find a tramp matching this description. See what he has to say for himself.'

'Do yer think he could be the one that attacked Selina?'

Lorraine snorted. 'Doubt it Carter, from the little we know about him, he's gotta be a scheming, conniving bastard with time on his hands He's got to plan his attacks. A vagrant might murder someone opportunistically, but not in this cold way. Nah, I think he's just a messenger, probably been paid a couple of bob to do the job.'

'Hmm, so we're stuck then.'

'Looks like it Carter . . . For the moment anyhow. But perhaps we could get a description, if I'm right, that is. In the meantime I'll try and get hold of Wade. See if he knows anything. If the bastard's chased him from Ireland without telling me, I'll have his friggin' badge.'

Carter walked alongside Lorraine for a moment, deep in thought. Suddenly he said, 'Don't yer think it's a bit strange that all this kicks off as soon as Wade comes over here to England?'

Lorraine stopped and looked at Carter. 'Yer don't think that it's Wade, do yer?'

Carter shrugged, 'Known stranger things happen.'

19

Mickey sat on the seat in the Broadway and watched as
Robbie negotiated with a couple of shoplifters. A few minutes
later, he came back swinging a plain blue carrier bag in his
hand and sat down next to Mickey.

'Got a good deal on some aftershave, a couple of tubes of
toothpaste, have yer seen the price of that lately? And that
special salon shampoo our Claire's always banging on about,
that should keep her happy for a day or two. Now all we need
is some fags for me mam, and I'll call it a canny day.'

'Cool.' Mickey answered, clearly not interested in
aftershave or toothpaste, and even less in shampoo. 'Aye, and
some free information . . . Acording to Stanners, it seems
there's a stranger about the place, and guess what, he's asking
about you.'

'Me!' Mickey swung his head round and stared at his friend
in amazement, 'Why would a bloody stranger be asking about
me? I don't know any strangers.'

Robbie hid a chuckle, stopped himself from stating the
obvious, and shrugging said 'Haven't a clue mate.'

'What did he say?'

'Stanners,' Robbie shouted to the boy he'd just bought the aftershave from. 'Got a minute?'

Anthony Stanners, a tall gangly youth with a wide grin and laughing blue eyes, in the middle of trying to sell his wares to three girls, glanced at Robbie, nodded and said, 'In a mo, bro.'

'I'm worried sick about Selina,' Mickey said, staring at the girls, but not really seeing them.

'Listen mate, from what yer told me and from what's in the *Echo*, it's a wonder nobody's been killed in the bloody place. I heard at least fifty were injured, but it was probably more cos the owner's paid the law to keep quiet. At least that's what people are saying.'

'Oh right, and by the time the gossip gets round Sunderland then makes its way to Newcastle and Durham then down to Middlesbrough, there'll be fifty thousand dead,' Mickey snorted. 'I know her dad's gonna blame me, he went mental when he saw us holding hands so God knows how he's gonna react to this. That's why I'm hiding at yours remember.'

'What do yer want mate?' Stanners said, waving the girls goodbye and sauntering casually over to Mickey and Robbie.

'Who's been asking about me?' Mickey asked quickly.

Stanners shrugged, 'Some creep with a funny way of talking.'

'What'd he look like? And, um, can I borrow yer phone?'

'Skinny, twentyish. Sinful ugly . . . Yer'll have no credit as usual, have yer?' Stanners handed his phone over to Mickey, 'One minute, one call, quick.'

'Cheers mate.' Mickey dialled the hospital, while he waited for the connection he went on, 'So what did yer say to him?'

'Said I didn't know yer of course. What do yer think I said, yer daft twat? Like I'm gonna tell a total stranger yer full name and address. Give me some credit.'

Mickey held his hand up for Stanners to be quiet, then asked the nurse on the other end of the phone about Selina. After having the nurse promise to tell Selina that he'd called, he handed the phone back to Anthony Stanners with a huge grin that was spread across his face.

'Cheers mate, she's still unconscious but they say she's comfortable, that's really all they would tell me. But do yer think they'll let her come home as soon as she wakes up? That means she might even be coming home tomorrow?'

'Sounds possible.' Robbie shrugged. 'I'm well pleased about that. If she does come home tomorrow, she'll be able to talk as well. She'll have told her dad that you had nothing to do with it. So pretty soon yer needn't hide away any more.'

'Yeah, good one, anyhow I think they would have lifted me before now if they thought I had anything to do with it, don't you?' He looked at Stanners and Robbie for confirmation.

Robbie was about to agree with him when Stanners said, 'That's him over there, outside the Golden Lion. Hasn't took him long to find the bloody shite has it. Look who the creepy git's hanging with.'

They looked across the road. Sure enough, a scruffy-looking skinhead was talking to Stevie Masterton and his gang.

Robbie and Mickey looked across the road. 'Him!' Mickey said. 'Looks like a right dirty manky cokehead to me, wonder who he is?'

'Yer gonna find out, cos that Stevie Shite's just pointed yer out to him,' Stanners said.

'I hate him,' Mickey said with feeling.

'Not keen meself,' Stanners laughed. 'Anyhow, I'm off, things to do if yer know what I mean . . . later guys.'

'Yeah,' Mickey and Robbie said in unison.

Interested in the stranger, Mickey and Stanners had not noticed Robbie lock eyes with Stevie Masterton. Masterton quickly looked away, knowing he was no match for a Lumsdon feeling protective over a sibling. Toad had bragged about his threats to Claire Lumsdon last night. And Robbie would lump him in with anything Toad did.

Robbie felt anger start to boil up inside of him, but he knew broad daylight was no time to catch Stevie Shite, he would be the one sitting in a jail cell and not that bastard.

Masterton, unable to help himself, glanced back as the stranger started to cross the road. Robbie was still staring at him. 'Gonna get yer,' Robbie mouthed, and Stevie Masterton left dust behind him as he quickly disappeared round to the back of the Golden Lion.

The stranger reached them and stared at Mickey, his top lip curled in a sneer. 'I've been told that you're having it off with my squeeze.' His accent was pure Mancunian.

Mickey just stared at him. He couldn't believe that his beautiful Selina had ever been with someone like him. Selina had told him something of her life before she had met him, and it sounded awful. To have the evidence, in front of him like this, made him realise how desperate her life had truly been.

'Got nothing to say for yourself, you fucking prick,' the skinhead sneered.

'Aye I have, fuck off.'

Robbie burst out laughing.

'You laughing at me twat? Think it's funny do yer?' The stranger squared up to Robbie. 'Cos I'll have the fucking pair of youse. I'm warning you don't fuck with me. I'm well known where I come from.'

Robbie stood up. He was only a couple of inches short of six foot and he towered over the stranger. 'Aye well, yer here now. And we don't want yer and I'm doubly certain Selina doesn't want yer either, so go away OK, back to where ever yer've crawled from . . . Come on Mickey.'

Keeping a wary eye on the stranger, Mickey got up from the seat.

The stranger spat on the ground at Mickey's feet. 'You're

going nowhere, mate, got that? Not till you understand what I'm fucking telling you.'

'Yer telling me nowt, OK. Who do yer think yer are? Piss off,' Mickey said, with a flash of stubborn temper as he started to walk away.

'I'm warning you,' the skinhead yelled after him. 'You keep away from her or I'll have you, I fucking mean it . . . She's mine. OK, *mine.*'

Robbie slipped behind Mickey in case he turned and faced up to the stranger. Mickey was not a fighter, but he was also not a coward and could be unpredictable, if provoked enough. 'Just ignore him, mate, OK? And don't worry, the Selina I've met is a different chick to the one he knew, she'll have nowt to do with the likes of him now.'

Praying his friend was right, Mickey kept on walking. They were round the corner and just passing Woolworths when the police car pulled up alongside them.

'Mickey Carson,' Sanderson said, as he got out of the police car, 'I'd like you to come with me to the station to answer a few questions, please.'

Mickey's face dropped.

'Just not your day is it Mickey?' Robbie shook his head.

20

It was half past two in the morning, and Kate Mulberry was sitting up late, grimacing at the screen on her computer. She had put in all the permutations of 'white rose', 'serial killer' and Dublin that she could think of into Google. She had then tried entering 'Houghton-le-Spring', but nothing was coming that looked even vaguely promising as a lead on this case. She blew her fringe out of her face, and sighed. She was on to something here, she knew it.

Kate lived in a one-room studio flat on her own. It was comfortable and clean, but very modest. She lived, slept and ate in it. The bathroom was a tiny cupboard off one side of the kitchen. Of course, she aspired to the type of flat that you could buy comfortably in London with the sort of six-figure salary earned by high-flyers such as Rebekah Wade, but, she rationalised, if you *were* a high flyer like that, you weren't going to spend much time at your own place, no matter how lush. No, you'd be at the coalface, staying at work until your story was ready to go off to press, following the best stories, stealing the scoops from your rivals, going to red-carpet affairs and hanging out with celebs. Your flat would simply be a place to sleep. Kate had a dogeared edition of Piers Morgan's diaries of his life as a newspaper editor, and she treated it as her bible. It was what she aspired to, an editorship on a big paper and all the luxury and prestige that went with it, and nothing was going to stand in her way.

Kate padded to the fridge in slippers, t-shirt and pyjama bottoms, her hair wound into a messy bun at the top of her head and fixed with a pencil. She yawned, opened the fridge door and peered inside. A limp stick of celery and a small pot of cottage cheese that was well past its sell-by date stared back at her. Misery. When she was famous, she'd be eating at the Ivy every night, wining and dining the rich and the famous, the great and the good. Kate grabbed an apple from the bowl on her kitchen bench and bit into it. What was her next move?

She'd have to keep an eye on Carter, that's what she'd do, but she knew he was too suspicious about her already. She sighed. She'd have to catch him off guard, try to gain his confidence in some way. But it had been a long day, and tomorrow was just about to dawn fresh and bright and she just wanted to go to bed so she could wake up and see if she could get to whatever it was Carter was hiding. Anything with the words 'serial killer' attached to it was bound to be her ticket out of here.

Just as she was about to shut down her computer screen, she thought of something else. She plugged in 'serial killer' + unsolved + ireland into her computer, still nothing, but this was addictive. She knew that she wasn't going to get much sleep that night.

For Lorraine, however, there was no sleep. She tossed and turned, drifted in and out, gave up, got up and made tea. She was sitting at the kitchen table, talking to Duke when, a few minutes later, she was joined by Mavis. Mavis wrapped her very hippy-ish dressing gown around her and smiled at her daughter.

175

'Enough in the pot for one more, love?'

Lorraine nodded, secretly glad of the company.

After Mavis had poured her tea and added milk and sugar, she came back into the sitting room and sat down opposite Lorraine. 'OK, spit it out. What's bothering yer love?'

Lorraine sighed, she knew these questions were gonna come eventually, if not from her mother then from her mate the Rock Chick. If she told her mother now then she might get a bit of peace from the pair of them for a while.

'Well, I've been really worried about Selina. The attack was really horrific, and yer should see her in the hospital, bandaged up like that. Luke's beside himself.'

Mavis tutted, pulling her dressing gown around her. 'Terrible business, that. Are yer any closer to finding who did it?'

Lorraine shook her head. 'We've got a couple of avenues to follow, but nothing concrete as yet.'

'Well, I hope you get the bastard and put him away for a very long time.'

Lorraine nodded, blowing on her cup of tea to cool it down. 'Otherwise,' she went on, 'it's mostly work problems mam, and bits and bobs, yer don't really want to know.'

'Course I do.' Mavis patted her daughter's hand and stared with concern into her face. Lorraine was looking tired and withdrawn, and she knew that she had hardly slept over the last couple of days.

'OK, Clark agreed to having a reporter tag along with me at the station and all points in Sunderland, without consulting me first, which is what he should have done.'

'A reporter, in the police station? Thought their place was outside on the steps?'

'Yeah, me too . . . Anyhow her name is Kate Mulberry, comes from Shiney Row, know any Mulberrys?'

'Actually, yes I do. Not bad people, the Mulberrys –

176

although Peggy would probably say differently. She had her heart broken for the twenty-fifth, or was it twenty-sixth, time by a Brian Mulberry, he belonged to Shiny Row.'

Lorraine cracked a smile. That didn't surprise her. 'I suppose Kate Mulberry's not what yer would call a bad person she's just so bloody nosey, and cheeky.'

'That's a reporter's job, pet.'

'Yeah, but she pokes her nose in everywhere, and gets underfoot. I can't wait until she's left the station, then we can finally relax.'

Mavis stared at Lorraine over the rim of her cup. Lorraine was gently stroking Duke's ears, and the dog was practically purring.

Might as well ask now when she's in a talkative mood, Peggy will never forgive me if I let this chance slip by. 'So, er, what's actually wrong with you and Luke?'

Lorraine shrugged, 'I suggested something stupid and the idiot took me up on it.'

'Something stupid?'

Lorraine looked at her mother. 'I said maybes we should cool it for a while until he and Selina sort themselves out.'

'And?'

'He didn't just cool it, he friggin' well froze it.'

'Oh dear.'

'Oh dear indeed.'

Mavis nodded. 'You jumped in with the best intentions and Luke without thinking took yer at face value.'

Lorraine nodded, 'Yeah and on top of that, we're not exactly sure mind, and yer can't tell anyone this, yer have to swear, I hope we don't but we might have a serial killer in town. From now on, I don't want you or Peggy going out alone, any night time pottery classes, drag her along with yer.'

'Oh God,' Mavis pulled her light-green dressing gown tighter around her body.

'*Please* keep that information to yourself. If this gets out, it might cause a panic. I don't want people to get too worried.'

'Does this weirdo have anything to do with Selina?' Lorraine put her forefinger over her mouth and made a small shooshing sound. Mavis understood and for the next fifteen minutes they talked about everything but Lorraine's work, Luke or reporters.

Mavis went up to bed first, followed a few minutes later by Lorraine. Before she climbed back into bed, she went to the window and looked out. 'Something's up,' she muttered. 'No rain.' Then she switched the light off and went back to bed.

Mickey was camped out on the floor of Robbie and Darren's bedroom. He lay flat on his back with his hands behind his head. The police had let him go at seven o'clock. Mickey was glad to see that they didn't seem to think that he had anything to do with Selina's attack, they just wanted to see whether he could remember anything important. They had also questioned a few others who had been in the nightclub, all of whom had confirmed Mickey's assertion that he had been separated from Selina.

'See, yer've got more friends than yer thought yer had,' Darren said, lying on his stomach with his chin cupped in his hands. 'Haven't yer?'

Mickey nodded, forgetting that neither Robbie nor Darren could see him.

Robbie rolled on to his back and unconsciously imitated the position of his friend. 'You deaf or what?'

'Sorry, I'm miles away. I've been trying to work out exactly what happened when I got outside and couldn't find Selina.'

'So what happened?' Darren asked.

'I looked round the back, cos there was some kids up the side, vomiting, and I wondered if Selina might have wandered round there, but I couldn't see her, I just went to the corner

178

and shouted her name. I should have gone right round, shouldn't I?'

Robbie grunted and Mickey, his heart sinking, took it as a yes. 'It's my fault isn't it,' he sighed.

'*No*,' Darren said.

'He's right Mickey, yer can't blame yerself for what some creep did.'

'Aye but . . .'

'No, yer can't. It's not your fault. Anyhow, yer probably disturbed him and saved Selina's life.'

'I never thought of it that way. Do yer really think so?' Mickey's heart flooded with hope.

A loud banging on the wall made them all jump. 'Are youse gonna shut up in there?' Kerry yelled. 'People gotta sleep yer know.'

'OK, OK,' Robbie answered. 'Goodnight Kerry.'

Kerry got out of bed and looked out at the dark sky before closing the curtains, then listened with her ear against the wall for a moment before giving a satisfactory nod and climbing into bed.

He leans against the wall, way back in the shadows where no one can see him and watches as the bedroom light comes on, slowly he smiles.

Think you are so clever don't you.

So smug.

So safe wrapped up tight in your little world.

He watches as she comes to the window, and laughs softly a moment later when the light goes out.

'Didn't even know I was behind you all the way home, did you. Ha.'

Part Three

21

It was early morning. Lorraine hadn't really been able to sleep after she talked to Mavis, so she decided to go to the station early. There were still a few police officers on the nightshift, and so the station wasn't quite empty, but it was still a far cry from the usual hustle and bustle of the day. As she walked down the corridor, she saw Carter from out of the corner of her eye. He was in an empty office, blearily looking at a video screen.

She opened the door and poked her head inside. 'Carter, what are yer on? Do yer ever go home.'

Carter yawned and stretched his arms over his head. 'I just couldn't sleep, and so I thought it was worth going over the CCTV footage one more time, rather than lie in bed staring at the ceiling.'

Lorraine walked into the office and closed the door behind her. 'You and me both. So, is there anything useful on the footage?'

Carter shook his head. 'I don't think there's anything that we can use. Here's the footage from outside the club when the alarm went off. See if yer can make anything out.'

Carter pressed a button and then rewound the tape. Then he

pressed play and pointed out the time and date at the bottom of the screen. 'This is about a minute before the alarm went at about eleven thirty.'

Carter and Lorraine watched, as first a couple of people, and then a whole stream of them, left the club, screaming and falling over each other. She leaned in. 'I can't really make out anything.'

'Nah,' said Carter, 'but here, I think this is Selina.' He pressed pause, and Lorraine thought that he might be right.

'Can we get it enhanced?' Lorraine asked.

'Yes,' Carter said slowly, 'but I don't think that it's going to help us very much.' He ran the tape again, until the image that they thought was Selina left the screen. 'Can yer see anyone strange?'

'Run it back for me again.' Lorraine leaned in once more as the few seconds of tape that Selina appeared on was replayed. She shook her head slowly.

'See what I mean, boss?' said Carter. 'Yer just can't make out anyone, there are too many people about. Yer can't see if one's grabbing Selina or not, it's just too chaotic.'

Lorraine sighed. 'How did yer get on with the footage from inside the club?'

'It's even worse. I mean, the picture quality is good and everything, better in fact than the CCTV camera outside the club but there are just too many people about. It could be any one of them. Do yer want to take a look?'

'Nah, Carter, I trust yer,' Lorraine sighed. 'Well, I thought we could have had him there.'

Carter shrugged. 'Me too. I'll just go over these tapes one more time, make sure that there isn't anything that I've overlooked.'

'Well, don't spend too much time if there's nothing more to be gained from it. Come and see me in my office, though, when yer finished.'

Carter nodded, turning his eyes back to the screen, and she left him to it.

Lorraine went into her office and closed the door. She took the e-mail from Collins out of her bag and read it once again. The bodies of the victims had all been found where the murderer had left them. In the e-mail, Collins had pointed out that not only were the victims mutilated in a cruelly clinical way, there would also have been a lot of blood involved. The killer must have been covered in it. How he left the crime scene, without drawing attention to himself, was the subject of much debate. Changing his clothes at the scene was one theory, or perhaps he wore a pair of overalls over his clothes so that he could pull them off once he had finished and be relatively clean underneath. But no such overalls had been found at the scene, which meant, if the theory was correct, he must have taken the overalls away to dispose of later. Searches through litter bins and rubbish dumps had led nowhere.

All the victims though, had had the same disturbing set of events leading up to their murder. They came from different walks of life, one was a nurse, one a banker and the other owned a small vintage clothes shop. The banker and the nurse were single and lived alone, while the third victim had a live-in boyfriend. There was nothing to connect the three women except for a disturbing chain of events that led up to the murder itself, which the police established by talking to their families and colleagues. A white rose was delivered, anonymously, to the victims' houses. Then, two days later, they received another anonymous delivery, this time, petals in an envelope. Two days later they were dead, a white rose placed in the cavity where their heart used to be.

Collins finished his e-mail by saying that what disturbed him the most about the killings was that, whoever had done this, clearly had the capacity for great anger which he then brought under control for his morbid surgery.

185

'This is,' Collins's e-mail ended, 'someone who can think things through, who understands cause and effect, and who is well versed enough in forensic techniques to not leave anything incriminating behind. We're dealing with a cold-blooded sociopath here. I very much hope, for your sake, that the attack on your sergeant's daughter wasn't him.'

Lorraine tossed the e-mail to one side and ran her fingers through her hair. She hoped very much that Inspector Collins was right, but she couldn't shake the feeling that what had begun with Selina was only the beginning of something far worse. It looked like Selina had had an extremely lucky escape.

A brisk knock sounded at the door. Lorraine said 'come in', and Kate Mulberry entered. Lorraine looked at her watch. Just gone twenty past eight. 'You're in early,' said Lorraine, suspiciously.

'I just thought I'd get started. Perhaps we could have that interview that I've been talking about?'

Lorraine sighed deeply. 'I just don't have the time today. I'm very sorry, Kate, this is not the day to catch me.'

'That's OK,' said Kate brightly, in a way that made Lorraine instantly wary. She didn't seem the type to let something like this drop so easily. 'Perhaps I could shadow Carter today instead? The story could be along the lines of the next generation of police officer replacing the old.'

Old? Cheeky cow, thought Lorraine. 'Carter's unavailable, I'm afraid. But yer might be able to go out with Sanderson today, I'll check.'

Lorraine noticed Kate's eyes slide to the e-mail that Lorraine had placed to one side of the table. Lorraine was sure that Kate wouldn't be able to read the main body of the e-mail, but slid a folder on top of it, just in case. Kate's eyes immediately rose to meet Lorraine's. Lorraine was sure that Kate was just about to say something, but instead the young woman smiled, and, with an exaggerated sigh, got out of her chair and said, 'Well, I shan't keep you, Inspector. I'm off to have breakfast in the canteen. Let me know whether or not you find any time today for that interview.' And with that, Kate left the office.

Luke, meanwhile, was still watching over his sleeping daughter. She had been given sedatives, and while Luke realised that all of this was part of the healing process, he really just wanted to talk to Selina, make sure that she was going to be OK, that this would be something she would recover from physically as well as mentally. He ran his fingers over his daughter's hair. Now that he had found her, he didn't want to lose her.

Someone gave a tiny cough to announce her presence. Luke looked up to see Amy Knowles standing in the doorway. Worry crossed her face. 'Sorry,' she whispered, 'I'll come back later, if yer like.'

Luke smiled, 'She's sleeping, but yer don't need to go, yer could sit with her for a bit, if yer want.'

Amy stepped quietly into the room. 'I can't stay for long. Me mam is looking after the boys for me downstairs. They're making one hell of a racket. I just wanted to drop this off,' Amy held out a large foil balloon that had 'Get Well Soon' printed in crazy letters on it. 'It's stupid, I know, but I thought it might make her smile, cheer her up.'

Luke was touched by Amy's thoughtfulness. 'I'll tell yer what,' he said. 'I'll tie it to her bed. It'll be the first thing she sees when she wakes up.'

Amy smiled.

Lorraine had spent a frustating morning going over forensics that went nowhere. The envelope had come back from the lab and yielded not a fingerprint, not a strand of hair or suspect DNA. Whoever sent the letter had dampened the seal of the envelope with water, not saliva and had probably handled it using gloves. The envelope was a very cheap kind that could be bought in any corner store and the ink was from a cheap pen. Aside from the petal inside the envelope, there was nothing remarkable about the envelope itself. Forensics had photocopied the front of the envelope and Lorraine had stared at the hand-written address for an age, trying to get a sense of Selina's attacker from the way he wrote. It was no use, the handwriting was blocky and deliberate, as if whoever sent the letter was trying to disguise his handwriting.

Carter came into her office not long after she had thrown the photocopied piece of paper down on her desk. 'No luck with that envelope,' Lorraine sighed. 'Forensics couldn't pull anything from it.'

Carter nodded in response, then said, 'Listen, boss, I've got the tramp that bought the flowers from that florist's, the Apple Blossom. He's in interview room 2, do yer want to interview him with me? He's in a bit of a state, the poor bugger.'

Lorraine followed Carter into the interview room. She held her breath as she entered. The tramp smelled earthy, musty. His clothes were mildewy and falling off him. He looked terrified. Lorraine sat down quietly opposite him. 'Don't worry,' she said gently, 'yer not in any trouble, I just want to ask yer a few questions. My name is Inspector Hunt and this is Constable Carter.' The tramp's head jerked towards her, then rolled back, an unfortunate nervous twitch that was probably heightened by being in an unfamiliar place. 'Carter, could yer get a cup of tea for him please?' she said in that same even voice.

Carter nodded and left the room. 'What's your name?' Lorraine asked, feeling as if she was talking to a particularly skittish horse. No sudden movements, no loud noises. The poor man was clearly mentally disturbed, probably had autism or schizophrenia, probably had been through the system and spat right back out. The man jerked his head in that peculiar way again. Lorraine noticed that his fingers were caked in mud and had cracked open painfully. She tried once more. 'What's your name?'

'Ned Hartley,' he said eventually, his statement followed by a jerk of his head.

Carter came in with a cup of tea and some sachets of sugar. Ned glanced up at him gratefully, and then emptied them all into the cup, and wound his hands around its warmth. His head jerked again, but Lorraine noticed that the twitch became less pronounced as he became calmer.

'Now, Ned,' she said, aware of keeping her tone steady. 'I need to ask yer a few questions about something that happened to yer the other day. Do yer remember someone asking yer to buy some flowers for him?'

Ned nodded vigorously, but this time, he seemed to have control over his movements. 'Yes, he gave me a tenner.'

Carter shifted in his seat and Lorraine could sense that the answer had excited him. But Lorraine played it cool. 'And he got yer to order some flowers.'

'Yeah,' he smiled, showing broken and blackened teeth through his dark-ginger beard. 'But he was scared I wouldn't remember so he wrote down the address.'

Lorraine and Carter glanced at each other. 'Do yer still have it?' said Carter. Lorraine could tell from his tone that he was trying not to sound too eager, but he was still coming across as a bit too enthusiastic. Lorraine hoped that his tone wouldn't scare Ned off.

But it seemed that they had gained Ned's trust. Holding his cup of tea in one hand, he patted his pockets with the other, until he found what it was he was looking for. He placed the cup of tea on the table and straightened it out, trying with his fingers to decrease it, then pushed the paper towards Lorraine.

189

Lorraine recognised the handwriting – it was the same as the writing on the front of Selina's letter, but she had already guessed that Selina's attacker had been the one to get Ned to order the flowers. It did, however, confirm her initial suspicions. 'Thank you Ned, this is very helpful. Can I keep this?' Ned gave her that same broken grin. 'Just one more thing, Ned, can yer tell us what the man looked like?'

Lorraine let him take his time, and he was obviously thinking hard. 'Tall,' he finally said. 'And he wore a . . .' he gestured at his head and looked as if he was grasping for the word.

'Hat?' Carter suggested hopefully.

Ned shook his head, 'No,' he pulled his fingers away from his forehead.

'Baseball cap?' Lorraine tried.

Ned nodded his head and smiled again.

'What about his hair colour? Eyes?'

'Couldn't see,' said Ned. 'Cap.'

'What about what he was wearing?'

Ned started looking anxious. Perhaps they were testing his memory more than it was up to. 'Dark,' was all he could say finally. 'Dark clothes.'

Lorraine smiled at him. 'Thank you very much for coming in,' she said. 'Yer've been very helpful.'

She made to stand up but then Ned said, 'Wait.'

Lorraine sat down again.

'The man,' Ned said, giving that characteristic jerk of his head. 'The man didn't sound like you, he sounded like, sounded like . . .' he was grasping for words, then finally, all his tweaks and twitchings ceased and he looked at Lorraine almost beatifically. 'He sounded different . . .' Ned sighed and looked helplessly at them.

A few minutes later, having questioned Ned Hartley as much as they could, Lorraine took Carter out of the interview room and said, 'I think that's all we're going to get out of him. Could yer take him to the canteen, give him a good meal? And then see whether any hostels have spare beds this evening. Poor bugger looks done in.' Carter nodded, and Lorraine continued. 'As do you. After yer've done that, get yerself to bed. I don't want to see yer back in the office until tomorrow morning, understood?' Carter nodded wryly.

After thanking Ned Hartley for all his help, Lorraine went to her office. The door was slightly ajar. *That's odd*, she thought, *I thought I had closed it*. She walked in, closed the door behind her. Everything seemed to be in its place, but, with a sudden lurch in her stomach, Lorraine remembered the print out. She lunged towards the desk and picked up the folder. The e-mail was still there, just where she had left it.

22

Selina slowly opened her eyes, she blinked twice before realising she was looking at the top of her father's bent head. She blinked blearily at her father. Her head hurt, and her ribs hurt when she breathed. In fact, everything hurt. 'Lu . . . Da . . .?' she whispered huskily.

Luke glanced up. 'Oh,' he smiled, full of relief. 'Selina, I thought yer were never gonna wake up.'

'What happened, where am I?'

'Can't you remember anything?'

She frowned, closed her eyes again, when she opened them, they were still full of questions. 'I remember being in the club with Mickey, then getting dragged out with the crowd. It . . . it was frightening, someone was wedged in the door and she was screaming, there was blood, some of the kids were slipping in the blood, and a . . . a few went down,' Selina shuddered. 'The fire alarm was going on and on, everybody was trying to get out . . .' She swallowed. 'Could I, could I have a drink please?'

'Yes, yes of course.' Luke hurried to the other side of her bed, poured a glass of water and helped her to sit up. 'Just sip it, no gulping mind you.'

She took a few sips, then with a deep painful sigh lay back on her pillow. 'What's that?' she said, pointing at the foil balloon.

'Amy dropped by. Thought you might think it was funny.'

Selina smiled weakly. 'That was nice of her.'

'I hoped you would be coming home today, but the doctor says you should stay in another night and come home tomorrow. You've been badly concussed, and I think he just wants to check that everything is OK.'

Selina slowly felt the bandage on her head, her fingers running over the material, then frowning her confusion, she ran her hand over the bandage on her arm.

This was not the first time Luke had dealt with a victim who was lucky to be alive. It was, however, the first time that the victim was his own daughter. He was loath to start asking her questions, but there was someone out there, perhaps someone close to them, who meant Selina harm. However difficult it was, he needed to ask Selina the same sort of questions he'd ask any victim. He tried to get straight to the point.

'Selina, you were attacked at some point after the fire alarm went off. You were badly beaten, and then you were found round the back of the building.'

'Wh—' Selina paused, letting it sink in.

It can't have been Eccles, surely she would have remembered if it were him, or perhaps the concussion had given her amnesia or something, she had seen people lose their memory like that in movies. She felt her head again, and winced, this time from her ribs.

'I feel . . .' she said. 'I feel awful. Everything hurts.'

'I'm not surprised. Whoever did this to yer, hurt yer pretty bad, the bastard. Yer arm's got thirteen stitches from a knife.' He stared at her for a moment, trying to keep his anger in check. 'We think whoever did this to yer was disturbed by someone, and whoever it was who disturbed him, probably saved your life.'

Clearly frightened, Selina started to cry, soft tears spilling down her face.

Luke felt his throat tighten. This wasn't the way he had wanted it to go. 'I'm sorry, love,' he whispered as he stroked her hair. 'But I have to ask yer a few questions. The sooner you are able to answer them, the sooner I can catch the bastard who did this to yer. Do yer think yer up to it?'

Selina breathed in deeply, wiped her eyes with the back of her hand, and smiled wanly, but bravely, at Luke.

'Yer just told me yer left the nightclub in the rush to get out. What do yer remember after that?'

Selina looked up at the celing. 'There was so much going on . . . I remember someone grabbing me arm and then . . . nothing.' She said the last word looking her father in the eyes. 'I'm sorry.'

'No, no, don't be sorry,' said Luke. Underneath his smile his heart broke as he looked at his courageous girl. He had known but had never really understood until now how young she was, how fragile. He placed his hand over hers and gave it a squeeze.

'I think I know who sent me the roses.'

Luke stiffened, was this, finally, a lucky break? If Selina couldn't remember the attack, then if she could name the person who sent her the roses, that was just as good. He tried not to let it show just how eager he was to hear her news, in case it scared her, 'Who, sweetheart?' he said gently.

Selina started to cry again, this time quietly, tears streaming down her cheeks. But her voice was strong when she said, 'His name is Eccles. He's a skinhead, from Manchester. We were, I was,' she gulped down a sob, and then continued, 'I was his girlfriend, well, I guess that's what you'd call it. I knew he was bad news, but he could supply me with what I needed,' Selina dropped her gaze to her hands, which were working the bedclothes in her fingers. 'He had this thing about roses, about anything romantic, really. But he'd mess you around, if he got you a stuffed toy, he'd rip the arms off or something like that. He thought it was really funny.'

Luke tried to keep his voice even, but his heart was going out to her. She had been through such a lot. 'So, yer knew who the petals were from . . .'

Selina nodded her head. Her breath was coming out in ragged sobs. 'But I didn't want to think it was him, I didn't want to think that he had found me.' She bent her head and started crying in earnest.

'Don't worry Selina,' he said gruffly. 'Yer won't be left alone for a single moment until we catch him.' He slipped his arm around her shoulder and she buried her face in his chest. Gently Luke stroked the top of her head. The lump in his throat thickened. He had been denied this simple contact with his own daughter for almost seventeen years. *And now some arsehole thinks he's gonna take it away, not gonna happen.*

Lorraine stood in the doorway watching them, she felt tears prick the back of her eyes and decided that this was a moment between Luke and his daughter. She walked quietly away until she was round the corner and out of sight.

She watched the minutes tick by on her watch and when she heard voices she made a noisy entrance into Selina's room.

She was rewarded by a brave smile from Selina and a welcoming one from Luke.

'Hi guys.' She walked up to Selina and put her arms around her. Over the top of Selina's head, she mouthed to Luke, 'How is she?'

Luke put his thumbs up, but she could see from his expression that there was more that he wanted to tell her.

'So, yer feeling all right kiddo?'

Selina let go of Lorraine and looking up at her said. 'Yeah, I'll get there.'

'Knew yer would. Look, I got yer a present,' Lorraine took a bag of grapes out of a plastic bag she had by her side. 'It's a bit of a cliché, but it's all they had at the shops.'

Selina grinned, and popped a grape in her mouth.

'Is there anything else yer want, anything I can do?' Lorraine continued.

Selina thought for a moment then, after giving a quick glance at Luke, she said, 'Can you get in touch with Mickey please?'

'Course I can, I know exactly where he hangs out.'

Lorraine saw Luke stiffen then, as if he'd finally realised that Selina was serious about Mickey, and because not accepting the fact would just make life miserable, he relaxed. After Selina had told him about Eccles, he realised that Selina could do a lot worse than Mickey. Perhaps he had been playing the overprotective father just a little bit too much. Perhaps he should finally start trusting Selina, after all. He took a deep breath, and then smiled at Selina. 'I'll tell him,' he said.

Selina gasped then smiled at Luke. And Lorraine felt her heart lift.

'OK great. Now that's sorted we've got to concentrate on catching the bastard . . . Do you mind very much if I take Luke away for a while?' She noticed Selina's eyes widen in fright, and hastily went on, 'Don't worry yer won't be alone, I have two officers sitting outside in a car, one will stay there and the other will sit outside your door. No one is gonna get in or out without someone knowing about it. We'll make double sure yer safe.'

Selina bit her lip. 'OK,' she said a moment later.

'Good girl,' Lorraine nodded, 'I'll get PC Mullins right up.'

Lorraine went out for Mullins and Luke turned to Selina.

'It's very brave of yer, and I'm proud of you. Roy Mullins is a big bear and he enters the boxing championships every year.'

'Does he win?'

'Yeah . . . Well.'

Selina smiled. 'Go get him . . . Dad.'

Part Four

23

Luke had spent his first night at home since Selina had been in hospital. Now that she was being watched around the clock, he felt a lot happier. He had told Lorraine the night before that Selina suspected that it had been Eccles who had sent her the petals. Lorraine looked unconvinced. However, she agreed to put out an APB to look out for any persons matching the description that Selina had given. Luke showered, shaved, and ate a hasty breakfast before a knock on the door announced Lorraine, who had come by to pick him up.

They were driving to the station when Luke's mobile rang. 'Say that again?' Luke said into his phone, his voice registering surprise. It was Sanderson on the other end, and when he repeated with great care what he had just said, Luke blew air out of his cheeks creating a whistling sound that echoed round the car.

'What?' They were pulling into the Seahills and Lorraine took her eyes off the road for a second, her eyes demanding to know what was going on.

Luke's face was grim when he said, 'A body has been found

near the children's home. A young female, heart cut out and replaced with a white rose in full bloom.'

'Shit!' Lorraine punched the steering wheel.

She spun the car round, put the siren on, practically frightening the life out of a flock of sea gulls which had come over from the coast for a breakfast of worms, and she headed quickly for Hall Lane Children's Home.

The usual crowd of onlookers were present as could only be expected at this time of a morning, from little old ladies to harassed mothers with babies in pushchairs, a few men dotted here and there and the odd teenager. Lorraine was pleased to see that incident tape had been erected over a wide space keeping the nosy spectators at bay.

But God only knows what evidence they've already trampled on, she thought pulling up next to Scottie's car.

A tent had been erected over the spot and two white-suited men were standing by with a stretcher. Lorraine and Luke moved towards Scottie, who was struggling to get his extra-large figure out of the white suit.

Scottie looked up, and smiled at Lorraine, but his smile didn't reach his eyes. Lorraine could only imagine what those eyes had just seen. And what she was about to. Scottie stepped out of his suit, and then said, 'This is a nasty business.'

'Sanderson filled us in on how the body was found,' Lorraine said. 'And let us know the state it was in.' Her stomach was churning. If this was a serial killer, then things in Houghton-le-Spring could get bad, very bad. She had to find whoever it was who was doing this, and find him before he killed again.

Scottie nodded, 'Aye it's certainly a grim one the poor soul,' he sighed. 'And Luke, everything all right? I heard Selina's on the mend,' he smiled.

Luke nodded, his gaze on the tent. The two men who had been waiting with the stretcher had come out of the tent with

202

the body, and were transporting it to the mortuary van. Luke gulped hard and stared as the two officers put the body in the back of the van.

'I'll tell yer what I know now, the rest will have to wait until I do a proper autopsy which will be sometime today. OK . . . From what I've deducted at the scene the victim is a white female, early- to mid-twenties. She was attacked from behind, and hit over the head with a blunt instrument.' He looked over to where a few uniformed policemen were searching in the area around the body. 'We found a wooden post with some blood and hair on it. I'd say that he picked up something to use either at the scene or along the way that he can discard after it's done its job.'

Lorraine felt Luke flinch beside her, knowing he was picturing what had happened to the poor woman in the van and what could have happened to Selina.

'She was cut open with a very sharp knife,' Scottie went on. 'I can't say for certain yet, but from the amount of blood, it was probably done while she was still alive. Her heart was removed, I suspect by someone who knows a little about anatomy, but I wouldn't necessary say that it was someone with medical knowledge. Yer can get a lot off the internet these days. And then, after death, a white rose in bloom was placed where the heart had been.'

Luke blanched and for a moment he looked desperately ill. 'If yer want off the case Luke,' Lorraine said quickly, 'I'll understand, Sanderson will . . .'

'No,' he practically snapped.

Scottie looked at the two of them, as he wiped his hands on a towel. 'What's going on,' he said quietly. 'Something you're not telling me?'

Lorraine looked at Luke with a question in her eyes. He nodded, then walked away and stood a little way apart from them, staring out towards the children's home. 'Scottie, I have some information about the killer. When yer hear it, yer gonna understand why I have to make sure that it's kept quiet.'

Scottie looked put out. 'Of course, Lorraine, yer know I don't go blabbing this kind of thing all over Sunderland.'

'I know. I know I can trust yer Scottie, but this is potentially explosive. Yer'll understand when I tell yer.'

She then told him what she and Carter had discovered, including the fact that, if it was a copycat, the killer would have needed access to the police database, 'Which means it could be one of our own,' she finished.

Scottie shook his head, as if trying to shake what he had just heard out of it. 'I just can't believe it's one of you guys.'

'Neither can I, Scottie, but it's something that we've got to explore. But there's something else. We think that Selina could have been one of his intended victims, but that someone disturbed him . . .'

He blanched, then looked over at Luke. 'How's he taking it?'

'As well as can be expected,' Lorraine sighed at the stock answer. 'It's happening just as he seems to have made a breakthrough with Selina, I think he's terrified of losing her, just when things seem to be going their way.'

He continued to shake his head. 'This is a nasty, nasty business but I'll see what I can find.'

'Scottie, Selina thinks that she was attacked by an ex-boyfriend, but I'm not so sure. She said that he had a thing about roses, especially white roses, but is it too much of a coincidence? That there's two people out there with this sort of obsession? Unless he's the copycat killer, of course. But then, how would he have known about the modus operandi?'

Scottie scratched his head. 'Well, I'm not a psychologist, but it seems to me that roses are a very potent symbol of romance and love. Remember what time of year we're in . . .'

Lorraine wrinkled her forehead and then it came to her. 'February. Of course. Valentine's Day's not far away.'

'This is only a theory mind you, and I'm making it up as I go along, but perhaps whoever did this had been rejected in the past and has decided to take it out on young girls. Yer say that Selina received a white rose in bud, then petals, and then a white rose was left at the scene? Well, that sounds exactly like the sort of ritualistic behaviour of a serial killer to me. If it was her boyfriend, well, then perhaps he's decided not just to punish Selina for her rejection, but other girls as well.'

'But I just don't get the link between him and the killings in Dublin. If I could understand that . . .'

'. . . then you could break the case wide open.' Scottie finished her sentence for her. 'I must say, I don't envy yer. My job starts and ends with the body, your job though . . .'

'Sanderson said that there wasn't an ID on the girl . . .'

'That's right, unless they find something,' he nodded at the police who were still looking through the bushes. 'But there was nothing on her, she didn't have a handbag, or she lost it, or the killer took it with him.' Scottie turned his gaze back to Lorraine. 'I'll run dental records, of course, but until we find out who she is, there's just only so much we can speculate on.'

Lorraine frowned, Scottie was right, they could theorise forever, but they had to start somewhere.

Luke walked back to where Lorraine and Scottie were standing. 'We need to start investigating ourselves,' Lorraine mused. 'Luke, yer can do that. See whether they've got an alibi for last night and the night that Selina was killed. Also try and find out whether they might have told anyone about the killer in Ireland. It's a long shot but perhaps someone let the details slip to a friend . . .' Lorraine couldn't help but feel that she was clutching at straws. 'Try and do it subtly, though. And we'll get Sanderson or Dinwall on to finding that ex-boyfriend of Selina's. Make it a priority.'

Luke nodded. He was clenching and unclenching the muscles in his jaw. Lorraine hoped that he wouldn't do anything stupid once the boyfriend had been brought in. She didn't care about Eccles, hell, once she was done with him, he could get run over by a bus for all she cared, but she didn't want there to be any 'accidents' that pointed to Luke and his fists. She wanted everything above board, so she could nail the bastard to the wall, and not have some wanker of a defence lawyer get him off on a technicality.

'I'll go to the hospital, see if Selina remembers anything at all.'

'But I've already . . .'

'Yer know full well Luke, yer'll not have been as relentless in your questioning of her as someone who is not related. In fact, she really should have been questioned by someone else entirely. Phone Carter, tell him to come and pick yer up, I'll go to the hospital by myself.'

'But . . .'

'Yer know I'm right, Luke. You're too close, and there'll probably be questions yer don't want to ask. I want nothing compromised in this case.'

He didn't like it, but Luke had to agree Lorraine was right. He watched her as she walked to her car, got in, started the engine and drove off. He looked at Hall Lane Children's Home for a long moment, and then, ducking under the incident tape, walked towards it.

Twenty minutes later Carter arrived at the scene and walked up to Scottie who was finishing up a few things before leaving for the morgue. 'Hello, Scottie, where's Luke?' Carter asked.

'Yer'll find him in the kiddies' home,' Scottie replied. 'I saw him heading that way and he hasn't come back out . . . Not that I know of, like.'

'OK Scottie, see yer.'

'Right. Oh, anybody looking for the young lass we've just sent to the morgue?'

'Nothing's come in yet, but it's only morning. At that age, it's sometimes a day or two before people start to worry where they are.'

Scottie nodded, 'OK, we'll just call her Jane then.' He watched Carter head towards the children's home and mused on how many Janes had passed through his hands. Jane Does and John Does of all ages, many remaining unclaimed forever.

Following the directions given to him by the gardener, Carter walked along the corridor of Hall Lane Children's Home towards the office, when he felt a sharp sting on the back of his neck.

'My God, a wasp,' he slapped the back of his neck and looked at his hand fully expecting to see a dead wasp. Nothing.

Shrugging he carried on, only to stop a moment later when another sting, this time to the back of his head, accompanied by the sound of giggling, caused him to spin round. 'OK, come out.'

At first there was silence then he heard what sounded like at least three kids laughing and running away.

'Little brats,' Carter muttered, though he couldn't help but smile.

He knocked at the office door and Luke opened it a moment later. 'Carter,' he said with a nod.

Carter stepped into the office and looked around. Metal filing cabinets lined one wall. All the office furniture looked knocked about, and the seat cushions were threadbare. It was obvious that any government monies that had been given to the home hadn't been spent on decorating. Someone had placed a bowl of brightly coloured pansies on the top of the filing cabinets, trying in vain to lighten the institutional atmosphere of the place. Cream blinds were up at the window and behind the desk were two people. One was a youngish

207

man with thick, dark hair and hazel eyes behind thick glasses, and the other was an older woman, whose thin, greasy grey hair clung to her scalp as if it had been glued on. Both looked up as he came in and smiled at him.

'Hello,' Carter nodded at the two people.

'Mr Hanson, and Mrs Rawhill, this is my colleague, PC Carter. Right,' Luke went on, 'yer say it was one of the younger boys who found the body and gave the alarm.' He directed the question at Mrs Rawhill.

'Yes,' her voice was thick and heavy with years of cigarette smoke. 'Simon Ashe. He is, as you can imagine, very distraught.'

'How old is he exactly?' Carter took his notebook out of his jacket pocket and was quickly scribbling his pen on one of the blank pages. When it refused to write he looked around helplessly. Hanson handed him a pen.

'Thanks.' He quickly wrote the boy's name. 'How old?' he asked again.

'Eleven,' Luke put in, already having asked the obvious but aware that Carter had a job to do. He moved over to the window and stood looking out, his hands behind his back.

The home was built in a square with an inner courtyard and wide enough on all sides so that a good portion of sunlight reached the kids who played there. The only occupants as the clock struck one o'clock were three boys of about ten to twelve years old, all three had home-made pea shooters and Luke smiled, been a long time since he'd seen kids with a pea shooter, most of them did their damage with mobile phones these days.

He was thinking alternatively about Selina and Lorraine when he heard Carl Hanson reply to one of Carter's questions.

'I've been back at work for about a week,' Hanson said.

Luke wheeled round to face Hanson. 'Been somewhere nice, then?'

208

Carl Hanson hesitated a moment, then with a slight shrug said, 'Just over to Ireland for a few days, visiting some relatives.'

'Oh aye, go there often do yer?'

Luke noticed that Hanson was avoiding eye contact. 'Well, just now and again.' He picked up a paper clip and started fiddling with it.

'Close family, is it, that yer go and see?'

Hanson finally lifted his head, stared at Carter and said 'yes' with such finality that Carter and Luke knew they would get nothing else there. Not at the moment, anyway. Not unless we have another reason to take him down to the station and question him further, Luke thought.

'Could yer give me a list of dates when yer were on holiday within the last year? And let me know whether or not yer were in Ireland.'

Hanson nodded, looking worried. 'Of course, but I'll have to look in my diary,' he said quietly. 'But could yer tell me what that has to do with the body that was found here?'

Luke shook his head. 'I'm afraid it's part of an ongoing investigation and we can't divulge the details at the moment. But if yer could fax or e-mail the details to my constable here, that should be enough to rule yer out.'

Hanson looked confused and Luke couldn't help but notice that he looked worried too. *He's definitely hiding something*, Luke thought, *but it could be anything. Maybe he's got a boyfriend in Dublin that he doesn't want his work to know about. Or maybe he's doing something in Ireland that he doesn't want* anyone *to know about*. Hanson took down Carter's e-mail address and told him that he would e-mail him the dates by the next day.

As they walked to the squad car, Carter asked Luke what he thought of Hanson for the killer.

209

Luke scratched the side of his head. 'I just don't know, Carter. He looks as if butter wouldn't melt in his mouth, but the coincidence is too strong. I've got to tell the boss about this.'

Carter gave a wan smile, 'And yer know what the boss will say.'

'Yeah Carter. "No such thing as coincidence".'

Smiling, the two men got into the car and drove away.

Hanson stared out of the window and watched the squad car drive away. When they had mentioned Dublin, a cold sweat broke out on his body.

'Are yer OK, Carl,' asked Mrs Rawhill kindly. 'It's a shock for all of us, a body like that being dumped on these grounds.' She reached out to place a hand on his arm, but he moved away before she made contact.

'Yes,' he said tightly. 'Dreadful business.'

Lorraine waited a minute, and smiled as he watched Selina, without her knowing that she was there. Sun was streaming through a window, and Selina was sitting up in bed, reading *heat* magazine. Lorraine knocked quietly on the door and walked in. Selina put down her magazine and smiled. She patted the side of her bed. 'Come to have a girly chat?' she said.

'Well, sort of,' Lorraine said quietly. 'Your father has told me that he questioned you about the other night, and that yer can't remember much about it. Is that true, Selina, or is there something that you're not telling me? Anything, however small it may be, will help catch the bastard who hurt you.'

Selina shook her head. 'Honestly, Lorraine, I've told him everything I can remember.' She twisted the bedsheet between her fingers. 'I'm sorry, I wish I could help you more.'

Lorraine smiled back at Selina. 'I just wanted to check.

210

Sometimes it's easier to tell other people stuff yer wouldn't tell yer family. I just wanted to check that there wasn't something that yer were leaving out, because it was your dad.'

'Honestly, Lorraine, if I could remember, I'd tell yer.'

Lorraine smiled, and clasped Selina's hand for a moment. 'Well, that's that. I'd better go.' She got up, shrugging her bag on to her shoulder again.

'Lorraine,' Selina said just as she was about to go through the door. 'He misses yer, yer know.'

Lorraine turned back, flummoxed. 'Did he say that?'

'Old moany face?' Selina snorted. 'Fat chance. Nah, I can tell. The way that he looks at you, the way he asks after you once you've gone. Is it because of me that you two aren't together anymore?'

Lorraine thought that she owed Selina the truth. 'Actually, it's partly to do with yer, but it's also to do with Luke, how he's coping with having a grown-up daughter suddenly arrive in his life. It's difficult for him too, yer know.'

Selina stared at her hands. 'I know,' she said simply.

Lorraine had got back to the office, and was sitting at her desk, mulling over some theories when Luke knocked on her door. 'Can I come in?'

Lorraine smiled, Selina's words ringing in her ears. *He misses you.* Even if they never got together again, those three simple words had meant a lot to her. 'Sure,' she said.

'While I was waiting for Carter to come and pick me up from the crime scene today,' Luke said, sitting down in his normal seat, 'I went up to the children's home and talked to Carl Hanson and a woman called Mrs Rawhill.'

'I met Carl Hanson,' interrupted Lorraine. 'At a charity dinner I went to with Scottie.'

'Yer went to a charity dinner with Scottie?' said Luke, incredulously.

211

Lorraine smiled. She loved that she could make him jealous. 'Just as friends,' she said. 'And I met Hanson. Nice guy, though he seemed a little uncomfortable, not with the company, but as if he was uncomfortable in his own skin.'

Luke nodded. 'That's just the impression I got too. Anyway, Hanson said that he had just been to visit Ireland, so I asked him to e-mail Carter with a list of dates. He just sent them through. Look at this.'

Lorraine studied the dates. He had been in Ireland at the same time each murder had been committed. 'What explanation has he given for this?'

Luke shook his head. 'None, but then, I haven't asked him.'

Lorraine sat back in her chair and looked at Luke. 'What's your feeling about Hanson?'

'As in, would I pick him as the murderer?' Luke shook his head. 'I don't know, it doesn't quite fit with me.'

Lorraine nodded. 'I agree. This is just circumstantial evidence, at the moment. And if we're wrong and he is the murderer, then we might scare him off by going in all guns blazing. No, I think we should hold off for a while, but keep an eye on him.'

Luke nodded. 'Will do, boss.'

'Carter!' a light voice echoed down the corridor. Carter, who had just been about to go and sit at his desk, shut his eyes and groaned. Kate Mulberry, dammit. Taking a deep breath, Carter turned and smiled tightly at Kate, who was dashing towards him as fast as she could on those high heels of hers.

'So,' she said without preamble, 'what can yer tell me about this murder near the children's home?'

'Kate—'

'I have talked to some of the onlookers, and they say that the body looked as if it was badly mutilated, though, of course, they couldn't get a good look—'

'Kate—' said Carter one more time. He had closed his eyes tightly shut and was rubbing the bridge of his nose between his thumb and forefinger.

'—at it,' Kate continued, as if Carter hadn't said anything at all. 'And then they erected a tent over it so I was wondering whether you could fill me in on any of the details?'

'Kate,' Carter almost shouted, which was so unlike him that the reporter shut up suddenly. 'Yer know cos I've told yer that I can't tell yer anything about an ongoing investigation.'

'Right,' said Kate again, with that steely look in her eye. 'Are yer sure about that? Because I'm going to print what I have to print, with or without a comment from the police. It's your chance, Carter, yer better take it, now or never.'

Carter remained silent, and, after a few moments, Kate smiled wryly, turned on her heel and walked out of the police station.

The phone rang and Lorraine picked it up. 'Inspector Hunt speaking.'

'Lorraine,' said a voice down the other end of the line. 'It's Wade, Ian Wade.'

'Well, well,' said Lorraine. 'I've been hoping to get in touch with you.'

'Glutton for punishment after the last time we spoke?' Wade laughed, obviously hoping they could get back to their easy banter.

'No,' said Lorraine. 'Not quite. You see, you're here from Dublin, and then, suddenly, we have a murder, and an attempted murder, which seriously mirrors what's going on in your neck of the woods.'

There was silence on the other end of the line. Then Wade finally said, 'All of that, that's confidential, yer know. How did yer get hold of this information?'

'I have channels,' Lorraine said primly. 'But what I want

213

to know is how much you know about this white rose killer?'

'Well, very little,' said Wade, who definitely seemed on the wrong foot. 'I've never been in homicide. I couldn't help you. Besides,' he said, 'that's what I was ringing to tell you. I'm leaving Sunderland and going back to Ireland tomorrow morning. I was wondering whether you wanted a quick bite tonight?'

Lorraine laughed. 'I don't think so, Wade,' and rang off.

Lorraine looked up to see Carter standing in the door. She beckoned him in and he closed it after him. 'It's that Kate Mulberry,' he said. 'She's been after me to give her some sort of statement of this murder down at the children's home. I told her to bugger off,' Carter said with a wan smile.

'Well done,' said Lorraine. 'Now, how do you fancy a trip down to Blacks?'

The first thing that hit Lorraine as she entered the club was the smell. Looking at Carter she wrinkled her nose and he nodded.

'Can I help you?' The voice came from the shadows on their right.

Lorraine and Carter turned and as their eyes adjusted they watched as a tall thin man with thick grey hair stepped out of the darkness and walked towards them. He wore a black shirt and black trousers, a thick gold chain around his neck and a matching one round his right wrist.

'Who are you?' Lorraine asked.

'I might ask you the same question, seeing as you are on my premises uninvited,' he replied with a slight sideways smile, that showed very little teeth.

'Police,' Lorraine answered, flashing her badge under his nose. 'And you are?'

'Gary Duffy,' he said. 'I hope yer found the CCTV camera footage useful? Carr told me that one of your lot came by to pick it up. From all accounts, whoever it was, wasn't quite as tasty as you,' he leered. Lorraine rolled her eyes. 'Do yer want to come into my office? It's much more comfortable there.'

Lorraine rolled her eyes at Carter, who grinned, and they followed Gary Duffy into the office.

The office wasn't much better than the rest of the club, as far as smell was concerned, although there was light coming in the windows. Duffy took some papers off a seat and indicated that Lorraine should sit there. Carter stood against the door, as there wasn't a seat for him. Duffy sat behind his desk, and placed the tips of his fingers together. Lorraine fought the urge to get out of there. The place was a dive and no mistake.

'So, what can I do for yer, Inspector?' The man made every question sound like a come on.

'First have yer any idea at all who it was that set the fire alarms off that night?'

He shook his head.

'You sure about that?'

'Of course, how would I know . . . What do you want me to do, bar everyone that was here that night.'

'That would be a start.'

'Oh yeah very good.'

Lorraine stared at him for a moment then snapped, 'I want a list of all your employees. A detailed list, meaning not only their names but their contact details.'

'That will take some time . . .'

'Oh I forgot to say, I want it now.'

'But . . .' he blustered, looking around him as if a list would appear.

Lorraine looked at her watch, 'Fifteen minutes tops . . . While you're at it we'll just take a look around.'

'But you can't just wander . . .'

'Why?'

'Well because . . . because . . .'

'Got something to hide have yer. Something yer don't want us to see.'

'Of course not.'

'OK, yer have fourteen minutes.'

Lorraine could practically feel the daggers in her back as she and Carter left and entered what would have been called in a gentler age the Ballroom.

The sharp winter sun trickles through the tree branches as he walks past the park. He passes the seats where a group of teenage boys are sitting.

The one he wants is not among them.

As he passes them he hears what they are saying, they are talking about a girl, a murdered girl.

He smiles to himself, a cold cruel smile that never quite reaches his eyes. He carries on into the main street then he spots him, hurrying to their meeting place outside the Blue Lion.

The apprentice. 'Ha.'

Part Five

24

It was cold but the sun was shining brightly and the recent heavy downpours had washed the Broadway thoroughly, giving it for the moment a fresh, brand new born look. Dave Ridley sat down and unfolded the newspaper that he had found lying on the bench. The headlines slapped him in the face:

KILLER IN OUR MIDST
Kate Mulberry
Sunderland Echo
A mutilated body was found yesterday in the grounds outside Hall Lane Children's Home. The woman, who has yet to be identified, is believed to be the latest victim of the White Rose Killer, a cold and implacable sociopath who has killed in Dublin and has evidently crossed the Irish Sea to come to Houghton, and to kill again.

The killer leaves a macabre calling card, a white rose, in the chests of his victims. It is unclear what he does with their hearts but, in the opinion of this reporter, the killer takes the hearts as some kind of keepsake, a memento of

221

the kill, which has powerful sexual associations with it, although none of the victims were interfered with sexually, prior to or after their death.

Although there has only been one murder in Houghton, I can confirm that the police believe another girl was attacked and badly beaten by the same man. I can also confirm that the police are, at this time, looking within their own ranks for the murderer.

The police weren't available for interview but in my research I have found that killers, such as the White Rose Killer, are almost always sexually impotent. The White Rose Killer has struck three times in Dublin, that's three families grieving over their dead daughters and sisters. But has his reign of terror come to Houghton?

This reporter must ask why the police have decided to keep the details of the killings secret, after all, the streets are not safe until the White Rose Killer is caught. But will he remain as elusive in Houghton as he was in Dublin? Only time will tell.

'Oh the nasty bastard.' Dave flicked the paper shut.

Mickey left the hospital on cloud nine. He'd visited Selina, and she was doing fine, just fine, so fine she was coming home just as soon as her dad picked her up. There had been a copper outside Selina's room. He had a big grey droopy moustache and had eyed him up suspiciously, but before he could question Mickey, Selina had yelled his name. 'It's OK, Roy,' she said. 'Mickey's my boyfriend.'

Roy had still stood in the doorway, until Selina had said, 'Roy, It's *OK*, I don't need babysitting.'

Mickey wasn't so sure about that. It was uncomfortable having a copper just outside the door, but at least that meant that Selina was safe, and that there wasn't a chance that anyone could get to her through the policeman who was, Mickey couldn't help noticing, like The Rock from WWF. Still, after Mickey had said goodbye to Selina and left her room, he couldn't help but notice that Mullins had looked him up and down, with suspicion in his eyes.

'What'd he think I was gonna do?' Mickey mused out loud, his eyes on the ground, as he took a short cut behind the hospital to the main road and the nearest bus stop.

'I'll tell you what I'm gonna do.' A swift punch followed the words and Mickey, his left eye already swelling, fell to the ground.

He rolled over quickly and the kick missed. He wasn't quick enough though to stop Eccles from jumping on top of him and knocking the wind clean out of his lungs. 'How is she?' Eccles demanded, grabbing Mickey's jumper in an attempt to shake the words he wanted out of him. 'How is she?' he screamed this time, spit flying everywhere.

Mickey dug his feet into the ground and lifted his body up. At the same time he punched out with both fists and succeeded in knocking Eccles off him. 'No better for you asking.'

Both of them jumped to their feet and Mickey's right eye met the next punch full on. Mickey groaned, pain shooting through his skull.

'I told you to keep away from her, didn't I? Didn't I?' Eccles demanded.

Mickey's hand caught the next punch as he landed one of his own on Eccles's head.

'Bastard.' Eccles grunted as Mickey, barely able to see, caught him behind his ear with a ringing blow.

'Fuck off, perve. She's my girlfriend now, not yours, and she wants nowt to do with a drug-taking freak like you. Yer horrible dirty creep. Got the picture, have yer?'

'Who're you calling a creep, you fucking bastard,' Eccles

sounded completely amazed that Mickey had the balls to stand his ground. Gulping in air he took another swing at Mickey, but Mickey was prepared for him. Ducking, he swung his left foot out and with a lucky swipe knocked Eccles clean off his feet.

Eccles fell heavily, the side of his head finding a hidden rock in the grass at the side of the path. He lay still, a pool of blood quickly forming under his head.

Mickey gasped, his face drained of colour and he wanted to vomit. He hated fighting and mostly managed to talk his way out of it, but this bastard had been out to murder him. Stepping over Eccles' prone body he squinted down at him.

'Oh God, oh God, he's friggin' dead!' Mickey's heart began to pound.

'I've killed him. I've fucking well killed him.' Mickey could barely breathe as waves of shock ran up and down his body. Wildly he looked around, tears stinging his already swollen eyes. 'He's dead . . . He's friggin' dead . . . What am I gonna do? Oh God, what am I gonna do?'

His instinct to help collided with his instinct for self-preservation which demanded he run, and now.

Adrenaline flooded his veins, making it impossible for him to keep still. In the grip of panic he turned and bumped into the corner of the wall, his elbow taking the full brunt, but he felt nothing but the burning need to escape. Crossing the car park at a mad gallop he fell over the bonnet of a bright red sports car, then only just missed being run over by an ambulance as it hurtled through the hospital gates.

Carter hurried into Lorraine's office clutching the early edition of the *Sunderland Echo*. Before he even spoke, Lorraine could see by his face that it was trouble.

'Boss yer gotta read this . . . Jesus.' He thrust the paper over her desk.

With mounting dread, Lorraine picked the *Echo* up and read Kate Mulberry's lurid account of the White Rose Killer.

'Shit, shit, shit!'

'Oh yeah,' Carter nodded. 'Plenty of it an' all.'

'What the fuck that lot out there are thinking, God only knows?' she shook her head as she got up from her desk. 'Come on Carter, gotta put this right now. Get them all together in the incident room. I'll be along in a minute.'

'OK, boss,' Carter scuttled out.

A few minutes later as Lorraine walked down the corridor she could hear a distant grumbling which stopped when she entered the room. She could see Dinwall, Sanderson, Peters, Travis and most of the others looking at her expectantly, some with bemusement, some with hurt disbelief and some with barely disguised anger. Copies of the *Sunderland Echo* were dotted around the room, Luke was holding one in his hands.

'OK, no beating around the bush, yer'll all have read the bloody article. I can imagine how distressed yer all must have been, but believe me, Mulberry only had one side of the story and what she didn't know she bloody well made up . . . I know what a great bunch of officers I've got here. But the fact is the Garda were keeping the fact that they have a serial killer on their hands extremely close to their chests. It was only through Carter searching through the police database that we found a link between the rose that was at the scene of Luke's daughter Selina attack and the killings in Dublin . . . And yers all know the only way to access the database is if you're a police officer.'

She paused a moment and to the accompanying silence took a sip of water from the glass Carter had put on the table for her.

'Bottom line,' she looked at her officers one by one. 'I don't for one minute believe that anyone in this room is, as Mulberry terms it, the White Rose Killer. But because of all,

all . . . this,' she pointed to the nearest newspaper, 'bloody shambles, you will all have to be questioned as to your whereabouts on certain dates. Of course there is a big possibility that the White Rose Killer has left Dublin and is now in Houghton. We do, however, need to verify each of your alibis, to rule yer all out of the investigation. As I say, I don't believe for a second that this killer has anything to do with this station, but we have to dot the is and cross the ts, as the saying goes. Any questions?'

She watched her officers as they glanced around each other, then Dinwall raised a hand. 'Who will be investigating us?'

Lorraine nodded over at Luke and Carter. 'DS Daniels and PC Carter. And I don't want yer giving them any trouble, I know they're hating this as much as you are.'

Dinwall snorted. 'Should have guessed the chosen two.'

Lorraine glared at him for a long moment until he stopped smirking and looked away. Then she said to the group, 'OK, show of hands. Who thinks Daniels would have attacked his own daughter? Who thinks Carter – this is *Carter* we're talking about, would have set the fire alarm off, waiting outside the club, and then – with his bare hands – beat Selina so badly she was in hospital for concussion. Go on, I want to see who thinks Daniels and Carter had anything to do with this.'

There were grumblings from the assembled group but no one put their hands up. 'Good,' said Lorraine. 'Any more questions?'

Sanderson raised his hand, 'Just one,' he said. Lorraine nodded and he went on. 'How the hell did Kate Mulberry get access to this information?'

Lorraine looked over at Carter who looked as if he was going to faint. She then turned her gaze back to Sanderson. 'Your guess is as good as mine.'

*

226

Lorraine had just entered her office when Carter came bursting in. 'You've got to believe me, boss, I didn't say a word to her, I swear I didn't.'

Lorraine indicated that Carter should sit. He did, but he looked sweaty and slightly green. 'Since I read the article I've been going over it and over it in my mind, but I still don't remember saying anything to her—'

Lorraine waved her hand. 'I believe yer Carter. I don't think it was anything yer did. In fact, I think Kate did a bit of "investigative reporting",' Lorraine made quotation marks in the air with her index fingers. 'The other day, she came into my office just as I had finished reading the e-mail from Collins. I popped a folder on it so that Ms Stickybeak couldn't read it, but when I came back, the door was ajar. I could have sworn I shut it on the way to the interview, but I wasn't sure. When I looked at my desk, it seemed to have been pretty much the way I left it . . .'

'Yer think she came in and read the e-mail?' said Carter. 'Shit.'

'Exactly. And yer told me yesterday that she was fishing for information about that poor Jane Doe, so she obviously put two and two together . . .'

Carter shook his head. 'Yer know, as much as I'm pissed off with her, you've got to admire Kate's balls . . .'

Lorraine grinned, 'You're a sucker for a pretty face,' and laughed when Carter, red-faced, denied any such feeling for Kate Mulberry.

A moment later, a PC stuck her head round the door. 'I've got an Inspector Harry Collins on the line,' she said to Lorraine. 'He's insisting that he talk to yer, now.'

'Put him through.' As she picked up the phone, Carter left his chair and shut the door behind him.'

'What the *fuck* do you think you're playing at?' came a voice down the other end of the line. 'My officers and I have been keeping this case under wraps for the past six months, and then you go and blow it all out of the water.'

'Inspector Collins, I am sorry, but the information was leaked out of my department . . .'

'Leaked,' roared the voice on the other end of the line. 'Well, I expect you'll be finding out and firing the little bastard who leaked this to the press, then.'

'It wasn't quite like that,' Lorraine explained. 'Against my better judgement, my super had a reporter tail my department for the last few days. It was supposed to be a look at the day-to-day running of a department . . .'

Collins cut Lorraine off. 'Let me get this straight,' his voice low but Lorraine could hear the anger in it. 'You had a *reporter* actually inside the station.'

'It wasn't my idea, and we kept everything as far away from her as we possibly could. But, with everything going on, we couldn't keep an eye on her twenty-four seven.'

'You're just asking for trouble, having a reporter at the station.'

'That's what I said to my super.'

There was silence on the other end of the line and then Collins sighed. In a voice more weary than angry he said, 'I heard about the Jane Doe. White Rose Killer or copycat, I'm sorry you've got this hell on your doorstep. He's a slippery bugger and no mistake. But I'm afraid that this is as far as our collaboration goes. I can't have anyone jeopardising our investigation, and I don't know how far you've put us back.'

'I'm sorry yer feel that way, Inspector,' Lorraine said, feeling guilty.

'Good luck with it all. I hope you find the bastard soon.'

'I hope you do too,' Lorraine said before she hung up the phone.

*

228

Lorraine was waiting outside of the hospital for Luke and Selina, wishing desperately for a cigarette. Would the longing for nicotine never leave her? The day had been difficult. She hadn't been able to get any work done as she was fielding calls from radio stations, newspapers and television reporters about the White Rose Killer. At one point Carter had knocked on her office door to tell her that Kate Mulberry was at the front desk, wanting to have a word, and Lorraine took great pleasure in telling Carter to tell Kate that she would be speaking to all other reporters, but not her. *I must get the name of that reporter, who was it? Alf Johnson, that's right, and give him an interview*, she thought vindictively. She rummaged in the glove compartment and breathed a sigh of relief when she found an old, already chewed pencil.

She stuck it in her mouth, and a moment later she spotted Luke coming out of the door, Selina hanging on to his arm and Luke carrying her things with his other hand. She flicked the sun visor down and fluffed at her hair, catching sight of the pencil in her mouth.

'Ugh.' She took it out and threw it back into the glove compartment.

'Hi, love,' she said to Selina as they reached the car.

Selina looked pale but smiled as she replied, 'Hello Lorraine,' and got into the back seat of her car. The front passenger door opened, and Luke planted himself down beside her.

'Home, boss,' Luke said as Lorraine pulled away. 'And if you would like to stop off at a pizza place, my daughter and I would love you to come to supper.'

'Sounds good to me. What topping?'

'You choose, Lorraine.'

'There's one just up ahead, will that do?'

Lorraine pulled outside the pizza joint, and Selina said, 'Give me the money. I'll go in and get it.'

'Are yer sure,' Lorraine said worriedly. 'Yer still moving a bit slowly . . .'

A look passed between father and daughter and then Luke said, with a smile, 'Aren't I the one who's meant to be overprotective and controlling? Besides, I can look out for Selina from here.' He reached into the back pocket of his trousers and drew out his wallet. Pulling out a couple of notes, he said, 'Lorraine, it's your choice.'

Lorraine shrugged, 'Pepperoni, I guess . . .'

Selina grabbed the cash and carefully got out of the car. As she pulled open the door to the takeaway and walked through it, Lorraine said, 'She's a changed girl, Luke, and not just because of the attack.'

Luke smiled. 'I know. You'll be pleased to learn that I've been taking your advice, trying not to be too overprotective, giving her some space, just like yer said I should.'

A cloud passed over Luke's face. 'I just hope that she'll be OK, with this killer on the loose . . .'

Without thinking, Lorraine placed her hand on Luke's thigh. 'We'll get him, Luke. We'll make sure that the bastard gets what's coming to him.' Then, she gasped slightly, as she realised that she had touched Luke, the first time for days.

Luke placed his hand on hers and held it. They didn't say anything for moments, Lorraine didn't dare to break the atmosphere with words. Luke finally lifted his eyes to hers and said, 'Lorraine, there is something that I've been wanting to say to yer for days, but I couldn't work up the nerve. I am truly sorry. I'm sorry for pushing yer away when I should have listened to what yer said. I know yer were just trying to help, and yer were right. I'm sorry for being a stupid, insensitive idiot, Lorraine. And . . . I love you.' He turned her palm over and kissed it. 'I want yer back, Lorraine, that is, if yer'll have me.'

Lorraine looked down. Her heart was flying in her chest.

Despite the dreadful day, she felt so happy, and tears pricked her eyes. She blinked them away, looked up and saw that Luke's eyes were also misted over. She laughed. 'Look at us, we're a couple of goons,' she smiled broadly. 'I love yer too, Luke, and of course I'll have yer back, there was never any question of that.'

Luke smiled and cupped her face in his hands. He leant over and gave her the lightest of kisses on the lips, she kissed him back, feeling like a lovesick teenager. Suddenly, there was a knock on the window. They broke apart.

Selina was at the window, grinning broadly. 'Thank *God*,' she said as she got into the back seat. 'Finally things are back to normal. Now, can we go home?'

Lorraine started the car and, grinning broadly, headed towards Luke's house.

Mickey threw a stone at Robbie's bedroom window.

'God I can practically hear them all snoring,' he muttered when he got no reaction.

Five stones later Robbie's sleepy face peered through the open curtain. Then Mickey saw that the bedroom light had been switched on, then the stairlight, then the sound of the lock being pulled back.

'Jesus, what the—?' Robbie said, looking at Mickey swaying in the doorway. He reached out his hand and helped his friend over the threshold. Then, after re-locking the door, he silently got behind him and pushed him upstairs into the bathroom. 'What happened to yer face?' Robbie asked, but Mickey waved him away and closed the bathroom door behind him.

Ten minutes later, washed and wearing one of Robbie's T-shirts, he entered the bedroom. Darren was sitting cross-legged on his bed and Robbie was rolling the sleeping bag out on the floor.

'I'm sorry mate, I didn't dare go home. Not this late, not like this. Me mam would have a fit. I've been walking and hiding for hours, me feet are killing me,' he sighed heartily and squinted pitifully at Robbie and Darren.

'And then a cop car came flying round the corner. I very nearly died.'

'Yeah, well yer do look a bit wobbly but not quite dead yet . . .' Robbie replied, sitting down on his bed. Mickey gratefully sank down next to him, feeling as if he would never regain enough energy to get back up again. 'Do yer think we should maybes go to the hospital?' Robbie said worriedly. 'Yer eyes look really bad and yer could get an infection in them if yer not careful.'

'*No!*' Mickey said in a panicked voice that sent alarm bells off in Robbie's head.

'Does it hurt?' Darren winced in sympathy. 'And what happened?'

'Eccles jumped me after I went to see Selina today.'

'The bastard.' Robbie punched his left palm. 'There's no need for him to do that.'

'Surely yer hit him back Mickey, say yer hit him back.' Darren pleaded.

Whatever they were expecting from Mickey, it wasn't him bursting into tears.

Robbie and Darren looked at each other and Robbie felt an icy feeling in the pit of his stomach. He'd been friends with Mickey since infant school, and knew him inside out. He was clumsy, very naive, and a lot braver than he gave himself credit for. For him to react like this meant big.

'OK, just take it easy, what exactly happened?

'Bastard, bastard, bastard.' It was as if Mickey couldn't sit still with agitation. He jumped up from Robbie's bed, and despite his sore and blistered feet, he paced the floor, backwards and forwards, over and over.

'Mickey, stop!' Robbie said, clearly scared for his friend. He got up and grabbed Mickey by the shoulders. 'What the hell's wrong with yer? Spit it out.'

'It's Eccles,' Mickey gulped. 'I think I killed him.'

'How dare she.' He snatched up the *Sunderland Echo* from the table and started tearing it into shreds.

'This is what you'll get.

'This.

'And this.

'And this . . . Ha.'

25

'Oh God,' Lorraine said to herself. It was eight o'clock in the morning and, although she had spent the night at Luke's, she had gone back home to shower and change. They decided to keep their relationship low-key, to avoid any station gossip. Now, as she pulled into the car park, she saw a gaggle of reporters crowded outside the entrance. She groaned to herself. *Exactly what I need.*

But no need to antagonise them either. She thought back to a media-training course that Clark had sent her on a couple of years ago. Friendly deflection of questions rather than coming back with a 'no comment' or insulting them was the way to go. She took a deep breath, grabbed her bag and got out of the car, girding herself for the onslaught.

When she slammed her car door, the reporters, like a pack of animals, turned as one towards the noise and ran towards their prey. Lorraine's normal stride was broken as the horde of reporters, thrusting microphones and recorders in her face, forced her to slow her pace. Questions were yelled at her. Lorraine held up her hand, 'One at a time, please.'

A red-faced young man with an accent that sounded as if he

came from Essex asked, 'Inspector Hunt, how concerned are yer that a serial killer seems to be targeting the young women of Houghton?'

Well, duh, Lorraine thought to herself, but turned to the reporter and said. 'Of course, I'm very concerned with the suspicious death of anyone. But I don't think we can call this a serial killing, not yet, anyway. There's only been one body . . .'

'With a remarkable similarity to the recent murders in Ireland,' a dark-haired woman with a Scottish accent said.

'We're following up on all leads, of course, but at the moment, I don't have anything more than what has already been in the papers.' Lorraine was almost at the entrance of the station by now. She looked at the double doors as if they led into the promised land.

'Inspector Hunt.' Lorraine didn't have to turn her head. She recognised the voice. *Kate Mulberry, the cheeky little . . .* Lorraine turned to Kate, with a forced smile on her face. 'What is your reaction to the news that, if this is a copycat killer, he might have some connection with your station.'

The little bitch. With a forced smile, and through gritted teeth, Lorraine answered, 'Well, I wouldn't believe everything yer read in the pages,' in a tone she hoped was light and breezy.

The reporters – all except Kate, she noticed – gave a laugh and Lorraine, now at the entrance to the station said, 'We'll be releasing a statement as soon as we have any information to give yer. For the time being, however, I'd appreciate it if yer didn't disturb the running of the station and let us get on with our jobs.'

And with that, she entered the relative peace and quiet of the station.

'What the hell is the matter with you?' Lorraine said an hour or so later as she almost bumped into Dinwall in the corridor.

'It can't just be the reporters outside. Yer've been moaning around with a face like a slapped arse for over a week now.'

Dinwall shrugged, 'It's a long story boss. And that report in the paper,' he shrugged. 'People have been looking at me strangely.'

'Have yer got something to tell me, Dinwall?' Lorraine joked, then wished she hadn't when she saw Dinwall's face. 'Listen, yer paranoid bastard, get yer coat. It's freezing out there. I'm on me way to see Scottie, yer might as well come.'

'Yeah OK. That's exactly what I need. The morgue will cheer me up no end.'

Lorraine ignored him, and waited while he ducked into the cloakroom and grabbed his overcoat.

'Brrr,' he complained when they were in the car park. 'It's bloody freezing out here.'

'For Christ's sake, Dinwall, all yer can do is moan moan moan.'

Lorraine was pleased to see that most of the reporters had left, either because of the cold or because of her short statement that she would let them have information when she could. The few who were there looked at her hopefully, but she put them off with a brief shake of her head. She had just pointed her keys at the car and heard the electronic beep to tell her that it was unlocked when she heard the tap of heels behind her. 'Inspector Hunt,' Kate Mulberry said. 'Can I have a word?'

Dinwall, when he saw who it was, gave an audible moan, and sat himself in the front seat. Lorraine stopped and turned to the young woman. 'Yer really pushing yer luck, Mulberry.'

'I just wondered, you know, because we have this rapport . . .' Lorraine raised a sarcastic eyebrow, Kate's smile faltered, 'that I could, you know, ride with you and . . .'

'Yer really think that after the stunt yer pulled that I'd let yer do that? You looked at confidential documents that yer had no business to see, and then yer disclosed them to the public. I have no idea yet what sort of panic you've caused, or how much yer article has damaged our enquiry, but I have no doubt in my mind that what yer did was hugely irresponsible.'

Kate's eyes took on that steely gaze that Lorraine recognised from the first time she met her. 'I happen to believe, Inspector, that the public has a right to know . . .'

Lorraine nodded her head. 'That's great,' she said sarcastically. 'Freedom of the press an' all. Just remember that when yer lying in bed at night, when another young girl has been murdered. I just hope your career is worth it.' Turning her back on Mulberry, Lorraine got into her car and drove off.

They left the police station, and in complete silence, drove past the school, turned left at the roundabout and got on the road to Sunderland. Dinwall's mood leaked into the car, and Lorraine was getting sick of it. 'OK, enough, spit it out,' Lorraine said.

Dinwall sighed. 'It's me wife. She thinks I'm having an affair.' Dinwall twisted in his seat and looked at Lorraine, 'But I swear to yer, boss, on everything holy, I am not.'

'Dinwall,' Lorraine shook her head. 'Yer got to have realised that your womanising was gonna catch up with yer someday. How many times have yer got away with it?'

Dinwall was silent for a moment, then suddenly said, 'But she's got nothing to worry about. I haven't touched anyone else, not for months.'

Lorraine believed him, not that that was any excuse for his past behaviour. 'So why has she suddenly started to give yer grief?'

He shrugged, 'Haven't the foggiest.'

'Come on, Lynn's not stupid, there must be something that's set her off.'

'Listen, there's nothing going on at the moment.' Lorraine could see that Dinwall was adamant.

'Well, yer gonna have to do some serious greasing to get back into Lynn's good books and that's a fact.'

'I wish yer would tell me how, cos me bloody back's going crackers with sleeping on the flaming settee.'

They pulled into Sunderland General and Lorraine said over the top of the car to Dinwall who was fastening his overcoat. 'Yer just gonna have to convince her that you'll never do it again.'

'But I haven't done anything,' Dinwall said, frustration showing in his face.

'But yer have before.' Lorraine turned towards the hospital and said over her shoulder, 'Take her some flowers.'

'Then she'll think I'm guilty.'

'Yer can't win OK, whatever yer do she's never gonna believe yer until yer get her trust back.'

Dinwall nodded glumly as they entered the hospital. A few minutes later they were outside Scottie's domain.

'Hello, lovely lady,' Scottie said, when Lorraine opened the door. 'Come in come in.'

Smiling, she entered and spotted Edna at her usual post. 'All better now Edna?'

'Getting there, but there's more life in here than there is at home, if yer know what I mean,' she sniffed loudly.

'Right then Scottie, what have yer got for me?' Lorraine asked, as she slipped her bag from her shoulder and placed it on the floor at her feet, the long leather handles making a slapping sound on the tiled floor.

Scottie pursed his lips and shook his head. 'Sorry love, but aside from what I already established at the scene, it's a big fat nothing.'

'Christ.'

'Yep . . . All I can say is who ever this guy is, he's good . . .

And I mean really good. He didn't leave one trace of his DNA on the body. It also looks as if everything was done calmly and clinically.' He rubbed the bridge of his nose for a moment before going on. 'It's as if it were a job he prided himself in doing perfectly. If yer know what I mean . . . Or it could even be a compulsion that everything had to be perfect. But I've got to say, there must have been a lot of blood. There's no way whoever did this could get away without getting blood somewhere.'

'So,' Lorraine shrugged. 'What yer saying is that we're looking for this really neat guy who tidies everything up as he goes along.' She shivered. 'What about the fact that he punches them out beforehand?'

Scottie shrugged. 'It's just speculation, but I suspect that he's full of rage. By hitting them, he gets rid of his aggression, so that he can fulfil his other compulsion, that of cutting out their hearts.'

Lorraine shuddered. 'God, that's creepy.' She walked around the body, paused once or twice to look from different angles. She reached the girl's feet, noticed the Jane Doe tag and felt a sense of pity for the young life that had been so cruelly wasted.

Dinwall uncrossed his legs and moved over to the side, giving Lorraine room to pass. When she was a foot away from Scottie she looked at him and said, 'I'm almost certain she was murdered on the spot, she's quite a heavy girl actually, to have been carried any distance. Plus with all the rain we've had lately the ground's pretty soft and all we've turned up so far are a few dog prints. If he'd been carrying her, I don't care how bloody careful he was, he'd have left some sort of print.'

'Yeah, I agree with yer.' Scottie said.

She sighed and looked at Scottie, 'Any other clues so that we might find out who she is?'

'One thing,' Scottie turned over the girl's arms. 'Track

marks. Not recent, but she was definitely a user at some point.'

Like Selina, Lorraine thought. But there the similarities ended. Selina was dark and small, while this girl was mousey and large. *But then*, she thought, *she's not that much older than Selina*. Could the link be the drug users' support group that Hanson took? He might be able to identify her at least.

Lorraine looked at Scottie, 'OK then, have you got any pictures of her yet?'

As if she'd predicted Lorraine's next question Edna already had a drawer open. 'Of course, here you go.' She handed a pale-green cardboard folder over to Dinwall who passed it to Lorraine.

Lorraine opened the folder. The face of the girl on the cold metal slab looked up at her. She studied it for a moment, wondering what her secrets were. Did she know the man who had murdered her? Or was this just a random killing? Could she have been connected with the club in any way?

She closed the folder with a snap. 'Right I've just had an idea . . . It's a long shot, but . . .' her words trailed off. She said her goodbyes, grabbed her shoulder bag and practically pushed Dinwall out the door.

26

Emma Lumsdon was sitting on the step, her bandaged foot stretched out in front of her. She had, so she claimed to her mother, fallen off the swing in the park and hurt it, and how can yer hobble to school and do P.E. with a bad foot? Much better to stay at home and read the latest *Harry Potter*, just to be on the safe side.

However, the way she jumped up a few minutes later and ran up the stairs proved she was fit enough to do a marathon.

'It's the Robocop woman,' she yelled, bursting into Robbie's room.

'Oh my God,' Mickey said, the blood draining from his face.

'OK,' Robbie took hold of Emma's shoulders and turned her round, 'Go downstairs and keep her occupied. If she asks for Mickey, yer haven't seen him for ages. Right?'

She shrugged her brother off. 'Might.'

'No mights about it, missy. Yer will if yer know what's good for yer.'

Mickey grabbed hold of Robbie's T-shirt. 'They must have found the body. What am I gonna do Robbie, what am I gonna do? She knows it's me . . . What am I gonna do?' Mickey's eyes flooded with tears as he became more hysterical by the second.

Robbie prised his friend's fingers open. 'Shh Mickey, we don't know what she's here for. It, it . . . It could be anything.'

'What, like she's popping in for a cuppa . . . I'll bet.' He sniffed loudly then followed with a huge sob.

'Stop it Mickey.' Robbie spotted Emma hovering in the doorway. 'You still here?'

She stuck her tongue out, but headed downstairs, to the spot she'd recently vacated.

'Hello Emma.' Lorraine smiled, as she walked up the path.

''Lo,' Emma replied.

'Is your brother in?'

'Which one?'

'Robbie,' Lorraine answered patiently.

Emma shrugged. 'Probs.'

Robbie arrived downstairs just then. 'Hi,' he said, giving Lorraine a small wave before putting his hand in his pocket.

'Hello Robbie, I was just wondering if yer friend Mickey Carson was around?' Without waiting for answer, she went on in a no nonsense tone. 'I have spoken to his mother. She says she hasn't seen him for a few days although she's had regular texts from him saying that he's here. And I have no reason to think she might be lying.'

Robbie swallowed hard. Lying was not something he was good at.

He pictured Mickey upstairs: terrified, battered and bruised and convinced they would lock him up and throw the key away. Even though it sounded as if it was self-defence and an accident.

He felt the palms of his hands begin to sweat and knew that he would fail the oldest crappiest lie detector ever invented. But he couldn't let Mickey down, whatever the consequences. 'Erm, no actually. Haven't seen him since the other day, when yer lot, er, questioned him.' He knew she was weighing him up, wondering whether to believe him or not. He smiled, hoping it was a convincing one, then when she didn't smile back he felt a worm start to crawl in the pit of his stomach. Jesus Christ. What would he get for obstructing the police?

'You sure about that?' Lorraine's voice convinced Robbie that she knew that he was lying through his eye teeth.

Robbie rushed on, 'Sorry, but I really haven't seen him . . . And I'm er, due at the job centre in a minute. Some sort of contract work coming up. I, er, don't want to miss it.'

Good God where did I get that from? Robbie wondered while Lorraine continued to stare at him.

After what seemed like an age, in which Robbie died a thousand deaths, Lorraine said. 'OK, Robbie, I won't keep yer then. But give him a message if yer do see him.'

'Sure.'

'Tell him he's in not in any trouble. I just want him to look at some pictures of someone who might have been there on the night at the rave. OK?'

'Yeah, yeah cool.' Robbie felt instantly relieved that she was not going to arrest him on the spot. He added quickly, 'But I don't know when that'll be.'

Yeah all right, Lorraine thought. *Methinks you doth protest too much, young man.*

'Also tell him that if I have to come looking for him again he *will* be in trouble,' she glanced at her watch. 'Yer have one hour to get him to the station.'

'What?' Robbie's mouth hung open for a moment, then he spluttered.' B— But I tol —'

'One hour,' Lorraine repeated, then turned and walked down the path.

She entered the station to find just about everyone in a flap. Spotting her as he came through the door, Carter hurried over to her.

'Boss.'

Lorraine's heart sank. Just the way he spoke and the buzz in the entrance lobby and the fact that she'd noticed the dog patrol pulling away as she came in, had her nerves jingling.

'OK, what?'

'I've been trying to phone yer for half an hour.'

'Shit, gotta get a new phone, so what's up?'

'There's been another body found, on the other side of the kids' home.'

'Anything to say it's the same murderer?' she looked intently at Carter, her blood chilling in her veins.

'Same MO.'

Lorraine groaned. It now looked certain that they definitely had a serial killer on their hands.

Robbie had been trying to get Mickey to see sense for fifteen minutes, but he was adamant. 'Can't do it, she's playing tricks. I know they're gonna arrest me soon as I walk in the door.' Mickey was shaking.

'Honest Mickey, she just wants yer to look at some pics. She certainly didn't go on as if yer were wanted for murder, and that's a fact. And to be honest, Mickey, yer don't know for a fact that he's dead.' Robbie shook his head. 'I reckon yer must have just knocked him out. Then he woke up and crawled back to whatever hole he came out of in the first place. Come on mate, think about it, somebody would have found him by now if he was still lying there. Yer not the only one who takes short cuts to the bus stop yer know.'

Mickey still looked unconvinced. 'I don't know, he looked dead to me . . . Robbie, what should I do?'

'Well, yer'll have to go to the cop shop, there's nowt else yer can do, cos if yer don't she'll only come back, yer can bet yer life on that one. Don't fret, I'll come with yer, there's no way I would let yer go alone.'

'But look at the state of me man . . . I look like a . . . a . . .'

'Yeah, yer look like a . . .'

Mickey held his hand up, palm out. 'Enough of that.'

Robbie couldn't help but grin. 'Come on it'll be . . .'

Whatever Robbie was going to say next was stopped by a crackling noise that sounded suspiciously like someone raking out the last crisp in the packet.

'Emma,' Robbie muttered.

Quickly he moved past Mickey and pulled the door open just in time to catch Emma hurrying down the stairs. 'Yer nosy little brat,' Robbie shouted, as he went after her.

He caught her at the bottom of the stairs just before she could disappear into a cupboard. He grabbed her shoulder and spun her round.

'What did yer hear?'

'Nothing,' she replied sullenly.

'Don't tell lies, Emma. What did yer hear?'

'Mickey thinks somebody's dead,' her lip trembled as she looked at her brother. 'Is Mickey a murderer? Is he gonna murder us?'

'No, no don't be silly . . . Now listen Emma, yer mustn't tell anybody what yer heard, promise.'

Emma hung her head.

'Emma, look at me,' he lifted her chin up so that she was forced to look him in the face. 'Yer know Mickey wouldn't hurt anybody; it was an accident. OK? But until we find out exactly what did happen and if anybody's even hurt at all, yer've gotta keep quiet, OK?'

Slowly she nodded.

'Promise?'

'Promise.'

Robbie heaved a sigh of relief. It was rare that Emma promised anything or readily co-operated with anyone, but he knew, as young as she was, that her word was good.

'Right, you'll have to go over Sandra's, cos mam's at her AA meeting OK?'

'Don't want to,' she stuck her chin out.

'But yer have to. I have to go with Mickey, and yer can't stop here by yerself . . . So for once do as yer told, OK?' He opened the door and ushered her out. 'Remember, yer promised,' he said as she passed.

He watched as she crossed the road, dragging her foot and limping badly, and smiled. There had been no sign of a limp when she'd run down the stairs.

27

Lorraine, with Scottie by her side, watched as the body of another young girl was carried into the ambulance. Dinwall was rummaging around, lifting debris off the ground with a long bare twig.

'It's exactly the same as the other one, Lorraine, and this guy's starting to drive me nuts. I know for a fact before I start and however hard I look, I'm not gonna find anything.'

Lorraine and Scottie swung round as the sound of screaming heading in their direction, grew louder and louder.

A fair-haired, middle-aged woman wearing a denim jacket and long flowing black skirt, followed by two small boys, was running towards them. Three other women, coats flying behind them and all three shouting at the woman in denim, were trying their best to catch up to her.

Everyone around had frozen into place as they watched the runners descend on them.

'*No!*' the woman screamed, setting Lorraine's teeth on edge, as she reached her. 'Say it's not her, say it's not my girl . . . Please, tell me it's not her . . .'

Dread swept over Lorraine. Obviously this woman thought it was her daughter they had just sent to the morgue.

The woman started pounding her fists on Scottie's chest. 'Tell me it's not my Amy.'

Then, almost in slow motion, she slid down Scottie's body, until she came to her hands and knees on the ground. Her sobs tore the hearts out of everybody standing there.

Oh no, sweet Jesus, Lorraine thought, and a sudden wave of horror ran through her. *It's Selina's friend. It's Amy. I thought there was something familiar about her. If the poor girl's face had not been so battered and bloody I would have recognised her right off. Oh, the poor woman.*

Lorraine and Scottie bent down to help the woman to her feet as her friends reached them. 'Say it's not my Amy, please say it's not so,' she begged between huge heart-rending sobs.

But no one could answer her.

Robbie and Mickey had reached the police station within the hour. They had been told by a uniformed policewoman to wait in a side room. Detective Inspector Hunt was out on a call and she would get back as soon as she could, meanwhile they were to stay put.

'How much longer?' Mickey said heaving a huge sigh, when they had been there for at least three-quarters of a hour.

Robbie, sitting with his head in his hands, declined to answer. Mickey had asked the same question at least forty times.

The door finally opened a few minutes later, but it was not who they expected. Instead, it was Detective Sergeant Luke Daniels.

Mickey died inside. *Shit.*

Luke moved to the interview table, pulled out a chair and sat down, resting his hands on top of the table, but not once taking his eyes off Mickey.

'Detective Inspector Hunt has been delayed. She asked me to interview you.'

'Wh— What for?' Mickey's throat dried up and he developed a nervous cough.

Luke opened a large brown envelope he'd been carrying and emptied half a dozen photographs on to the tabletop. 'Would yer take a look at these photographs and tell me if you saw her in the club the night the fire alarm went off, or any time before or after. Then yer can tell me where yer got the black eyes from, and why you have not been round to visit my daughter, who is giving me real grief about you.'

Mickey coughed into his hand, 'Er, well yer see. It's like this . . .'

'Photos first,' Luke said sternly as he pushed them closer to the edge of the table. 'Then yer can tell me why yer look like a panda.'

Eager to please, anything to get out of there, Mickey picked the first one up, stared at it, then looked suspiciously at Luke. 'Why are her eyes closed?'

Robbie stole a quick glance over Mickey's shoulder, let out a gasp and said quietly, 'She's dead.' He looked at Luke, 'Isn't she?' Luke nodded.

Seeing this confirmation, Mickey hastily dropped the photograph and shook his head adamantly, 'Never seen her before.'

'Never?'

Mickey shook his head again. 'Never.'

'Robbie?'

'Sorry, me neither.'

'OK all right, do youse two know any of the kids that grew up in the children's home?'

'Yeah, a couple were in our year at school,' Robbie answered. Mickey was still traumatised by the dead girl's photograph, and was finding it difficult to focus.

'Good kids? Bad kids?'

Robbie shrugged, 'They were all right mostly, liked to kick a ball around, though Tom wasn't as good as he thought he was.'

'Any idea where they are now?'

'I know that Tom's left Houghton, don't know where the other ones are.'

'They didn't talk to yer about the home, did they? Did they ever have any problems?' The boys looked bemused, and shook their heads.

Luke tapped the table again, it had been a long shot, sometimes they paid off sometimes they didn't. He looked at Mickey and wondered whether or not to tell him that there was another body found, that of Selina's friend, Amy. Perhaps now wasn't a good time. He looked shattered by the picture that he had just seen. He stared at Mickey for a moment and watched as he squirmed. Shaking his head he thought, *Poor bugger, what a bloody mess, somebody's definitely had it in for the kid, without doubt.* 'OK, who beat yer up?'

Mickey froze, he'd been dreading the question coming. He sighed, then managed to sputter, 'I, er I tripped over, that's right, that's what I did.'

'Yeah, right.' If his daughter was going to go out with anyone, better that person be a useless liar than a really good one. He could see through Mickey as clearly as if he had been made of glass.

'No, honest, didn't I, Robbie?'

'Yes, oh yes, man,' Robbie replied, nodding his head convincingly, as his brain tried to catch up with his mouth and co-ordinate what was coming out of it. 'So spectacular, really man. He tripped at the top of the stairs and bounced all the way to the bottom and hit his nose on the banister . . . Better than a circus act.'

Luke smiled, plausible story but highly unlikely. But it was clear he wasn't going to get anything more out of Robbie. He sighed. 'OK, come with me.'

251

Mickey started to shake, and even Robbie was starting to look worried. 'Where, where we going?' Mickey managed.

'To visit my daughter, OK? I need some peace and it seems you seeing her is the only way I'm gonna get any. But don't look too happy about it, there will be a police officer in attendance at all times.'

'Cool. Yeah.' Mickey felt so relieved that his head was in danger of falling off he was nodding it so hard.

'What about me?' Robbie asked.

Luke raised an eyebrow, 'Don't yer want to see her?'

'Well, er, yes. But I'm not gonna play gooseberry to the love birds am I?' Luke made a sort of growling choking sound in the back of his throat.

'Tell yer what,' Robbie added hastily. 'Yer can drop me at the Broadway, if yer want to, that is.'

'Yeah, right. Get walking, it's only fifty yards away.'

'So it is.' Robbie grinned. 'Er, how do I get outta here?'

'Follow me.' Luke turned at the doorway, Mickey was still sitting in his seat. 'You an' all.'

'Oh right.' He jumped up and followed Luke and Robbie out of the door. It was drizzling rain outside but to Mickey the sun was shining. He was going to see Selina.

He spreads the polish evenly on the cloth and lovingly applies it to his shoes and begins the serious business of bringing a shine sharp enough to use as a mirror.

But no matter how hard he polishes, it is not good enough. It never had been. Nothing he did ever pleased the blonde bitch. He rubbed harder, his thoughts boiling in his head.

Why, he asked himself for the countless time, *did she stand back and let it happen?*

He picks up the photograph and stares. The woman in the photo is wearing blue jeans, her long hair tied back in a ponytail, she is walking along a country road, her dog by her side.

She was so beautiful, yet so treacherous, the bitch. Just like the one now, except the one now isn't half as frightened as she ought to be.

But I'll scare her, he thought to himself, *I'll let her know who's really the boss of this town. She'll pay for what she did to me. They'll all pay.*

28

Amy Knowles did belong to the woman in denim and as Lorraine and Luke walked up the path through the neatly kept garden to the blue front door, Lorraine couldn't help but feel slightly guilty for feeling so happy that she and Luke were together again.

Shaking herself inwardly, she prepared herself for the job in hand. It was always harrowing to meet the parents of someone who had been the victim of such a brutal murder. But Lorraine always reminded herself that however harrowing it was for her, it was a hundred times worse for the loved ones of the victims.

She knocked on the door. It was opened a moment later by a small, slim man with a large mole on his left cheek, and dried blood in his right ear. It was obvious that the man had been crying. The red eyes and the slight sob as he opened the door, convinced Lorraine that this obviously heartbroken man was Amy's father. But what was the story with the blood in the ear?

'Mr Knowles?' Lorraine said gently. 'I'm Detective Inspector Lorraine Hunt, and this is Detective Sergeant Luke

Daniels. Can we come in? I'd like to speak to yer about yer daughter.'

Mr Knowles nodded, and ushered them into his house. 'I'm so sorry for your loss,' Lorraine said as they followed him down the hallway. He didn't answer, just shook his head, as if he himself couldn't quite believe what he was going through.

The sitting room was very clean and tidy. Lorraine got the impression that it was kept for best, the room the family sat in when people came to visit. The actual, day-to-day living went on elsewhere. Mr Knowles asked them to sit down. The house was strangely quiet and there was no sign of Amy's mother and the two small boys.

'Would,' he cleared his throat, 'excuse me, would you like tea?'

Knowing that sometimes the recently bereaved needed to keep occupied, Lorraine and Luke both said yes.

As tea-making noises came from the kitchen, Luke picked up the newspaper that Mr Knowles had so obviously been trying to read and Lorraine looked around the sitting room. It was simply furnished with plain cream walls with a matching sofa and a red carpet. She was surprised to see a piano against the back wall, long time since she'd seen one of them in someone's living room.

Mr Knowles arrived back with a tea tray, two white china cups on saucers, and a matching milk and sugar bowl. Luke did the honours and handed Lorraine her cup. When Mr Knowles sat down Lorraine took a sip, smiled at him and was about to speak when Mr Knowles broached the subject of his daughter himself.

'My Amy loves – loved – her tea. She loved music as well,' he continued, turning his head to look at the piano. 'Believe it or not, she could bang a hell of a tune out of that old thing. All this silly bang bang modern stuff as well . . . It belonged to my wife's mother, the piano.'

'Where is your wife Mr Knowles?' Luke asked.

For a moment he stared at them, his eyes vacant. Lorraine didn't press him, just waited until he was ready to speak. He came back from whichever memory his mind had played back to him, gave a weak smile then said, 'She's at her sister's. Her and the boys.' Unconsciously he touched his ear, the one with the dried blood. 'She's . . . the doctor has sedated her, she gets violent sometimes, only when she gets upset, mind you,' he rushed in his wife's defence as again he touched his ear.

'All right Mr Knowles, I am sorry to bother you at a time like this . . .'

'I only came back because you phoned to say you were coming. My wife's sister Kath is mostly sorting things. We haven't told the boys yet that their mam is dead.'

Lorraine sat back in her chair. She felt awful for the poor family. *Those boys are gonna grow up with some legacy, with a mother dead. I will catch the bastard responsible and he will go down forever if I have my way.*

'Mr Knowles, I should let yer know that Sergeant Daniels and I did know Amy. She was a friend of Luke's daughter, Selina.'

'Oh,' Mr Knowles said gently. 'Selina. I only met her the once. But Amy is—' he caught himself on the tense, '—was, very fond of her. I heard about her trouble. Is she better now, Sergeant Daniels?'

'Yes, she's out of hospital now, Mr Knowles, thanks for asking.'

'How old was Amy, Mr Knowles?' Lorraine asked.

'Twenty-three. She had the boys when she was eighteen and couldn't cope, not with twins when she was on her own. And then she got into trouble with a bad lot. But she got herself out of that, didn't she? That was how she met Selina, at that support group?' Mr Knowles was answering Lorraine, but his eyes were on Luke. His voice was steady, though his eyes were filling with tears.

Lorraine glanced at the photograph on the mantelpiece. The boys were about two and Amy, who would have been twenty, looked about fifteen.

'You are gonna catch him, aren't yer?'

'We'll do our best,' Lorraine replied, 'but any help yer could give us would be much appreciated.'

'OK, well yer know that club what was in the paper the other day?'

Lorraine nodded.

'She liked going there, she went the other night cos she liked the DJ, said he was the best around.'

'OK then,' Lorraine said. Luke was silent, staring at the photograph of Amy and her boys. 'Can yer think of anything else? Has she recently upset anyone?'

He shook his head. 'Sorry no, but if she had, it would have been a pretty spectacular upset, don't yer think, to do that to her . . . Jesus Christ,' he dabbed at his eyes as he started crying softly.

Lorraine sighed, she rose and gently touched Mr Knowles on his shoulder. 'We'll catch him, don't worry . . . Will yer be all right on yer own?'

He nodded, 'My brother in law will be here to pick me up shortly.'

'OK, Mr Knowles, thank yer for yer time. We'll be in touch. Don't get up, we'll see ourselves out.' He didn't answer so Lorraine nodded at Luke and he led the way to the door.

'Where to now, boss?' Luke asked when they had got into the car.

Lorraine chewed her bottom lip for a moment, then looked at Luke. 'The club Luke, let's pay the heartless bastards a visit.'

'I need to go home Lorraine. I just want to check on Selina again. I don't think she knows yet about Amy.'

'That's fine. I'll phone Carter to meet us at yours and he can come to the club. OK?'

Staring straight ahead, Luke nodded.

29

The sun had finally come out, bringing an unseasonal warmth to the day. Claire Lumsdon and Katy Jacks were approaching the shop where a few days ago Katy had, after much humming and hawing from Jim Stanhills, started her mural.

Jim Stanhills was standing with his back to them, his hands on his hips staring at the wall.

'I hope he likes it,' Katy wailed. 'Do yer think he likes it Claire?'

'Course he will, what's not to like? It's absolutely fab,' Claire assured her for the umpteenth time.

They reached Mr Stanhills, but when she saw his face, she saw him looking grim. Perplexed, Katy and Claire looked at the wall, and their faces drained of colour.

'Jesus.' Claire gave out a startled yelp. 'What the? Oh . . . Oh my God.'

'Yeah, exactly,' Mr Stanhills said, finally tearing his eyes from the wall and looking at them.

All Katy's hard work had been destroyed. Someone had taken a can of white paint, and had sprayed a large white rose on the mural that Katy had only just finished.

'Toad,' Katy whispered. 'It's gotta be him.'

Mr Stanhills shook his head. 'Sorry, but Toad was locked up yesterday afternoon, caught shoplifting in Woolies. Anyhow the wall was fine then. Who else have yers been upsetting girls?'

'Nobody,' they both cried indignantly, just before Katy burst into tears.

'Could be his evil bunch of mates taking the bloody piss,' Jim said, looking in dismay at Katy. 'They've seen that article in the *Echo* and are just trying to scare yer. But for what it's worth,' he said kindly, 'I thought the mural was great.'

'Yer did?'

'Oh, yeah, don't worry,' Mr Stanhills patted her shoulder. 'You'll be able to paint over it. It'll be as good as new in no time.'

'Shouldn't yer call the police first?' Claire asked.

'Don't think they'll come out for graffiti do yer.'

'Aye but what if it's more than graffiti? What if it wasn't Masterton and his gang who had done this? What if it's the . . .' she gulped. She didn't even want to say the words.

Mr Stanhills sighed. 'I wouldn't get too worried about that. I doubt that it's this guy that all the papers have been banging on about. Probably all wind and water pet. Don't fret too much girls,' he soothed them. 'Just clean it up and I'll fetch yer both a can of coke and some choc, how about that?'

They didn't answer so he left them to stare at the wall. The pale lemon background had been filled in with a poor resemblance of a white rose in full bloom, a black dagger dripping black blood over the top of it and underneath in large black capitals someone had written

GONNA GET YOU

'I don't care what Mr Stanhills says,' Claire said to Katy. 'That's bloody scary, that is. Even if it is just Masterton and his gang of cronies.'

'Here yer go, girls,' said Jim Stanhills. He gave them a can of coke each and a dairy milk chocolate bar to share between them. Katy followed him back into the shop to get the paint tins she used for the background. When she returned she took a sip of her coke then picked up her paintbrush and started going over the graffiti with a vengeance.

'What if it is the White Rose murderer?' Claire said after they had been painting for a few minutes.

'Claire! Stop it . . . Anyhow why would he be after us? He doesn't know who we are. It's just Masterton trying to scare us.'

'How do you know that? And anyway, don't yer remember what he did to that girl? I read about it in the paper. Cut her heart out and stuck a white rose inside her.'

'My dad says they should get sued for printing that. He says some people are terrified to go out now. He says it's probably made up anyhow, cos oniy the cops would know what he did.'

Claire, more frightened than she was letting on, let Katy babble as she continued painting.

30

Selina sat with her arm around Mickey. He had comforted her while she had cried about Amy. She could hardly believe it, Amy was dead. She hadn't known her for very long, but they had become such good friends, in such a small amount of time. Selina couldn't believe that her kind, gentle friend was murdered. It sent chills down her spine. But everything seemed to be turning upside down. Nothing seemed right any more. Amy dead, and Mickey scared senseless and hardly able to talk in case he had killed Eccles.

They were on the settee in front of the fire, the policeman on duty was reading his paper in the kitchen with the door open. However awful she felt about Amy, Selina knew that she had to persuade Mickey that he hadn't killed Eccles. That Eccles was like a cockroach, nigh indestructible. Why was it that the good ones died so young while scum like Eccles just kept going, no matter what you threw at them? Selina sighed and squeezed Mickey's hand. 'Don't worry so much Mickey. I'm telling you that horrible evil bastard won't be dead. And if he is, which I'm sure he isn't,' she quickly added before going on, 'I know a lot of people who'll be celebrating.' She squeezed his hand again.

Mickey stared at his feet for a moment, then said with deep feeling. 'But Selina, he wasn't moving. There was blood all over the place.'

'No, listen to me Mickey . . .' Gently she turned his face to hers, 'he'll have crawled away like the worm he is. Honest Mickey he's got more lives than a cat.'

Mickey calmed down a little under Selina's comforting words. He transferred his gaze from his feet to Luke's guitar, stared at that for a moment, then looked at Selina, 'That's what Robbie said.'

'Robbie's right.'

'But what if he is dead and one of his mates came looking for him and dragged him away?'

'Why would they do that? Trust me, they won't be bothered about that prick. If they'd have found him they would have ransacked his pockets for their next fix.'

Mickey sighed. 'I hate the horrible creep Selina, honestly.'

'Yeah, I do know Mickey, and I know yer would only have been acting out of self-defence. Believe me, he'll have really meant to hurt you. I've seen him kick people over and over in the head when they are down,' she paused for a moment thinking back to more than one dank and dirty night. 'And,' she swallowed hard, 'and I'm ashamed to admit that I did nothing to stop him, he had what I needed . . . But believe me he won't, wherever the creep is hiding, be worrying about you, not one little bit, and that's the truth.'

She did not tell him but she suspected that, in fact, Eccles would most likely be hiding out in some dirty stinking shit hole, fairly plotting his revenge against Mickey.

Mickey heaved a sigh, then nodded, 'Guess you're right.' He looked at Selina, saw the strain in her face and felt a pang of guilt. He'd been banging on about his troubles, totally forgetting hers and what she had just gone through. And Amy,

God, how awful was that. To think that she had been killed by the same person that tried to do in his girl, it sent cold shivers down his spine.

'Sorry, Selina, how about you? Feeling any better?' Gently he rubbed his fingers over her bandaged arm.

Selina shivered. 'I'm having nightmares.'

'Oh, I'm sorry.' It was Mickey's turn to comfort Selina, and he did so with the utmost tenderness.

Selina suppressed a sob of happiness, despite everything else that was happening around her. Happiness was an emotion she had rarely felt in her seventeen years of life. It all seemed too good to be true: she had found a father after all these years and now she had found Mickey. The nightmares she'd been having since the attack were terrifying, but she was sure that once whoever had attacked her had been caught, they would, hopefully, go away. And if it was Eccles, and Selina was in no doubt that he was twisted and evil enough to be the White Rose Murderer, then he was not gonna take this happiness away from her.

She snuggled further into Mickey. 'Can't we just forget about everything? About dead people who aren't even dead for a little bit?'

Mickey was about to answer when he was beaten to it.

'Who's dead?'

They had both been sitting with their eyes closed. They hadn't even heard Luke come in. Selina groaned and Mickey felt dread wash right through his veins and collect in the small of his back.

'Who's dead?' Luke repeated.

Selina looked at her father stubbornly. 'Don't know what you're talking about.'

Superintendent Clark burst, without knocking, into Lorraine's office to find her standing over Carter reading what he had up on the screen. They both looked up at the interruption. Lorraine straightened up, smoothed a stray lock of hair behind her ears and crossed her arms. She looked coolly at her superior officer.

'Superintendent Clark,' she said. 'What can I do for you?'

'I have,' he spluttered, 'just run a gauntlet of reporters, all asking me when we're going to bring in the White Rose Killer. Not just that, but the whole police station believes one of *them*, one of us, that means, Inspector Hunt, had something to do with the murders. The station is awash with speculation and paranoia, my officers are getting pulled aside each time they go out to take a cigarette break, and yet there has been no more movement, that I can see anyway, on catching, this, this White Rose Killer. What have you got to say for yourself?'

Lorraine took Clark's onslaught in her stride. 'If yer remember, Superintendent, yer insisted on having a reporter in the station, even though I relayed my concerns to yer. If she hadn't been here, she wouldn't have poked her nose into confidential files, and that article wouldn't have been written.'

'So, it's my fault,' the super spluttered.

Lorraine sighed heavily, 'I never said that. But Kate Mulberry is ambitious. And she's a reporter. Sticking her nose in where it doesn't belong is what she does. Maybe we should have been more careful, but I'm not sure we could have been more careful. We've got an investigation to run which is difficult enough without having to look over our shoulders the whole time. Anyway, it's done now. We can't get rid of the reporters, they're perfectly entitled to camp out in the car park if they want to, and there's no point in antagonising them, they'll just give us bad press. So we just have to carry on trying to find the killer, which was what we were doing just before yer interrupted us.'

Clark spluttered further, looked as if he was going to burst a blood vessel, and left the room without further ado. Carter was looking at Lorraine with admiration. 'Well, that's that,' she said. 'So, back to the matter in hand. Donald Carr – the barman at the club?'

'Yes,' said Carter. 'It turns out he goes back and forth. Has family in Dublin. Not only that, he's got form. GBH. Probably why no respectable club would want to take him on, not with that record. He might be worth another look.'

Lorraine wasn't quite convinced. It felt as if they were clutching at straws. Sure, Carr had form, but there was no mention about violence against women. *Anyway*, she reasoned, *Carter's right. No harm in looking.*

Ten minutes later they were outside the house in Grasswell that Donald Carr was renting.

Carter banged on the door. When there was no answer, he banged on the door again. A moment later, they heard somebody moving about, then the sound of at least three stiff rusty bolts being pulled back one by one. Finally, the door was opened, by a blond-haired man with long sideburns and a moustache.

'Mr Carr, is it all right if we come in?' Lorraine asked.

He looked up and down the empty street before looking back at Lorraine.

'What for?'

'We need to talk to yer for a few minutes.'

'Haven't done nothing,' he muttered but stepped back and allowed them to enter.

They followed him along the passageway and into the kitchen, passing a door on their left. *That must be the sitting room*, Lorraine thought, trying to peer through the one-inch gap. There wasn't much to see, a television with an empty flower vase on top of it was about all she could make out.

In the small kitchen, sheets of newspaper were spread out on the table with two polish cloths on the far side. The rest of the space was taken up by a few cream-painted cupboards, an ancient washing machine and a cooker that tilted to one side like a resident drunk.

Carr indicated for Lorraine and Carter to pull a chair out each from under the table, while he sat in the one nearest to the cloths. He took up a pair of boots and started to polish them.

Carter took his notebook out and looked expectantly at his boss.

'Mr Carr,' Lorraine said before she was even properly seated. 'You have recently come over from Ireland, and you work as a barman in Blacks, a rave club?'

'That's right,' his voice was soft and only slightly accentuated.

'Can yer tell me where yer were on the night the fire alarms were set off?'

'In the club.'

'And you escaped unhurt?'

'Yes.'

'Mr Carr, did you see anyone attempting to abduct a young woman?'

'No. I was too busy trying to get out meself. Listen I've told all this to yer before. I know yer asking me because yer want to see whether I fit the profile of yer killer or not.' He was polishing his boots with great care as he spoke. 'Listen, I've been working every night solid for the past fortnight. I need the money to get out of this dump.'

'Yer have witnesses?'

'Of course, Gary Duffy can verify where I was.'

'OK, thanks for yer help.' Lorraine rose abruptly, startling both of the men.

'We may be back Mr Carr, just to verify a few things.'

He nodded as Carter snapped his notebook shut and followed Lorraine.

They were sitting in the car before Lorraine spoke, staring

out of the window and gently stroking her chin between her thumb and forefinger. 'We just seem to be going round in circles, Carter. Nothing's panning out,' she said, completely frustrated. 'There are too many leads, and none of them seem to be going anywhere. Dammit!' she yelled, hitting her hands on the steering wheel.

Carter just looked at his boss, wishing that he could offer her some word of wisdom, but he found himself at a loss for words, for once.

'I'm sorry, Carter,' Lorraine said. 'It's just so damn frustrating.' She took a deep breath. 'We'll stake out the club tonight, Carter. See if anything comes out of that.'

'You bloody stupid man!' Vanessa Lumsdon shouted at Mr Stanhills. 'The kids are terrified now, why the hell couldn't yer get the coppers in the first place, or better still have painted the damn thing over before anyone saw it. Claire came back home crying her eyes out, thinking that the White Rose Killer was going to target her and Katy next.'

'Now Mrs Lumsdon, we all make mistakes, granted I should have painted it over myself. Tell the kids not to worry.'

'"Tell the kids not to worry",' Vanessa repeated in amazement. 'Are you for real or what? We all know why yer didn't call the coppers, in case they saw the duty-free fags yer selling under the bloody counter.'

Mr Stanhills bristled. 'I'll have yer know, Mrs Lumsdon, I do not sell duty frees.'

'Piss off, yes yer do. I buy the bloody things from yer, remember.'

'Well, what's done is done . . .' Stanhills handed a grinning customer his change, closed the till drawer with a snap and turned back to Vanessa.

'It's painted over now . . . And I don't think the bloody White Rose murderer would take time out to paint a friggin' rose on my wall . . . It's just been that idiot bunch of dope heads what hang around here with nowt else to do.'

'Aye, be that as it may, enough people saw it before Claire and Katy had the nous to paint over it. Yer've now got half the estate terrified. The bairns will probably have nightmares now.'

'Well, Vanessa, yer should take that up with the police. It's covered up now, that's the best I can say or do.'

'Well, it's not bloody good enough.' Vanessa stormed out of the shop, where a sizeable crowd had gathered.

'He thinks it's the druggies playing tricks, and he's probably right, yer know,' Mr Skillings said.

'Aye, that's what I think an' all.' Doris Musgrove nodded, although she refused to let go of her granddaughter Melanie's hand.

31

'For the friggin' hundredth time I am not having it off with Kate Mulberry, will yer please believe me,' Dinwall pleaded. Tears of frustration and anger filled the corners of his eyes.

His wife stood with her arms folded across her chest and her face set in a stubborn mask.

He moved towards her, 'Please believe me.'

'No. I know you,' she sneered. 'Any piece of skirt will do. I bet yer thought all yer Christmases had come at once.'

'You're being paranoid!' Dinwall wanted to tear his hair out. 'I don't know where yer got this from, but yer making a huge mistake. I haven't touched her.'

'Sandra Gilbride saw yer, but didn't tell me until today. She saw yer in the café.'

'. . . that was days ago! I was just doing me job! She was shadowing me for an article she was writing . . .'

'Yeah, and what article was that? Yer divulged all yer secrets about the White Rose Killer to her, did yer? Was that how she got her "exclusive report"? Pillow talk, was it?'

'No! I didn't know anything about it meself, not until the papers went out. And I never touched Kate Mulberry.'

Lynn snorted. 'Sure you haven't. Just like you never touched all those other girls I found out about. Well, fool me once, shame on you. Fool me twice, heck, fool me a dozen times, shame on me. I've had enough. I want yer out of the house.'

'Lynn, love, I'm telling yer the truth . . .'

But she was having none of it. She kicked the suitcase she had packed earlier. 'I want you out of here and I want yer out now. Right now.' Each word was punctuated with a kick to his suitcase.

'Please, Lynn, I'm beggin yer . . .'

'No . . . Go and live with yer poxy slapper and I hope yer have a fucking good time together. Go on,' she was screaming now. 'Go on, I hate you. And I never want to see yer again. Fuck off.'

He knew then that there was no talking to her at this moment in time. He had never, not in his three years of marriage, heard his wife swear. Yeah, he'd flirted once or twice, well more than once or twice, but it hadn't meant nothing. Just a little excitement, the thrill of the chase.

She was crying now, fat tears dripping off her chin, huge sobs tearing at her chest.

'Please,' he whispered, but she ignored him. Slowly he bent down and picked the suitcase up. Shoulders drooping and head down he headed for the door, looked back at her once but she was staring in the opposite direction.

Outside he flung his suitcase into the boot of his car. 'Damn that bloody Mulberry woman,' he muttered. 'She's not only turned me wife against me, she's turned the force against me too.' He slammed the boot, went round to the front and got in.

If I ever get my hands on her, he was thinking as he banged the door so hard the glass in the window rattled, *I'll kill the bastard.*

*

271

It was full dark when Lorraine and Carter left the police station to go to the club, but two plain cars called in from Sunderland Gill Bridge station had been on duty since three that afternoon, one at the club and one at the children's home. Neither had so far reported anything suspicious.

Lorraine and Carter pulled up next to the curb, facing one of the cars. A moment later Lorraine exploded, 'What the fuck is Kate Mulberry doing here?'

Wary of any shrapnel coming his way, Carter said meekly, 'She probably put two and two together, and realised that we'd be staking out the club at some point or another.'

Lorraine breathed in deeply, and tried counting to ten to get her temper back. She had just managed to get to three when she thought *Fuck this*, then flung the door open, jumped out and approached the reporter.

'Uh oh,' Carter whispered.

'What the hell are yer doing here?' she asked Kate Mulberry.

Kate drew herself up to her full height, which was still inches below Lorraine's, and said, 'Inspector. As you haven't given me any information I decided to go where the action is.'

Lorraine took a deep breath and glared at Kate Mulberry. 'Yer not staying here. Yer too visible and yer'll scare the killer off. Yer need to go back home.'

'What?'

'Yer heard right the first time. I want you to go home. You are not needed nor wanted here tonight . . . Can I be any plainer?'

Mulberry bristled. 'I'm only doing my job.'

'So am I . . . And the best way I can do my job is with you outta my hair.'

'Yer can't make me do anything. I'm a private citizen, minding my own business. I have every right to be here.'

'Listen,' Lorraine snarled, 'and listen good. If yer not outta

272

here within ten seconds, I'll have yer arrested for obstructing police business. I'll get Sanderson to take yer down to the station, which is another good policeman off the job, looking after you, when we've got a real killer to catch. Lives are at stake here, don't yer get that? And they're worth more than yer poxy career.'

'Can I quote yer on that?' said Kate, her steely side coming out once again.

'Yer can plaster it on a billboard, for all I care,' Lorraine shot back. 'Yer can broadcast it on national TV. I don't give a shit. Now get the hell out of my face.'

Kate harrumphed, and pulled her coat tighter about her. Lorraine watched her walk down the road. When she was sure that Kate Mulberry was on her way, she walked back to the car and got in beside Carter.

'The cheek of some people, fucking beyond belief. Drive round the block and come in the other side, no doubt we've been clocked.'

Lorraine took out her mobile, dialled a number and put the phone to her ear. 'That's strange, Dinwall's not answering. I know he's off duty, but he rarely misses the chance of a bit of overtime.' Frowning, Lorraine put the phone on the dashboard.

'Stop here,' Lorraine ordered Carter. 'This will do.'

They had a good view of Blacks, which looked as if it had once been a warehouse of some sort. The walls were faded red brick, and the peeling paint on the doors and blocked out windows were a dirty grey-green.

As Lorraine and Carter watched, a group of five kids all wearing chav gear, baseball caps and assorted tracksuits, walked up to the club entrance and began to queue outside the doors. A few minutes later more kids began to converge from both sides of the street. Lorraine and Carter settled in for a long evening.

*

273

Luke had tried his best to get an answer out of Mickey, but he had proved stubborn and Selina even more so, although Luke guessed that if Selina had not been there to prop him up, Mickey would have certainly caved after a few minutes. *Who the hell were they talking about?* he asked himself. *Who's dead?*

Feeling hungry, Luke went into the kitchen and opened the fridge, 'Jesus,' he muttered, staring at the empty shelves and a dry shrivelled cucumber. 'Got to do a big shop.'

Opening the cupboard on the wall above the fridge, he found his choice was limited to a can of peaches which had been there since the Christmas before last, or a can of recently purchased tomato soup. He settled on the soup. Selina and the police officer had eaten two cottage pies for tea. Mickey had gone home to escape his relentless questions, and now Selina had shut herself in her room and wasn't speaking to him.

'So what's new,' he muttered, opening the can and pouring the contents into a small pan.

A few minutes later, soup and a rather dry bun on a tray, he went into the sitting room, hoping she'd calmed down enough and came back downstairs to talk and get back on the footing they'd enjoyed these last few days. He stood in the doorway, the room was empty and a strange feeling wrapped around him. He took a few moments to realise it was loneliness. And he didn't like it.

Selina must be in a real huff, he thought, his long legs crossing the space to the chair by the coffee table in moments. He put the tray down, then sat. The feeling was still there, made even worse by the fact that he would not be seeing Lorraine tonight either, because she was staking out that bloody snake pit of a club.

He finished the soup, and still feeling restless, he decided to try and patch things up with Selina. Lorraine would probably kill him if he didn't. Although he would swear his life away that when he came in they were talking about somebody being dead. *For a fact something's happened, Carson wasn't born with two black eyes. And there was bruising on his neck. Fell down the stairs, a likely story. Somebody's beaten the shit out of the kid, but who and why?* 'Do the bloody pair of them think I was born yesterday?' he muttered.

Sighing, he dropped the spoon into the empty bowl. What the hell could he do, short of arresting them and bringing them in for questioning, which he knew was the worst idea possible. *Talking about dead people and having two black eyes is not an offence, but it's damn suspicious. Never gonna find out if we're not speaking to each other, just sitting here. Shit, time to make amends.*

He went to the bottom of the stairs. 'Selina,' he shouted.

There was no answer, bar the echo of his own voice. *Keep calm, don't say nothing to set the ball rolling again,* he thought as he slowly walked up the stairs. Reaching her bedroom his fist was poised at her door to knock.

He chewed on his bottom lip for a moment. 'Selina?' he asked quietly.

Again, no answer. Though he fancied he heard a voice so he put his ear to the door. Then felt relieved as her voice droned on. Oh good she must be on the phone. *At least she's talking to somebody.*

He went back downstairs. Soup was not going to be enough, so he picked up the phone and ordered pizza. He then flopped on the settee, kicked his shoes off, switched the television on and tried to lose himself in a repeat of *Taggart.*

Lorraine said, give her space. OK, that's what I'll do, and if she doesn't come downstairs when she smells the pizza, tough!

He loosened his shirt and removed his tie, and tried very hard not to think about the two women in his life.

Kate Mulberry glanced behind her, certain she'd heard footsteps, but in the darkness she could see nothing. She took a deep breath and carried on down the unlit street, fuming at Lorraine but fuming even more at herself for not standing her ground and insisting that she stay at the club. And then she heard it again, for definite this time. Yes, footsteps.

Frowning she walked faster. She shoved her hands deeper into the pockets of her light-blue coat and walked progressively faster until, for some instinctive reason, she was terrified, and practically running.

She knew someone was following her.

No matter how many times she told herself to stop being silly, she was just imagining it. One more street, that's all, then the main road and the bus stops just around the corner.

Where the hell is everybody, OK it's cold but it's not cold enough for the whole world to hibernate, for God's sake! Shit what's that?

She shook herself, it was just an owl.

The ice in her spine and the prickles on her scalp made a lie of her previous statement that no one was there. There was somebody there; she glanced around again and peered into the dark.

Selina regretted climbing out of the window as soon as her feet hit the ground. Her ribs hurt like hell. She wondered if she could even manage to walk very far. She hadn't said anything but it seemed as if they were getting worse instead of better. She took a moment, her hand on her side, and waited until the pain subsided.

She gazed back up at her bedroom window. How the hell was she ever gonna get back in?

Shit, fuck . . . Worry about that when the time comes. She started walking to the end of the road, she wore the hood on her red jacket up, which made a pyramid shape on top of her bandages. She had to see Mickey, she just had to or she would die. Old moany-head had done it again, creeping about the place and cocking his ears.

There would be hell to pay for this escapade, but it wasn't fair, Mickey would have stayed longer if moany-face hadn't gone straight into police mode at the mention of somebody being dead.

She heard a sound behind her and glanced round, peered hard into the darkness, shrugging, she turned back. 'Must have been a dog or something,' she muttered as she strode forward.

Ten minutes and I'll be at Mickey's. What can happen in ten minutes? she asked herself. But still she could do nothing to suppress the cold shiver that ran down her back. *Eccles won't be anywhere near here, no way. He'll be licking his wounds in some crack den like the creep animal that he is.*

So why do you think someone's behind you? She heard sounds behind her again, someone walking quickly. *What if* . . . And then her heart stopped for one deadly moment as the footsteps were beside her.

Thought I'd forgotten . . . Thought I would just let it go. Thought you could slag me off in front of the whole world . . . Bitch.

He watched hidden in the shadows as she passed him in the dark street. Waited with a unique patience, knowing the dark would hide him. His knives, his friends safe by his side, polished and shining, ready and waiting.

He stepped out behind her. Knowing she had heard him, wanting her to hear him.

Wanting her to fear him.

He stood perfectly still when she turned and peered into the dark. He knew that, dressed all in black as he was, that she would hardly be able to see him.

He smiled. It was fine that she had heard him, she would not escape.

She would pay, and then he would show that bitch what fear truly was.

32

'She's still in bed,' Luke said to the WPC with the cropped brown hair and large hazel eyes, who would be sitting with Selina today. Luke was pleased because Selina and WPC Carol Burns seemed to hit it off but he could have sworn she wasn't coming today, she had a doctor's appointment or something. 'I, er, thought Dinwall was here today?'

WPC Burns had brought two supermarket bags of shopping with her, and she placed them on the ground by her feet. 'Haven't yer heard the news?'

Luke felt a sinking feeling in the pit of his stomach 'No, why? Something I should know about?'

'Guess they were waiting to tell yer when yer get in. Sorry sir, but there's been another murder.'

'Oh Jesus.'

'Yeah,' she kicked the bags. 'And yer owe me twelve pounds, fifty-nine pence. Me and yer daughter gotta eat.'

Luke grimaced. 'Oh yeah, sorry about that. It is rather bare in there. I was gonna find some time today for a shopping spree.' He fished in his pocket for his wallet, handed her a tenner and three pound coins.

'Got no change,' she said, taking the money and putting it in her pocket.

Luke smiled, 'No problem. Thought yer had a doctor's appointment today?'

'I changed it, don't worry about it.'

'Thanks for that, better go.' He headed past her and once he reached the gate, turned. 'Tell her ladyship when she finally rolls out of bed that there's cold pizza in the kitchen for brekkie, and I hope she enjoys it.'

Carol Burns laughed, then said 'Bye sir' as she went into the house.

Ten minutes later Luke pulled up outside the station. Quickly he hurried to Lorraine's office.

Lorraine looked up and smiled at Luke when he came in. She was talking on the phone. Luke could see she was tired, and from her side of the conversation, guessed she had Scottie on the other end.

'I heard the news from Burns,' Luke said as she put the phone down. 'What's happening?'

She sighed and picked a pencil stub up and chewed the end for a few moments. She took it out of her mouth and then said, 'Last night, a young woman was attacked and murdered. According to Scottie, it's one of the most brutal murders he has ever seen in all his time as a pathologist.'

'Shit, any idea who she is?'

Lorraine shook her head.

'Is it the same as the others?'

'Well,' she said slowy, 'Scottie says that if it is, he's changed his MO. This poor bugger has been slashed practically beyond recognition, and I've never heard him say this before, but he reckons, God help the parent that has to identify this poor soul. He says the attack must have been frenzied, there's at least forty slashes on her face and body. And none of the wounds were fatal, she bled to death, slowly and in the most intense kind of pain.'

'Jesus Christ, Lorraine, what the hell is going on in Houghton?'

'I wish I knew, Luke.' Sighing she threw the pencil in the drawer, grimaced, then went on, 'Scottie wants us to go to the morgue right away. Come on, I need you to drive me. I'm knackered after the stakeout.'

'Anything come of that, Lorraine?'

She shook her head. 'No, quiet as the grave.' She winced when she said that, and Luke squeezed her shoulder.

'Don't be too hard on yerself, Lorraine, yer can only be in one place at a time.'

Lorraine gave him a wan smile. 'What I really need is to stop at home for ten minutes, just to have a quick shower and get changed. That should revive me.' Luke nodded. 'And if Mavis or Peggy ask yer to stay for a full English, the answer is no,' Lorraine continued. 'Not even a slice of crispy. I'll only be ten minutes if that.'

They pulled up outside the hospital forty-five minutes later. Lorraine, her hair brushed into a bun at the nape of her neck, wearing a fresh white blouse and navy suit, looked anything but as if she'd been up most of the night. As they were walking towards the entrance, Luke's phone rang.

Lorraine was at the steps leading up to the door when she realised Luke wasn't at her side. She turned to see Luke frozen on the spot, listening to his mobile.

'What?' he shouted.

'Problem?' Lorraine walked back to him.

'OK,' he said to the phone before closing it and putting it back in his pocket. All the while his eyes never left Lorraine's.

'What's wrong?' The way he was staring set Lorraine's heart beating faster.

'It's Selina. She . . . she's not at home. Her bed's not been slept in.' His tormented eyes lifted from Lorraine's to stare at the blanked-out window where he knew Scottie would be working on the murdered body of a young woman. Lorraine glanced quickly at the window and knew instinctively what Luke was thinking.

'Bloody hell, Luke,' she rubbed his arm. 'For God's sake, get that idea out of yer head. It won't be her. Now, go on, go and find her. I'll bet yer anything yer like she'll be with Mickey Carson. I'll see to this business, go on love, please go home.'

Luke was silent for a moment, his eyes bright with fear, then he swallowed hard and shook his head. 'Can't Lorraine. I have to know. One way or the other I have to know, now, if that's her in there. If, if that's Selina.' He stared into Lorraine's eyes a moment longer, then strode past her to the door, Lorraine hurrying to keep up with him.

'Lorraine, Luke—' Scottie said, but Lorraine and Luke ignored him and moved to the table. A white sheet covered the body, which was easily identified as female.

Luke stared at the white sheet, he could hear his heart pounding in his ears, he hesitated a moment, took a deep breath then slowly, dreading what he would find, pulled the sheet back.

But it was Lorraine who gasped out loud and grabbed hold of the edge of the table. 'Oh no,' she whispered, staring at the body. 'Oh no . . . Jesus Christ!'

Even though her face was slashed and her skin was hanging down like crushed red ribbons, Lorraine could still tell who it was.

'Kate Mulberry,' Luke whispered.

Part Six

33

Darren Lumsdon quickly pushed the last of his newspapers through the door of 66 Daffodil Close, then, running down the path, he hurried home.

Good thing it's a teacher's training day, I would never have made it to school in time this morning. He waved at Mr Skillings as he passed.

The reason he was late, was that he had some monumental news. And couldn't he just picture all of their faces when they heard this!

He burst into the house knowing that everyone would be in the kitchen, diving into their cornflakes. Robbie reached into Darren's paperbag as he passed and fished out a bottle of milk.

'Only one . . . You're as bad as our Claire was.' Robbie was referring to the 'perks' of being a paperboy. Each Lumsdon who had a route would nick a couple of bottles of a morning, making sure to vary the homes that they nicked the milk from.

Darren did not answer. He had more important news to tell.

'Guess what?' he all but shouted. 'That bloody white rose is only back on the shop wall.'

'That's it,' Vanessa jumped up, spilling her cup of tea in the process. 'I'm off to tell the coppers and stuff Stanhills and his duty frees.'

'Way to go, mam,' Robbie said from the doorway.

'Darren, run over and see if Sandra's decent, tell her to come right over.'

'OK, mam.'

Claire reached into the sink to get a cloth to wipe up the spilt tea. Her hands were shaking. She was convinced that the White Rose murderer was out to get her and Katy.

A few minutes later Sandra came over. 'The bairn's told me all about it,' she said as she walked through the door.

'Aye why, I'm calling the coppers this time. I'm not one bit bothered what Stanhills says. Any one of us could be in danger here, he's already murdered God knows how many women, and his calling card's a white rose. It could be for any of us.'

Suzy started to cry.

'Shh,' Kerry patted her arm. 'She doesn't mean us, as in us in here.'

Vanessa looked at her Suzy. 'I'll not be long pet. Come on Sandra, Stanhills could be keeping valuable information from the coppers. Or it could be nowt. Either way, we'll have done our duty.'

Sandra nodded, then followed Vanessa out of the door.

James Dinwall stretched and groaned. Every muscle he moved screamed at him. He looked in his rear-view mirror. 'Christ almighty,' he muttered to his reflection. He wearily rubbed his bloodshot eyes, before peering more intently at his cheek.

Is that a scratch? He rubbed at the two small patches of dried blood on his left cheek. Now where the hell did that come from?

A car and a bottle of whiskey, he shook his head. 'No substitute for a warm woman.'

Where had he been last night? He vaguely remembered

being in the White Lion bar with a couple of mates from work, but sometime after nine things became a blur. How much had he drunk?

Quite a lot judging by the smell. Ugh, he wanted to vomit. He opened the window to let some fresh air in and noticed the empty whiskey bottle lying on the path. 'Shit.' He groaned loudly, wondering who the hell he might have upset, and startled an old man passing by with a newspaper tucked under his arm.

He never drank whiskey, it was like fire water to him and made him very argumentative. Groaning again he looked at his watch next. 'Shit.' It was ten o'clock. He was over three hours late for work.

His keys were still in the ignition, thank God for that small mercy. He twisted the key, started the engine and headed towards the police station. He would clean up in the toilet, stop at the shop first and get a Bic razor and a pint of orange juice. Dehydrated wasn't the word. His mouth felt as if something half dead and furry had crawled in overnight and staked a claim on his tongue.

Twenty minutes later, after shopping and taking a change of clothes from the suitcase that he had in the back of the car, he was sitting in the canteen with a cup of coffee. He stared at the headache tablets in his hand that he had begged off the canteen cook and wondered how they would mix with God knows how much alcohol he had still in his system.

'Better not,' he muttered, slowly shaking his head. He'd just have to suffer through it. He had poisoned himself enough with alcohol without adding more chemicals to the mix. He stuffed them back in his pocket as he took a deep drink of his coffee.

His eyes met the startled look of Sergeant Allan Peters as he came through the canteen doors and, spotting Dinwall, did a double take. *What the fuck's wrong with him?* Dinwall wondered, still staring at the sergeant, whom he vaguely remembered seeing last night.

Instead of coming over, Peters backed out of the canteen leaving the door swinging behind him. *Oh for fuck's sake*, Dinwall thought. Since that little bitch's article had come out, the station was in a state of unrest with everyone wondering whether they could trust their colleagues, wondering whether there was a killer in their midst. Although Luke and Carter had interviewed everyone at the station, and had been convinced that no one was a suspect, there was still a high-level state of anxiety, and paranoia had affected even the most level-headed of policemen.

34

'I think it's the same knife, Lorraine.' Scottie was staring
down at the mutilated body of Kate Mulberry. Luke had
gone in search of his wayward daughter, and Lorraine and
Edna were sitting on the stools. Edna had poured Lorraine a
restorative cup of tea, and Lorraine had taken it gratefully.
She was hugely shaken by Kate Mulberry's murder. The
thought that she had sent her to her death wouldn't leave
her. She was hardly registering what Scottie was saying.
Come on, buck yer ideas up, she said to herself. *Yer've got to
stay on the ball, if yer ever gonna catch the bastard who did
this.*

'In fact I'm pretty certain it's the same one,' Scottie
continued. 'If you look here,' he pointed to a deep wound in
the centre of Kate's chest. Lorraine got off her stool and came
over. 'It's in the exact same spot as the other ones, almost as if
he was going to cut her heart out just like the others, then for
some reason became angry and started slashing. The thickness
of the blade where she's stabbed,' he pointed at a couple of
places on her body, 'matches the thickness of the stabs on the
other bodies.'

'Uh huh,' Lorraine nodded. 'What if he intended to slash her anyhow and out of habit started there?'

'That could be so,' Scottie stared at the spot for a moment. 'In fact yer probably right Lorraine. He'd have been angry with her over that piece in the newspaper, wouldn't he?'

'It all sounds logical to me. And I very much doubt that there'd be two frenzied killers on the streets of Houghton. I'm betting it's the same man. And he had motive enough. But we're still only speculating on what his motives were for murdering the others.'

'Now, there yer have me. Cuts I can match up, reasons, well kiddo, that's your territory.'

Lorraine sighed. She felt dreadful that Kate Mulberry had been murdered. She turned away from the ruined body of the reporter. She sat back on the stool and put her head in her hands.

Edna touched Lorraine's hand. 'Are yer OK, Lorraine, love?'

Lorraine licked her dry lips. 'I sent her away Edna, I sent her to die.'

Scottie was immediately by her side. 'Nonsense. Whatever yer did, yer did not knowingly send that young woman to her death.'

Lorraine shook her head. 'I should have sent her away in a police car, but she had just wound me up too much.' She flicked a tear away.

Scottie put his arm around her and Edna leaned over and flicked the switch for the kettle to boil for another cup of tea.

'Come on girl, what exactly happened?'

Lorraine told them. When she had finished, Edna handed her a cup of tea. 'Yer were only doing yer job Lorraine. Here, love, drink this.'

'God bless the poor soul, but she was obviously a nuisance,' Scottie said. 'Yer were just doing yer job, and I would have sent her away too, after all the trouble she caused. But yer

290

can't go blaming yerself for this. No way, I won't let yer. You are a damn good copper, Lorraine, one of the best I have ever met, and I won't have yer blaming yerself for any of this.'

Edna looked from Kate Mulberry's body to Lorraine and shook her head. 'Looks to me like he was out to get her one way or the other. If it hadn't been last night it would have been tonight or tomorrow. Yer can't predict an attack like that. Not your fault at all.'

Lorraine sighed. 'I know . . . I know but . . .'

'No buts. Finish that cup and get out of here. You've got a murderer to catch so the rest of us can sleep safe in our beds.'

Lorraine dutifully drank the tea, but inside she knew that she would carry a small kernel of guilt for the death of Kate Mulberry for the rest of her life.

Peters with Sanderson in tow crossed the canteen floor and stood in front of Dinwall. 'James Dinwall, I am arresting you on suspicion of murder.' Sergeant Allan Peters held out a pair of handcuffs.

'Yer what?' Dinwall couldn't believe what he was hearing.

'You heard,' Peters replied. 'Hands please.'

'Is this a wind up or what?' Dinwall asked in amazement, looking from Sanderson to Peters.

'There's no need for those.' Sanderson stepped forward, but his voice was serious. 'Come on James, please.'

'But what the hell . . .?'

Before Sanderson could answer, Peters jumped in. 'The woman you swore you would murder as soon as yer got yer hands on her, in front of at least a dozen witnesses, *five* of them police officers, well, she's been found dead. Kate Mulberry's body was found early this morning slashed to bloody bits, yer fucking savage. That article in the paper just too much for yer, was it? I should have known that the traitorous killer in the office would be yer.'

291

'That's enough Peters,' Sanderson warned. 'We don't need to arrest him, even. We just need to question him at the moment. We have nothing to go on but his drunken rants last night, OK?'

Dinwall's face drained of all colour. His complexion was so grey that Sanderson thought he was going to faint.

'Give yerself a minute James.'

'But what . . . I don't understand,' he spluttered. 'I haven't got a clue what the fuck yer going on about.'

'Kate Mulberry was found murdered this morning. You threatened to murder her. Now where did yer go last night after we left yer crying into yer beer?' Peter snapped, the handcuffs still in his hand.

'How the fuck do I know.' Dinwall shouted. He was starting to shake. 'I woke up in the car with the mother of all hangovers. I don't even know how I got there,' he shook his head, his eyes pleading with Sanderson.

'Is that a scratch on yer face?' Peters asked, staring at the red mark on Dinwall's cheek.

Dinwall ran his finger over the mark. He gulped. Surely he would remember murdering someone last night, but then he couldn't remember getting the scratch on his cheek either, nor how he had got to the car. His mind was still blearily trying to process the information. They couldn't seriously think that he was the killer?

'Well, come on, then.' Peters took hold of Dinwall's elbow.

At first Dinwall resisted. 'Get off, yer fucking mad you are . . . So yer actually think I done her in? Jesus!'

Sanderson leaned forward and said gently, 'Come on son, there's nothing concrete yet. I'm certain there will be an explanation.'

Though even Sanderson looked a little worried as he studied the scratch on Dinwall's face.

*

Twenty-five minutes later, Lorraine, still with a twinge of guilt about the death of Kate Mulberry that she managed to put to one side, was listening to Carter who had arrived to pick her up. They were sitting in the car outside the hospital.

'No way . . . No way . . . Dinwall! Have they gone bloody mad up there? Arresting Dinwall?'

Carter nodded. 'But yer know what the station has been like with rumours flying everywhere. I think that everyone went a bit nuts, looking for someone to blame. He was crying, boss, when they finally got him out of the canteen, screaming about kicking a man when he's down.'

'Get me to the fucking station at once. It wasn't Dinwall, unless he's the White Rose Killer an' all, which is not fucking likely. Who's the instigator of these rumours?'

'Peters.'

Lorraine frowned. 'Peters is a good man. But he and Dinwall aren't the best of friends.'

'They say Dinwall was threatening to murder Kate in the pub last night.'

'That doesn't mean he fucking did it, for God's sake. If I had a penny for every time somebody's threatened murder in the heat of the moment I would be a billionaire. Stop at this shop.'

Carter pulled up outside a newsagent's and Lorraine jumped out, returning a few minutes later with a packet of cigarettes.

Carter's jaw dropped. 'Oh, yer not, boss.'

'Just watch me.' She fought with the cellophane wrapper. 'For fuck's sake, don't they want yer to smoke the damn things?'

'Must be an omen.'

'What?'

'Yer know a sign saying . . .'

'I know what a fucking omen is.' At last she got the cellophane off, opened the packet, took a cigarette out and

293

stared at it. 'What you looking at?' she snapped at Carter who was staring at the cigarette every bit as intensely as she was.

'Nothing boss.' He quickly swung his eyes back to the windscreen. 'But er, think of all those pencils yer've chewed, all the trees wasted.'

'Trees!!! A fucking sapling wouldn't cover it yer cheeky monkey . . . Why are we still here?'

Carter started the engine and headed towards Houghton, every minute expecting her to use the cigarette lighter in the car to light up.

'Mr Hanson, Mr Hanson,' Jamie Kirkton yelled.

Carl Hanson turned and frowned at the ten-year-old boy who had called his name. 'What?' he snapped. Then softened his voice as the boy's face fell. 'Sorry Jamie, a few things on my mind, how can I help you?'

Jamie gulped, then started to cry.

'What's wrong Jamie? I'm sorry if I shouted at you.'

Jamie shook his head. 'Tom says he ate the gold fish that we won at Houghton Feast.'

'What? Of course he didn't, he's just teasing you.'

'Tom also says that the murderer is gonna come tonight and get me.'

'Jamie, Jamie,' Hanson knelt down so that he was on the same level as the boy, 'Tom is just winding you up, I've told you this before.'

'But the fish isn't in his bowl.'

'The fish died yesterday while you were with the Prices. I buried it myself.'

'Really?' Jamie sniffed.

'Really. Now how did it go with the Prices?' The Prices were a middle-aged childless couple from Shiney Row who were looking to foster Jamie. Hanson and the rest of the staff were all praying for it to work out. Jamie was a good kid whose parents had been killed in a car accident, and his only living relative – his paternal grandfather – had Alzheimers and was in a home himself. Sometimes the older boys teased Jamie because he was so gullible and far from streetwise.

Jamie lightened up a little. 'Good, I like them. They give me cakes. Will the murderer come tonight?'

'No, Jamie, of that I am sure. Now go on, it's nearly lunch time.'

'Poor fish.'

'Yeah, poor fish.' Carl Hanson watched as Jamie walked along the corridor to the dinner room. Once he saw that he was safely inside, he made his way to the staff room.

He picked up the early edition of the *Evening Chronicle* that someone had brought in and sat on the chair beside the window. Staring at the headline that proclaimed the horrible murder of reporter Kate Mulberry, he sat unmoving for a moment, then crushed the paper in his large strong hands and scowling, threw it into the bin.

35

Luke had spent frantic hours searching for Selina. Of course none of Carson's friends had seen them. *Like they would tell me if they had.*

'Where the hell is she?' Angrily he took a bite out of the toast he'd just buttered. 'I'll throttle the bloody pair of them, for God's sake, with everything that's going on.' He banged his fist down on the kitchen bench, just as the back door opened and Selina followed by Mickey came in.

Luke swallowed nearly choking on his toast as he stared at them, not knowing if he wanted to bang their heads together or hug them.

'Hello . . . D . . . Dad.'

Before he could say anything Selina took a deep breath then went on. 'The truth is Dad, we simply fell asleep.'

Overcome with emotion for the moment, Luke looked from one to the other, Mickey quickly hung his head. But Selina stared back, her eyes clear.

'Do you know something?' Luke said gruffly a moment later. 'I actually believe you.'

He could see their face's light up and held up his hand in a

cautious manner, and said more sternly, 'That doesn't necessarily mean yer off the hook, either of you . . . Can you
imagine how worried I've been with a bloody murderer out
there? Jesus Christ, Selina, yer think yer would have learnt
your lesson from being in hospital. Yer think yer would have
learnt yer lesson from Amy.' Even though he'd promised
himself he would be calm, Luke began to pace back and forth.

Selina looked shamefaced and then said quickly, 'I know
and we are really, really sorry. Aren't we Mickey?' Mickey
nodded and Selina went on, 'But we fell asleep, we woke up
and here we are. And before yer say, stop being flippant, I'm
not trying to be, I'm just telling it like it was. We're both sorry,
really, really sorry. And there's nothing else I can say Dad.'

Luke felt a lump form in his throat. He stopped pacing and
looked at her. He ached so much to hold her. So many years
apart. But would she let him, or would it embarrass her in
front of Mickey? So much so that she would push him away
and widen the rift that was just beginning to slowly close
between them?

'Dad,' Selina stepped forward until she was in touching
distance of Luke. 'I am sorry.'

Luke's breath caught in his throat. He opened his arms and
Selina hugged him, while a bashful, grinning Mickey watched.

'OK,' Luke said a moment later, a huge grin on his face. 'No
harm done this time, but you must promise me never ever to
be so bloody stupid again.'

'OK. I promise. So what now?' Selina held her side, the hug
had cost her.

'So now I'll phone PC Burns, get her back here and I'll go to
work so that we can eat.'

'OK, could you please ask Carol to pick up a McDonald's
on the way, me and Mickey's starving.'

'So, it's Carol now, is it?'

'Yeah, she's cool.'

'Hmm. Well, I've got good news. Carol's already been to the supermarket, yer can feed yerself from what she's brought in.'

Twenty minutes later, spotting PC Burns pull up in her car, Luke went into the hall, shoved on his jacket and came back to Selina and Mickey who were holding hands and smiling at each other.

'Just one thing, I may be late back, probably very late, but when I get back, I want and need the full story on those panda eyes of yours Mr Carson.'

That's wiped the smile off his face, Luke thought with just a pinch of satisfaction as he left the house.

Lorraine stormed down the corridor to interrogation room 3, where Peters and Sanderson were with James Dinwall.

She had never before seen such a look of utter and complete relief on anyone's face when she opened the door and Dinwall turned in his chair to look at her.

'Boss,' he practically wailed. 'Thank God . . . tell them it wasn't me.'

Lorraine got the distinct impression that Dinwall was about to throw himself at her feet and plead his case. He relaxed for a moment, convinced common sense had arrived, then full of righteous indignation he went on. 'The fucking stupid bloody idiots think I killed Kate Mulberry. I've been trying to tell them, if I killed her, wouldn't I be covered in blood? Wouldn't I have more than a scratch on me face?'

Sanderson looked as relieved as Dinwall was to see Lorraine. Peters, watching Dinwall's every move, remained calm and Lorraine could tell that he seemed to really believe that Dinwall could be capable of such an atrocity. *Or*, she pondered to herself, *was it more that he wanted to believe it?*

Frowning, she said, 'Yer look a bloody mess Dinwall,' she wrinkled her nose, 'and I can smell last night's booze coming out of yer very pores.'

Dinwall swallowed. 'I know, boss. What can I say? I got drunk in the car and fell asleep, that's all I remember . . . Didn't even know until I got into the station that Kate was dead.' He paused for a long moment, obviously thinking about Kate Mulberry. Sadly he shook his head and looked at Lorraine. 'It wasn't me, boss.'

'I know, Dinwall.'

'See, yer fucking pricks,' he yelled. 'I told yer it wasn't me.' He glared at Peters, 'Bastard, just you wait, I'm lodging a complaint about you!'

'No, yer not,' Lorraine said.

'Eh?'

'Listen, the station has been in turmoil ever since that bloody article came out. Everyone has been blaming each other, everyone has been looking over their shoulders. This was why Luke, Carter and I were so careful to keep everything between ourselves – not because we thought that there was a killer amongst us, but because we didn't want to create suspicion amongst the ranks. I want you two to put this behind yer. Peters,' she turned to the uniformed officer, 'yer have to make a public apology to Dinwall, and once you've done that, that's it. It's the last I'm going to hear about it. And Dinwall, yer going to accept his apology. Now, shake hands, the two of yer.'

Peters and Dinwall glared mutinously at Lorraine, and then grudgingly shook each other's hand. Sanderson looked on with amusement.

'Right, Dinwall, go home. Take a day or two to sort yer life out. Then I need yer back on the job . . . You are no good to me at all in this state.'

Dinwall nodded. 'Thanks, boss.'

'Seeing as yer slept in the car, I take it yer've been thrown out?'

Dinwall nodded again, more slowly this time.

Before anyone could say anything else, Luke knocked on the

door and walked into the interrogation room. 'Looks like trouble outside, boss.'

'What?'

'Vanessa Lumsdon and Sandra Gilbride are outside, demanding to know what yer gonna do to stop the White Rose murderer drawing on the Seahills shop walls.'

'Come again?'

'Yer heard right. Some clown has been spray-painting a white rose on Stanhills' shop.'

Lorraine sighed heavily. 'God almighty.'

'What a bloody day,' Lorraine said, resting her head on Luke's bare chest.

'And yer handled it brilliantly, as always, my love.' He smiled into her hair as he kissed the top of her head.

Lorraine wriggled with delight, then lay still thinking of Dinwall. 'Yer know, I never thought Peters had it in for Dinwall that much. I know James can be a bit of an arsehole at the best of times, but he's not a bad man on the whole.'

'Peters is an old woman, always has been.'

Lorraine sighed. 'And whoever it is graffiting those roses on the Seahills, I'll personally strangle the git when I catch him.'

'Good idea to send the extra patrols round tonight. It'll keep the estate happy.'

He could feel Lorraine smile, and then heard her breathing change as she fell asleep. Luke was quiet for a moment thinking of Mickey Carson. He and Lorraine had not got in until late, so Carson had gone by the time they got back.

But there's always tomorrow. He leaned over the top of Lorraine and switched the light off.

36

Mavis handed Peggy a cup of tea, then switched channels on the television.

'What yer doing, I was watching that!'

'And how many times have yer seen it? Jesus, as if Orlando Bloom would ever look at you.'

'It does a girl good to dream.'

'Girl?' Mavis snorted.

'Hey, what's this?' Peggy craned her neck to look out the window, and Mavis turned round.

A white florist van had pulled up to the curb, and a young man got out and went to the back of the van.

'Ee, it's February the fourteenth, Mavis. It's St Valentine's Day.' Peggy grinned, nodding her head.

The young man came down the path, carrying a single white rose in bud. Peggy hurried to the door.

'For God's sake, don't get yer hopes up. I can guarantee it's not from Orlando Bloom.'

'Yeah yeah.'

She came back a few moments later with a puzzled frown on her face. 'It's for Lorraine.'

'What? Did yer really think it was for you?'

Peggy shrugged. 'Yer never know yer luck . . . But it doesn't say who it's from.'

'Gotta be from Luke.'

Mavis had barely got her words out when another florist's van pulled up, this one bearing the logo, Apple Blossom. They watched as the florist carried a bouquet of red rose buds down the path. Then both of them stared at the single white rose in bud.

Lorraine played with the packet of cigarettes she'd bought the day before. Tapping first one side of the packet on her desk then turning it over and tapping the other side. She'd never succumbed and lit one yesterday, but she was fairly tempted today all right.

'No bloody further forward,' she thought, staring at the brass handle on the drawer. 'Now, Sanderson has gone home to bed, the poor sod looked absolutely knackered. That's what comes of insisting on spending two nights in a row, staking out a club. Dinwall is off licking his wounds, God knows where, and Luke's back at the kids' home checking out a few things.'

Her fingers hovered over the drawer handle, made contact and slowly slid the drawer back open. *Just one.* 'No.' She slammed the drawer shut just as her new mobile rang.

'Hello. Oh hi, Mam. What?' she yelled a moment later. 'A white rose bud came addressed to me?'

'Yes, love,' Mavis replied, her voice shaky with fear. 'I think he's after you now. Oh, what are we gonna do?'

'Don't worry, Mam, nothing's gonna happen to me. It's probably just a show-off thing, it happens. Sometimes these people crave attention, trying to frighten me is just another way for them to get it. Now, please stop worrying and I'll see yer tonight.'

302

Mavis said goodbye and Lorraine put her phone down. 'Well, we've got one cheeky bastard here all right,' she said to herself.

Carter knocked and hurried in. 'Yer wanted to see me, boss?'

Lorraine shook her head. 'Sorry, Carter, I've got a lot on me mind and I can't remember what I wanted yer for. But it looks as if the White Rose murderer has now targeted me.'

Carter was stunned for a moment then he managed a rather strangled, 'What?'

'Yes.'

'Jesus, boss.'

'Yeah, cheeky bugger or what? I want yer to put a car on my house. I want to make sure that Mavis and Peggy are OK.'

'Righto, boss.'

'And tell them to be discreet. I don't want me mother or Peggy getting wind of this. It'll just worry them unnecessarily.'

Carter nodded, and left Lorraine's office. She thought of the White Rose Killer, and how he had got a tramp to order flowers for delivery to Selina. Is that what he did this time too? Suddenly, something clicked into place in her head. What was that she heard about a man talking to a tramp? Where had she heard it? She sat bolt upright in her seat. That was right. Dialling Scottie's number, she tapped her fingers on the desk impatiently while she waited for him to pick up. 'Edna,' she said finally, 'thank God yer in. Do yer have any contact details for Lady Sybill? No, that's fine, I'll hold on.' She grabbed the cigarette substitute from the top drawer of the desk and put it in her mouth while she waited for Edna. Finally she came on the other end of the line. 'No phone number? No, that's OK, I'll go to see her. Thanks very much, Edna.' Putting down the receiver, Lorraine grabbed her coat and her bag, and ran out of the office.

*

Luke left the children's home no wiser than when he'd gone into it. None of the kids had seen anyone acting strangely about the place at any time on or between any of the murders. A couple of wise guys had even complained about being questioned again, cheeky little sods.

He headed back to the station, changed his mind half way there and made his way home. He would find out one way or another just who the hell had beaten Mickey Carson up.

He walked in to find Mickey, Selina and PC Burns playing cards. The constable put her hand down when he entered the room and stood up. 'How long do yer plan on staying sir? Only if it's gonna be a while, could I pop out for a minute.'

'I'll be an hour, tops,' Luke said. 'But I need to go out after that. Do yer think yer could be back here by then?'

'Will do. Thanks, sir.'

She quickly left, grabbing her bag on the way out, and Luke sat down next to Mickey. 'OK, son, now we have time to find out exactly what happened to yer. If yer think for one minute I bought the falling down stairs story, yer're sadly mistaken. So out with it.'

Mickey groaned inwardly and quickly glanced at Selina, who shrugged. They had talked it through more than once, and Selina had told him to tell the truth; after all this time a body would have turned up somewhere. So it stood to reason that Eccles was still alive. Robbie too had been urging him to tell the truth.

He blew air out of his cheeks, looked once more at Selina, then back at Luke, and blurted out, 'It was an accident. I didn't mean to kill him, honest, I didn't.'

'What?' Luke gasped. 'Kill who?' This was the last thing Luke had expected, and he stared at Mickey. 'I think you better explain yourself.'

Mickey sniffed, ran his tongue over his dry lips and, heart

beating fast, he said, 'Selina's old boyfriend, Eccles. He, he jumped on me when I came out of the hospital, after I had seen Selina. We had a fight. I didn't want to, but . . .' He looked down at his hands and wiped his sweating palms on his jeans.

'Dad, he can't be dead,' Selina quickly said. 'I keep on telling Mickey that he's not dead, but he won't listen to me. Eccles will have crawled away somewhere and he'll be planning some way to get his own back. I know it. It'll be him that's painting the walls in the Seahills, it's gotta be. He's got this thing about white roses, always has had. He's crazy enough to be the White Rose murderer . . . And I'm surprised he hasn't wrote Mickey's name under the bloody roses . . . Probably because he hasn't even thought of it yet. He is *not* dead,' Selina went on adamantly. 'I know he's not, but Mickey won't listen. Tell him, Dad, tell him they would have found a dead body behind the hospital by now, wouldn't they?' She pleaded with her eyes for Luke to understand and agree with her.

Luke didn't know what to say. He looked slowly from one to the other, shook his head in amazement and muttered, 'My God,' under his breath.

Mickey choked on a sob, took a deep breath, then went on, 'Selina and Robbie keep saying he's not dead.' He shook his head slowly and looked into Luke's eyes, the pain in their depths clearly visible.

'But he hit his head and blood was all over the place. I didn't mean to kill him, Mr Daniels, and that's God's honest truth.' Then, totally drained of energy, his face pale with worry, Mickey sagged against his chair.

In the ensuing silence, Luke stared at Mickey's hands. *The poor kid's shaking like a bloody leaf.*

Selina broke the silence, 'Will you be able to help him, Dad?'

305

'Why the hell didn't yer tell me any of this before?' Luke demanded when Mickey had finished giving Luke every detail of what had happened outside of the hospital.

But Mickey was all talked out. Full of misery and fear, he hung his head.

Seeing this, and knowing he would get nothing more from him for a while, Luke turned to Selina. 'And just what sort of character is this Eccles?'

She sighed. 'The worst.'

'Yer know, if youse kids would just tell people when yer get terrorised like this, it would make life a lot easier.'

'Do yer think he's dead, Mr Daniels?' Mickey suddenly spoke up.

Luke looked at Mickey, and thought, *Yer just can't help but feel sorry for the hapless sod.*

'No, Mickey, I don't think he's dead.'

'Really?' Mickey gasped. 'Honestly Mr Daniels?'

Luke nodded. 'I think you've been worrying yerself over nothing. I would have heard if a body was found near the hospital.' Luke studied Mickey's face. 'You probably would have got away with self-defence anyway. To do that sort of damage, he must have hands like bell metal.'

'He uses knuckle dusters,' Selina said.

'What? They were banned years ago.'

'Like that's gonna bother him . . . He found them one night when he bro—'

Luke held his hand up. 'If you were with him, I don't want to know any more, thank you.'

Selina looked at the ground. 'Sorry, Dad,' she muttered.

A moment later, PC Burns came back. Luke stood up, 'Just in time Carol. I need to head off.' He pulled a twenty-pound note out of his wallet, 'Get what ever takeaway youse want, OK?' He handed the money over, then motioned for PC Burns to follow him into the kitchen.

306

'Don't, whatever yer do, let either one of them out of your sight for a second. OK?'

'Yer sound worried.' Burns frowned.

'I am. I don't think for one minute that this is over for these two. I also think we have a loose cannon running amok.'

'As well as the White Rose murderer sir?'

He nodded. 'As well as.'

'Don't worry sir, I'll take care of them.'

Luke smiled at the young constable. 'Thanks Carol. I really appreciate it. And I know that Selina likes having yer around. Right then, I'll be off.'

He stares at his hands, rubbing his thumb over his fingers, he smiles.

'Think you're so clever bitch, think you can catch me, I know how you think.

'Pretty soon you'll figure out that I have an apprentice. Pretty soon you'll come looking. But I hear every breath you take. I know you.'

He pats his tool wallet. 'Everything ready and waiting bitch . . . Ha.'

37

Lorraine pulled her car into the driveway to Lady Sybill's house. It was amazing. The frontage was hugely impressive, three large leaded windows looked on to well-mown lawns, and there was a round turret on the left-wing of the house.

Rapunzel, Rapunzel let down your hair. Lorraine pictured Lady Sybill complete with wrinkles and yards and yards of hair sitting at the top window of the turret, and smiled.

She got out of the car, slung her bag over her shoulder and walked towards the house. She rang the door bell, and leaned back resting her weight on one foot, giving the other foot a break. *New shoes, bloody well killing me.*

'Come on, yer old dear.' She rang the bell again impatiently, this time moving forwards and easing the other foot. 'Come on, come on.'

A moment later, a young man opened the door. He looked Lorraine up and down, then said, 'Can't you read?'

'Yer what?'

'The sign, no hawkers or canvassers.'

'Oh yeah, I did see that.'

'And?'

'And what?' *Yer pompous git.*

'Did you read it?'

Fed up with playing games, Lorraine got her badge out and snapped, 'Couldn't help but read it, right in me face. Can you read that?' She practically shoved her ID under his nose.

Before he could reply they both heard someone behind, then Lorraine smiled, recognising Lady Sybill's laugh. Then the old woman poked her head around the young man's arm.

'It's all right Simon. Don't you two recognise each other? You met at the charity dinner for the children's home.' Simon looked down his nose at her, and they shook hands briefly. His handshake was as weak as she remembered it. 'Off you go, there's a good boy.'

Lorraine hid a smile as Simon, who bristled at being spoken to like a small boy, left them without another word.

'Come with me,' Lady Sybill said.

Lorraine followed her along a hallway glittering with chandeliers and into the first room on the right. It was one of the front rooms with a view of the lawns.

As in the hallway, the walls were painted a rich cream. It was a beautiful room and a very welcoming one. Lorraine sank gratefully into the dark-cream settee with what seemed like dozens of silk cushions. Lady Sybill sat in a chair facing Lorraine.

'Please take no notice of Simon my dear, he is a snob. If he'd been born on cobblestones he would still have been a snob, but he means well.' Lorraine reflected on how 'he means well' was a term where all types of bad behaviour and manners were swept aside. And anyway, one look at Simon and she could tell that he had never actually meant well his whole life.

Lady Sybill continued, 'Well then dear, so what can I do for you?'

'It's just a few questions, if yer don't mind?'

'Not at all,' she replied. 'Anything to help the police with their enquiries. Now, would you like a cup of tea?'

'No, thank you. I'm sorry, I really must get going soon. I'm really pushed for time.'

'Of course my dear, fire away,' she clapped her hands together and smiled at Lorraine. 'As they say in all the best detective films.'

'OK. The night of the dinner, you mentioned that yer saw someone who was helping a tramp, and that he had been at the children's home. Do yer remember anything more about him?'

Lady Sybill took a deep intake of breath, and suddenly didn't look as happy anymore. 'In actual fact, yes I do. My stupid memory, playing up. I could have kicked myself afterwards.'

'Why's that, Lady Sybill?'

'Because that man, the one who had tortured the cat as a young boy, well, I forgot that he had a brother at the home too, and, well, Hanson was his brother.' Lorraine could feel prickles on her scalp as pieces of the puzzle began to slot into place in her mind. Lady Sybill didn't see the reaction that her words were causing and continued, 'But I got so confused, because when he came for the interview with the board of governors, he confessed that he had been at the home, but under a different name. And to tell you the truth I can't really remember which brother tortured the poor cat.'

'What name was that?' Lorraine could hardly believe what she was hearing.

'What was it now, it's on the tip of my tongue . . .' Lady Sybill paused, patting her chin with her delicate fingers as she stared into space. She then said, conversationally, which was an odd tone considering what she was to say next, 'He changed his name, he said, because of the abuse he had suffered as a young boy. He didn't want anything to remind

311

him of his father, but of course we needed his earlier name to pull his files. Now, what was his name again?'

'I don't mean to pressurise yer, Lady Sybill, but it's really important.'

Lady Sybill dropped her gaze to the floor. 'Don't worry, dear, I've remembered. Wade. His name was Wade.'

38

Eccles paced back and forward, the ecstasy coursing through his veins, filling his body full of false energy. He, Masterton and the others were in an empty house on the Seahills. It was the worst kind of squat, broken, decaying floorboards, water leaking all through the house from the holes in the roof. All the rooms had a greenish-grey pallor and smelt like vomit and shit. Bundles of bedclothes lay at the sides of the room, with slack-jawed boys, eyes dead to the world, lying on them in a drug-induced haze. Eccles was the only one with any energy. 'I'm gonna have her now, gotta have her now, fuck the rose painting, that crazy bastard can fuck off an' all. What the fuck does he think he is, telling me what to do. Well, it's my turn to make the rules.' He was walking up and down, unable to stop pacing. He had also taken some crystal meth along with the ecstasy, and his synapses were snapping. But Eccles felt right in control, he felt strong, he felt powerful.

'Why don't yer just leave it?' Stevie Masterton said. He was nervous, for once right out of his depth, all this talk of rape and murder, way, way out of his league.

'Leave what?' Eccles demanded, then went on without waiting for an answer. 'Leave her? Is that what you are saying? No way, she's mine. And when I've doled out what she's getting, I'm looking for that bastard. Yeah, the legendary White Rose Killer himself,' Eccles sneered. 'He's the one that's already tried to kill her, and when it went wrong he's happy for the coppers to think it's me. The bastard. Thinks I don't know, he's trying to set me up, doesn't he.' He stopped pacing long enough to snatch a joint out of one of the other boy's mouth. 'Give me that you, greedy bastard.' He aimed a kick at the boy's shin and took a long drag.

Stoned out of his mind, the boy just looked at him and grinned, showing a mouthful of green teeth.

'Fuck off.' Eccles took three deep draws of the joint then threw it back at him. The boy squatting next to the first saw his chance and scrambled for it.

'Bunch of fucking wankers the lot of youse. How the hell did I ever fucking get mixed up with you losers.'

Wish to fuck yer hadn't, Masterton was thinking.

'Yer think I can't do it, don't yer? Yeah, I know where the bastard lives, I know what he does, and how he does it.'

'How would you know that?' *This bugger's a first-class nutter,* Masterton thought, staring at Eccles. 'A murderer's not gonna show the likes of you what he does, is he?'

Eccles got down on his haunches and faced Masterton. 'I followed the bastard, that's how I know. I watched him cut her heart out, saw exactly what he did.' He smiled, and the smile chilled even Masterton. There was no emotion in Eccles's eyes. They were as dead and blank as a shark's. He took his mobile from his pocket and waved it in Masterton's face. 'And,' he said quietly. 'I've got it on here.'

The boy who had snatched the joint from the floor looked suitably impressed. 'Yer mean, like watching yer very own snuff film?'

'You betcha,' Eccles answered him, but didn't take his eyes from Stevie Masterton's face.

'What?' Masterton gasped. 'You've videoed it?'

Eccles grinned an evil grin and pressed a couple of buttons on his mobile. Masterton gazed in wonder, then turned away as the full horror of the video was exposed. Three of his gang members were entranced though, however, and were giggling. Their faces were lit up by the greenish glow of the light from the mobile. Suddenly Masterton felt sick, at the evil life he had led, at his friends, at the chain of cause and effect that had led him down a path to a stinking house, in a room full of druggies, who were watching the sickest kind of video you could possibly get, for entertainment.

But then came another noise, as the door downstairs was kicked in. The boys looked round, as one, and someone said, 'Shit, it's the fucking police.'

Eccles went to the window and kicked out the glass. He was halfway out when the police ran up the stairs, and swore as he realised that his mobile phone, which he had hastily shoved in his back pocket, had fallen out and was lying on the floor. But there wasn't time to waste going back and getting it, not if he wanted to deal with the bitch. He dropped to the ground.

Masterton, seeing his chance, grabbed the phone and shoved it in his pocket. He might be able to use this. He yelped as the door to the room was kicked open and in rushed three burly coppers in uniform.

39

'Mam . . . Mam . . . Guess what . . . There's a fucking raid going on across the road,' Darren Lumsdon yelled as he ran down the stairs three at a time to the sitting room. The whole household turned to stare at him.

'What did you say?' Vanessa asked.

'Hurry up, you'll miss it, there's a raid. I saw Stevie Shite and his gang going into the house ages ago.'

Vanessa grabbed hold of his ear, 'What did you say?' she repeated, slowly twisting his ear.

Darren thought for a moment. Shit . . . 'Sorry, Mam.'

'Don't bloody well forget it either.' She gave his ear another twist for good measure, before asking. 'Now, what raid, where?'

'Where them Bronsons used to live, before they won all that money, the one out the back what's still boarded up, there's coppers crawling all over it.'

Without another word, the whole family jumped up and ran upstairs to the backroom. 'Don't switch the light on,' Kerry yelled to Emma. 'They'll be able to see us.'

They all huddled round the window, pushing and shoving

for space, then quietened down when the back door opened and Stevie Masterton and his gang tried to make a run for it. In minutes they were handcuffed and led round to the front.

'Get in,' Darren yelled, his fist in the air.

'I couldn't see properly cos of all the rain,' Claire said. 'Was that Eccles creep one of them?' No one said anything for a moment, thinking, then Emma spoke, 'No, don't think he was.'

Darren shook his head. 'No'

He crushed the sleeping tablets with a rolling pin until they disintegrated into a fine white powder, then he added some to the spaghetti bolognese which was heavily laced with garlic just the way his brother liked it.

He himself hated garlic so there was no reason for his brother to suspect anything when he didn't have the meal. The garlic would hide the bitter taste of the sleeping pills.

Some of the powder he kept for another time, for someone else.

For the apprentice.

'For the bitch. Ha.'

40

The storm, which had been wreaking havoc in the west for most of the day, had crossed over the Pennines losing none of its fury, and was now venting its wrath on the north-east. Lorraine pulled up outside Hanson's house, after calling into the station and getting the address off Carter. She'd decided that Carter would have to stay on home base to liaise with everyone, seeing as the mobile phones only seemed to be working when they wanted to.

Thank God the land lines had not been affected, though with the gales that were buffeting her car she guessed that one or two poles might come down.

She eased the car into a gap between two identical Renaults, praying that she didn't crunch one of them; the lashing rain had visibility down to practically zero. The house was in darkness which meant nothing. She knew that most people lived at the back of these terraced houses, down a long passageway. She tried her mobile. Just like before, no signal. 'Damn.'

She threw the mobile into her bag, got out of the car, shivered then fastened her coat up to her neck to keep out the wind and rain, and practically had to fight her way up to the door.

God, when was the wind ever as bad as this?

The door opened as her hand was poised to knock. 'I saw you coming.' Ian Wade said by way of explanation as he opened the door to her.

'Wade?' Lorraine said. More pieces of the puzzle were falling into place, although it was by no means complete. As soon as Lady Sybill mentioned that Carl Hanson had once been called Carl Wade, Lorraine had wondered where Ian fitted into all of this; perhaps he had in some way helped to keep Hanson out of the Garda's eye, or perhaps his involvement was much more sinister.

Wade smiled, although Lorraine noted, not for the first time, how the smile failed to reach his amazing green eyes. 'I owe you an explanation. If you come in, I'll do my best to put you in the picture, as it were.'

Feeling slightly apprehensive, Lorraine stepped over the threshold.

'So, enough crack cocaine to set the whole of Houghton and Hetton reeling.' Luke frowned at Masterton.

'I didn't know it was there, honest. I swear to God I didn't know about it. The fucking greedy bastard was keeping it for himself, he must be dealing,' Masterton whinged. 'Yer can catch the bastard, I'm not going down for him.' He folded his arms across his chest.

'Well, looks like yer are, you and the rest of the motley bunch of cretins.'

'No fucking way.'

'Talk to me then.'

'I want me solicitor.'

'Where is he?'

'Newbottle Street, yer'll have the address somewhere.'

'Don't get cocky, kid, yer know who I mean.' Luke was getting exasperated. He had dealt with Stevie Masterton before, and was used to his delaying tactics.

'I want me solicitor,' Masterton repeated, but a little less cockily this time.

Luke gritted his teeth. 'I'll add withholding information to the rest of it.'

Masterton digested this for a moment then, leaning forward said, 'I've got some information. I've got evidence to back it up, and I wanna do a deal.' He paused. 'But I won't do it without me solicitor present.'

'What on earth would you have that would interest me enough to want to do a deal with a snail like you?'

'Fuck off, then,' Masterton said sulkily.

'I thought so; add wasting police time to the list, might get yer another three months on top of everything else, especially if I really stress to the judge just what a horrible bloody nuisance yer are . . . Yer don't like it inside do yer, Shite?' Luke used Masterton's commonly used nickname, the name that he was known by throughout the Seahills.

Masterton's face changed colour in rapid succession, a sickly grey at the thought of hard time, then a bright livid red at the use of his hated nickname.

'Fuck you, and yer fucking daughter. I hope the bastard does what he says he's gonna do.'

Luke was on his feet in an instant. Quickly he reached across the table, grabbed Masterton by his throat and hauled him up off his seat. Peters opened his fingers to let his pen, conveniently, fall to the floor, and got down on his hands and knees looking for it.

'What?' Luke yelled.

Masterton squirmed, and tried to wriggle free. 'Nowt, I didn't mean nowt,' he managed in a high-pitched squeak.

Luke shook him, his face barely an inch from Masterton's,

and growled, 'I've asked yer once and I won't ask again. And I won't be responsible for my actions if I don't get an answer. *NOW!*' He screamed the last word full in Masterton's metal-bound face.

'All right, all right, I'll tell yer . . . I'll tell yer.'

Luke let Masterton drop on to his chair, then towered over him. Masterton shook himself, glowering at Luke.

'Spit it out.'

'He's gone looking for her.'

'What!?'

'Eccles, he says he's gonna kill her . . . And . . .' he swallowed hard, knowing he was in deep trouble and that this man in front of him would kill him if anything happened to his kid . . . And he knew that if he didn't tell them about the murder they'd bang him up for life.

'He knows who the murderer is,' he blurted quickly.

'What?' Peters said, as he came up from under the table, knocking his head on it. 'Ow, yer bastard.' He stood up, rubbing the bump on his head and glared hard at Masterton.

'Not my fault, yer dummy.'

'You'll be sucking one if yer don't mind yer manners yer cheeky git,' Peters threatened.

'Enough,' Luke shouted, banging his fist on the table. 'Talk and talk now.'

'OK, keep yer lid on . . .' Masterton said without thinking, then seeing Luke's face he knew it was time to start looking after number one, all thoughts of getting his solicitor were forgotten. A moment later he took a deep breath then said quickly, his words tumbling over each other, 'He's got it all on his fucking mobile, the whole friggin' event, yer can see him cutting her heart out, he followed him and . . .' Masterton gulped and shook his head. Luke and Peters could see that he was, for once in his life, genuinely disgusted. 'I couldn't fucking look at it, but the others . . . They'll tell yer what's on it.'

'Yer mean he calmly filmed the whole thing . . .' Peters frowned his amazement. He was a hardened copper, who thought he'd seen it all, but the whole idea of this was mind blowing. He stared at Masterton.

'He says he's the apprentice now and that . . . And that he needed to video it for perfection.' Masterton shivered, 'He even had a white rose stencilled on his chest ready to fill in when he does his first murder. It, it's weird, it's like they were fucking blood brothers or something.' He took Eccles's phone out of his pocket and passed it to Luke. 'He dropped this when he ran out the window as you lot came in. Yer can see it for yerself.'

'How?' Luke coughed, his mouth had dried up. 'How does he know the murderer?' Luke demanded.

'Cos he disturbed him. When the murderer had tried to . . .' he glanced up at Luke. 'When he had tried to get yer daughter.'

Luke was becoming agitated. 'How long before we brought yer in had he been gone?'

Masterton shrugged, 'He had just left. But the perve likes to spy on people for fucking ages before he does anything.'

'You better pray that I'm in time boy.' Luke looked at Peters and said quickly, 'Put him in the cells, put them all in the cells and then follow me home.'

Luke ran along the corridor at breakneck speed. Pulling his mobile out of his pocket he phoned Lorraine. It was still ringing when he reached his car. 'Come on, come on precious, answer the damn thing.'

Although to everyone's relief, the network was finally up and running, Lorraine's mobile had switched itself off when she threw it into her bag.

'So, why did yer return, Ian?' Lorraine said, in what she hoped was a conversational manner. Ian Wade was staring at her in a way that she found almost uncomfortably intense.

He smiled. 'It's nice to see you, Lorraine, but why are you here? You didn't track me down, did you? Missing me?' He laughed, but to Lorraine's ears the laugh was mirthless, hollow.

Lorraine quickly thought on her feet. 'Actually, it was Carl Hanson I wanted to see. He's been helping Selina get on her feet. I just wanted to thank him, really. In person.'

'Did yer realise that Carl and I are brothers?' Wade said suddenly.

'No, I didn't,' Lorraine lied. 'I didn't know. You don't look very similar.'

Wade smiled. 'Well, the resemblance is there. He just looks a lot older than he actually is.' Lorraine nodded and waited for Wade to continue. 'He had a harder life than me, I guess some would say.'

'Really?' Lorraine said. 'Why sort of harder life?'

Wade looked around, and then, as if he had only just realised that they were standing, pointed at the couch and said, 'Where are my manners? Why don't you take a seat? Would you like a cup of tea?'

'Yes please,' Lorraine said, putting a grateful tone into her voice. 'Milk two sugars, please.'

As soon as Wade was out of sight, Lorraine took her phone out of her bag and swore when she realised that it was switched off. She turned it on. 'Come on, come on,' she said under her breath.

Suddenly Wade was in the room. Lorraine quickly slipped her mobile into her pocket. 'Just checking my messages.'

Wade sat down. 'There's no milk,' he smiled, and carried on confidentially, 'and we've run out of tea bags as well. Two bachelors in one house, doesn't make for an organised fridge.' He grinned.

Lorraine smiled back. 'So,' she prompted. 'Yer were going to tell me about your brother.'

'Carl, yes,' Wade leant back in his chair. 'Well, it's a bad business really. In fact, I didn't come to Houghton on holiday. I left the Garda to care for him.'

'Really?' Lorraine said as innocently as she could. But she knew about Wade, she knew that when he was a child, he had tortured innocent animals. Could people change? Which brother could she trust, if either? *And which one is really the torturer, you or your brother?*

'We had a pretty horrible time growing up,' Wade said. And then his voice took on a different quality, as if he was going back through time. He sounded younger, more fragile. 'Our father, he was the kind of guy who . . . the kind of guy who was used to taking what he wanted. And what he wanted,' he paused and looked down at his hands. 'And what he wanted was the both of us.' Wade looked up at Lorraine. She could see his Adam's apple bob as he swallowed. 'I,' he said finally, 'I was lucky. Carl was always good to me, he took care of me. He didn't let our father touch me. He offered up himself instead, he was my protector.'

Lorraine leant forward, seeing Wade as a young boy, feeling his pain. 'Yer knew what was going on the whole time?'

Wade nodded and sniffed. He had started crying, and he angrily wiped his tears away with the cuff of his sleeve. He took a deep breath and carried on, 'I knew what was going on. You see, whenever,' he stopped again, took a deep breath and then said, 'whenever it was going on, for a long time, I could hear Carl fighting back, trying hard to stop him. But he was only a boy, and Dad was a big man. Then one day,' Lorraine could see the pain that was going through him, just talking about this. 'One day, I could hear him, my father, breathing outside my bedroom. And then Carl went up to him, told him that he would do it, willingly, if only he wouldn't do it to me. And then I never heard Carl fight, never again.'

'Jesus, Wade, that's awful,' Lorraine said. 'What about yer mother, where was she, in all this?'

Wade snorted. 'She,' he looked up at Lorraine, 'she was worse than him. By a fucking mile. And why was she worse? Because she knew. She knew, the bitch, and she didn't do a fucking thing to stop it. We were just boys,' he said, swallowing again, 'and despite it all, we loved our father. We couldn't tell anyone, we didn't want him to go away or be put in prison. But she, she,' he said, lifting red-rimmed eyes up to Lorraine. 'She could have stopped it. But she didn't lift a finger. I hated her, I hate her still. I lived in fear that Carl couldn't stop him and what happened to him would happen to me. And then our mother disappeared, and our father killed himself, and so Carl and I were put into a home. And that's it really. As soon as he could, Carl changed his name to Hanson, which was our mother's maiden name. I guess he didn't want to be reminded of him. And now,' he stared at his hands, 'after he protected me for so many years, I guess it's now my turn to protect him.'

Lorraine blinked. 'What are yer saying, Wade?' she asked quietly.

Wade seemed to shake himself out of his mood. He turned to Lorraine and smiled. 'Are you hungry? There's some spaghetti bolognese in the oven. Let me get you some.' Before Lorraine could object Wade was on his feet and already in the kitchen.

Going over Wade's story in her head, there were still two or three questions in Lorraine's mind, not least just what it was that Wade felt he had to protect Carl from. Lorraine rose and followed him into the kitchen. She stopped in the doorway. The kitchen was small but was immaculately clean, and the smell of the bolognese certainly had her mouth watering.

'So, where is Carl now?'

Wade turned quickly, the sharp knife in his hand catching the light from the spotlight just above his head.

*

Eccles slipped quietly into Selina's bedroom; the climb up the shed and into her open bedroom window had been easy. A three-year-old child could have managed it.

He knew exactly what to do, he had been well trained. The rose was safe in his pocket, the knife strapped to his side, he had watched his mentor over and over on his phone, but seeing it for real, wow that had been something else. He shivered with anticipation. There was a line he was going to cross. A line which, after you had crossed it once, there was no going back from. He was going to kill for the first time.

Slowly he crept along the landing, counting the rooms. One, two, three, four.

One of these must be a bathroom.

He found it behind the third door. Good, good, pray there isn't another downstairs.

His plan was simple. If Selina came up to use the bathroom first, then the others would live.

The bathroom was large and tiled in blue. Behind the door on two pegs hung two dressing gowns, a pink one and a white one. Luck was on his side. There was a walk-in cupboard on the same wall as the door, which was exactly what he had hoped for. He had watched long enough to know there were three people in the house, at the moment all alive and kicking.

'But not for long,' he whispered to himself, his eyes glistening as he breathed in and out, just as he had been taught, slowly, slowly.

'Where is he?' Lorraine asked again, frowning as Wade stared at her, the knife clasped in his hand.

It took a moment for him to answer, then he said with a shrug, 'Oh er, he's at work. He won't be long.'

He took a plate out of the cupboard and began to scoop the

spaghetti bolognese on to it. Lorraine's stomach rumbled. But however hungry she was, she was damned if she was going to share food with Wade. Something in his story didn't quite ring true. 'Thanks, but I can't, sorry.'

'Nonsense, you must try it. I promise you, it'll be the best spag bol you've ever tasted.'

'No. It's Peggy's night to make dinner, she'll skin me alive if I don't eat it.' Lorraine turned and walked back into the sitting room but not before she'd seen Wade's scowl.

Wade was starting to worry her now. 'Where's the phone?' she asked over her shoulder as she looked quickly round the room.

'It's not on,' Wade said in her ear. 'BT said sometime this week.'

'Oh.' Lorraine felt the hairs rise on the back of her neck and gave an involuntary shiver. Then the door opened and a man dressed all in black stepped in.

41

Mickey put his Monopoly money on the board, stood up and stretched. 'I'm going to the loo, so no nicking me money while I'm gone.'

'Yeah, like we would,' Selina laughed, eyeing Mickey's neat little pile of money.

'Please . . .' WPC Burns jumped up. 'Ladies first.'

Mickey gave in at once. 'Be my guest,' he said, waving his arm in a chivalrous flourish.

'Proper little gentleman you've got yerself here, mind you.' She smiled and winked at Selina as she headed for the stairs. Mickey blushed as he sat back down, and Selina playfully slapped his thigh which made him blush even more.

Eccles heard Carol confidently taking the stairs two at a time. Calmly he slipped the knife from its sheaf at his side. As the door opened, he took a deep breath and waited until she passed the cupboard and her back was to him. Then, carefully, silently, the air still trapped in his lungs, he stepped out and, using both his hands and all of his strength, plunged the knife into her back. As the knife touched her heart the air exploded out of Eccles's lungs. Without knowing the reason or the why, with a soft sigh, Carol folded over and fell to the floor, dying almost instantly.

Keeping the knife in her body so that the blood didn't leak out, Eccles dragged Carol's body over to the bath and put her in it face down, then, with his feet braced solidly against the side of the bath he pulled the knife out with both hands. It reluctantly released its cold grip on Carol's still body with a soft, sucking sound.

So it hadn't been Selina. But it still had been something. Adrenaline pumped round his body, better than any drug. He let the feeling surge through his veins for a moment, and then prepared himself for the next one. The world, for him, became more lurid, more intense. Sights and sounds were more vivid than they had ever been before. Picking up the small bath mat, he noticed how blood had dropped on it and spread into tiny petal-like shapes, which he marvelled at for a brief moment, then threw it into the bath after Carol, taking as much time as he dared to stare at the body and savour the buzz.

Oh, this was so much better than watching. He shivered with delight before pulling the shower curtain along and consigning WPC Carol Burns's still warm body to the cold, plastic bath.

Stepping back he stared at the closed curtain, and with an icy smile, muttered, 'No longer the apprentice.'

Hanson lunged forward, his eyes blazing, his left hand outstretched towards Lorraine, his right hand raised in a fist.

Quickly Lorraine ducked and swung to the left. Easing most of her weight on to her left leg, she shifted her balance and shot her right foot out, which connected solidly with Hanson's shin. Hanson yelled out, and Wade took the sudden opportunity to launch a left hook at Hanson's chin. Hanson folded

330

and hit the floor as if in slow motion, almost in the same way as WPC Carol Burns had.

Lorraine relaxed and breathed deeply.

'Thank God you're here Wade,' she muttered, before rising and turning to him.

'Jesus,' she gasped out loud, her eyes widening and her heart going into overdrive. Wade was moving in on her with a large knife, its blade catching the light as he slowly waved his right hand.

'Shit!' she shrieked, as she snatched up a kitchen chair and held it in front of her body.

How the fuck could she have been so wrong? Hanson had been trying to help her, and she had helped Wade knock him out cold, which meant that it was just her against the man who had attacked Selina, who had killed all those women. The final jigsaw piece fell into place.

Wade edged forward. Lorraine shook the chair as if she was facing a lion, thinking the chances of coming away from either conflict would be about the same. Wade smiled. That cold clinical smile that never quite reached his eyes. 'Ha.'

Mickey untangled himself from Selina's arms. He really couldn't wait a minute longer. What the hell was Carol doing up there?

'I've gotta take a wazz. I'm gonna see what she's doing.'

'She has been a long time.' Selina picked up a magazine and started to flick through it as Mickey got up from the settee and went to the bottom of the stairs.

'Carol,' he shouted, then waited a moment before shouting again.

'She's not answering.' He turned to Selina. 'Do yer think I should go and knock on the door?'

Selina shrugged. 'She might be taking a shower.'

'Why aye, when she knew I needed to pee! Anyhow I can't

hear the shower going.' He stood on the first stair, cocking his ear. 'I think I better go and knock, yer never know she might have taken poorly or something.'

Engrossed in her magazine, Selina nodded, and Mickey made his way up the stairs.

'You all along.' Lorraine stepped over Hanson's prone body, not once taking her eyes off Wade.

'Ha.'

Realising that she was being backed into a corner, Lorraine stopped. She knew the chances of getting out of here unharmed were slim, but she would not cower in the corner. She would rather take her chances and come out fighting.

But that was the last chance scenario. She'd talked herself out of bad situations before, and Wade loved to talk about himself.

Come on Hanson, for God's sake wake up.

'Yer set him up.' She met Wade's stare, her eyes as unflinching as his. 'Yer needed to kill all those women, but yer did it when Hanson was in Dublin, so that yer could blame it on him.'

'Knew you would figure it out . . . Far too bright for your own good, little lady.'

'So what was it? Why did yer start killing women? Couldn't get it up? Is that why yer did it? So yer could have power over them?'

A muscle in Wade's jaw twitched 'It would seem that simple to you. You wouldn't understand. I've been rejected all my life,' he started to shout. 'First by my father, then my bitch of a mother wouldn't save us, and then you,' he sneered. 'You couldn't even remember me when I first saw you. Did you know how it made me feel? Well, I'll tell you. It made me want to kill you, but not before I had killed everyone you had ever possibly cared about.'

Wade was shouting too loud to hear anything but his own

angry words, but Lorraine was closer and she heard Hanson groan softly. *Come on Hanson wake up wake up, for frig's sake come on . . . Come on.*

Mickey knocked on the bathroom door. 'Are yer all right Carol?'

He strained his ears but heard nothing. He knocked again and shouted this time. When there was still no answer, he frowned his puzzlement, then went to the top of the stairs and yelled down them. 'Selina, I think yer better come up here.'

Hearing the worry in Mickey's voice, Selina put her magazine down and followed him up the stairs.

She looked at the door, then at Mickey, 'What's wrong?' she whispered.

'I've tried knocking and everything, but there's been no answer.'

'What do yer think we should do?'

Mickey shrugged.

'We better go in,' Selina whispered, and Mickey nodded.

Selina took hold of the handle, opened the door and pushed it right back. Leaning forward she looked around, and then again before saying, 'She's not here.'

'What?' Mickey looked into the bathroom. 'That's odd. Where the hell can she be?'

'Carol,' Selina shouted, her voice echoing around the bathroom. When there was no answer Selina looked at Mickey and shrugged.

'Well. I've still got to go.' Mickey went in and closed the door behind him.

Selina decided to go downstairs and look around outside. *Carol wouldn't have nipped out to the shops without telling us, would she? No, Dad would go mental if he thought she'd left us on our own. Don't think she would do that anyhow. It's pissing down out there.*

333

She opened the back door and looked around the garden, not that there was much to see in the dark. She grabbed her coat and clutching her ribs made her way down to the back gate and got soaked through before she even reached it. Opening the gate she looked down the street. A young mother, struggling to push a twin buggy, was the only person in sight. Quickly Selina closed the gate and locked it. Frowning, she hurried back up the path.

She had nearly reached the back door when she heard a flapping noise. Looking up she saw her bedroom curtain blowing in the wind. Her window was open.

'Friggin' hell, everything will be soaked.' She hurried as best as she could inside and up the stairs, wondering when she had opened her window, but somehow knowing that she hadn't.

Passing the bathroom door, she banged on it with her fist. 'You still in there?'

'In a minute,' Mickey said. He zipped up his fly, and then washed his hands. Out of the corner of his eye, he saw the glint of something sharp and metallic, and some primal instinct made him stand aside. He dodged to the left as the knife came down, but he was slightly too late. He screamed as the knife caught his side and sliced it wide open.

'Mickey, what's the matter?' Selina yelled as she ran back to the bathroom and pushed the door open.

'Keep out,' Mickey yelled. 'Run, Selina, run.' But it was too late. Selina was already in the bathroom.

42

Carter was beside himself. He had phoned Lorraine over and over but her mobile was switched off.

'Bloody hell,' he muttered, putting the phone back down yet again.

The storm was finally abating but it had brought its own havoc with it. There had been three car accidents on the A19 just outside Houghton, one which had been fatal, and a full-scale battle in the Blue Lion had the police resources stretched to the limit. Carter was worried. Since Lorraine had called asking for Hanson's home address, he had not been able to get in touch with her, which wasn't like Lorraine at all. Carter called another station, but they had their own problems, and could only supply one police car with two officers. It would have to do.

It took them five minutes to reach Hanson's house, which was all in darkness.

'Keep behind me,' Carter warned as he tried the door handle.

The door opened easily. Surprised, Carter stepped in.

'Hello,' he shouted.

'Carter,' came the muffled reply from a room down the hallway. 'In here, quick.'

Carter set off at a run, the two officers dogging his heels. He could see light coming from a thin strip at the bottom of a door. He pushed it open just in time to see Wade make a last frantic attempt at slashing Lorraine with a knife. Lorraine quickly side-stepped and swung the chair, but Hanson had been conscious for some moments, waiting his chance. He rose quickly and knocked his brother to one side.

Facing him he screamed, 'After all I did for you, I protected you, my life was ruined so that yours would be better, and this is how you repay me?'

He fell quiet for a single moment, in which Lorraine quickly looked from one brother to the other.

In a voice suddenly calmer and quietly pleading, Carl Hanson looked at his brother and went on, in a hushed voice, 'Why . . . Why after all I did? Every thing I went through, it was all for you. So you would have a better chance, wouldn't have the weight of it to carry around all your life. To lie in bed night after night thinking of the horror of it all.' He sobbed, and brushed large tears off his face as Wade just continued staring at him.

Hanson's shoulders slumped. Slowly he shook his head. 'It was all for nothing.'

'Ha.' Wade looked for a way out but there was none, the two WPCs had each advanced around the side of the room. He was surrounded. Still staring at his brother, he held his hands out and the nearest WPC cuffed him.

'I won't forget you,' he snarled at Lorraine as they led him out. 'Yer blonde bitch. Yer'll be sorry. One day I'll be back.'

'Yeah, you and a few others. What the fuck took yer so long, Carter?' Lorraine demanded as she sank gratefully into a chair.

Carter's heart sank and he spun round to face his boss. 'Sorry, sorry I didn . . .'

Lorraine smiled, a weak one, but still a smile. 'Yer done good Carter.'

Luke, with five officers in tow, ran into his house. He heard his daughter scream, and hurled himself up the stairs. Eccles ran out of the bathroom and into Selina's bedroom.

Luke pointed to three officers, 'He's going out the window. You and you out the back now, you,' he pointed at the third officer, 'you follow him.'

Luke ran into the bathroom just as Selina screamed again. She was holding the shower curtain back and staring into the bath. Mickey was hunched up on the floor holding his side with both hands; blood was seeping through his fingers.

Taking stock of the situation, Luke pulled his phone out and quickly asked for an ambulance then walked over to his trembling daughter. He took one look in the bath, saw the poor, ruined body of WPC Carol Burns, then pulled Selina close to him. He calmed her down and sat her on the toilet. She watched as he knelt beside Mickey. 'Let me see.'

Mickey, face pale, eyes wide and staring, shook his head. 'No. I can't, it'll all spill out.'

'Oh Mickey.' Selina sobbed. 'It's all my fault.'

'No it's not,' Mickey muttered, just before he passed out.

Finally, the press conference is over, thank God, Lorraine thought, as she, Luke and Carter went back to her office.

'Well, at least Clark gave us some credit this time,' Luke said, pulling up his chair.

'Only because the smarmy bastard was in friggin' Ireland playing golf,' Lorraine answered, looking out the window at the brilliant sunshine.

'Who would have thought that it was Wade? Though, mind

337

you,' Luke added hastily, 'I didn't like him much from the beginning.'

'Rejection and jealousy are two very powerful emotions, people have murdered for less.'

Wade had confessed all, had confessed to murders that they didn't even know had happened. It was spooky, though Lorraine refused to let him know that he had phased her, the way that he had stared at her when he had described how closely Lorraine had resembled his mother, was spooky but she wasn't going to let him see that. When he relayed how much he had hated his mother, and how that, in his own eyes, she was worse than his father, he stared straight at Lorraine, as if physical resemblance meant that Lorraine was somehow responsible for what had happened to him. When he was fourteen, his mother had been the first of his victims, he confessed, and then he had killed his father, making it look like suicide. It had been so easy and he had got away with it scot free. In fact, the only punishment he had ever received was when he had tortured that cat.

In Ireland, he had battened down the compulsion for years, to finally kill again. He had been responsible for the three deaths, plus one other. They all looked like Lorraine, he said, staring straight at her. And he had timed the deaths to coincide with his brother's visits to Dublin, so that he could frame him, if he needed to. And then, when he had seen Lorraine in Ireland, and she hadn't even remembered him, all the feelings of jealousy had come up again. He wanted to kill Lorraine, but first he wanted to make her suffer. By killing Selina and her friends, he could make Lorraine feel bad and still pin the blame on his brother. And Kate Mulberry, well, she deserved to die after what she wrote about him. There was nothing wrong with his manhood.

'Fancy the mother looking like you though boss, that's amazing innit though,' Carter piped up from beside the filing cabinet where he was looking for papers. 'He blamed her for standing by and letting it happen didn't he?'

Lorraine sighed, 'Aye, but according to Hanson, the woman was terrified to death of her husband. She did what she did to protect herself.'

'She hid behind a kid and created a murderer, that's what she did,' Luke said, before taking a drink out of his can of coke.

'I thought it was Wade all along, didn't I boss?' Carter said.

Lorraine nodded solemnly at Luke, who looked impressed. 'Well done Carter.'

'Yeah, and if he hadn't come when he did, we might have had a different tale to tell.'

Carter blushed, basking in the praise. 'Em how's Mickey Carson?'

'Twenty-four stitches in his side, but nothing internal, more like a deep slash. That Eccles is mad as a bloody hatter an' all. He was still screaming that he wasn't an apprentice no more when we had him in the cells . . . He's probably still screaming.'

They were quiet for a moment, all three of them thinking of Kate Mulberry, whose funeral they would be attending later today.

Then Carter said, 'Bet Mickey's enjoying all the fuss.'

Luke groaned, 'You bet, regular little hero.'